Masters of My Desire
The Doms of Genesis, Book 2
Jenna Jacob

Published by Jenna Jacob

Copyright 2013 Jenna Jacob
Edited by Seraph Editing/A.Pfau
ePub ISBN 978-0-9885445-2-9
ISBN 978-0-9885445-3-6

All rights reserved. No part of this book may be reproduced, scanned, or distributed in any printed or electronic form without permission. Please do not participate in or encourage piracy of copyrighted materials in violation of the author's rights.

This is a work of fiction. Names, places, characters and incidents are the product of the author's imagination and are fictitious. Any resemblance to actual persons, living or dead, events or establishments is solely coincidental.

DEDICATION

To Jenna's Sultry Street Sirens,
You ladies ROCK!

To all my amazing readers,
Your support and encouragement is phenomenal.

To A. Pfau,
Your editing magic is miraculous ~and~ you have the patience
of a Saint.

To my Incredible husband,
Loving family, and Beautiful friends,
You are my rocks
My anchors
My life preservers

THANK YOU!

Take a peek at the end of this story for other Jenna Jacob titles
soon to be released.

CHAPTER ONE

"Oh my God, I just killed Bambi." My body trembled as tears stung my eyes. Guilt and sadness replaced the adrenaline that slowly bled from my veins. I couldn't blot out the image of the regal brown eye staring at me, or the sickening thud of flesh exploding against my bumper. The thunderous beat of my heart and the cacophony of shrieking metal still echoed in my ears.I peered through the web of my shattered windshield. Blood and chunks of fur-mixed-flesh covered the hood. The front of my SUV looked like something out of a bad horror movie. I shouldn't have looked. Saliva pooled in my mouth and I swallowed rapidly, refusing to vomit on my leather Benetton jacket.

"Oh, Bambi, I'm so sorry. You probably have a mate and babies that will wonder where you are." My vision blurred as I mourned the poor buck's death.

Even the ache in my shoulder, where I'd bounced against the door frame, paled in comparison to the anguish I felt for taking the animal's life. I was a murderer.

Unsure of how long my SUV had been sitting in the middle of the road, I shook my head and attempted to clear the disoriented feeling. I needed to find help. As I glanced at the passenger seat, I found that my purse had slid onto the floorboard. Unbuckling my seatbelt, I gingerly reached across the console and retrieved it. My head throbbed with a million jackhammers and my stomach pitched like a kayak in a stormy sea. I sat up, inhaled a deep breath, and pulled out my cell phone.

A growling engine and crunching gravel drew me from my task. I jerked my head and peered in the rearview mirror, catching glimpse of a huge red truck that pulled up and stopped. When the window lowered and the passenger stuck his head out, my heart nearly stopped.

He was handsome to the point of devastating. Long, blue-black hair, sun-kissed skin and high exotic cheek bones left no doubt that he was of Native American descent. The look of concern in his erotic charcoal eyes caused butterflies to dip and swirl in my stomach.

I pressed the button to lower my window, a *thank you* poised on my tongue, but the damn thing wouldn't budge. I raised my finger, motioning for him to give me a second, then slung my purse strap over my shoulder.

When I opened the door of my SUV, the frigid wind almost took my breath away. But the sight of the driver's hypnotic blue eyes, as he poked his head around the stunning Native man's shoulder, had me all but sweating. With ashblonde collar-length hair and a rugged jaw dusted in a light scruff, the driver looked dangerous and delicious. The two men were scrumptiously hunky, the exact type that caused me to get tongue-tied and act like a fool. But, Lord… were they ever gorgeous.

"No. Wait," The passenger bellowed. His deep voice flowed over me like rich chocolate.

My brow wrinkled in confusion as I eased from my seat. A nauseating squish echoed in my ears as my foot plunged, ankle deep, into the warm, thick center of the deer's bloody carcass. My eyes grew wide and a pitiful moan seeped from between my lips.

"Ewww," I whined.

Revulsion crawled up my spine and landed like a brick in my stomach. I jumped over the remains of the deer and ran toward the back of my SUV. Quaking and retching, I was unable to erase the slippery sensation or the grotesque sound from my mind. My stomach protested with a violent swirl. My hands slid to my knees as I doubled over and promptly puked every drop of my four dollar and eighty-seven cent cup of coffee on the side of the road.

"Hold her hair," ordered the passenger with that deep erotic voice. Fingers gathered my mane as broad hands gripped my hips in a sturdy hold. "Let it out, little one," the Native man whispered. His hot breath fluttered over my ear and I trembled.

Another wave erupted and I coughed it out, followed by a rather un-ladylike spit.

"I'm sorry," I groaned. Embarrassment flooded my veins.

"You have nothing to be sorry for," reassured the blue-eyed man who gripped my hair. "I think we need to get you to a hospital."

"No, please. I don't want… no hospitals," I begged. Holding my frigid fingers to my pounding forehead, I swallowed the bitter taste left in my mouth. "I'll be okay."

"You're shaking like a leaf. Do you think you're done here?" The deep-voiced man still clutching my hips asked.

I nodded and slowly stood upright.

"Good girl."

His innocent words sent a blast of heat straight to my core. My nipples hardened with a sharp ache. I swallowed back a gasp, blown away by my potent sexual response. I peered over my shoulder. The dark-skinned man wore a mask of worry. I was entranced by the decadent heat rolling off his rugged, muscular body.

"I'll call for a tow. Why don't you take her to the truck, Dylan," the Native man directed.

"No, ambulance, please," I begged the handsome stranger. His black hair whipped over his face. He gathered the wild strands of it into a wide fist then tucked it down the back of his tightly-drawn T-shirt. I ogled at his massive, sculpted chest like an idiot.

"You need to be checked out, pet," the Native man stated as he stepped toward me and wrapped his broad, warm hands around my cheeks.

Pet? Oh God, was he a Dominant? My mouth was dry and a sturdy tremor wracked my body. In all the books I'd read and all the sites I'd perused on the web, *pet* was a common name that a Dom addressed his submissive by. They also fancied terms like *girl, precious, kitten,* or *little one*. Wait, had he'd already called me 'little one'? *Oh shit, he did!*

I couldn't breathe. It felt as if the air had been sucked from my lungs. A black-spotted veil clouded my vision and my stomach swirled. I was going to pass out or throw up again, maybe both. My heart hammered like a drum line in my chest and I closed my eyes.

"Easy," his rich velvet voice echoed in my ears as his hands tightened upon my face. "Relax, little one. Take a deep breath. What's your name?"

Little one. He'd said it again. I knew in my bones, he *was* a damn Dom. My heart clutched and my head swam.

Despite being a relatively assertive career woman, I yearned to be gagged, bound and spanked as I submitted to a pair of Doms' deviant sexual whims. Cruising on luxury yachts in Morocco, as the sex toy of two rich Dominant Sheiks, was my favorite 'private time' fantasy. But what were the odds of finding a Dom on a deserted county road in the middle of Iowa? Was this some kind of divine intervention… a sign to break free from my inhibitions and live out my depraved BDSM ménage fantasies? *As if.* I could never get *that* lucky.

"S…Savannah. Savannah Carson," I stuttered. Tongue-tied as usual. I never knew what to say to beautiful men. When I opened my mouth, I usually ended up sounding like a complete moron. And suspecting he was a Dom only doubled the risk I'd say something stupid.

"I'm Nick Masters." He smiled and eased his hands from my face.

Master Masters? I almost snickered, but cried out in surprise as I was hoisted off the ground and into the burly arms of… what was his name? Oh yes, Dylan.

"Come on, let's get you inside the truck and warm you up." The blonde man's smile was filled with compassion and reassurance. And silly me, I stared up at him with my mouth hanging open, clutching his steely shoulders as a host of lurid images of him 'warming me up' flitted through my head. But oh, it felt glorious nestled against his rugged chest… too glorious.

"I'm Dylan Thomas," he introduced as he carried me toward their big red pickup.

I blinked in surprise. "Like the poet?"

"Yes, like the poet," he chuckled with a nod. Easing me onto the bench seat, Dylan turned up the fan on the heater then shut the passenger door.

The lush air inside the truck felt heavenly. I leaned forward, warming my fingers against the dashboard vents. Dylan reappeared on the other side of the truck and climbed in next to me, behind the steering wheel.

"Where were you headed before the accident?"

"Kit's Korner. It's a bed and breakfast down the…"

"I know where it is. Nick and I are staying there, too. We stay there every year."

"So do we."

His brows drew together as his piercing blue eyes studied my face. "Do you need to call someone? Your husband? A boyfriend?"

"No, neither. I… I'm meeting my sister, Mellie, tonight. Ohmigod, I bet she's going to be worried. I need to call her. See, it's our annual 'Sisters Getaway.' We meet in the summer, when it's warm, you know? We couldn't do it until now because we've been busy."

Even I couldn't follow my manic rambling. My brain wasn't firing on all cylinders and I wondered if I was making a lick of sense. Gazing into his dangerous eyes, it was a miracle that I was able to string more than two words together without tripping over my tongue. I turned my attention toward the sight of poor Bambi lodged beneath my Escalade. My throbbing head and aching shoulder were unrelenting, but the gnawing suspicion that Nick was a Dominant was taking precedence over the pain. I was far more apprehensive about my conjecture of Nick than worrying about what dork-wad impression I was making on a hot guy sitting next to me.

"We're out of cell phone range now. You probably already know the area around Kit's is a dead zone, right?" After I nodded, Dylan went on. "Nick carries a satellite phone. I'm going to get it from him so you can call your sister, okay?"

I nodded again like a damn bobble head doll, but at least I wasn't trying to talk. Dylan flashed a panty-melting smile and patted my leg. I tensed at his touch and tried to ignore the current of electricity that darted straight to my core.

"Don't worry. We're here to help you. So you just sit back and relax. We'll take good care of you, kitten. I promise."

I swallowed tightly as he sprung from the truck and shut the door. Dylan had just called me *kitten*.

"No way," I whispered as a new wave of anxiety tingled in my veins. "Surely they can't *both* Doms, could they?" The question had my hormones swirling like an F5 tornado. Pain, guilt and fear made for a potent emotional cocktail. This was either a fabulous dream or a goddamn nightmare…I just wasn't sure which.

As both men climbed into the toasty truck, I tried not to tremble. Nick, the dark swarthy man, handed me his satellite phone. I placed a call to Mellie, but she didn't answer. I felt bad that I had to leave a condensed message of my disheartening episode but reassured her that I wasn't hurt. After placing calls to my insurance company and securing a rental car to be delivered to Kit's, Nick asked what personal belongings I needed from my demolished SUV. Of course, neither of them allowed me to lift a finger. They loaded my things into the backseat of their truck as sirens wailed in the distance.

I turned in my seat, pinning Nick with a stern glare. "You didn't tell them to send an ambulance, did you?"

"Oh I did, pet. And you *will* be checked out, even if I have to tie you to the gurney myself. Do you understand?" A smirk curled one side of his mouth as his sinful eyes flashed with hopeful promise. My blood spiked, my body hummed, and a rush of honey spilled from inside me.

"Yes, Sir," I mumbled then gasped, dismayed at my submissive response.

"Very nice, pet," Nick purred. "I knew the minute I gazed into your eyes."

"Knew what?" I huffed. I couldn't retract my initial response, but prayed I could blow enough smoke to hide my true longings.

"We'll talk later, after I know you're all right, girl. We have a lot to discuss."

The knowing smile that adorned his face was maddening. I wanted to lie, to refute his assumptions, but an ambulance and patrol car were barreling down the road. Now wasn't the time. My head wanted to explode as the sirens screamed in a bone-rattling pitch.

The EMT's poked and prodded announced I had no broken bones, but suggested I be transported to the hospital for further evaluation. I adamantly refused. It was only a headache and a few sore muscles, definitely not life-threatening injuries that would warrant a hospital visit. I was warned to seek medical assistance if my headache got worse or didn't go away. I assured the EMT's I would if I needed to, which placated them to a degree.

Nick, too, promised to hog tie me and take me to a hospital if any lingering side effects from the accident remained. I rolled my eyes at his overprotective mien then watched as my SUV was hoisted onto the back of a tow truck—wobbling over the remains of the poor deer—and limp down the road. After answering a zillion questions, the officer handed me a copy of the accident report then informed me that I was free to go.

Before climbing back into their truck, I dug through my makeup bag until I found the bottle of pain pills I'd thankfully packed.

"Do you have any water, by chance?" I asked Nick, who was watching me as if waiting for me to explain the meds in my palm.

"Sure thing." Dylan smiled as he flipped open the lid of cooler in the bed of the truck and plucked out a bottled water.

"What are those?" Nick asked, nodding toward my hand.

"Pain pills."

"Why do you carry pain pills?"

"I had dental surgery a couple of weeks ago. It flared up last week so I wanted to be prepared in case." I shrugged. "Guess it was a good thing I did."

"You were a girl scout, weren't you?" He grinned as he retrieved the bottle of water and handed it to me.

"No." I chuckled, shook my head then swallowed the pills.

It felt like hours before we were finally on our way to Kit's. Seated between the buff men as we drove down the gravel road, their combined warmth and masculine scents had me reeling like a poster child for schizophrenia.

"So what happened back there? How did you manage to pulverize that big bastard?" Nick asked, capturing me with his sinful black eyes.

"I didn't mean to… to kill the poor innocent thing." The weight of my guilt was oppressive.

"Innocent, huh? Kind of like you?" A wolfish nuance laced Nick's smile.

"I'm not innocent," I protested, but my tone was far from convincing.

"Right," he said with a derisive smirk. "Tell me something, how innocent was that buck when he demolished your Escalade?"

"It wasn't his fault. I should have been paying attention."

"What were you paying attention to?" Dylan asked, glancing at me for a brief second.

"I'd taken my eyes off the road to turn up the heat, but it was just for a second. When I looked up, he was right in front of me. There was nothing I could do."

"Do you need us to turn up the heat?" Nick's decadent, velvet purr left no doubt he wasn't talking about the heat of the truck.

Desire slashed through me like a hot knife and scalded my cheeks. I lowered my head to hide my embarrassment. "No thank you, I'm fine."

"You're not fine, kitten. You've just been in a wreck. Don't lie to us. We don't tolerate that very well." Dylan warned.

"How long have you been in the lifestyle?" Nick's forthright question caught me off guard.

Suddenly the air in the truck was as thick as mud, at least for me. "I don't know what you're talking about," I lied.

"Hrmm, I bet you don't." Nick scoffed. Suddenly he leaned in; his lips close to my ear. "You don't need to run from it, little one. If it's something new and little bit scary, talk to us. We'll help you through it."

I shook my head in furious denial then thrust out my chin. "I'm not running from anything."

"Ordinarily, we spank little subbies for lying, but we'll give you a free pass on the off chance you really don't know what you are." Dylan's smiled. His expression was warm, but his voice teemed with command.

Staring at his broad hand gripping the steering wheel, I had no trouble envisioning Dylan's beefy paw spanking my ass. That thought had my brain spinning like a ballerina on crack. *No.* I couldn't confess that I knew about Dominance or submission for fear it would lead me to profess the kinky fantasies tucked deep in my brain.

I sucked in a deep breath and mentally hiked up my big girl panties. "I know exactly what I am. I'm a successful businesswoman who has no intention of handing over her power to a couple of Neanderthals who want to subjugate her."

Nick's eyes flashed wide and a brilliant smile exploded over his face. "How do you know it's a power exchange, pet?"

Fuck! Me and my big mouth. "This discussion is over," I announced in a haughty, ice queen tone—the one I reserved for assholish lawyers who assumed I was an incompetent adversary.

"Oh it's far from over, little one. But we'll table it until you're feeling better." Nick's dazzling smile was so intoxicating, I felt like a drunken sorority pledge.

With a non-committal scoff, I deemed my best course of action was to keep my mouth shut and not say anything stupid. Not give them any leverage that would lead to me succumbing to the dark, forbidden desires laid buried inside.

As the pain meds began to take effect, my eyes grew heavy. They slid shut and I rested my head on the back of the seat while my brain whirled.

I'd somehow managed to be in the midst of two Doms. Doms that exuded an aurora of power, more power than I'd felt before. Either seemed more than capable of fulfilling my deviant dreams. And while a part of me felt like a kid in a candy store, another part felt like a scared rabbit stalked by a couple of hungry wolves.

On the other hand, they didn't know a whit about me or my boring life. I could be as wild as Mellie, if I wanted to. She was forever trotting the globe as an interior designer to the world's rich and famous. I'd stopped counting the number of flings she'd had with filthy rich men from exotic continents. Unfortunately, I was nothing like my sister. Dylan and Nick might be floored to discover my last dating disaster had been nine long months ago, with a boring paralegal from Topeka. I was the first to admit I lacked in sexual prowess, but nothing had prepared me for Wayne. He pegged the needle on the Nerd-O-Gram. Compared to him, I was a promiscuous sex-kitten. Lucky for me, Wayne's sinuses began to drain half way through our date. When he put the metholatum strip across his nose in the restaurant, I knew he'd be lucky to get a handshake when the night was through.

It was a sad fact that my love life sucked. So why couldn't I have a BDSM ménage fling? What was stopping me? *Your fears, you idiot.* That tiny of voice of reason echoed in my head. But it wasn't like I'd ever see them again. There'd be no awkward "Thanks, we'll have to do this again sometime" or "I'll call you in the morning" bullshit. Nothing was stopping me from living out my fantasies if I really wanted to. And thinking about the two men I was wedged between… I really wanted to. Maybe I could break free of my chaste shell for a few days. I'd have a steamy bounty of memories to take back home and re-live at my leisure…Like every flippin' night with BOB, my battery-operated boyfriend.

My thoughts grew fuzzy, shrouded in a dark haze that seemed determined to drag me under. Absorbed by the hum of the diesel engine, I faded into nothingness.

Pulling me from the inky blackness was a rich, smooth voice. Disoriented and floating in a thick fog, it took me a moment to realize I was no longer in the truck, but flat on my back in a warm, soft bed. I wasn't at home because it didn't smell like my room. And I knew I wasn't in a hospital, either. There was a strange familiarity to the scent of cinnamon and spice, and as I opened my heavy lids for a moment, calmness settled over me. I was at Kit's. My eyes fell closed as I struggled to clear the drug-induced blanket that enveloped my brain. Focused on the deep, lustrous tone, I attempted to decipher the words resonating in my ears.

"No, I do *not* want her rescheduling the damn deposition again, George. This is bullshit. She's playing the victim card and I'm sick to death of it. She signed the pre-nup without an ounce of reservation. She stole from me, lied, and cheated. As per our agreement, she took everything she walked in with: Pimp-boy's Bentley and a fucking closet full of designer clothes and shoes. I will not give her a goddamn penny!"

Nick. Yes, it was the russet-skinned Native man talking, but his voice sounded funny. Tight and brittle and bathed in sharp but controlled anger. Battling my brain, I searched for a clear path through the twisted labyrinth of residue that the pain pills had left behind.

Pre-nup? As in divorce?

"She needs to find another stupid bastard to sink her talons into. I'm done."

Forcing my lids open, I spied Nick sitting in a chair at the foot of my bed. Sat-phone pressed to his ear, his expression was grim as he pinched the bridge of his nose between his thumb and finger.

After forcing my lids to remain open, I inhaled a deep breath. The familiar spicy scent of the barn drew a smile. It wasn't really a barn, but a modernized outbuilding, a separate structure to house guests across the gravel parking lot from Kit's early 1900's Victorian mansion that accommodated even more customers.

Mellie and I always opted to stay in the barn on our yearly trip. Its seclusion ensured we could stay up late, giggling, sipping wine, and talking trash without worry of keeping other guests awake.

Overpowered by the mighty weight of my lids, my eyes slowly eased shut once more. But I continued to listen to

Nick's decadent voice and tried to ignore the tingles of need his tenor induced.

"Thanks, George. I appreciate you handling this for me." Suddenly his tone softened to a more familiar timbre. "How are things going at Genesis? Is little Leagh still keeping you on your toes?" I could hear the echo of George's baritone voice through the sat phone, but not clearly enough to make out what he was saying. There was a long pause before Nick issued a deep laugh. "She loaded your toy bag with clothespins and bunny floggers? Whoa damn, that little vixen. I'll be anxious to hear how you punished her for that when we get back. *If* we get back, that is. There's a hell of a nasty storm that got us in its crosshairs. If it's headed your way… stay safe my friend." Nick paused, again. "Okay, man. Thanks for everything. I owe you a bottle of Macallan or Dalmore, your choice. Later, man."

"Who are George and Leagh?" I asked. My tongue felt like rubber and my words came out slurred. "What time is it?"

"Ah, you're awake. They're friends of mine. Well, mine and Dylan. It's about four-thirty in the afternoon. How's your headache, little one?"

The bed dipped and I forced my eyes open, determined to stay alert as I gazed up at Nick sitting alongside me. Lord, the man was gorgeous. His long, inky hair hung over his shoulders and I wanted to reach out and touch it, to rub the glistening strands through my fingers.

I swallowed back the longing with my dry throat. "Headache's gone, but I feel loopy. I think I've been sucking on sand. I need water."

"Good. I'm glad your headache's gone. Stay put, I'll be right back."

It was a chore, but I pulled my arms out from beneath the blankets and eased against the headboard. The covers pooled around my waist and I gasped to discover I was buck-ass-naked. I yanked the sheet up to my neck as Nick swaggered from the bathroom with a glass of water in his hand.

"Where the fuck are my clothes? And who the hell undressed me?" I screeched.

Nick blinked than narrowed his eyes, his brows slashed in an angry scowl. "Seems I forgot to get the soap from the bathroom to wash your filthy mouth out with, little one."

"The hell you will," I gasped.

"Dylan and I took your clothes off and washed the blood from your foot before we tucked you into bed. Your clothes are up at the house. Kit's trying to get the stains out. And your shoe is in the dumpster on the driveway."

Nick thrust the glass toward me with a disapproving frown. I guzzled the cool, refreshing liquid and tried to ignore his stern expression. A wave of guilt washed over me and though I probably owed him an apology, they'd seen me naked… without *my* permission. I had no idea if they'd touched me or fondled me, I was knocked the hell out on pain meds. I didn't know a damn thing about either of them. They could have violated me anyway they'd wanted to, and I'd never have known.

I glanced up at Nick and was surprised to see a hint of hurt in his expression. I suddenly realized, if they were indeed Doms, they wouldn't have taken such liberties with me. They would adhere to the BDSM code of conduct, which was "safe, sane and consensual." My stomached churned and embarrassment spiked for thinking they'd done anything but care for me. Still, they were strangers and dammit, they'd seen me naked.

Even the two men I'd had clumsy sex with back in college hadn't seen me totally nude. I'd made sure the lights were out before I'd worked up enough courage to peel off my jeans. My inept sexual experiences were less than exciting. It obviously wasn't for either of the nerds, because they never came back for a second round.

Nick crossed his arms over his massive chest as I drained the water from the glass. Gazing at his russet muscles bulging from beneath his tight black T-shirt, I prayed I wouldn't choke. He looked forceful and imposing and I had the overwhelming desire to trace my tongue over every defined ridge of his body.

"You know, you're not the first woman I've seen naked. And I can safely say you won't be the last."

"I'm sorry if I seem unappreciative, but I was surprised to wake up nude. I'm a modest person. I don't prance around naked in front of people. I can't even remember the last time my own doctor saw me without a paper gown on." My words tumbled out, clipped and bitter.

"We didn't undress you with sexual intent, little one, if that's what you're worried about."

"I'm not worried." I lied. "But you two certainly could have done anything you wanted and I'd be none the wiser now, wouldn't I?" I hissed. Cursing my burning and aroused body, I longed for them to touch me, comatose or not.

The smile Nick bit back infuriated me even more.

"Trust me, little one. When we explore your body, we're going to want you wide awake for every sweet caress."

"You're forgetting one key element, Mr. Alpha Dom... it has to be consensual."

"Consensual, indeed. Which brings us back to the question I asked in the truck, girl. How long have you been in the lifestyle?"

I clenched my jaw, determined not to answer.

Nick sobered. "Why do you do that?"

"Do what?"

"Pull up walls and hang 'no trespassing' signs the minute you realize you're not in control?" He leaned down and stroked a warm finger over my cheek. "You know being out of control, especially for someone like you, is usually an amazing experience."

"Someone like me? I have no idea what you're talking about," I lied, as I jerked back and set the empty glass on the bedside table with a heavy thud. "I'm sure you think I'm some type of repressed submissive. I hate to burst your bubble, pal, but I'm not a sub. Not in the least. I am always in control and I like it that way."

"You've already used your free pass, little one. That lie is going to cost you." A wicked grin spread across his gorgeous lips. "Not tonight, but soon."

I swallowed down desire, then inhaled a deep breath. "Look, Nick. I'm not here to play games. I'm here for a week of relaxation with my sister."

But the entire time I tried to reason with him, fantasies of those Dom/sub games involving him and Dylan filled my mind. I closed my eyes and with a slight shake of my head, vanquished the images. The reality was, I'd never be brave enough to confess my submissive desires to Nick, Dylan or anyone else. And his dogged questions about my experience of BDSM, or rather lack of, only served to breed doubts and insecurities in my brain. Why was Nick showering me with flirtatious overtures? Did he derive some kind of sick thrill out of? Or was he pretending to be interested in someone like me, assuming I'd be a quick, convenient conquest?

Nick had already commented about me being innocent—even though I'd refuted it with an abysmal lie— I wasn't naive enough to harbor hopes that eye candy like he and Dylan would ever look twice at me. And why was I allowing such lofty thoughts to burn up my brain cells in the first place? Nothing was going to happen because I was too big a chicken. But it didn't diminish the fact that he'd seen me naked, seen every one of my imperfections, and still taunted me with sex-laced innuendos. Could he honestly be interested in me?

Fat chance.

Insecurities swirled like a twister inside me, but one thing was certain: Nick's powerful command tested my restraint. It was paramount that I shield myself in a thick layer of armor, until I figured out what game he was playing, lest I do something stupid like beg him to teach me the ways of submission.

Nick walked to the end of the bed, pulled back the curtain, and gazed out the window.

"Speaking of your sister, she called on the sat phone while you were asleep. They had to divert her flight to Oklahoma City because the storm has already hit Omaha and their airport is closed. She's not sure she can make it but thanked me for helping you out." He turned, a wolfish grin tugging his lips as he gazed into my eyes. "I promised her we'd do everything in our power to take good care of you."

Assaulted with a combination of arousal and despair, my heart sank and my shoulders sagged. I hung my head, blotting out his innuendo, as the force of Mellie not coming to Kit's slammed me hard. This was supposed to be *our* time. It was the most important event in my boring life. I looked forward to this week the whole damn year and now…it wasn't fair. Since our parents died, I drew strength from Mellie. I counted on her to prop me up and make me feel like I could survive another year of work and sleep, work and sleep. She was all I had left and she wasn't coming. Tears stung my eyes and slipped down my cheeks.

"Aww, little one, don't cry," Nick consoled as he turned and sat next to me on the bed. Placing two wide fingers under my chin, he raised my head, forcing me to look into his eyes. "I'm sure she'll try to get here in a day or two. I see your time with her means a lot to you."

"It does," I sniffed, clutching the sheet to my breasts. "I've looked forward to this vacation with her for such a long time."

Nick released my chin then wiped my tears with the broad pads of his thumbs. How could he could be so tender, yet so incredibly powerful? He was frightening and enigmatic in a surreal way and the longer I was in his presence, the more I could feel him delving inside my soul.

"Where's Dylan?" I asked, unable to mask the quiver of insecurity.

He held me in a commanding yet compassionate gaze. "When we carried in your purse, it slid off the table and some of your things fell out. As we were putting them back in we saw your grocery list so he ran to the store to pick up the things you wanted."

"You looked in my purse?" I screeched, in disbelief.

Nick raised his palms. "I know. I know. We breached the most sacred place a woman possesses. But you'll be pleased to know we put everything back in while keeping all your secrets intact. No wars were started and no children or animals harmed in the process," he explained as that dazzling smile spread across his lips.

I couldn't help but chuckle. "You're a smart ass, you know that?"

"So that's what it takes?"

"That's what *what* takes?" I felt my brows furrow in confusion.

"What it takes to make you smile."

My face warmed and I lowered my head. They had taken charge of everything. I didn't know if I should be happy or mad about it. Having decisions made for me felt…awkward.

"He didn't have to do that. I could have borrowed Kit's car."

"He wanted to, pet, besides you're in no condition to drive."

"I feel fine now. I *could* have driven." Nick issued a look rife with skepticism and I sighed in frustration. "Do you mind stepping out of the room so I can find my robe?"

"Yes, I mind. I have no intention of leaving you alone after the dose of pain meds you took. They knocked you out cold. I'm not about to let you stumble and fall. What if you hit your head?"

He was the most infuriatingly pigheaded man I'd ever met. But I could be as equally stubborn.

"I'll be careful. I promise. Now get out so I can use the restroom."

"Go." He raised a hand toward the bathroom, like a restaurant Maître D' ushering guests to their table.

"I'm not getting out of this bed naked. Not with you in the room."

"And I've already told you, I'm not leaving you alone. I don't like to repeat myself, little one. It goes against my nature."

"Ah, yes. Your big-bad-Dominant nature. How silly of me to forget," I taunted with a sarcastic smile. "You may have seen me naked once, but you won't see it twice. Now leave."

He studied me in silence, his lips pursed, and I could almost hear the cogs of his brain turning. Those decadent charcoal eyes seared deep, and the thin sheet I clutched to my breasts, wasn't near the barrier I needed to hide from his scrutinizing Dominant scalpel.

He took a step back then widened his stance, squared his shoulders and placed his hands behind his back. His eyes shimmered with untamed exactness and dominance rolled off of him in a wave so powerful, I thought it would flatten me like a paper doll. A sizzle of excitement blistered my core and hot, slick nectar oozed from between my folds.

"You have two choices, little one. You can either get out of bed and walk your sexy ass to the bathroom, or you can lay there and soil the sheets. I don't care which you decide but listen and listen well. I'm not leaving you alone. So you make the choice. What's it going to be? "

My face burned in embarrassment. His tone was reminiscent of my father, *God rest his soul,* when he caught me trying to shave the family cat when I was six. Maybe I *was* acting like a petulant child, but he was *not* going to see me naked again. My body contained way too many imperfections for me to strut around nude before an audience. Even an audience of one. If I didn't work fifty hours a week, I'd spend more time at the gym and have a tight body. But I would never in a million years lay there and urinate on the sheets—I'd have to be on my death-bed before I would succumb to *that*.

I jerked my head and issued a seething glare. "Fine!"

Flicking my wrist, I ripped the sheet from my body, swung my legs over the bed and stood up. At that exact moment, Dylan stepped into the room, his eyes wide with surprise. I yelped. Consumed with embarrassment, I slapped one arm across my breasts while my hand dipped to cover my pussy.

"No need to be shy, kitten. We've seen every gorgeous inch." Dylan smiled, his enticing dimple claiming my attention before the room began to spin and my vision blackened. My knees felt like Jello-O and I tried to take a step as I blinked through the inky veil that was closing in fast.

"Shit!" Nick cursed. Before I could get my bearings, both men had me locked between their muscular bodies. I stood helpless, sandwiched between what felt like, two marble statues. Hormones zinged and pinged and it was the most divine moment of my entire life.

"Back to bed," Nick barked.

"I'm fine," I argued, shaking off the rush of lust. "I just stood up too fast."

"You're a stubborn little kitten, aren't you?" Dylan growled.

"No, I just need to go pee."

Their combined heat enveloped me and an arc of fire burned deep in my womb. Proportionately huge erections pressed and warmed my mound and ass. I closed my eyes, trying in vain to shove the image of tandem cock worshiping from my mind.

They led me to the bathroom and after convincing them I was capable of taking care of my business without their help; they left me alone and closed the door. I envisioned them standing on the other side, hovering like a couple of mother hens. While I didn't know why, they seemed bent on coddling me. Funny thing was, I thoroughly enjoyed it—all except for the part of being nude—which hadn't seemed to turn them off. They'd continued to flirt with me… at least I thought it was flirting. I couldn't be sure. A part of me wondered if they were simply trying to put me at ease after my hellacious day. Without a lot of exposure in dealing with the opposite sex, I wasn't completely sure what they were up to. The only way to find out was to ask, and I certainly wasn't about to do that.

As I washed my hands, I noticed my toiletries had been neatly aligned on a glass shelf, inside an alcove by the sink. They'd unpacked for me, too? *Oh my god. Where's my vibrator?* Embarrassment consumed me and I could only hope that they'd left my suitcases alone. I brushed my teeth and started to brush my hair when a tiny tap came from the other side of the door.

"You okay in there?" Dylan called out to me.

"Yes, mother, I'm fine." I sighed and rolled my eyes.

Gooseflesh peppered my arms at the sound of his sardonic chuckle. "Just so you know, princess, we're both wearing belts and we found some cotton rope, not to mention a whole drawer full of wooden spoons and spatulas in the kitchen."

"Are you implying that you'd try to tie me up and spank me?" I asked as I wrapped a fluffy white towel around me.

"Oh yeah," Dylan replied in a sexy drawl from beyond the portal.

I opened the door to find him wearing a dangerous smile, dangling my silk robe on the tip of his finger.

"Is that your idea of a threat?" I asked as I plucked the garment from him.

"No, kitten. That's a promise." He said with a wink.

I flashed a patronizing smile, then closed the door in his face.

CHAPTER TWO

Emerging from the bathroom, with my robe cinched firm around my waist, I felt more in control until Dylan slid his arm around me. His touch was tender, as if cradling a delicate porcelain doll. A shiver stormed down my spine. Nick reappeared at the doorway carrying a mug of hot tea and ordered me back to bed.

Their overindulgence was near claustrophobic, but I sipped my tea beneath their watchful gaze, thankful for the TLC they extended.

"We're going to go relax in the other room so you can rest," Dylan announced as they both stood and turned for the door.

I felt a little guilty for the wave of relief that washed over me.

"Hey guys?" I called out. "I just want to say thank you both for… everything."

Their matching broad smiles warmed my heart.

"We'll let you shower us with appreciation later." Dylan winked with a devilish grin then closed the door behind him.

My heart drummed in my chest. Surely he wasn't talking about showering them sexually, was he?

Oh, you wish.

"Right," I whispered aloud. They were far too suave and urbane for a plainJane like me. They had swag, and lots of it. I had GPS coordinates and typographical maps.

But they don't know that about you, and they'll never find out, unless you tell them.

Me, me engage in a meaningless fling? "Honestly." I mumbled aloud. "More like…turn tail and run."

And why was I thinking such ludicrous thoughts in the first place? They weren't interested in having sex with me. This was all some grandiose game they got off on playing. They had no intention of following through with their sexual innuendos, did they? Doubts volleyed through my brain like a tennis ball at Wimbledon. And trying to find an answer to any of them was next impossible, not to mention pointless.

Restless, I was no longer tired but bored, vegging out in bed. I made my way to the window and pulled back the curtains. The snow was coming down in a violent rage and the ground was covered in a thick, white virgin blanket.

Disheartened that Mellie wasn't with me, I was relieved she was safe in Oklahoma. Still, I had no idea what to do without her. I sat on the end of the bed and watched the snow pile up.

Lost in my daydreams, I jerked in alarm when a wide palm clasped my shoulder.

"Sorry, kitten. I didn't mean to scare you." The smile on Dylan's face was warm and reassuring. His hand trailed up and down my arm with a compassionate caress. There was nothing sexual in his touch, yet my body responded as if he'd meant it as foreplay and I tingled with the underlying surge of power infused with his fingers.

"No need to be sorry, I didn't hear you come in," I replied with a slight smile. The spicy scent of fish and herbs filled the room and my stomach growled.

Dylan stared down at me. His reassuring mien ebbed and a somber expression lined his face. "Damn, Savannah. You're so fucking beautiful." Absorbed in his cerulean eyes, I wanted to drown in them for hours. "Come on, kitten. Dinner is ready."

I cleared my throat and longing erupted inside. "I can't believe you guys know how to cook."

Dylan wrapped his hand around my elbow as he led me toward the door. "What a treat we have in store for you this week. You may not know it, but you have the pleasure of being snowed in with two of the world's most amazing chefs."

I laughed. "So that means we're having soup and sandwiches for dinner?" I teased.

He clutched his heart and a mock expression of pain distorted his handsome face. "Your lack of faith in us wounds me deeply, kitten."

"Oh so you two pulled out all the stops, huh? You've prepared soup and grilled cheese then, right?" I mocked with a cheeky grin.

Dylan escorted me to a large dining table. As I glanced over the freestanding island centered in the kitchen, Nick looked up. He flashed a heart-stopping smile then focused his attention back to a large steaming pot on the stove. The combination of the delicious aromas and his dazzling smile made my mouth water.

"No, smart ass, something better than grilled cheese and soup. You just wait and taste what we've created for your dining pleasure, kitten." Dylan pulled out a chair for me. "Sit. Your dinner will be served in a moment."

My brows drew together in confusion as I settled in the chair then looked up at him. "But I thought…"

"You thought what?"

"Never mind." I bit my lips together.

I didn't want to bring up the subject of Dominance and submission with them. Serving was a submissive's job. Dom's weren't supposed to wait on a submissive, at least not in any of the info I'd read. There was something fundamentally wrong with the whole picture.

"If you have something to say, speak up. We're damn good at a lot of things, kitten, but mind reading isn't one of our strong suits." Dylan smirked.

"I don't doubt that for a second what you two are good at." The innuendo rolled right off my tongue. I wasn't sure who was more surprised, me or Dylan. The look on his face was pure intrigue. I wanted to die. "I mean… I don't doubt that you guys are good cooks. It smells delicious."

Dylan leaned in close to my ear. His warm breath wafted over my neck and drew a shiver up my spine. "For some reason, you have it in your head that we won't make you pay for your little white lies. Let me tell you something, kitten…you couldn't be more wrong."

He's playing with you. He's not serious. The voice in my head screamed it in an effort to calm my galloping heart. But it didn't work. My palms were sweaty and my throat was dry. I didn't respond, because I didn't know what to say. Instead of stumbling out a reply, I leaned forward and began to fill the empty glass next to my plate with wine.

Dylan reached out, wrapping his wide hand over mine, ceasing the flow of the deep, red liquid, then forced the bottle back to the table.

"What do you think you're doing, kitten? You can't drink alcohol. You might need another pain pill after dinner."

"No wine," Nick bellowed as he made his way to the table, carrying plates laden with food.

"I can have one glass. Besides, I'm done with the pills. I feel fine," I protested as Nick set a steaming plate before me. "Ohmigod, this looks amazing. You really can cook."

"Brat," Dylan chuckled.

I continued to press for wine with my meal, refusing to beg but rather cajole. They grumbled in disapproval but relented and allowed me *one* glass. Dictating my every want felt awkward and uncomfortable, but after one bite of the herb-crusted white fish, my focus centered on the amazing meal.

We ate and talked in a relaxed, casual way. I learned more about them and felt more at ease by the time dinner was done. Dylan had a quick wit and spouted funny one-liners. He reminded me of a sexy game show host. Nick was the more serious and pragmatic of the two but then I remembered the conversation he'd had with his friend George. I couldn't help but think his divorce was the reason for his more subdued mien. Between the two, I could relate more toward Nick's quiet and reserved demeanor. But I found it refreshing the way Dylan made me laugh so easily.

They wouldn't allow me help clean up the kitchen; instead they positioned a large leather couch in front of the fireplace and instructed me to relax. I stared into the dancing flames, wrapped in a soft cotton blanket. My belly was full and for the first time all day, I felt at peace. It wasn't long before they sat down beside me, and once again I found myself nestled between their rugged bodies. Dylan handed me a mug of hot chocolate and I sipped the rich, frothy sweetness as our conversation flowed.

Nick reached his hand back to gently massage my neck as we talked about our lives. Dylan feathered his fingers along my arm and I found myself calming even more beneath their blissful touch.

They'd been best friends since first grade and each claimed the other as a brother. Nick owned a construction company in Chicago. His smile told me he was very proud of the work he did. Dylan had been a sniper in the Marines and served three tours in Iraq. After being honorably discharged, he joined on with Nick as his foreman.

I explained my job as an archeological activist, which after learning about Nick's company filled me with anxiety. I'd lost count of the number of construction company owners I'd pissed off over the years, having slapped injunctions on their dig when something of historic importance was discovered at the site. Nick was sympathetic when I explained most of the artifacts unearthed were Native American in origin.

It had been difficult to tell them about losing my parents at sixteen. I'd never told anyone other than Myron, my boss, how they'd died on an icy Ozark road. Witnesses said my dad had been driving cautiously but hit a patch of black ice at the top of a steep hill. The car slid down a steep embankment and flipped numerous times. They died instantly. It was a freak ice storm they'd encountered on their way home from closing up our cabin for the winter. Mellie was away at college but transferred schools and moved back home, where she raised me until I graduated high school.

I hadn't realized I was crying until both men leaned over, pressed their lips to my cheeks, and sipped away my tears.

An arc of electricity zipped through my veins then centered beneath my clit, scaring the living shit out me.

"Is there any more wine?" I blurted. My body stiffened even as their fingers continued to caress and soothe.

"Not for you, little one. We want you clearheaded when we discuss our next topic."

I wiped my cheeks, swallowed tightly then glanced up at Nick. He was wearing his bad-ass Dom face. A powerful tremor shook my entire body.

"Are you cold, kitten?" Dylan asked.

"No, just scared," I confessed without thinking. "Isn't it getting late? Maybe I should go to bed. We can always talk tomorrow."

"It's barely ten o'clock, little one. Surely you can manage to stay awake a bit longer. Hrrrmm?" Nick cajoled with an arch of his brows.

"Okay," I whispered.

"Good girl." Dylan smiled.

Why did they have to keep saying that? Each time the phrase rolled off their tongues, it was like being punched in the stomach and suffocating in a blast of sexual heat, all at the same time.

"No more evading the question, pet," Nick prefaced with a warning. "What have you experienced in the lifestyle?"

"Nothing," I said in a shy voice. Dropping my gaze, I clasped my hands together to keep them from trembling.

"How do you know about it?" Nick pressed. His calm carefree timbre never altered, nor did the sublime pressure of his skillful fingers on the back of my neck.

"I've read books about it and looked it up on the internet."

"What intrigues you about the lifestyle?" Dylan asked, sidling closer, both hands caressing my non-injured shoulder and my forearm.

While their questions drove my anxiety level through the roof, I'd never felt so safe and protected since my parents were alive. It was as if the ground beneath me had crumbled, but for some unknown reason, I knew in my heart that they'd never let me fall. Maybe it *was* time to put on my big girl panties and be honest about the desires I'd spent so long hiding.

"Everything," I whispered on a shaky breath. "I'm always in control and I dream about letting it all go."

Nick fingers stilled before he palmed my nape. With firm but gentle pressure, he guided me until I faced him. Placing his palm along my jaw, he spread his fingers along the side of my neck in a silent declaration of possession.

Without a word, he leaned in and claimed my lips in a warm, passionate kiss. My head swam and my body ignited as his sensual lips melded against mine. A moan splintered the silence…my moan. Controlled by some unknown force, I slid my hand up his sculpted arm, and threading my fingers through his long, black mane, I savored the contrast of his thick, chiseled body and his soft, silky hair. His gentle force intensified, demanding more. Growing bolder, I matched his passion, giving back every sizzling emotion, reveling in the growl of approval that vibrated over our conjoined lips.

"Fuck, yes," Dylan whispered in encouragement.

Nick's mouth curled into a smile atop mine and I attempted to pull back, but he held tight and kept me captive. The smile disappeared as his tongue traced the seam of my lips, coaxing them open in gentle persuasion. I parted them in timid consent. Without hesitation, his tongue delved deep. His fingers tightened upon my nape as he explored every crease and crevice with a slow languid glide.

Dylan slithered his hand down my arm, massaging his fingers over my stomach and legs, kneading and squeezing with a palliative touch. Engulfed in a thick haze of surrender, I relinquished control. Enveloped in serenity, the heady sensation felt like a powerful drug, one I could become addicted to, if not already. One demanding kiss had drawn out my submission and had me sailing higher than the clouds.

Nick eased back and my eyes fluttered open. He held me prisoner with his decadent gaze.

"Thank you for being honest, little one. It means a great deal to us."

"Uh-huh," I moaned on a quivering sigh as lava-like fire pumped through my veins.

"I need a taste, too," Dylan announced, in a raspy voice teemed with demand.

Nick's hands slid away and Dylan took over, as if they'd rendered this exchange a hundred times before. He didn't say a word, he didn't have to; his hungry expression spoke volumes.

Dylan's soft lips pressed against mine. There was no gentle coax as his tongue claimed my mouth. I could taste his urgency. I clutched his shoulder and wrapped my fist in his shirt, anchored to him for the wild ride.

"That's it, little one. Let him explore your sinful mouth," Nick growled against my ear. His lips left a trail of fiery kisses along the sensitive column of my neck before stopping to nip at my thundering pulse point.

For the first time in my life, I felt truly alive. My body hummed as they set blaze to yearnings that I'd kept locked away. Desire to unleash every single hunger clawed and screamed to be set free.

Dylan skimmed a broad palm over my throbbing nipples. He swallowed my muffled whimpers as his hand stilled, gently cupping one breast. His tongue swirled with mine before dragging me into his mouth, granting permission to explore as he had done to me. With a tentative flick of my tongue, I perused his mouth in an awkward probe, grateful when he assumed control and suckled me deep inside, once again.

With a slow torturous glide, Nick slid his lips up the side of my throat then nipped the fleshy lobe of my ear. My swollen clit throbbed in time with my pounding heart. The little bud, desperate for relief, longed for their skillful fingers to delve between my cream-soaked folds and rub its misery away. The necessity to come filled my soul and I thrust my hips with a wanton roll. Desperate for release, I heard my pitiful whimpers filling the air, and I cried out in frustration when Dylan released my lips.

"Shhhh, kitten. Everything is okay, calm down. We're not going to push you. Let's just sit here and talk." Dylan soothed.

Talk? Was he on crack? I didn't want to talk. I wanted to fuck! Fuck long and hard for hours on end. Feel them driving their glorious hard cocks into me until I lost count of orgasms…lost consciousness. They'd inadvertently unlocked Pandora's Box and dammit, she was primed...and far beyond ready to unleash herself upon their licentious shafts.

"Talk?" I whimpered, panting like a porn star. My head swiveled back and forth as they exchanged a look of disbelief.

"How long has it been since you've…been with someone?" Dylan asked.

Oh hell. Swallowing tightly, I tried to steady my breathing. No way in hell could I confess I hadn't had sex in over four years. They'd fall out laughing and think I was frigid or lousy in bed, which I probably was. I had no idea if I was a good lover or not. I suspected I was pretty lousy, since neither guy from college wanted a repeat performance. But how did one know if they truly sucked in the sack? It's not like I'd handed out score cards at the end of the deed. Christ, I didn't want to think about my lack of sex, much less discuss it.

Nick cleared his throat. When I turned to look at him, he pinned me with an impatient stare. "You're stalling, little one. Stop processing or trying to candy coat it. We know it's been…awhile. We simply want to know how long."

"How do you know it's been awhile?" I snapped with indignation. "I could have had sex last week. It's not stamped on my forehead like the expiration date on a carton of milk, for crying out loud."

"I have no doubt you *could* have. You're a beautiful, alluring, and extremely erotic woman. But you *didn't*." Nick smiled, seeming pleased with his ability to read me like a goddamn book. "You're making me repeat myself, little one. Just so you're aware, I'm keeping track. Now answer me. How long has it been?"

There it was again, that commanding, demanding, Dom voice that made me turn into a gelatinous pile of marshmallow fluff. *Damn him!* I shot a glance at Dylan. He was the jovial one...the more patient and tender of the two, at least that's what I'd witnessed so far. No doubt he possessed a dominant aura, but it wasn't nearly as chokingly palpable as Nick's.

Dylan studied me for a moment and then chuckled. "Oh, kitten. The games you're trying to play will never work. It's best you know that up front. You can't play us one against the other. That's never going to happen." The amusement left his face. "Now answer the question," he demanded in the same stern voice I'd grown accustomed from hearing from Nick.

I didn't want to see the look of pity or disbelief on their faces, so I lowered my head and sighed. "Four years."

"How many times have you had sex?" Dylan asked in a gentle coax.

I closed my eyes as all my grandiose dreams of pretending to be a free and wild spirit swirled down the drain like a flushed turd. And with them went my hopeful Dom/sub ménage fantasies. Dylan and Nick would soon discover that I was nothing more than an inexperienced geek, not a thing like the women they were likely accustomed to. Gorgeous men like them didn't fantasize about having sex with "nerd-girl." And there was no amount of smoke I could blow up my own ass—no matter how alive they made me feel—that could convince me otherwise.

I took a deep breath. "Look guys, it's late and I've had a horrific day. Whatever this is…it isn't going to work. So let's just call it a night and save ourselves from any more awkward conversations. I'll hang out in my room until Mellie gets here. Maybe I'll come out from time to time…we can play cards, or watch TV, hell…I'll even let you give me cooking lessons. But let's stop wasting each other's time playing pointless games, okay?" Without waiting for them to respond, I started to stand.

Before I could lift my butt off the couch, Nick leapt to his feet. He turned and faced me. Anger blazed in his eyes. He thrust out his arm and extended his hand. A rolling wave of fear and indecision gripped me by the throat.

"If you're ready for bed, we will escort you to your room," His voice was low and bathed in warmth but his eyes still held a powerful edge of fury. Dylan stood as well, and looked down at me. His expression was unreadable, but his gorgeous blue eyes had dulled, gone lifeless. Their matching chagrin filled me with dread.

Maybe I'd seen too many horror movies, but the savage expressions etched in their faces ensured taking a shower ranked last on my list. They'd blown the intimidation factor clear off the charts. Still, I refused to sit there and cower. I squared my shoulders, lifted my chin, and stood without the aid of either man.

"I'm quite capable," I replied in a frosty, detached tone.

Nick wrapped his hands around my waist, shifting my robe, and exposing more of my breasts than I felt comfortable revealing. I couldn't erase the fact that they'd both seen me naked, yet the power of his commanding hold stripped me far beneath my surface flesh. I felt sliced open and far too vulnerable.

"We've no doubt you're quite capable of…a lot, little one. But the one thing you consistently show us, the one attribute you have down to a science, is slapping up walls and closing yourself off. Our questions weren't meant to make you run and hide. They were intended for quite the opposite, in fact."

Dylan's fingers feathered through my hair before he tucked a long strand behind my ear.

"We wanted to know if you'd like us to teach you about submission, kitten. We were just about to extend the offer until you slammed the door and locked us out. Which makes us wonder if you were being honest with us in the first place."

I opened my mouth to speak but Nick shook his head, silencing me.

"We can't take you on the journey until we know what makes you tick. The only way we can do that is through communication. If you've investigated the lifestyle, you should know that by now. Wasn't the topic of communication covered in any of the books or articles you read?"

It had been. Almost everywhere. The need for open, honest communication had been driven home like a nail hammered into wood. The cornerstones of a good BDSM relationship were honesty, trust, and communication.

I hadn't been honest with them for fear they'd reject me. I didn't trust them because I didn't know them, at least not well not enough to let them see the real me. And I hadn't communicated anything beneath surface level, aside from the loss of my parents...again, because of my fears.

"You wanted to train me?" I gasped, unable to hide my astonishment.

"No, little one, we *want* to train you, but only if it's something you desire. Is it?" Nick eagerly asked, his face no longer reflecting a hint of its previous fury.

My head bobbed on its own accord before my brain could begin to process why their offer was probably a bad idea.

"Good girl. The first thing you'll have to do is knock down your walls and let us in. Can you do that for us, kitten?" Dylan traced his fingertips up my arm. Gooseflesh pricked my flesh.

"I don't know. I'm scared. I think I want to try, but I already know I'll probably screw it up. There's so much I still don't know."

"We don't expect perfection, little one, just the willingness to learn and to grow and not keep anything hidden. And I do mean *anything*...not your joys, sorrows or fears. Do you understand?"

"I have a lot of fears," I confessed in a small voice.

"We know that. But we're patient. We will help you work through them," Dylan reassured.

"But I don't know that much about you two."

My excuses were fears, rising to the surface. Try as I might, I couldn't stop them from rolling off my tongue.

"Which means you're taking a risk. That makes it doubly difficult, no doubt." Nick nodded. "We want to earn your trust and we'll do all we can to put your mind at ease. We'll never hurt you, Savannah. Never take advantage of the power you give us. On that, you have our word."

"But a minute ago, you were so angry, I didn't know what you were going to do to me. You guys scared me."

"It wasn't anger, little one, it was frustration. You open and close yourself like a revolving door. We keep trying to find ways to stop the damn thing, but we can't. Not without your help." Nick issued a consoling smile. "We can't force your submission. We can only take what you're willing to give us, girl. I think you already know that."

I couldn't help but smile. His analogy was dead on. I could see so very clearly how confusing my behavior had been. "Yes, I do."

"Come on, kitten," Dylan smiled and extended his hand. "Let's get you tucked into bed. We'll start your training in the morning."

Butterflies dipped and swirled in my stomach as I placed my fingers in Dylan's broad, calloused palm. He helped me to my feet then slid his arm around my waist, holding me tight to his rugged body. Nick closed the safety doors of the fireplace and turned off the lights, then draped his arm over my shoulders. The room glowed in the dancing firelight, much like the simmering lust inside my core. I knew sleep wasn't going to come easy, not until my fingers relieved the blistering orgasm bubbling inside me.

They stood at the side of my bed expectantly. Nick leaned down and untied the sash of my robe while Dylan nimbly slid the silky fabric off my shoulders. I sucked in a gasp and gripped the ebbing fabric before it exposed my breasts.

"No. Let go, little one. You're perfectly safe," Nick whispered as he wrapped his fingers around my wrist and eased my hand away. "We're tucking you in. Nothing else."

The robe fell away on a gentle sigh and I fought the urge to cover myself with my hands. Nick leaned over and pulled the sheets down then patted the mattress. With a timid nod, I settled into the middle of the big bed. As Nick drew the covers up, Dylan crawled over me and lay atop the blanket, next to the wall. I turned and stared at him with wide curious eyes. He simply flashed me a smile as Nick slid onto the covers along my other side.

"Sleep, kitten. We promise to keep you safe," Dylan whispered.

Safe. Oh I felt more than safe, a hell of a lot more. Humming with need that I couldn't sate as planned left me feeling safe but horny as hell.

Nick turned on his side and threaded his fingers through my hair then began to massage my scalp. Dylan also turned, propping his chin in one palm before tracing the tips of his fingers over my cheek in a tender caress.

I closed my eyes. A moan of delight laced my heavy sigh. The abstract patterns their tranquil fingers painted, lulled me into the calling darkness.

CHAPTER THREE

A shrill screech filled the room, jerking me awake. I tried to sit up but was tangled in a web of heavy arms and legs. Nick groaned and pawed at a leather case on his hip as the incessant alarm continued to blare. Glancing over my shoulder, I watched as Dylan scrubbed a hand over his face, lifted his head off the pillow, and opened one eye.

"Good morning, gorgeous," he said with a lazy drawl as both eyes popped open and a slow smile spread upon his lips.

"Hello," Nick growled into his sat phone. "Yeah, just a sec. It's for you," he announced, handing me the phone.

"Hello?"

"Sanna? How bad are you hurt? Please tell me you're okay. How bad is your car?" Mellie's questions rushed out in one long string.

"I'm fine, Mellie. Nothing's broken except my SUV." I smiled.

"Thank god! Is that guy who answered in bed with you?"

"Yeah, I mean…no," I stammered as I tried to sweep the cobwebs from my mind. "Not like you think. Where are you?"

"I'm home," she said with a dejected sigh.

"No," I whined as I sat up and tucked the covers beneath my arms. "Why?"

"Have you looked outside? Of course you haven't. You're in bed with Mr. Dreamy Voice," she laughed. "I was up all night watching the news in the Oklahoma City airport. I just got home a few minutes ago. You're in the middle of a blizzard of biblical proportions up there. Mother Nature is being a bitch. I don't think there's any way I can make it at all, sweetheart."

"Shit," I sighed. Nick cleared his throat and I glanced over at him.

"Soap," he mouthed with a scowl.

"I'm sorry to wake you two up so early. I sure hope I didn't interrupt anything," Mellie teased with a wicked giggle.

"Three of us," I mumbled, still fighting the sleep fog saturating my brain. I cringed when I realized what I'd just confessed.

"Oh, little sis, we're going to have a nice long talk when you get home," her voice dipped to a clandestine whisper. "I want a play-by-play of all your sweaty deeds."

"There's nothing to tell," I replied in a soft hiss. "So you're really not coming?"

"Baby, they've shut every airport down across the northern plains. You can't even get back to Kansas City. At least not for a while."

"Oh, Mellie," I groaned.

"I know. I know. Look, since I've already got the week off and since I can't get to you, I'm going to crash for a few hours then repack and head to Cancun. Alejandro has a yacht and we're going to spin up Baja for a few days."

"You lucky bitch," I giggled.

"Oh, kitten," Dylan warned in a low growl.

I rolled my eyes at him and huffed. Nick pinched my nipple through the bedding and I jumped in surprise then flashed him a hateful scowl.

"I don't blame you for chasing the sunshine and warm temps. Oh and just for your information, we are not planning our trip here in November *ever* again. It's cold as fu--" I amended my words when I caught the look of censure etched on Nick's face. "It's cold here."

"I hear you, baby. Hey, when is Myron planning on shutting down the office this year?"

"He already did. The last case was wrapped up a couple days ago. He and Helen should be in the Caymans by now."

"Oh, good. So you don't have to go back to work until February, right?"

"Yeah,"

"Great! Come stay for Christmas. I'll talk Alejandro into taking us on a cruise to someplace sinfully warm."

I could hear the excitement in her voice, and I hated to dampen her plans, but I'd feel like a third wheel spending the holidays with Mellie and her current *flavor of the month*.

"We'll see," I answered vaguely. "Let's talk about it when I get home, okay?"

"Hey, I'll see if he has a friend for you...maybe two, since you're obviously into that," she giggled.

"No!" I gasped. "Please Mellie, don't. We'll discuss this *later*."

"Or you could bring along the guy with the sexy bedroom voice and whoever else is in the sack with you. Damn, Sanna. When you break out of your cocoon, you go balls to the wall. I never would have suspected you were a closet sex kitten."

"Mel, dammit, just quit will ya?" I warned.

"Aww, okay. I'll stop pulling your chain. But dammit, you're so much fun to tease."

"You're not funny," I groaned.

"Just promise me one thing?"

"What?"

"Don't do anything I wouldn't enjoy." Her sweet laughter made it impossible for me to stay grumpy.

"I won't," I insisted with a soft chuckle.

"Hey Sanna?"

"Yeah?"

"Please don't try to drive anywhere until they get the roads cleared. Promise me." I knew by the tone of her voice...she was worried.

"Cross my heart. I won't even think about it until it's safe. You've got my word, sweetie."

"Thank you, baby. Okay, I'm gonna go crash and burn. I'm exhausted. I'll try to give you a call when I get back from Baja. Is it okay to call on this number again?"

"I'll call *you* when I get home, okay?"

"Give me a break, sis. I wasn't going to steal him, just ask him to talk dirty to me." She giggled.

"*Good bye*, Mellie," I sighed.

"Bye baby."

After ending the call, I handed the phone back to Nick, who was sitting on the side of the bed wearing a cheeky grin.

"What?"

"First, I want to know how you're feeling this morning. Is your headache back?"

"No. I feel fine. My muscles are a little sore, but other than that I feel perfectly…great." I was going to say normal, but me in bed with two studly men was anything but normal.

"By the way, that was an interesting conversation, little one."

My face felt hot. "You heard it?" I gasped as my eyes grew wide.

"Every word. The bad thing about sat phones is that even with the earpiece pressed up tight, you can still hear what the other person is saying." The knowing twinkle in his eyes had me rewinding the conversation in my mind. Had I said anything embarrassing or too revealing? I couldn't remember exactly what had been said, but more than likely it was damning and humiliating.

"So, are you ready to keep breaking out of your cocoon, kitten?" Dylan asked with a broad smile. "We're more than ready show you how to spread your wings and fly."

"Spreading my wings to fly" wasn't the lurid thought flashing in my mind. But spreading my legs and flying to the heavens was…in living color. Damn my pent-up orgasms.

"Who wants coffee?" I squeaked. "Either of you hungry? I'll make breakfast." I was just about to scramble from beneath the covers when I remembered I was naked. "Nick, could you please hand me my robe?"

A devilish smile spread over his lips as he reached out and cupped my cheek. "You will address us both as Sir from now on and your safe word is red."

My guts seized and I swallowed with an audible gulp. Submission 101 had begun.

"I assume you know all about safe words?" he went on. I nodded and noticed the smile had fallen from Nick's face. His tone took on a commanding edge and his eyes conveyed stern authority. "We will ask or give an order only once. If you fail to meet our request, you will be punished, unless of course you call your safe word."

"Don't think about calling 'red' unless you're in physical or emotional pain, kitten. That will earn you an even harsher punishment," Dylan issued in solemn warning.

"You won't be wearing your robe today, pet. If fact, you won't be wearing clothes for quite some time." A wolfish grin spread over Nick's mouth.

"But…" I swallowed tightly. "It's cold."

"Then your nipples will be deliciously hard for us, kitten." Dylan quipped with an equally hungry smile. "Never fear, pet. We'll keep the barn nice and warm."

Nick stood and extended his hand. "Coffee sounds wonderful, little one. Please go to the kitchen and make some for us."

What had I gotten myself into? Last night the thought of submissive training sounded like heaven. But morning brought with it the stark reality that I was in way over my head. Suddenly, learning submission felt more like a prison sentence. Surely they didn't expect me to frolic around all day in the nude…did they?

"You're not already testing the rules, are you, kitten?"

I shook my head as I stared at Dylan. "No…Sir."

"Good. I'd hate for us to get started off on the wrong foot, princess." He smiled.

I sucked in a courageous breath then slid the covers off my body. My nipples beaded instantly and the steady throb of the turgid peaks had nothing to do with the cool air. Before I could begin to rise from the bed, Dylan cupped my shoulder.

"Wait, before you go." He leaned down and covered his silky, hot mouth around my nipple. Sucking it deep, his tongue swirled over my rippled flesh then flicked my turgid bud.

"Ahhh," I cried out on a breathy sigh.

He pulled back with a satisfied smile as he gazed down at my slickened peak. "That's to keep you focused on us while you make coffee, kitten."

"Yes, Sir," I whispered on a shaky breath.

As I eased out of bed, I prayed my trembling legs didn't give way and cause me to eat the floor, face first. Luckily, I made it out the door without any clumsy moves. That was probably because I was too focused on wondering if they were gawking at the cellulite on my naked butt as I left the room.

My wet nipple burned to be immersed in Dylan's hot mouth again, and my hands trembled as I began to make the coffee. I could hear their deep, muffled voices coming from my room but couldn't make out what they were discussing. "Probably plotting all the ways they can think of to make me squirm." I whispered under my breath.

As I filled the carafe with water, my arm brushed across my turgid nipple. A soft moan rolled from the back of my throat.

To keep you focused on us...

"You have no idea how focused I am right now, dude." I hissed quietly. "And it's not on coffee, that's for damn sure."

A rich aroma filled the kitchen as I arranged cream, sugar and various sundries upon a serving tray and when the coffee maker stopped gurgling, I filled three mugs. Taking careful steps, I made my way back to the bedroom and made it without the inky brew sloshing over the rims.

Dylan and Nick sat clustered together in matching wingback chairs. Between them, a pillow lay on the carpet. They expected me to serve them in true submissive style. Even though I'd never attempted them, I'd read about serves, and was determined not to fail my first lesson. Gliding my knees to the pillow, I kept my eyes cast downward as I slowly set the tray down in front of me. Catching a glimpse of my beaded nipples, a tiny smile tugged my lips. I'd been so centered on my task, I'd almost forgotten I was nude.

Panic swarmed in a sudden rush. Not because I was kneeling at their feet in my birthday suit, but because I had no clue who I was supposed to serve first.

"Very nice, little one," Nick praised as he leaned forward, trailing his fingers over my cheek.

"Beautifully done, kitten," Dylan complimented with a matching caress.

I sat frozen, my mind whirling with indecision.

"May I ask a question?"

"May I ask a question, *Sirs*," Nick corrected.

"Right, sorry. May I ask a question, Sirs?"

"Yes, of course. Raise your head, kitten and ask away."

I peered up at Dylan then cast a wary glance toward Nick. "I don't know who to serve first, Sirs." My confession was soft, mirroring the smallness I felt inside.

"Ah, sorry, kitten. We forgot to explain that. You will always serve Nick first. He's more of an Alpha-Dom. That's not to say that I'm not a Dominant, but Nick is wired a bit more demanding than I am."

I'd already surmised *that* from their opposing traits, but having it confirmed somehow made Nick's dominance even more intimidating.

Nick laughed softly as he glanced at Dylan. "That was very... tactful."

Dylan shrugged, his familiar impish grin curling over his lips. "I try."

"Thank you, Sirs," I replied with a nod then turned my attention all on Nick. "How do you like your coffee, Sir?"

"Cream, with lots of sugar. I like sweet things, pet...like you." He smiled.

A shiver chased up my spine as I prepared his mug. I could feel his gaze following my every move. With trembling hands, I turned the cup until the handle faced toward him then raised it above my head. Keeping my eyes cast toward the floor, I prayed the coffee wouldn't slop and burn his thigh. I exhaled a grateful sigh of relief as his broad hands encased mine, stilling the wobble.

"You're doing fine, kitten." Dylan's praise bolstered my confidence. "I prefer mine black, please."

"Yes Sir. Thank you."

Nick's touch may have calmed my trembling hands but did nothing to still my thundering heart. I wanted to please them, to prove I was worthy of their tutelage. Their calm patience and reassurance were an added bonus. They'd brought my yearnings bubbling to the surface and with it a strange feeling of being whole. And while I couldn't quite wrap my head around it, I knew I'd been bestowed with a precious gift...their Dominance.

Nick released his hold on my hand and accepted the cup. "You may serve Dylan now, little one."

Raising the second mug of coffee above my head wasn't as difficult or as scary. Dylan kissed my fingers as he drew the cup from my hands.

"Excellent job, kitten. You may enjoy your coffee now, as well."

"Thank you, Sir." A wave of satisfaction filled me as I prepared my own mug. Sipping the sweet, hot brew warmed me and I was grateful not only for the coffee infusion, but that I'd actually succeeded in not screwing up my first lesson. I sat back on my heels as we chatted, wondering what their next task might be.

Their greedy gazes roamed over my breasts and between my legs. I tried not to squirm as my body reacted to each stirring caress. Before our mugs were empty, Nick stood.

"We're going to fix some breakfast, little one. Why don't you go relax in the tub and we'll come get you when it's ready."

"Yes, Sir. Would you like me to take the tray back to the kitchen for you?"

"No, kitten. We'll take care of it. You run along and relax for a bit. Rest up for your first day of training."

"I will, Sir." I smiled. This submission stuff was great. Well, all except for trekking around nude.

As the tub filled, I brushed my teeth then poured my favorite jasmine bath oils into the steaming water. After shoving my hair into a clip, I stepped into the luxurious water, engaged the jets than immersed my body. My eyes all but rolled to the back of my head as pulses of liquid bliss drummed over my sore muscles.

Nick entered the bathroom long before I was ready to leave the soothing tub, announcing that breakfast was ready. Holding open a big soft towel, his eyes sparkled as I stood and flipped the drain. Heat rushed through me as I tried to shove my insecurities of being naked aside and stepped from the tub.

Nick didn't dry my body with sexual purpose, but with reverent affection in a bonding sort of way. And for some strange reason, it felt more intimate than the kiss we'd shared the night before. Steam clouded the mirror as I released the clip in my hair and set it by the sink. On instinct, I looked around for my robe before I remembered their "no clothes" rule. I steeled myself to leave the warm, humid bathroom, naked as a jay bird.

"I picked out some clothes for you. They're on the bed. Dress and then join us, little one." Nick winked as if he could read my mind.

"Oh, gawd, thank you." I rejoiced.

He raised his brows. "Thank you, who?"

"Ah, I mean, thank you, Sir."

"Much better. Hurry up. We've fixed a feast and we want you to enjoy it while it's hot."

"I will, Sir. Thank you." I nodded as he left my room.

I sighed in delight when I spied my cotton pajama bottoms, a long sleeved thermal shirt, and a pair of socks upon the bed. *No panties? No bra?* It didn't matter, I was just thankful I had warm clothes to wear.

Breakfast was incredible. Fluffy blueberry pancakes, country ham, hash brown potatoes, orange juice and coffee. The conversation was light. Dylan and Nick seemed unusually quiet, which troubled me. Maybe they were in Dom mode and trying to keep my on my toes. The thought excited me and scared me a bit.

When the meal was done, I stood and started to gather the dishes.

"Sit down, kitten," Dylan instructed. When I eased back into the wooden chair, he forced a tight smile. My anxiety spiked. "Do you know why we let you wear clothes this morning?"

"No, Sir." Why *had* they allowed me to get dressed? Were they throwing in the towel? Had I done something wrong, failed the first test without even knowing it? One derisive thought after another hammered through my brain.

"Why do *you* think you've been allowed to dress, little one?" Nick asked with an intense stare.

"Because I failed," I whispered, then hung my head.

They both scoffed softly, which led me to peek up beneath dark lashes. "No," Nick began. "We wanted you to feel more secure. More safe, so to speak. We're going to ask you some questions and we expect absolute and total honesty. Understood?"

Great. I'd rather have done the damn dishes in the nude, than participate in their Dominant inquisition. "Yes, Sir," I said on a bitter sigh.

"I detect some resistance, kitten. Why is that?" Dylan tilted his head as he pinned me with an expectant look.

"I'm afraid that once you find out I'm nothing special, you'll decide this training stuff is a waste of time."

"Thank you for your honesty." Nick replied, his midnight eyes delving into mine as he wrapped a broad hand over my fingers. I drank in his heat as my body trembled. "That's the last thing we'd ever think. Everything about you is special. When we came upon you on the road yesterday, before you even opened your car door, we knew you weren't like any other woman we'd met."

Boy he's good. Nick blew smoke so smooth and lush, I almost believed him.

"So, our first question is one we asked last night. How many times have you had sex?"

His words hit me like a freight train. They wanted all the gory details of my non-existent sex life. I suddenly realized I didn't have near enough clothes on. Rife with scenarios of rejection, I tried to imagine what their reaction would be when they found out I was as sexually inexperienced as I was green of the lifestyle. I figured they'd laugh and I'd feel like a fool, but they wouldn't hurt me, at not least physically.

This test wasn't nearly as easy as serving them coffee. They'd gone from baby steps to pushing me off a fucking overpass. This was going to end one of two ways: they'd catch me or I'd end up splattered on the ground. The odds were fifty-fifty. I sucked in a deep breath then raised my head. Staring across the room, I focused on a putrid oil painting hanging on the wall that I'd never noticed before. Big gaudy flowers in unnatural tones held a certain symmetry that aligned with my feelings of inadequacy.

"Two," I confessed on a modest whisper, then prepared myself for the worst.

"Okay. Can you tell us about the two men? What were they like?"

That was it? Just "okay?" Nothing more about my huge, ugly confession? They didn't fall out laughing. Hell, they didn't even snicker. It obviously took a shitload to shock them. There wasn't a doubt in my mind they'd each had more than two lovers…two hundred probably. And I was certain they'd never gone four days without sex, let alone four years.

To my surprise, they didn't respond; they just moved on to the next question. *Shit. What did Nick just ask me?*

"I'm sorry, Sir. What was the question?"

Nick raised his brows and his lips drew into a tight, thin line. "You know the rules. If I'm forced to repeat myself, then stand and bend over the table, girl."

"I… No. I mean, I was thinking about something else. I didn't hear your question, Nick, honestly."

A devilish smile curled on his lips. "It's Sir, little one. Consider this a reminder to focus on my words."

My body shivered—not with fear—but arousal. Finally I was going to feel what a spanking was really like, not by a hairbrush bent over the bathroom sink, but by a real Dominant's hand. Filled with trepidation and delight, I couldn't speak. I simply stood and waited while Dylan pushed the dishes aside and placed his wide palm between my shoulders. With firm but insistent pressure, he pushed me flat against the polished wooden surface; gathered my wrists and extended my arms high above my head.

"Don't move, kitten," he breathed in my ear before he placed a kiss on my shoulder.

Self-conscious about my ass proffered in such a vulnerable position, I didn't want to focus too keenly on whether they found it repulsive. As if reading my mind, a sound slap landed over my butt cheeks, followed by a brilliant fire that spread over my ass, sluiced down my legs, and crawled up my back. I'd expected the pain but what I hadn't predicted was the needful throb of my clit, or the deluge of slickness that spilled from inside me.

"Oh, yesssss," I hissed as I sagged against the table while arching my ass high in the air. "More. Please."

Nick swore under his breath as Dylan expelled a gravelly chuckle.

"This is supposed to be punishment, little one,"

Unable to miss the humor in Nick's voice, he leaned over my body and brushed the hair from my nape.

"It feels good, Sir," I confessed on a dreamy sigh.

Savoring the lingering sting, I didn't object when my cotton pants were eased from my body. As I shivered at the contrast between my heated flesh and the cool air of the room, chairs scraped over the tile floor. I wanted to sneak a peek and see what they were up to, but kept my forehead pressed against the smooth table…waiting. Anticipation soared as kinky thoughts saturated my mind.

"Spread your legs, kitten," Dylan instructed as a pair of hands gripped my thighs, widening my stance. "You're already wet, pet. I can smell your sweet cunt and fuck if it doesn't make my mouth water."

Dylan's crude language was like an aphrodisiac. I moaned my affirmation as I ground my hips against the table's edge.

Without warning, another sturdy slap landed on my ass. I sucked in a hiss, welcoming an even brighter surge of fire. I exhaled with quick hard puffs as I basked in the swelling tide, wanting nothing more than to drown in its torrid bliss.

A quick succession of wicked slaps lit up my flesh and I cried out as I writhed.

"Your safe word is red. Do you need to use it, little one?" Nick asked in a feral growl.

"No, Sir," I gasped as tears spilled from my eyes. "More. Please."

"Look at that," Dylan said with a hint of awe.

"Son of a bitch," Nick moaned. "I think maybe you should help her out, man."

Enveloped in a haze of fire and demand, their voices were distant. Hazy.

Thick fingers spread my labia and I cried out in surprise as my body took control over my mind, demanding what it needed. My hips ground a hungry rhythm atop the table as a wide palm soothed in unhurried circles over my inflamed orbs.

"Touch my clit, oh please. Please. I need it," I begged with a brazen plea.

"Yes, kitten. I'll touch it and a whole lot more." Dylan promised from somewhere below the table.

I was jolted by his warm, slick tongue as it slid up my center in a slow, languid swipe. My knees buckled and my aching pussy pressed over his face. No man's mouth had ever touched me there. It was a savagely intoxicating sensation and I growled like a feral beast.

"Easy, little one," Nick murmured in my ear as he wedged his arm between the table and my belly, securing my waist in a tight grip. My whole world centered on Dylan's wicked tongue as he lapped my swollen folds, guzzling my nectar and toying with my clit.

"Why don't you date more men?" Nick growled in my ear.

"What?" I panted, lost in the euphoric splendor of Dylan's masterful mouth.

Nick landed a harsh slap upon my ass.

"Oh Christ, no," I wailed.

Another brutal smack brought me up from the table as a cry of searing delight tore from my throat.

"Answer the question," Nick whispered in my ear as he lowered me back upon the table.

Two fingers plunged deep inside my core, driving through the fiery heat in search of… "Oh my god," I wailed. Dylan's fingers tapped upon some unknown, hypersensitive place inside me. Lights flashed behind my eyes. My entire body seized then surged like a tsunami beneath his fingers.

"You don't have permission to come, girl, and if you don't answer my question, I guarantee we'll keep you poised on the edge for hours. I asked you a question and I expect an answer." The foreboding tone of Nick's voice only served to drive me higher. Dylan's fingers stilled and I moaned in frustration. It took a long minute before Nick's words registered in my brain.

"They don't like me," I cried out as I thrust my hips against Dylan's fingers in silent petition.

A brutal spank rocked me to the core. Crying out in pain, I began to sob.

"I expect an honest answer, girl," Nick thundered.

"It is honest," I implored. My tears spilled onto the table.

"Explain your answer, little one," he demanded as his hand soothed the sweltering pain that consumed my orbs.

I needed to focus. Engage my brain. The sooner I answered his relentless question, the sooner they would free me from this frenzy of demand. At least I hoped so.

"I don't know. I mean, I don't know why they don't see me...I don't see them."

"Breathe, pet," Nick coaxed as the wicked tongue beneath the table flicked my clit.

"I can't," I gasped. "Please, let me come. I swear I'll tell you everything."

"You don't make the rules, girl," Nick purred. "We're waiting."

I whimpered and sucked in a ragged breath.

"Dusty courthouses. Ancient security guards. Married lawyers. Assholes. My last date...nerdy paralegal. I suck at sex. There."

It felt like I was reciting shorthand for the short bus. I prayed Nick wasn't going to insist I explain it all again. I knew I'd fail. I needed Dylan's lips...his fingers...his obscene pleasure like I needed air to breathe.

"What do you do for fun?" Nick pressed. I groaned and rocked my hips in need.

"Nothing. I mean, I read."

"You don't go to clubs or out to dinner with friends?"

"No. Please, Dylan.?"

"But I love to hear you suffer, kitten," Dylan growled. "Besides, you didn't ask me correctly. Without showing the proper respect to your Sir, I might just leave you like this."

"No! Please don't, Dylan Sir. Please…"

"Please what?" Nick challenged.

"Touch me. Lick me, Sir."

"Touch what? Lick what?" Nick teased.

"Ohmigod," I moaned. "Don't make me say it."

"If you don't say it, kitten, you don't get it." Dylan warned with a hit of humor.

My mouth was dry as I panted with demand. "Please Dylan, Sir. Touch my pussy with your fingers and your tongue again."

"With pleasure," he roared before his entire mouth enveloped my oppressed pussy. He extracted my honey with ruthless possession.

I bucked and writhed, lost in the splendor of every sizzling sensation. Nick gripped my hair and pulled me upright, his brawny chest like marble against my back.

"Arms above your head, pet," he instructed, releasing my waist only to snake his fingers up my shirt, where he pulled and rolled my beaded nipples.

Soaring to heights I'd never known, I closed my eyes and savored each wicked sensation.

"I can't wait to taste your nectar, little one. Your scent is like sweet wine and I want get thoroughly drunk on you," Nick's warm breath fluttered over my ear. His fingers floated from one turgid peak to the next, teasing with delicate tugs as he plucked a carnal melody that made my body sing.

Dylan's tongue zeroed in on my clit as his fingers found their way back to that magical bundle of nerves deep inside. My limbs grew numb and my body hummed as the gathering storm centered deep in my womb, swelling with stupendous pressure. My wanton cries escalated, higher and faster until my keening whimpers of need filled the air.

"Let it consume you, little one. Fly for us, sweet pet. We want to hear you. Feel you. Watch you come undone."

Dylan pressed his fingers against that secret place as he sucked my clit between his lips and scraped his teeth over the swollen bud. Nick stretched my nipple, rolling it between his finger and thumb. He gripped my hair and tugged my head back before sinking his teeth into my throat.

Lightening exploded down my spine, through my limbs, detonating deep in my core. My screams of deliverance filled the room as my tunnel clutched and seized Dylan's fingers in violent spasms. Wave upon wave exploded through me as they continued to coax my convulsing body, forcing me over the edge again and again.

Nick's rich velvet voice whispered depraved and immoral words as Dylan slurped and lapped my flowing cream. The room spun in a carousel of carnal splendor as they slowly eased me down with gentle strokes and glowing praises.

Nick held my boneless and quivering body as Dylan crawled out from under the table, his face glistening and eyes sparkling. Nick scooped me up into his arms as Dylan stepped in, meshing me between them before he pressed his slick lips against mine and plunged his tongue deep inside my mouth.

I could taste and smell my own essence. It was warm and a bit salty with a hint of spice undefined. Tasting myself was strange but not repugnant and I greedily swirled my tongue around his, capturing more of the unique flavor.

"Let's go to the bedroom," Nick moaned with a needful growl.

CHAPTER FOUR

I was still basking in the afterglow as Nick eased me to the mattress. My butt cheeks were tender, but I barely noticed as I floated on astral clouds of bliss. Nick tugged off my shirt before I snuggled into bed and closed my eyes.

"It's not nap time yet, kitten. We're just getting started." I opened my eyes to find Dylan gripped the hem of his shirt, then shucking it over his head. I was wide awake then.

I turned on my side to gaze over each tanned ridge and rugged muscle of his incredible body. With an inward sigh, I longed to run my fingers over his unyielding flesh. He tossed his shirt across the room with a flick of his wrist and I grinned.

"What? No butt wiggling? No hip thrusts? What kind of strip tease is this?" I laughed.

A muffled chuckle came from behind Nick's shirt as he peeled the tight material off then over his head. My gaze locked onto the toffee-colored planes and rippling muscles of his chiseled form. The two of them looked as if they'd stepped right off the pages of a fitness magazine.

"Where's your money, kitten?" Dylan teased as I rolled to my belly, cradled my chin in my palms, and watched them strip with rapt attention. I licked my lips, still anointed in my salty nectar, as a coy smile blossomed over my mouth.

"I can pay with kisses, Sir," I giggled.

The taunting smile fell from Dylan's face and he wasted no time kicking off his shoes and unfastening his jeans. Nick's unveiling was a scant heartbeat behind his friend. Neither wore underwear, and as they shed their jeans, two glorious cocks sprang forth. They were engorged, erect and ready. I marveled at the stunning sight, captivated by the twin crystal beads clinging to their broad, swollen crests.

"What is it you want to kiss, kitten?" Dylan asked with a feral smile as he stepped forward, fisting his turgid cock. The crystal swell of indulgence grew atop his wide brim.

A sizzle of lust pulsated through my body. I was barely able to peel my eyes from the enthralling sight when Nick stepped in close to me. His eyes blazed with desire. As my gaze dropped to the thick veins lining his wide pillar, his shaft jerked in need.

My palms itched to glide over their straining flesh. Yearned to slide the tip of my tongue over those irresistible beads of pre-come and feel them slide deep in my mouth. My body ached to feel their engorged sabers.

Acting on instinct, I eased off the bed and onto the floor. Tucking my feet beneath me, I thrust my shoulders back and cast my eyes to the floor, waiting their command. Submissive surrender surged.

"Raise your eyes and tell us what is it you want, little one." Nick commanded. His voice was enticing and thick with hunger. A shiver of fear mixed excitement slithered up my spine as I raised my head and stared into his lethal eyes.

"Please, Sirs. I need to taste you…both."

A beastly growl rumbled in Nick's chest as he gripped his shaft, pumping the generous length with ruthless jerks. A trickle of clear fluid seeped from the swollen purple crown and dripped along his fist.

Stepping in front of my face, still stroking his steely shaft, he cupped my jaw. "Open that wicked mouth of yours, little one," he instructed in a low whisper.

"I…I…" My fear surged.

"You've never done this before, have you?" he asked in a compassionate voice.

"No, Sir," I mumbled. Embarrassment spiked.

"We'll teach you," he replied. "Stick out your tongue and slide it over my cock. Taste me, little one."

Nick guided my trembling hand to his cock, wrapping my slender fingers around its girth. His shaft was warm and pulsed beneath my fingers. A powerful intimacy washed over me. It was as if this one touch linked me to his soul. I felt his need, his hunger. It was savage.

I opened my mouth and extended my tongue. With a timid swipe, the clear compulsion exploded over my taste buds. I savored the crystal bead, sliding my teeth over its slick texture. It tasted salty, but laden with a potent musk.

"Oh, my," I whispered, dragging my tongue over his crest, restless for more.

"That's it, pet. Take your time. Satisfy your curiosity," Nick coaxed as his fingers thread through my hair and massaged my scalp. "When you're ready, open up and take me inside. Just remember to relax your throat and breathe through your nose."

Delighting in the unique flavor collecting on my tongue, I nodded.

Growing bolder, I swirled my lips over his broad crest and traced the smooth skin beneath the wide flange with the tip of my tongue. I felt a rush of power when he hissed in approval.

Dylan guided my free hand to his shaft. I began to stroke him, rubbing my thumb over his silky, wet cap. Cupping my fingers over the slick tip, I coated them with his emollient then slid my fist up and down his throbbing shaft.

"Fuck," Dylan snarled. His powerful fingers encased mine, setting the tempo and pressure he desired. "Stroke it just like that, kitten," he murmured, as he guided my hand up and down his hot, slippery stalk.

My confidence bloomed. I opened my mouth and wrapped my lips around Nick's wide, dripping crest. He gripped my hair as I suckled the tip, drawing out more of his tangy essence.

"You're killing me, pet," Nick growled as he tilted my head back with his tangled fist.

Filled fuller with the new position, I rolled my tongue over each distended vein and continued to stroke both their cocks. Nick wrapped his hand over mine, stilling my movement, before he guided me to the base of his cock, squeezing my thumb and finger tightly around him.

"Hold me like that, pet. No more stroking. Your hot mouth is the most motivation I can take right now. I don't want to embarrass myself this soon. Keep me wrapped tight with your fingers, okay?"

I grunted my affirmation, feeding inch after glorious inch of his turgid cock into my mouth. The texture of his velvet steel, his masculine scent, and the veins alive and quickening upon my tongue slashed all modesty. The feel of their cocks called to some inborn, primordial feminine craving, compelling me to sate.

"Yes, kitten. Suck him deep. Convince him how fiercely you want to please him," Dylan encouraged. He disengaged my hand from his shaft and I emitted a whimper of dismay over Nick's cock.

"Fuck," Nick hissed, then gripped my hair and shuttled a frenzied tempo before he pulled from my mouth with a feral roar.

"On the bed, kitten. It's time to brand you as ours," Dylan directed.

Brand me? Fear thundered through my veins. Glancing around the room, I searched for whatever nefarious tool they intended to use. Surely they weren't planning to carve my flesh with a branding iron or knife…were they? I swallowed then skimmed a scared glance between them.

"You're going to do what?"

"Brand you, little one, with our come. Mark your breasts, your belly. Your flesh with our seed." Nick explained, his eyes glazed in desire as he jerked his cock with vicious strokes. "We're going to claim your power as we brand your mind, heart, body and soul."

My…heart? *No.* They could have my mind and body all they wanted, but I'd never give them my heart or my soul. This was a training exercise, not a love connection. If I allowed them to crawl inside my heart, I'd never survive the death outside this magical cocoon. They could only take what I was willing to give. As long as I shrouded my heart, everything would be fine.

With a timid nod, I forced a smile then rose from the floor and climbed onto the bed. They joined me atop the mattress. Nick knelt on my left and Dylan assumed the same position on my right. I stared up at their rugged bodies proffering myself like a sacrificial virgin.

Nick gazed down at me, command and power flashed in his eyes. Hunger etched his face.

"Who do you belong to?" Dylan asked. Their fists blurred, pumping up and down their angry shafts.

"You, Sirs," I whispered, unable to look away from their forearms bunching and flexing with their punishing strokes.

"What is your purpose, pet?" Nick pressed. His rich voice was thick with lust.

"To please, Sirs."

"Very nice," he moaned, sweat glistening upon his impeccable body.

"Spread your legs. Use your fingers and open your pussy for us, sweet slut," Dylan demanded.

Slut. It was such a filthy word, but Dylan's tone held such idyllic passion, it slashed away all vulgar implications. I'd never felt so aroused. So debased. So calm. So submissive.

No longer coaxing, they meted control with deliberate precision. Stretching my thighs wide, I spread my saturated folds open, watching as their eyes flared and bore into my pink parted flesh. Inspecting my wet slit, Nick's eyes narrowed in concentration as their labored breathing filled the room.

Clear fluid dripped from their bulbous tips glazing my breasts and stomach. This torturous precursor filled me with anticipation. Watching as they bludgeoned their weeping cocks, anticipating of their hot come splatting over my flesh, was maddening. Aching to feel claimed…owned, even for the briefest moment in my life, was piercing. Spreading my labia wider, I toyed with my clit. It was hard, in distress, and ready.

"Beg for us to claim you, sweet slut," Dylan choked as sweat beaded his forehead. A grimace of lust distorted his features. Power. Demand. Control. He wore each expression like a fine tailored suit.

My tunnel contracted and my heart soared at the sublime splendor of it all.

"Please, Masters. Please mark me. Make me yours," I moaned on a ragged whimper.

"Oursss," Nick cried as streams of thick, hot nectar erupted from his shaft, spewing over my nipples, my throat, painting my chin.

Almost simultaneously, Dylan's eruption followed. He cried out as silky, warm seed splattered lower, glazing my stomach and breasts with his sultry offering. Ropes of creamy come spurted from their cocks, bathing me in their fiery brand of possession.

Tears stung my eyes and a whispered mantra of "yes, yes, yes," spilled from my lips. The magnitude of the moment blindsided me as sobs tore from my throat. Nothing could have prepared me for the onslaught that fused my heart, body and soul. *This is submission.*

The last of their vestiges dripped over my skin. I dragged my fingers through their hot seed then drew the slick offering to my lips. Collecting their creamy treasure, I sucked on their fingers and filled my belly with their silky imprint.

Nick climbed from the bed and returned with a towel. With reverent tenderness he wiped me dry, yet couldn't erase the indelible mark branded to my soul.

In perfect synchronicity they eased beside me, a glaring testament to the number of times they'd dispensed this exact bounty on other women. Before childish jealousy could stab me too deep, Nick wrapped me in his arms, curled me onto my side and held me tight against his chest. Dylan pressed his warm body against my back. Encapsulated in their steely bodies, I felt small and slashed open in ways I couldn't begin to articulate. Overwhelmed with emotion, tears spilled from my eyes

"I don't know why I'm crying," I whined. And I didn't. Unable to compartmentalize or reconcile the barrage of feeling that ripped through me, I felt as fragile as bone china. Something amazing and far beyond my comprehension had been unlocked inside me. I felt vulnerable, raw, and strangely at peace, which did nothing to stop the avalanche of emotions crashing down on me.

"It's okay, kitten?"

"It's not okay. I don't know. What is wrong with me? Why can't I stop crying?" I sobbed, wishing I could sort the myriad of indescribable feelings pinging through me. But I was powerless. "Thank you for giving me this. I know it sounds stupid, but I never would've had this experience if it weren't for you both. Thank you. I'm sorry…God, I sound so pathetic," I choked as the tears continued surge.

"What's happening is perfectly normal. Tell us what you're feeling and we'll help you through it," Dylan soothed as his wide hand trailed up and down my hip.

"I don't know how to describe it. I don't have words that encompass all these feelings. They're too big and it's all so foreign." I sniffed.

Their understanding of what I struggled to comprehend…it was like a safety blanket. They eased me down from my emotional high with tender words and indulgent caresses. Before long, I'd regained my composure and settled down, nestled between their rugged bodies.

My thoughts swirled as I tried to dissect and analyze each emotion. As my mind wandered down a convoluted labyrinth, tendrils of fear took root in the pit of my stomach. How was I supposed to go back to my uneventful life after experiencing such wonderment? The void was sure to be staggering. Tempering the surge of panic even as it clawed to break free, I focused on the rhythmic pattern of their breathing, concentrated on the soothing cadence of their fingertips, and put a lid on thoughts of the future.

You're here now. Bask in every sensation while you can.

I nuzzled Nick's chest and closed my eyes. I inhaled his masculine scent, branding it into memory. I threaded my fingers through Dylan's hand, still resting on my hip. I imprinted the feel of his gentle and reassuring squeeze to my soul. I may not have been able to live this fairy tale forever, but I could take these memories with me and pray they'd be enough. Tears seeped from my eyes once again. I couldn't hide from the fact that they'd changed me. Freed me. Opened me to something magical. Forced me to see that the parts I'd tucked away were beautiful and natural. With a clarity I'd never known before, a veil had been lifted. I was a submissive and it was pointless for me to deny it ever again.

I had six days…six short days, to learn all I could about submission from these two amazing Doms. And I had no intention of wasting a single moment. I sniffed and inhaled a ragged breath, welcoming the sudden calm, centered feeling washing over me.

In a tangled web of arms and legs, we talked for a long time. My plague of insecurities gone, at least for the moment, I found it easy to confess all the curiosities I yearned to experience. My list wasn't long and their eager remarks made it clear they were going to take immense pleasure in introducing me to the joys of paddles and bondage. Their gentle words, wicked chuckles and reassuring mien filled me with nervous energy. A flash of anticipation tore through me at their promise of testing my limits. I was anxious to being the journey.

It was several hours before we ventured from the bed. I peeked out the window as they slipped back into their jeans. Snow had drifted half way up the large rectangular window "Unbelievable," I muttered, in awe of Mother Nature's frenzy. "You guys have got to see this."

As they peered out the window, Nick shook his head chuckled. "Guess we'll have to find a way to occupy our time while we're snowed in."

"I bet we can come up with something fun." Dylan winked then flashed a sordid grin. "Like dishes."

"Oh yeah, that was the first thing on my list," Nick quipped with a sarcastic roll of his eyes.

They were shirtless and virile in their low-slung jeans, making it was pure torture to join them in cleaning up the breakfast dishes. The desire to glide my tongue over every inch of their sharp, defined muscles was driving me insane. Catching the glimpse of heated desire in Dylan's azure eyes, I spread my legs and bent at the waist while stowing the frying pan and grinned as he cursed under his breath. That was all the encouragement I needed. Teasing and tormenting with overt poses as I put the clean dishes away, their playful swats and broad-handed gropes made my hormones zing from head to toe.

While wiping down the stove, I noticed Dylan dash down the hall only to reappear a few moments later with a large black duffle bag slung over his shoulder.

"Excellent idea," Nick drawled with a mischievous smile.

"What's that, Sir?" I asked.

"A good Dom is like a boy scout, kitten. They always come prepared," Dylan replied as he plopped the bag down on the dining table. "And trust me, girl. We're damn prepared."

"Prepared for everything," Nick chuckled in agreement. "Even curious pets stranded on the side of the road. When did you bring that in?"

"Yesterday when I unloaded the groceries. I hoped we might need it," Dylan's eyes twinkled in devilish delight.

"Why do I have the feeling there's something dangerous inside?"

"Is that how you address us, little one?" Nick's brow arched.

"I mean, Sirs," I amended with a grimace.

"Only dangerous for kittens who forget to show proper respect," Dylan chided.

"Yikes," I gulped. "I promise to do better, Sirs."

"Then nothing in there is dangerous for you, little one...only fun."

I inched close to the table as Dylan took his time pulling back the heavy-duty zipper. The tick of its teeth filled me with anxiety. I couldn't bring myself to attempt a peek inside.

He reached into the bag and pulled out several thick bundles of white cotton rope. My heart sped up as a smile formed over my lips.

"Dylan is a master in the art of Shibari. Have you read about it, little one?"

I shook my head. "No, Sir."

"It's Japanese rope bondage. It's quite lovely to look at and even more impressive for the sub that's bound and trussed up beneath its knots."

A quivering sigh fluttered from my lips as I stared at the innocuous bundles. Dylan unwrapped various lengths of rope and draped them over the table. With a crook of his finger, he smiled. "Spread your legs and raise your arms out to the side."

He wrapped the soft rope around my waist, lacing the smooth cotton under my arms and beneath my breasts while Nick helped cinch the braided cord in place. The combination of gliding coils and their warm hands grazing my flesh lulled me into a place of peace. Dylan worked silently, threading rope beneath lines already established and tying knots at various intersecting intervals. He continued to wind the rope around my torso and between my breasts, securing me in stunning diamond pattern. They worked in tandem, trussing me up in ties and lines. A trail of neatly aligned knots extended down my body, each one constricting me tighter. Each precisely placed strand forced my flesh to bulge and as he wrapped the rope firmly, I exhaled, closing my eyes, lost in the splendor of being bound. The lack of mobility wrought by the restraints induced a state that felt like being drugged. As I surrendered to their masterful hands and the soft reassurance of the rope, I was soon floating in a silent corner of my mind.

My eyes fluttered as a strand slid between the cheeks of my ass then up my center, pressing a fiery kiss upon my clit. Dylan mumbled something about my wet pussy, but I was too far gone to piece his words together. Suspended in an ethereal cloud of tranquility, I sailed free, never wanting to touch back down.

A sturdy tug on my nipples caused me to flinch before warm mouths engulfed my breasts, and sucked my steepled buds. Their soft slick tongues pressed each one to the roof of their heated mouths before they nipped and laved my pebbled areolas. Issuing a sultry moan, I rolled my hips as a provocative burn blossomed beneath my clit. The knotted rope strategically placed atop my pearl burnished like a lover's thumb, chasing streaks of lightning through my veins. Pressure surged as I ground against the cluster.

A sturdy slap landed on my ass. I squealed as my eyes flew open and their persuasive mouths abandoned my breasts.

"Welcome back, kitten. I take it you're enjoying the ropes?"

"Mmm," I purred. "Yes, Sir. They're amazing."

"I think you like this knot the best, little one," Nick teased as he reached down, giving a tug on the rope that bisected my core.

"Ahhhh," I hissed. "Especially that one."

My admission brought a smile to their faces.

"Are you doing okay? Tell us what you're feeling," Dylan's hypnotic blue eyes studied me with an intense gaze.

"I'm doing wonderfully, Sir. I feel like I'm floating in clouds. The ropes are tight but they don't hurt, in fact, they feel incredible. I'd always dreamt of being bound, although not in this way. I never imagined I would feel so safe and whole." I sighed in frustration. "It's more than that, but I can't find words to describe how blissful I feel right now."

"In what way had you dreamed about bondage, little one?" Nick asked with a leering grin.

"Just the regular, Sir. You know, tied to the bed.. that sort of thing."

"You're doing a fine job, kitten." Dylan smiled. "Are you brave enough for me to bind your arms?" I nodded in anticipation of even more rope encasing my flesh.

"No more stimulating your clit, Savannah, that's our job. You do it again, and we'll cut the rope between your legs. I'll personally see to it that you suffer a good long while in orgasm denial. Do you understand?"

"What's orgasm…oh," I amended as a mental picture of his threat filled my mind. "I don't think I'd like that, Sir."

He laughed. "I'm sure you wouldn't, but it's a very effective tool, little one."

"I think edging might be more effective," Dylan interjected as he guided my arms down in front of my body and pressed my wrists together. "Hold your arms like that and don't move, kitten."

"I won't, Sir. What is edging?" I asked as he began to wrap my wrists and looped the rope between them.

"Edging is a bit more sadistic than orgasm denial." His cerulean eyes sparkled as he glanced up at me. "It involves taking you to the brink of orgasm then bringing you back down, over and over, until the combination of frustration, delirium, and need has you all but pulling your hair out."

"Oh," I whispered. That didn't sound enjoyable at all. "Don't either of you implement fun punishments?"

"Doesn't that defeat the purpose of a punishment, little one?" Nick grinned. "But there are times when a punishment backfires on a Dom. Like your spanking earlier."

"How did that backfire?" I asked as Dylan's hands secured a tight, exact row of stunning knots from elbows to wrists.

"You enjoyed it," Nick growled.

The ropes felt incredible but I found that engaging in conversation kept my mind from floating back to that ethereal place I'd visited before.

"This isn't the type of Shibari I'd put you in for a suspension scene at Genesis, but I wanted you to get a feel for the ropes, kitten."

"What is Genesis?"

"It's our BDSM club back home," Nick responded as his gaze trailed up and down my snugly bound body. "You look absolutely gorgeous."

"Damn, I wish I had a lift for you here. It's amazing how fast you fly to subspace with the few things we've tried so far. I would love to watch you float away, suspended high in the air."

I blinked at Dylan. *Subspace?* Was that the dreamy feeling I kept experiencing?

He must have read my mind, because he smiled and combed his fingers through my hair.

"Yes, kitten. We can tell by the way your eyes get all glassy and unfocused. You wear subspace well."

"It's peaceful. My mind goes quiet and I just…feel what you're doing to me. I like it."

"That's how it's supposed to be, little one," Nick nodded soberly.

A shy smile curled on my lips. "So, now what am I supposed to do? You've got me trussed up like a turkey."

"Greedy, aren't we, little one?" Nick teased.

"Yes. I am. We've only…" Dylan arched his brow. I didn't want to remind them about the disquieting amount of time we had. Like a sponge, I wanted to absorb every sensation and emotion they were willing to share, in our limited days. "I'm anxious to learn is all, Sir."

Nick swatted my butt and growled. "Honesty, girl. This all stops if you can't be totally honest."

A gasp of shock filled my lungs. "We only have a few short days, Sir. I want to learn it all."

"Much better. Thank you, little one." Nick's voice held a disquieting edge and a blind man couldn't miss the dismal look they exchanged. "We'll teach you as much as we can in the time we have, girl."

My heart clutched as my eyes stung. With a solemn nod, I lowered my head. Drawing attention to the scant number of days we'd share, I'd inadvertently given credence to the elephant in the room. And with it, the disquieting realization that I'd allowed them to bind not only my body, but my heart. The realization sent a rolling rush of panic through me.

"I'm sorry to ask this after you've gone to all this trouble, Dylan Sir, but I need to use the restroom. Could you please untie me now, Sir?"

CHAPTER FIVE

It was a cowardly way out, but I needed a few minutes to gather my thoughts…to cordon off my heart and set some desperately needed internal boundaries. As they released the ropes, I closed my eyes. My freedom was bittersweet. With each snug line they peeled away, a layer of my submission went with it.

The slap of reality was far too harsh. I wasn't equipped to handle this. They'd stolen my heart so fast—even after I'd vowed not to let them—that the need to reclaim it was essential. The power they wielded was more persuasive than I'd ever dreamed possible. I never imagined drowning so easily into submission.

As the last rope slid from my flesh, I had to force myself to walk, not run, to my room. I closed and locked the bathroom door then sat on the edge of the whirlpool tub. I scrubbed a hand over my face, desperate to compartmentalize the swirl of emotions.

I'd not sorted a damn thing before the door knob twisted and rattled.

"Open the door, Savannah." Nick's deep voice thundered on the other side.

"I'm almost done," I choked out as I lurched to my feet and flushed the toilet in ruse.

"You've just earned a round of edging, pet. Open *now* or you'll be racking up even more torture."

I swung the door open and was met by two faces etched in blatant disapproval. My stomach twisted into knots, and not the fun Shibari kind. "What did I do?"

Dylan walked to the edge of my bed and pointed to a spot on the floor. "Not another word, kitten. On your knees… over the bed,"

"But, I…"

"You were told not to speak," Nick interrupted with a paralyzing scowl.

Somehow I managed to assume their instructed position even as my body trembled and my knees felt like Jell-O.

Spying the black duffel bag on the floor near the end of my bed, I was certain it contained a plethora of wicked devices for unruly subs. But *I* wasn't unruly… I was just confused and desperate for some alone time to sort out my feelings. Why couldn't they understand that?

Because you didn't tell them, dumb ass.

"Arms above your head and keep them there. I don't want to see a pinky twitch, pet" Nick's voice teemed in command, and my tunnel contracted in arousal.

Pressing my forehead against the mattress, my hair shrouded my face as I placed my arms above my head. Trepidation galloped through me and I battled to contain my fear.

A heavy foot slid between my legs, nudging my knees apart once, twice, three times, until I was wide open to accept my punishment. Cool air wafted over my exposed pussy. I had no doubt they'd see how wet I was.

A broad hand splayed over the small of my back as the bed dipped. Nick's scent surrounded me as his warm breath danced over the shell of my ear.

"You shut down on us like a light switch, little one. You have ten seconds to explain what trigger flipped in that beautiful head of yours."

His terse demand had my pussy oozing like sweet, thick honey.

No. They could use soothing words, pull every deviant trick out of that little bag of tricks, but I would not confess I'd lost hold of my heart. I might as well have *pathetic looser* tattooed on my forehead. I'd take their punishment then find a way to recapture my heart.

With unyielding pride, I pressed my lips together.

"Nothing to say, kitten?" Dylan prodded.

I shook my head without uttering a word. Every muscle in my body tensed in anticipation of eminent pain.

I jerked with a start as two fingers plunged inside my slick core. A masterful thumb began to strum my clit.

"Oh, God," I moaned.

"No, kitten, we're not gods, just two tenacious Masters determined to tear down your walls. You can't escape us, girl. You'll tell us what's bothering you, if we have to keep you here all night."

There was no malice in Dylan's tone, just a buttery promise. Validation that they intended to prod, gouge, and split me wide open, at least emotionally. Decadent fingers toyed with my pussy, setting me on a collision course with the stars. Trying to force aside the rising tide of desire, something cold and slippery slid over the puckered ring of my ass hole. All prospect of rejecting their pleasure went up in a cloud of elusive smoke.

"No," I cried out in fear, trying to rise up from the bed. Nick's splayed hand held me in place, like an anvil atop a fly.

"Shhh," Nick murmured in my ear. "It's lube. Your ass is virgin, isn't it, little one?"

"Yes Sir," I gasped squeezing my eyes shut, counting the seconds before an invasion of pain.

"How did you think you'd be able to accommodate both of us at once?" Nick pressed.

"I didn't," I lied.

The sinister fingers withdrew from my pussy. Morass with need, my hips writhed and a moan of despair seeped from my lips. A buzzing sound filled my ears then someone pressed a cold vibrator mercilessly against my clit.

"Simmer for a bit, kitten," Dylan chided. "Then maybe we can get some straight answers from you."

Within minutes, I was on the cusp of orgasm. Squirming, I tried to escape the vibrating demon. Desperate for release or reprieve, my limbs grew numb and my tunnel expanded. The orgasm was barreling down on me like a freight train. I keened in panic as I clamored to hold back my release. The vibe was pulled away and I slunk to the mattress as a groan of frustration bubbled in the back of my throat.

"Why did you shut down earlier, little one?" Nick pressed in a deep, honey-sweet voice.

So, they wanted to play twenty questions with my arousal again. Dammit, I sucked at this fucking game. Sucking in a deep breath, I was determined to hold out even as my clit screamed in demand.

"I had to go to the bathroom," I hissed. Why wouldn't they let me have just one little white lie? We could move on to bigger and better things...like the gargantuan orgasm clawing inside.

Nick let out a humorless chuckle as the buzzing vibrator whirred to life. "You don't have permission, little one."

"I assumed that the first time," I snapped in defiance as the wicked toy was pressed against my clit once more.

It only took seconds before the threat of release thundered through my veins. Cries of demand tore from my throat.

"Don't do it," Nick barked. His bellicose tone melded with the carnal shriek roaring through my veins.

"I can't hold it," I screamed.

And just as I crested the peak, the vibe was jerked away.

"No more, please," I sobbed.

"You hold the power, kitten," Dylan replied, his warm hand trailing up and down my spine. "Answer the question, and you'll finally be allowed to crash headlong into that sweet release you're primed and ready for."

"I don't want to answer the fucking question, I just want to come," I wailed.

"*Why* don't you want to answer it, you filthy-mouthed girl?" Nick growled.

"Because it's personal," I whined, sagging against the mattress.

"That's all the more reason to tell us, little one."

"Look, there are things that I need to keep private, okay? This isn't a relationship, it's just lessons."

Nick slung his burly arm beneath me, flipping me onto my back. His face hovered above mine as he seared me with a lethal gaze.

"Oh, you're so wrong, little one," he hissed between clenched teeth. "If you don't think we're emotionally invested in each other, no matter the length of time, you're seriously mistaken. There's nothing you can't tell us. Nothing you can't confess. There's no part of you, past or present, that we don't ache to own."

My heart hammered in my chest. His words sliced me open like a scalpel.

"We're not going to let you fall, little one. Not today, not tomorrow, not even next week."

"You can't promise me that." My voice cracked and tears filled my eyes. "You and Dylan will be back in Chicago next week and I'll…"

"You'll what, baby?" Dylan asked as he climbed onto the bed, kneeling next to me. His eyes brimmed with warmth and compassion. God, he undid me with just a look.

"I'll go back to…to dreaming about all this," I sobbed.

"You can do more than dream about it." Dylan smiled as he bent, sipping my tears between his lips. He sat up and glanced at Nick, whose expression was grim and unreadable. "Nick and I talked this morning about…things after this week. We've got a friend, Mika. He owns Genesis. We're going to reach out to him and get some people you can contract who are in the lifestyle back in Kansas City. We want you to connect with them when you get back home. There's no way in hell we're going to open you up without a safety net to fall into. Unfortunately, it won't be our safety net."

His words burned as if he'd doused me in acid. They intended to pass me off to some unknown Dom, and expect me to hand my control over to him? What if he decided he didn't want me? What if I wasn't experienced enough for anyone else? How had this connection with Dylan and Nick grown so strong in such a short amount of time? And when had I allowed myself to envision more from this "arrangement" than they had offered?

When you lost your heart to them, dumbass.

I didn't want reality rearing its ugly head. Not now. Not yet. In a week…I'd welcome it with open arms, let the emptiness run its course, but not yet. Until I found a way to insulate my heart, I knew I'd be a fool to take one more step down this precarious path with them.

With a gulp of steadfast determination, I braved back my tears. I *would* find a way to rescue my heart and carry on with my training. Then once back home, I would seek out my own Dominant…if and when *I* decided. They didn't need to fix me up with a stranger. I didn't want a stranger. I wanted Dylan and Nick. And if it was only for a short while, then so be it.

"Thank you. I really appreciate you guys being concerned about how this is going to affect me. But I don't want you to call your friend, Mika. I'll find a Dom on my own."

"Nobody said anything about us fixing you up with another fucking Dom," Nick snarled.

"Easy, bro," Dylan warned with a cautious stare.

"No," he challenged. "If we expect her to be open and honest with us, than it's only fair we do the same."

"Nick," Dylan chided, his cerulean eyes flashing in silent warning.

"Savannah." Nick gazed down at me, ignoring Dylan's caveat. His charcoal eyes softened as he smoothed a hand over my hair. "We're not looking to hook you up with a Dominant. The thought of you kneeling before someone else and looking up at him with your beautiful, trusting brown eyes makes me want to slam my fist through a lead wall."

"I don't understand," I was afraid to breathe…afraid to hope.

"I'm telling you that you've touched me, little one. In here." He patted a broad hand over his heart. "And when this week is done, I'll be carrying a piece of you with me."

His words made my mind whirl like a carnival ride. Nick wasn't making a declaration of love by any stretch of the imagination, yet it garnered a palpable tension between him and Dylan. I was more than surprised by Nick's confession. Dylan had impressed me as more in touch with his feelings, yet Nick's words obviously bothered him.

"And you with me, Sir," I replied in a timid voice. I couldn't keep from gazing up at Dylan and wonder if he, too, would think fondly of our time together.

"I'm sorry, kitten." Dylan's expression was filled with sorrow and guilt.

The last thing I wanted was for any of us to walk away shrouded in guilt.

"For what?" I painted on a soft smile. "You've nothing to be sorry for, Sir."

"I'm good with a joke, pet. But I've got a lousy track record when it comes to relationships." Dylan gave a minimizing shrug and for the first time, I caught a glimpse of *his* emotional fortress. Seemed I wasn't the only one hiding behind walls of self-preservation.

Memories of college days popped into my brain, Psych class in particular. We'd had a discussion about masks people projected to hide inner pain or personal trauma, and how those who projected excessive humor were often the ones hiding the deepest scars. The predominant motive was to keep others at arm's length to shield their heart or stave off pity. My heart ached for Dylan, not with pity, but sorrow for what whatever pain life had dealt him. I surmised his experiences in Iraq could have been the reason he wanted to hide pieces of himself. War had to be a life-altering experience, and not in a good way.

I raised my hand, cupped his cheek, and gazed into his eyes. "I promise I won't ask you to marry me, then." Shock played over his face. I couldn't help but grin.

He laughed then reached down and tweaked my nipple. "I like this sassy side of you, kitten. Claws and all."

"I'll remind you of that, Sir, the next time you decide to torture me with edging. That suc... stunk." I tossed a glance at Nick then flashed an innocent smile.

"You're getting better little one, but you obviously have a long way to go," Nick warned. "Where did you learn to curse like a sailor?"

I shrugged. "I grew up in a house filled with colorful language and sometimes it just slips out."

"Like when you talk to your sister?" Dylan grinned.

"Sometimes," I replied in a defensive tone then shook my head. "You can't tell me that you two choir boys haven't cursed. I've heard you."

"True, but we don't like to hear you curse."

"You're in construction, for crying out loud. It's not like you've not heard those words and worse. I was at a site once and a guy asked if I wanted to see his purple headed yogurt slinger. I was like...seriously?"

Dylan started to laugh. Nick cupped his hand over his forehead and gaped at me as if I'd grown a third eye.

"Did you tell him yes?" Dylan choked out in his fit of laughter.

"Oh, for the love of... no, I did *not*!"

I giggled when Nick threw his head back and laughed. The weight of our awkward discussion had been purged and the buoyant laughter was a balm to my jagged nerves.

"Fair enough, little one. Just watch your mouth with us. And Dylan, make a note to talk with the crew about language when we get back," Nick instructed with a velvet chortle.

"Speaking of business, don't you think it's time we got back to it?" Dylan smirked as he cupped a breast and leaned down.

"Yes Sir. I think that's a marvelous idea." I sighed and thrust my shoulders back, greedily lifting my breast to his approaching mouth.

Nick eased from the bed, stripped off his jeans and positioned himself between my legs, spreading my thighs wide.

"You're dripping wet, little one. Your claims of it being tortured tell me otherwise. Were you lying to us?"

I gasped on a quivering breath as Dylan sucked a nipple in deep, flicking the sensitive tip with his tongue. The sizzling current surged straight to my clit. "I wasn't lying, Sir. My body has a mind of its own when I'm with you two. Trust me. I enjoy what you're going to do a whole lot more, Sir." I moaned.

Nick chuckled. His breath whirled over my anxious pussy. "Ah, but you don't know what we have planned, pet. And I don't remember saying anything about you enjoying it."

"Please Sir, I've had enough torture for one day."

"You haven't yet begun to suffer for me, little one." His words were like rich, dark chocolate. Decadent and delicious.

I had no doubt that Nick could make me suffer a wealth of untold agony, and that thought alone made me even wetter. A whimper of delight slid from my throat when Nick's broad thumbs spread my folds, and he swiped his hot, wet tongue up my center. His rumbling growl of approval made my heart sing.

I opened myself to his desires, and he devoured me like an animal starved. Fingers filled my quivering tunnel as his tongue laid siege to my clit. A wet finger rimmed my anus as Nick circled the gathered flesh in a delicate massage. Pulses of electricity arced in a dazzling fire, spreading outward from my virgin hole in an obscene ripple. Dylan nipped and laved my turgid nipples with urgency.

Lost in every sensation they commanded, I was at their mercy. Fingers, tongues, teeth, and hands worked at exacting my surrender. And like a baby sapling in a hurricane, I yielded to their demands. I welcomed the building pressure; basked in the gathering current that numbed my limbs, and savored the carnal fire pumping through my veins.

"Please. Please. Please," I mewled in an urgent mantra.

"You beg so fucking sweetly," Dylan praised as he tugged my throbbing nipple between his teeth. "Shatter for us, kitten. Come now. Come hard!"

His words, like scissors, clipped the unraveling threads of my control. As I sailed over the edge and into oblivion, Dylan sank his teeth into my nipple, pinching the other with a brutal squeeze.

Nick's broad finger breached my puckered rim, driving deep inside my dark passage as I splintered into a thousand shards of molten glass. My screams of ecstasy echoed through the room. Arching my hips, my tunnel and ass gripped Nick's nimble fingers, locking him deep. Blue and white lights exploded beneath the spotted lace obscuring my vision. Locked and frozen, a prisoner to the orgasm's brutal assault, oxygen burned my lungs. My heart thundered in my ears and without warning, my uncontrollable spasms sucked and clutched the embedded fingers that still coaxed for more.

A feral roar splintered the air as Nick ripped his fingers from within me. My tunnel fluttered in abandonment. A mournful wail tore from my throat.

"Hang on, baby," Nick hissed in a tight, impatient voice. "I have to feel you, pet."

Faint sounds of a condom wrapper slowly registered in my brain. I writhed; the sudden emptiness was savage. I was burning alive. Something cold and hard pressed against the fiery lips of my pussy.

"Yes, please. Fuck me, Nick. Fuck me hard."

"Fuck her, Nick. Christ. Yes," Dylan demanded on a feral whisper.

Nick slapped the broad head of his cock against my clit and I screamed as the orgasm continued to toss me in its tempest.

"It's Sir, my luscious little slut," Nick roared. Pressing the bulbous crest between my swollen folds, he drove deep into my clutching core.

"Sir...Sir, fuck yes. Oh yes, Sir. Fuck me hard," I choked, rocking my hips and meeting each of his slow languid strokes in a piqued frenzy.

His cock was huge and the pain of my yielding tissues was exquisite torture.

Lost in the sensation of Nick, I was only half cognizant of movement near my head. Nick forged his bountiful cock in and out, dragging over that roaring bundle of nerves, hidden so deep inside me. A wide hand wedged beneath my shoulders blades, lifting my back off the bed. I slitted my eyes open and watched through the rapturous haze. Dylan, now naked as well, stuffed a pillow behind my back then lowered me down upon it, slightly elevating my head.

My breasts were thrust toward the ceiling in sovereign offering as he settled in behind me. Leaning forward, his engorged cock seeped in need beneath his pounding fist, directly above my face.

"Open, kitten. Swallow me down that glorious throat. Suck my cock, baby."

Pressing the top of my head to the mattress, I opened wide and stuck out my tongue. The muscles in my throat tightened as I gazed at Dylan's shorn sac, tightly drawn in narrow ripples; separating his orbs was a thick rigid line. As I inhaled his potent, spicy aroma, he threaded his saber between my lips.

Our hisses, grunts, growls and moans melded with slapping flesh, marking time to the most salacious symphony of indulgence I'd ever heard. Thick and pungent, the scent of sweat and sex filled the air. Never before had I felt so replete and profoundly feminine.

Dylan's cock nudged the back of my throat in a poetic dance. I reached up and gripped his hips as I breathed in his savage musk. Nick drove deeper and faster into my blazing core, surging the crescendo higher and harder.

Unable to focus on each individual sensation, I surrendered shamelessly to their lashing shafts, giving over to every deviant desire they longed to sate.

Nick brushed his finger over my sensitized clit and once again, I took flight. Lost in a prurient fog, I spiraled higher and higher within their mastery. My muffled moans of demand vibrated over Dylan's cock.

"Now!" Dylan thundered as his thickness swelled upon my tongue. An animalistic cry of triumph tore from his lungs and his hot, thick come jettisoned down my throat.

Nick bellowed a thunderous growl as he pounded deep into my cunt, spilling his blistering seed into the rubber barrier. I swallowed and screamed, gurgling on Dylan's slippery seed as I shattered over Nick's driving shaft. My entire body convulsed as if possessed, while my pussy gripped and milked Nick's cock. Panting and sweating, I forced my heavy lids open and dropped my arms to the bed as Dylan withdrew from my mouth. His body was covered in a glistening sheet of sweat and an expression of total bliss reflected upon his face. I smiled then peered at Nick as he eased from my fluttering pussy wearing a satisfied smile over his tawny lips.

"You're amazing, little one." He winked then rose to his feet and strolled to the bathroom as my tunnel quivered in glorious aftershocks.

Dylan flopped onto the bed besides me, flat on his back. He panted as if he'd run a marathon. My breathing was much the same. Nick returned within moments and gently wiped my sensitive folds with a warm cloth before dropping to the bed alongside me. I reached out and rested my palms on their wide chests. Their fingers entwined mine and I closed my eyes to savor the connection. I felt limp and wasted, yet more alive, more invigorated than I could ever remember.

The shrill sound of Nick's sat phone caused all three of us to jump in surprise.

"I'm going to throw this fucking thing out the window," Nick groused as he sat up, snatched his jeans from the floor, and freed the phone.

"Hello," he barked with a scowl.

"Are you three doing okay? How is Savannah feeling today?"

I could hear Kit's voice through the ear piece and watched Nick's expression soften. A slow smile tugged the sides of his mouth.

"She's doing fine. I know she's sore, but she's not complaining." He grinned mischievously. "She cries out now and then in a moan or whimper."

His body shook with silent laughter as my eyes widened in horror. I had to bite my lips between my teeth to keep from screaming at him.

"Do you have enough groceries? If not, I can try to dig a path and bring you some food."

"We've got plenty. There's nothing we need. Stay inside and keep warm. We're just hanging out down here and getting to know Savannah better by the minute." Nick flashed me a wicked smile. "Other than that, there's nothing much going on down here. Just waiting for the storm to pass. Is everything okay up at the house?"

"Me and these two cuties from Des Moines are doing fine," Kit laughed.

"You're not corrupting them, are you?" Nick teased.

"I wouldn't remember how," she chuckled before her voice dropped. "I haven't heard a word from Mellie. Is Savannah freaking out yet?"

Nick explained that Mellie had called and was safely back home. Kit reminded him there was dry wood in the mudroom, for which Nick thanked her before saying their good-byes.

"I can't believe you just did that," I gasped.

"What?" Nick blinked in a poor attempt at feigned innocence.

"You told Kit I was sore and moaning and that you were…" I raised two fingers on each hand and wiggled them in a quotes symbol. "Getting to know me better. She's going to think we're down here having sex."

"Well, we were."

"Argh," I groaned. "She doesn't need to know that!"

"She doesn't. She thinks I was talking about the accident. And why does it bother you if she knows the truth?"

"It's private." Blood heated my cheeks.

"And?"

"And…" *Dammit*! Why did Nick have to keep digging at me? "I just don't want her to know."

"That's not a reason, pet." Nick frowned.

"Do we embarrass you, kitten?" Dylan asked, a frown tugging his mouth.

"No. God, no!"

Nick bent down, picked up the vibe and turned it on. "Need another reminder about being honest, pet?"

"No. Put that away," I demanded.

Nick tsked and shook his head as Dylan sat up and spread my legs wide, gripping my thighs tight. Holding the buzzing vibe, Nick rubbed it along the inside of my thighs. "Issuing orders now, are you, little one?"

"No more, Sir. Please. I'm begging," I groaned.

"Then answer the question, girl. Now." Nick snarled in impatience.

"Because I'm not a slut that engages in one night stands, or one week stands, or any other kind of stand." I blurted out.

Without a word Nick turned off the vibe, stood, and walked to the bathroom. Dylan issued a heavy sigh and released my thighs.

"What?" I gaped at Dylan and his vexed expression. "Dammit! You're the ones who wanted me to be honest."

"Nick, bring back the vibe." Dylan barked.

"No!" I huffed as I sat up. "No more edging."

Nick stood in the frame of the doorway. My gaze skittered over his naked body, greedily absorbing the bounty of tight muscles stretched beneath his toffee skin. When I glanced at his face, he pinned me with a look that screamed Dominance *and* disappointment.

"Okay, look. I'm really trying here, you two. But you can't expect me to open up and vomit out all my feelings then turn around and get pissy when you don't like what I say."

"Nobody's gotten pissy except you, kitten." Dylan smirked.

"You two are wearing pissy expressions. I can see them."

"But we're not the one throwing the tantrum now, are we?" Dylan's blue eyes twinkled as a sarcastic smile spread over his lips.

"Did you forget who you were addressing, little one?" Nick's dark brows slashed as he scowled and walked toward the bed...vibe in hand.

"No, Sir. I'm just trying to communicate. That's what I'm *supposed* to do, right?" I snapped.

Okay, so maybe that wasn't the tone I should have used, but they were backing me into a corner and my innate reaction was to push back.

Dylan wrapped his hand in my hair and stood, promptly lifting me off the bed with him. A wicked grin curled on Nick's lips as he turned on the vibe.

"Shall we start this conversation over, little one?"

I swallowed the lump of fear in my throat and nodded before casting my eyes toward the floor. Well, as best I could. Dylan's hand was so tightly cinched in my hair, my scalp burned.

Nick silenced the vibe and placed it on the nightstand next to the bed. "Much better. Replacing your combative attitude with this stunning submission is guaranteed to make things go smoother."

He caressed my cheek. The defiant brat inside me wanted to nip at his fluttering fingers. He'd stung my pride. But instead, I closed my eyes and tried to center myself and let his silky compliment calm my overbearing resolve.

"You're very beautiful when you let go, little one." Nick's lips pressed against my ear drew a shiver down my spine.

"Thank you, Sir."

Dylan released my mane, his warm hand settled on the small of my back.

"We're not angry, kitten, we're upset that you equate what we're doing to something as insignificant as a one night stand," Dylan began. His hand moved slowly up my spine, resting on my nape. With two fingers under my chin, he raised my head and gazed into my eyes. "If all we were interested in was sex, we wouldn't waste our time to dig into your soul and uncover the buttons necessary to push your submission. And we certainly wouldn't shower you with tender touches, reassurance and praise, if all we wanted was just a piece of ass."

"This goes much deeper than a casual fuck, little one," Nick interjected. "Do you honestly not feel that? Did you not capture the depth of my words earlier?"

I turned to look at Nick, overwhelmed by the rejection reflected in his eyes. An oily, black wave of guilt consumed me. The roots of submission weren't planted in sex, but rather finding fulfillment in bringing the Dom pleasure. I couldn't afford to think my submission would ever lead to something more with their pleasure. Our paths had crossed for this short time, and I was a fool to hold onto illusions. Facts were facts and although it pained me, I knew I would be just a memory for them, if even that, in the very near future.

"Yes, Sir. I understood. You've touched me, too. But I wasn't…I didn't mean it the way you're making it sound," I stammered.

"What did you mean, then?" Dylan asked with a tender squeeze of my neck.

"I meant that Kit knows me. She knows I'm…inexperienced. We're girls. We talk about things like that, especially after a shi... a load of Merlot." I closed my eyes and exhaled, finding it hard to censure my words, especially when I was trying to make a point. I looked up at Dylan. "I didn't want her to find out what we were doing because I didn't want her to think I was a freak."

"What does it matter what people think, kitten?"

"It doesn't. I mean, it shouldn't…but Kit's like a friend in a lot of ways. I couldn't share this with her. I don't even know if I can tell Mellie about all this. The way you two make me feel, or how submission fills this empty place inside me…I don't have words for it." My gaze flittered back and forth between them, searching for a glimmer of understanding

"We don't want to be your dirty little secret, kitten. Nor will we ever allow you to be ours," Dylan replied in a censuring tone. "We hope that what we're sharing will help you grow past your fears, and erase the preconceived notions of how you're supposed to behave or conform. Our hope is that by the end of the week, you'll see yourself and your desires in a whole new light. Do you understand what I'm saying?"

"Yes, Sir," I whispered with a slow nod.

"All right. Let's all go soak in the tub for a bit. You can't tackle it all in one day, little one. I think you need to relax and let things unfold as they will." Nick's reassuring words filled me with hope. I might get this submission stuff down, after all. Thank goodness they were both patient.

Dylan cupped my chin and claimed my lips in a powerful, drugging kiss. "Don't forget, kitten…we'll be right here beside you every step of the way," he promised.

Yes, they would. For a week, at least.

CHAPTER SIX

The giant tub was designed for two people but was spacious enough for three. The hot, bubbling water soothed my sensitive folds, but the avid attention Dylan and Nick dispensed was far more luxurious. They cleansed my body with tender care and shampooed and rinsed my hair. Passing me from one to the other, their reassuring hands never left my flesh.

Tranquil and boneless, I laid atop Dylan's brawny chest with Nick's strong body draped over my back. If I'd had the ability to stop time, cocooned in their silent affection, I would have chosen that moment for it. The entire adventure was unchartered territory, yet nothing in my life had ever felt so right, or garnered this level of inner peace.

"How sore is your little clit, pet?" Nick asked in a low, enticing whisper.

"Mmmm," I purred. "Just a little bit."

Nick nipped the lobe of my ear. "Just a little bit, what?"

"Sir. Just a little bit, Sir," I replied with a dreamy moan.

"Then we'll let it rest for a while and begin your anal training."

My eyes flew open wide and I jerked my head from Dylan's chest, nearly colliding with Nick's chin. "My what?"

A devilish grin spread over Nick's lips. "Your anal training."

"Oh, no, Sir. You misunderstood. My clit is fine. Honest." I protested.

He slid off my back and sat next to Dylan, cupping his hands around my face, Nick shook his head. "You remember what lying gets, don't you, pet? I thought you didn't like edging."

"I don't. I mean…" I exhaled a heavy sigh. "My clit is a little bit sore, but not so sore that we have to do something else, Sir."

"That's not your choice, girl. Tell me, what has you so frightened about anal training, little one?"

"I'm afraid it's going to hurt."

"Have we hurt you yet, kitten?" Dylan asked, knowing full well the answer to his question was a resounding *No*.

"Of course not, Sir."

"Then you have no tangible reason to fear it." Dylan winked.

He was right. They worked hard to bolster my trust. The misunderstandings we'd had so far were born of *my* fears and insecurities. Secure in the fact they'd never intentionally hurt me, it still didn't erase my apprehension of them shoving things up my butt.

"How does it work, Sirs?"

"That's my girl," Nick smiled. "We'll show you shortly. But don't worry, we'll start out small."

An hour later I found out that *small* was a matter of perception. Small for Nick was *huge* and severely uncomfortable in my opinion. After we'd retreated from the tub and dried off, they eased me to my knees and bent me over the bed. With soothing words of encouragement, my tiny puckered rim was slathered in cold, slick lube. Dylan showed me the slim, silver butt plug, adorned with a sparkling purple jewel on the base, then shoved the damn thing straight up my ass.

I never knew how much concentration it took to clutch my dilated muscles around the invading plug. Every movement was a war between my body and my brain. My body demanded that I expel the vile intruder, while my brain petitioned it remain.

Shuffling to the couch and easing down slowly, I was grateful for the armistice and only had to cope with the dull throb of my stretched tissue. My Doms found great pleasure in my discomfort. I wasn't quite so thrilled. In an effort to appease me, Nick built a fire so I could warm myself then swaggered to the kitchen to help Dylan prepare dinner. I listened to their banter and grinned as I watched the flames dance and flicker. A part of me longed for the storm outside to rage on forever. The fantasy they'd created was nearly perfect...all except for the plug up my ass.

As darkness fell, the common area was filled with warmth from the roaring fire. The plug was less distressing as we cleaned the dinner dishes. However, I was no longer bending in provocative taunting fashion, too scared the damn thing would pop out.

Retiring to the couch as we'd done the night before, we shared a bottle of wine. With my first day of training under my belt, they were anxious for feedback. Trying to put it all into words was a struggle but I managed to relate the peace I found being bound. I made no bones about my aversion to edging, but after a load of ribbing from Dylan, confessed the end result was somewhere between heaven and life-altering.

"And what about the plug, little one?" Nick chuckled. "Does that rate low on your list, as well?"

"No, Sir. It's doable because I know it's part of the preparation." *Preparation to fulfill my ultimate fantasy. Well, one of them anyway.* I dreamt of visiting a fetish club almost as much as I yearned to experience double penetration. The latter filled me with trepidation even with anal training. I wasn't sure I could accommodate both their massive cocks. Before letting my fears get the best of me, I steered my brain back to thoughts of their club.

"What is Genesis like, Sirs?"

"It's amazing," Dylan began. "The members are genuine and kindhearted. It's hard not to think of them as extended family."

I could feel the love reflected in his words and I smiled. "What do they do there?"

"Everything you can think of," Nick chimed in. "From soft and poignant exchanges all the way to blood dripping, ear piercing edge play."

A shiver skittered up my spine. "That sounds scary."

"It's all consensual and negotiated, kitten. We have a private room. A lot of the regular members there do. But nothing is more educational than sitting in the dungeon and watching the various sessions played out."

"A private room? I guess you two have played with a lot of submissives, huh?" I tried to hide my sudden feelings of jealousy but must have failed because Nick turned and studied me for a long moment. His eyes reflected a hint of sorrow.

"Yes, little one, we have. But that doesn't diminish what we're sharing here with you. Do you understand me?"

"Of course, Sir. I honestly didn't think you two were *really* choir boys." I smiled, trying to make light of my callow insecurities. "So, what kind of stuff do you have in your private room?"

"We have a large play space and bathroom. In addition, there's a cross, different types of suspension equipment, a bondage bed, spanking bench, and a large regular bed. It's similar to the equipment that's in the main dungeon but on a more private scale," Dylan replied.

Images danced in my mind of all the deviant ways they could use me in a room like that. I needed to change the subject before I left a puddle on the leather couch. "George, your friend on the phone…is he a club member, too?"

"Yes," Nick smiled and nodded. "And also my legal advisor. He's an older gentleman with a young, vibrant, and extremely mischievous sub, Leagh. Her club name is Dahlia. She keeps him on his toes."

Dylan's laugh was loud and robust. "That's an understatement, bro. She's a hellcat. But just exactly what he needs. Dahlia's antics breathe life into George. You can almost feel the energy in their dynamic. They are so in love."

"I remember you laughing about bunny floggers or something," I grinned and nodded.
"He's a lot older than she is?"

"Yes, he's in his late sixties and she's…probably mid-twenties, I'd say." Dylan nodded thoughtfully.

Forty-some years was quite an age difference. I wondered why the woman, who was close to my age, chose to be in a relationship with such an older man.

Nick watched with a broad smile as I pondered. "There's no age limit or restrictions when you connect with someone in the exchange, little one. Much like the vanilla world, we're all puzzle pieces. And when you finally find the one that's a perfect fit for you, nothing else matters."

The way he read my mind was almost eerie. I nodded at his analogy. It made sense.

"I'd love for you to have the chance to meet Emerald, kitten."

"Emerald?"

"She mentors new submissives and is extremely dedicated to the lifestyle. Emerald is her club name. A lot of the subs and Doms chose alternate identities to ensure their privacy. Even though there is a rigorous vetting process, one of the cardinal rules—at nearly every club—who you see and what you see remain within the confines of those four walls. There are a lot of high-profile members and keeping their anonymity is paramount. People don't want to lose their jobs or their children," Dylan explained.

"I see. Do you have club names, Sirs?"

"No, pet. We don't." Nick replied.

"And you think there is a club like Genesis in Kansas City?"

"Maybe not exactly like Genesis, but I know there are lifestyle groups in your area and like-minded people tend to welcome their own kind with open arms, kitten."

I nibbled my bottom lip and gave a silent nod as my mind whirled. The fit with Dylan and Nick felt so real and so right. Were there other Doms out there that would make me feel the way they did? Would I experience this powerful connection with another? As I lowered my head, lost in thought, a subtle smile tugged my lips. I'd been naked almost the entire day and not been the least bit embarrassed by it. For some bizarre reason, it suddenly felt like the most natural thing in the world to be stark naked between them. Had they changed me that much, in two short days? Was there a chance I would ever be this relaxed around another Dom or Doms? The thought of kneeling for anyone other than Dylan and Nick made my heart ache. But then I remembered; I had to keep my heart out of the mix. If I wanted to continue this new path they were leading me down, and continue to revel in the serenity it brought me, I'd have to find a Dom or two of my own...Doms that would teach *and* claim me. Dylan and Nick would be forever etched in my heart, but a mere scratch on the surface was as deep as they could ever be.

"You're thinking awfully hard, little one. Share with us," Nick coaxed.

"I'm just trying to take it all in. The thought of being in a club like Genesis is...well, it fills me with excitement."

That was an understatement. My pussy had been weeping since we'd first started talking about Genesis. I was all but squirming.

A tense and awkward silence fell over the room.

"Once I get home, I think it would be fun to find a club I could join."

A fierce scowl appeared on Nick's face and his body tensed. Even Dylan's relaxed demeanor took on a distinct edge. I wasn't trying to demean their training, but my attempt to convince them I was self-reliant had totally backfired. Then I remembered what Nick had said about me kneeling before another. What was I supposed to do, just erase all these wonderful feelings they'd unlocked inside me and go back to *reading* about the lifestyle? That wasn't fair.

"You don't like that idea much, do you, Sirs?" I turned my head and took inventory of their expressions. No, they didn't like it at all. "Do you have some other alternative I don't know about? I'm going to pursue the lifestyle when I get home. It's too important to me to try and shove it back inside me."

They'd been the key that unlocked a whole new world. I had no intention of slamming the door shut and walk away from what they'd awakened.

"We realize that, kitten. But doesn't mean we have to like it," Dylan grumbled.

"I don't like the idea of having to get comfortable with another Dom either, but I'll do it. I'm a strong-willed woman and I'll do whatever it takes to find a Dom or Doms who will be patient and teach me the way you two have." I gave them both a reassuring smile and without asking permission, I reached up and kissed each of them on the cheek. "Thank you for doing all this for me."

Nick gripped my hair and pulled my lips to his, searing me in an urgent claim. He tasted like power and demand. At first, I met his frenzied kisses head on then relaxed and opened for his tongue. A growl rumbled in his chest as he devoured me in fervent command.

I clutched his broad shoulders. His silky black mane danced over my fingers as he slammed me like a freight train of power. Dylan skimmed his lips and tongue up my spine then nestled at the column of my throat. His teeth scraped my flesh. As he nipped my pulse point, a hungry moan rolled from the back of his throat and vibrated through my blood. My pussy clenched, and my ass muscles constricted around the plug. Fire blazed beneath my clit and I climbed my way up Nick's body, straddling his lap while he devoured me with blistering kisses. I whimpered, grinding my needy pussy against the swollen erection trapped beneath his jeans.

"Fuck, Savannah," Dylan whispered as he moved off the couch and knelt behind me. Nick swallowed my cries and Dylan tapped the jeweled base of the plug, making a lurid melody drum over my electrified nerve endings. Need clawed beneath my skin as I tore my lips from Nick's mouth.

"Please. Masters. Please help me," I begged. Dylan's lewd symphony was driving me insane. Like a cat in heat, I writhed on Nick, rubbing my beaded nipples over his dense chest.

"Fuck! I need a condom," Nick roared before gripping my hips and lifting me off his lap. He held me tight with one hand as he freed his cock in a frenzied rush with the other.

Gazing at the glistening wet tip, I wriggled free and slid to my knees. The plug tugged in a divine avalanche of pleasure. My desperation grew to demand.

Dylan had disappeared but I knew he'd be back. Mesmerized by Nick's weeping erection, the need to taste his salty essence and glide my tongue over the angry, distended veins drew desperate whimpers out of me.

"No. Not yet," he barked as he fisted my hair and lifted my head. With an impassioned gaze, he looked into my eyes. "Tell me what you want, girl. You don't get to take from me. You beg for what's driving you half out of your mind."

"Your cock, Master. I need to taste your cock, please," I panted.

"Such a sweet, insatiable slut," Nick praised with an animalistic growl. "No. You'll do far more than taste me, girl. You'll worship my cock. Worship it with all your heart."

Cinching my hair tighter, Nick forced my lips to the smooth, slick cap. I opened wide and engulfed his steely pillar, moaning in delight as his familiar tangy flavor glazed my tongue.

"Mother fu…" Dylan exclaimed from behind me. The heavy duffle bag hit the floor. "Ass in the air, kitten. It's time to play."

I rose to my knees. Nick issued a slow tortured hiss as I cupped his sac in my palm, stroking the base of his shaft with my other.

Dylan tapped the inside of my thighs and I spread my legs wide. Without altering the steady tempo of my mouth, I sucked and swirled my tongue over Nick in reverence. I was determined to make him feel the unmitigated hunger clawing within, and my overwhelming need to please him.

"You're dripping wet, kitten," Dylan said with depraved approval in his voice. "I think you like this little plug, pet."

Dylan gripped the base and began to spin the torturous plug like the hands of a clock. I cried out over Nick's cock before he yanked my mouth off him with a curse.

"I want to hear your cries of splendor, little one. Sing for us as Dylan prepares you for a bigger plug."

"A bigger one? Oh God," I moaned as Dylan continued to swirl and tug on the metal plug. Shards of electricity exploded from my sensitized ring spreading outward, each bolt racing up my spine and down my legs. My clit throbbed in need as Dylan eased the plug out. Involuntarily, my puckered ring constricted and released as it attempted to condense back to normalcy.

Cold lube plopped upon my gripping rim and a broad, thick finger breached the tender tissue…then another. It was excruciating and rousing. I needed to come.

"Excellent, kitten. You've dilated beautifully. I think you'll be able to handle the larger plug just fine," Dylan whispered as his wicked fingers thinned my puckered flesh.

"No, please. Put the other one back in, Sir. I can't stretch anymore down there."

"Oh, you can, little one, and you will...because it pleases us." Nick smiled. "Put your mouth back to work on my cock, girl. No more screaming over my dick. You're killing my control."

Nick settled my mouth over him once again. Dylan's finger circled my gathered ring, opening me up even more. The sensation was absolute ecstasy. With gentle persuasion, he widened and stretched my fragile passage with his beguiling fingers. My nerve endings screamed in pleasure mixed with pain and I reveled with each glorious gliding swirl upon my inflamed tissue.

Bobbing up and down on Nick's cock, I slurped and moaned. My hips rocked in shameless thrusts as my hungry virgin hole milked upon Dylan's fingers.

"We're almost there, kitten. Just a little bit more." His ragged, warm breath fluttered over my butt cheeks. Consumed with need, I launched back, impaling his fingers. "Christ, I want to bury my cock inside your silky, tight ass. It's going to feel so fucking good."

"I can't wait to feel us both inside her, man. She's going to blow our minds and we're going to love every fucking minute of it." Nick's gravely tone teemed with lust.

"Fuck, yessss," Dylan hissed as his fingers slid free. Smearing on more lube, he pressed the cold metal tip against my hungry rosette. With painstakingly slow determination, he applied pressure while swirling the new plug.

Flashes of light exploded behind my eyes. My body trembled and quaked. Tremendous pressure blossomed beneath my clit. It was too much. Too intense. I needed relief. Lowering my hand to my pussy, I swallowed back a moan of relief as I strummed my swollen clit, then thrust back against the marauding metal saber.

"Place both hands flat on my thighs, little one. You don't have permission to touch *our* clit." Nick released my hair and gripped each wrist, drawing my hands away from my sodden pussy and his tightly drawn sac.

I rocked my hips in frenzied frustration as I tried to force the plug through my taut tissue. I kept feeding on Nick's stalk, the voracious lust driving me to madness.

"Relax, kitten." Dylan consoled my desperation by running his fingers from the small of my back to the crack of my ass. "We're almost there, baby. Don't force it. I don't want you to tear. You're doing beautifully kitten, and we're so fucking proud of you."

His words of praise calmed my panic-laced-anxiety. Soon, I was floating in a vaporous, serene silence. Liberated from the shackles of conscious thought, I hovered in the buoyant clouds of surrender and basked in each and every euphoric sensation. Nick's veins pulsated on my tongue and brilliant colors flashed behind my eyes. I could taste the sweet salacious hum radiating from his heated shaft. As Dylan slid the plug into place, I reveled in the depraved narrowing of my throbbing, taut ring.

"Get your cock in quick, bro. Her lush mouth is making me fight to hold out," Nick warned.

Dylan grunted as he pressed his cool, latex-sheathed crest between my fiery folds. "You want me to fuck you, don't you kitten? Fill you full of my hot, hard cock."

I moaned a muffled gurgle then bore my hips down, imploring Dylan to drive in his massive shaft. Bellicose curses filled the air. Fingers plucked and pinched my nipples as Dylan drove balls deep into my fluttering core. The pressure of his ample cock and the dense plug was glorious torture. I'd never been stretched so tight or felt so full in my life.

Surrounded by their hot bodies, the carnal grunts and groans of imbibing flesh and the thick, sultry scent of sex that clung in the air was sublime. My dark forbidden fantasy had come to life. It was more surreal than anything I'd ever imagined, alone in my bed.

With each smooth thrust of their sabers, they marked my heart...my soul. These two incredible men had severed the chains that held me prisoner to a muted existence. Peeled away the beige and cast me into a rainbow of colors. They'd brought me to life. I would never be the same woman again.

"Feel us, little one. Feel the power you give us," Nick hissed. "It's all coming back to you, pet. We're giving you back your precious, precious gift. Touch your clit, Savannah. Take us with you and shatter for us, my gorgeous little vixen."

Sliding my hand from his thigh, Nick seized my hair and lifted his hips, shuttling his cock deep into my throat as I strummed my swollen, needy clit. I soared higher and higher. Dylan cinched his beefy hands onto my hips and launched his cock into my dripping cunt with unrelenting strokes. Power surged in a conflagration of possession, driving dominance into every cell of my body. Permeated with their command, my milked Dylan's driving shaft as I shattered.

Nick pummeled my mouth with rapid thrusts and my cunt locked upon Dylan's cock, imprisoning him as the brutal orgasm ripped through me. Their animalistic cries echoed in my ears as they filled my mouth and pussy with hot, thick streams. Ecstasy blinded me as wave upon wave crashed through my core. Gulping down Nick's thick treasure through screams of rapture, my body sang an exalted rhapsody.

The orgasm was colossal. Each exchange we shared was more brutal and potent than the one before. Their claim scored deeper each time they took me to the stars. Now spineless, I collapsed over Nick's lap. His turgid cock lay hot and twitching against my cheek. Dylan eased from my quivering tunnel and I jerked in surprise when he pressed a warm cloth against my enflamed folds, tenderly cleaning me. When he was done, he leaned down, smoothed the hair off my neck and placed a sweet kiss on my nape.

"I'm all sweaty," I mumbled, still absorbed in the afterglow.

"I like making you sweat, kitten," he chuckled. "But I *love* hearing you scream."

"I like the way you two make me sweat and scream," My words were slurred. I felt drunk and zapped of all energy in a delicious, foggy haze.

Dylan lifted me from the floor and cradled me in his arms. From beneath my lashes I watched Nick stand and refasten his jeans. Dylan sat back down on the couch, his hard cock nestled against my hip.

A wry grin tugged the side of Nick's mouth as he gazed down at me. "How are you feeling, little one?"

"Dreamy," I sighed with a smile.

A wide grin burst over his mouth. The man defied the gods with his unadulterated beauty and I couldn't help but stare at him for a long while. When Nick sat back down, he pulled me onto his lap and cradled me in his arms. I snuggled against him, drinking in the heat of his body. Dylan placed my feet to his lap and began to massage my arches. With a soft moan, I closed my eyes and reveled in their luxurious aftercare. The crackling fire echoed in the stillness of the room. It was several silent moments before either man spoke.

"Is she asleep?" Dylan asked.

"I think so," Nick replied. "Savannah?"

Curiosity kept me from responding. I could feel a palpable tension in their exchange and right or wrong, I wanted them to think I'd fallen asleep in hopes of determining what was bothering them.

"We're in over our heads, man, especially you. You know that right?"

"Don't pin it all on me. I saw the look on your face when you were balls deep inside her pussy. This whole thing is getting FUBAR'd beyond belief," Nick whispered, punctuating his emotions with a heavy sigh. "It's going to be hard to leave all this."

"You mean hard to leave *her*," Dylan corrected.

"Exactly."

"I think I've figured out how she knocked the knees out from under us."

Nick's body tensed and I felt him turn his head, his warm breath no longer wafting over my face. I remained lax, listening.

"So it's not just me?" Nick asked with a hint of sarcasm in his tone.

"No, man."

"So tell me what you've come up with, Doctor Dylan," Nick teased.

"Fuck you. Don't bust my balls just because I happen to be in tune with my feelings. It doesn't make me a pussy, it makes me cautious. Keeps me from getting in too deep with women like her."

"You mean its mortar for your walls, asshole." A soft chuckle rumbled in the back of Nick's throat.

"That, too. You want to borrow some? I think you need it."

"Nah, I'll be fine. We both will."

The tone of Nick's voice left me wondering if any of us would be fine after this powerful connection. I was stunned by the revelation that I had touched them so deeply. My heart quickened but I kept my breathing level and deep.

"You know as well as I do that this can't go anywhere, right?"

"Do you always have to be so fucking negative when you can't cover something up with a joke?"

"Do you know why you married Paige?"

"Oh Christ, do we have to go there?" Nick grumbled. "Yes, because I was a stupid fuck-knuckle, thinking with my dick."

"Well, there's that," Dylan softly chortled. "You're in love with the idea of marriage, family, and taking care of the little woman."

"Should I carry Savannah to bed and lay down on the couch for this analysis, Doc?"

"Come on, Nick. You've helped me see the forest for the trees plenty of times and I always do the same for you, man." Dylan lectured as Nick grunted. "I get it. I know you want to settle down and have a family. Even before you married Paige and we went through our shit, I secretly hoped that she'd come around to the idea of us sharing her, because you've wanted it for so damn long."

"I know, man. And I'm sorry for what it did to us. I learned a lot of lessons from that mistake. The biggest one being, we're no good alone and that I have lousy judgment when it comes to women."

"No you don't. Look at that woman in your lap. She's perfect," Dylan replied in an awed tone. "But I'm not a poster child for any damn wedding chapel. The minute anything starts to feel like a ball and chain, I'm asshole and elbows running the other way," Dylan sighed. "But that one there...she's so fucking real. That's how she blindsided us. She's like an oasis in the middle of the desert and so different from the subs we play with at Genesis. She's like a breath of fresh air. Honest and pure."

"So why aren't you running for the hills?" Nick pressed.

"Because I can't--I don't want to. Believe me, I've tried. She's like a magnet. I'm so fucking drawn to her. Do you know how perfect she'd be for us, if only..."

"If only she didn't live in another state and wasn't set on finding a Dom when she got home."

Their entire conversation had me fighting back my hope and a whole host of unnamed emotions. I curled on my side and nuzzled my face against Nick's chest. With the revelations being unearthed between the two, I didn't trust that I could hide my facial expressions, so I hid.

"Savannah?" Dylan whispered.

Shit. If they ever found out I was eavesdropping I'd probably earn a whole damn day of edging. I couldn't answer him now. They'd know I'd been listening to them all along. Besides, I had the distinct impression their conversation was far from over.

You shouldn't be doing this. It's deceitful. Leave it to that pragmatic voice inside my head to dump a truckload of guilt. But curiosity reigned supreme. *And what did curiosity do to the cat, dumbass?*

"She's still out," Nick whispered. "There's nothing we can do, man. We'll teach her as best we can with the time we've got left. Pray she finds a group and keeps growing and maybe visit Kansas City from time to time to check in on her."

"Christ," Dylan swore in disgust. "And how are you going to feel when we show up at one of the clubs in Kansas City and see her with a Dom? You know as well as I do that somebody is going to snatch her up in the first five fucking minutes."

"Listen to you, 'Mister Don't Tell Her How You Feel'." Nick taunted. "Shit. I can't go there, dude. Her with another Dom? Fuck."

"You're going to have to stash that shit, man," Dylan warned.

"We both are. The last thing I want either of us to do is hurt her. All that innocence…we've got to be careful, bro."

My head spun. They had feelings for me far outside the realm of just teaching me. That powerful connection between the three of us wasn't my imagination. Yet they weren't going to act on their feelings. They were going to pretend it all didn't exist. I hadn't said a word about finding another Dom, just a club I could join to keep learning. They had no clue that I didn't want another Dom, I only wanted them. But I didn't live in Chicago. The distance thing wouldn't work. So they were just going to ignore the giant elephant in the room, and what? Think I wouldn't notice? God, men were so clueless.

"So we have a few more days. We'll do the no strings, no promises route and enjoy her as long as we can and then say good-bye, right?" Dylan asked with a flat monotone voice void of emotion. Nick didn't respond for a long time. He issued a long heavy sigh and brushed his fingers through my hair.

"Yeah, if that's how it has to go."

So that was their game plan. Close off their hearts and ignore their emotions. It didn't make sense. Doms were supposed to be open and honest.

People in glass houses.

I inwardly cursed that annoying little voice in my head for pointing out the obvious—and for playing such a stupid game of subterfuge, my heart ached. Making a conscious effort to grab hold of my gratitude, I realized I'd still be locked in BDSM dreamland if not for them. I'd be ignoring all the desires they seemed to effortlessly pluck from within me. It would be so easy to plop my ass down on the pity pot and wallow in despair for not having a long-term relationship with them, but the harsh reality was… it wasn't in the cards.

Dylan eased off the couch and returned a short time later. The smell of scotch wafted through the air. Their conversation veered toward work and upcoming projects they'd bid on. Their voices held great passion as they talked about a community center for underprivileged youth, scheduled to break ground in the spring. The big bad Doms had a soft spot for children and those less fortunate. It was somewhere during their discussion of politics, City Hall, bureaucratic red tape and corruption that sleep pulled me under. Rousted awake, I discovered Nick was carrying me back to my room as the fireplace glowed with dying embers.

"I'm sorry we have to do this to you, little one, but we need to get that plug out before you go to sleep." Nick placed me onto the cold sheets then turned me to my side. I shivered when he pressed my knees up. "We'll get you warmed up in a minute, little one. Just take a deep breath and as you let it out, push for me, okay?"

I closed my eyes and as Nick's broad fingers gripped the wide base, I exhaled and bore down, anxious to get the wicked plug out of my body. A soft whimper escaped my lips as the widest part slid free. Nick strolled off to the bathroom as Dylan drew the sheets around my shoulders.

"We're proud of how brave you've been with the plugs, kitten," Dylan praised as he threaded his fingers through my hair.

But not proud enough that I earned a way to keep you.

Driving the cynical thought from my brain, Nick returned and washed my sensitive rosette with a warm cloth. I was still shivering as they climbed into bed, but warmed up quickly once wrapped in their sinful warmth. I drank in their heat, drowning in the bliss of their chiseled form and convincing myself I was too tired to wrangle the myriad of emotions. Within minutes, I'd drifted off to sleep.

CHAPTER SEVEN

Blinding sunlight streamed in from beneath the curtains. The storm had passed. A melancholy ache filled my heart. No matter how desperately I wished it, time wasn't going to stand still. Peering to my left, I saw Dylan laying on his back, snoring softly. With care, I rolled to my side and gazed at him, taking in every contour of his rugged features. Blonde stubble covered his jaw and chin and I longed to draw my nails over the coarse hairs, feel them prickle upon my fingers. Light lashes rested against his cheeks, shrouding his beautiful azure eyes beneath the smooth lids. Staring at his full lips, I remembered how soft and compelling they felt beneath my own. My gaze wandered down his wide neck, over his broad tanned shoulders, resting on his flat, dusky brown nipples. Hard muscles bulged beneath his flesh as if a master sculptor had spent a lifetime chiseling him out taupe granite.

Curling my arm beneath the pillow, I elevated my head while I drank in the rest of his features. He'd kicked most of the covers off and they lay in a twisted ball at the foot of the bed. A beam of sunlight spilled from the curtain's edge, illuminating his impressive, flaccid cock resting upon his thigh. My palms itched. I'd never felt a soft cock before and I stared in utter fascination.

"No matter how long you look at it, kitten, it isn't going to suck itself," Dylan teased in a sleepy voice.

I jerked my head up at him and blinked. A goofy smile spread over his gorgeous face as that sexy-assed dimple grew more pronounced.

"Morning," Nick mumbled in a gravely tone as he sat up and placed a tender kiss on my shoulder. "Starting lessons before coffee?"

"Maybe," Dylan smirked. "I think Savannah might need breakfast in bed. She looks kind of hungry."

"Very funny," I said in a dry tone. "I was just looking at…"

"My cock, yes, I know, kitten. Crawl on down there and take a closer look. It won't bite."

"I need to brush my teeth first," I said and began to scamper out of bed.

"Bring the tube back with you, little one." Nick instructed with a mischievous twinkle in his eyes.

"The tube of…toothpaste?" I asked as my brows wrinkled in confusion.

"You mean, the tube of toothpaste, Sir, don't you?" Nick reminded as he pursed his lips as if pondering some unpleasant form of punishment.

"Yes, Sir… that's exactly what I meant." My words rushed together as I remembered the brief but formidable lesson of edging. Nope, I didn't need any more punishments.

"I thought so, girl." Nick winked and flashed a dazzling smile. I swallowed back a wanton moan and hurried to the bathroom.

After my morning rituals, I ventured from the bathroom, toothpaste in hand. Their gazes clung to my body with every step I took. My nipples pebbled and my heart beat faster as both cocks sprang to life. Devilish smiles adorned their faces and I knew they were up to something, I just hoped there was a happy ending in it—for all of us.

"So, do you have some kind of kinky tooth brush lesson planned?"

Nick chuckled. "Something like that, little one." He extended his hand and I passed him the paste. "Come, lay down."

I eyed him with suspicion as I climbed over his stretched out legs, taking my time to gaze upon his thick erection, before settling in between them. Nick removed the cap as if he were opening a container of plutonium, slow, and careful. Evident by the smirk on his face, his dramatic mien was meant to heighten my anticipation. It was only a tube of toothpaste, for crying out loud. How deadly could it be?

"Spread your legs, kitten," Dylan instructed with an equally devilish grin.

"I hate to break this to you, guys…but I don't have any teeth down there." I couldn't help but laugh as I spread my legs.

"Guys?" Nick admonished.

"Oops, sorry. Sir's."

"We're well acquainted with your cunt, girl and can both attest to the fact that there are no teeth in or around your slick, hot pussy. But we also know how much you're going to squirm when we lick that minty toothpaste off your sweet, sensitive clit."

"You can't put that on my girl parts." I gasped and slapped my thighs together.

"Of course we can," Dylan refuted. "And it's your clit, kitten."

"I know what it's called. I mean why would you want to put it there, Sir?"

"That's what we intend to show you, kitten. Just breathe and enjoy the sensations." Dylan's strong hands pried my legs apart as Nick smeared a fingertip of paste upon my turgid nub. I yelped, startled by the cold cream. But then a strange tingling sensation enveloped my nub and I gripped the sheets and anchored and ready for any other qualities the paste might contain.

Dylan climbed between my legs and lowered his head. His wet, warm tongue swirled over my pearl and when he blew a gentle breath over the swelling bud, I nearly launched to the ceiling fan. A shrill cry ripped from my throat. I could have sworn he'd pressed an ice cube straight over my clit. As the shock to my system diminished, the tingling sensation started again, accompanied by an enticing burn. Repeating the process over and again, Dylan licked and sucked with spellbinding precision while Nick iced and nibbled my nipples with the paste. Currents of electricity pulsated through my cells, crashing headlong upon one another, before pooling beneath my sweet spot in pulsing urgency. Every touch, lick and kiss spiked my need to come. The demand grew higher and harder, like a rolling ocean tide, surging and racing toward the craggy shore.

"Have you ever read about orgasm denial, little one?" Nick asked as I panted and writhed.

"What?" I gasped as I opened my eyes. I tried to focus on his face hovering close to mine. Even with my mind thick like syrup, I recognized the flash of disapproval in his eyes as a smile of retribution tugged his lips. *Crap!* I wasn't paying attention, again. Why had he chosen that exact moment to start asking me questions, anyway? He knew I was close to coming undone. They'd been fervent with the toothpaste. Coupled with Dylan's magnificent tongue and his nimble fingers, it was a miracle I'd not failed them and cum like a virgin bride. "No. No, Master. Please. No edging."

"I love it when you call me, Master, little one. And there will be hours of edging if you don't answer my question." Nick stroked his cock in long, slow glides as he glanced down at Dylan, who still devoured me with a vengeance.

I had to focus and think about what he'd asked me. Something about orgasm denial. "No Sir, I haven't."

"Haven't what, little one?"

"I haven't read about orgasm denial, Master."

"Very good, pet," he praised as he leaned in and pressed his lips to mine with a rough and hungry kiss.

I opened to him in greedy invitation, yet his tongue simply teased the rim of my lips, never advancing inside my mouth. I wanted to suckle him deep, but he wouldn't allow me. I mewled in frustration, desperate to feel his control.

He pulled back and actually laughed. "Oh, little one, you're not calling the shots here. Don't tell me you've not figured that out yet."

"No, Master. I mean, I'm not calling the shots. I know who holds the power." I whimpered and writhed as Dylan continued his blissful torture.

"Your power, precious, and it's delicious. But it's time for more anal training." His brows arched as an evil smirk tugged one corner of his mouth.

I groaned and tossed my head from side to side in protest as I ground my center against Dylan's deviant mouth.

"Oh, but it is you sexy, rebellious wench," Nick replied with a chuckle.

Suddenly, Dylan abandoned his playful torture and sat up. Thick cream glistened upon his lips and chin. He gave me a playful wink then eased from the bed, no doubt in search of his bag o' wicked tricks.

I wanted to scream. Their incessant toying and teasing and denying me an orgasm was not going to make me a better submissive, just a frustrated, pissed off woman. And that damn plug! What was the thrill of shoving that thing up my ass? I was certain I could accommodate them just fine, *if* they went slow. And if I failed to seat them both, *then* bring out that annoying metal bastard and shove it up my backside.

"Remember pet, this isn't all for you. It's for us, too." Nick soothed.

With a deep sigh, I closed my eyes and nodded. I'd never get past the doorway of submission, let alone begin the journey if I expected to always get my way. But dammit, did they have any idea how uncomfortable that damn plug was? Of course not! Dominants didn't parade around wearing jewel encrusted plugs up their butts. A giggle threatened at the visual dancing in my brain.

"On your knees, kitten," Dylan instructed with a roguish gleam in his eyes.

"Yes, Master," I grumbled before I rolled over, and braced on all fours.

Nick assumed the role of 'Master butt plug shover' as Dylan's decadent fingers assuaged the lurid burn. The conflagration consumed me and the demand for release snarled inside. And as the broad flared section of the plug passed my impossibly stretched rim, Nick landed a sharp slap over each butt cheek. I begged and wailed for permission to come and wasn't prepared for what happened next. Nick wrapped his arm around my waist and pulled me upright.

"Let's go make some breakfast, little one."

"Now?" I screeched, panting and dazed. "You can't be serious, Sir!"

"Oh, but I am," He smirked.

"But…I need…what about…"

"I asked if you'd read up on it, little one. You told me no, so I decided you should experience it firsthand. Welcome to orgasm denial." His deep laughter reverberated in my chest. I had to clench my teeth to keep from cursing.

"Come, kitten. It won't be quite so frustrating when you allow your mind to focus on something else for a bit. We like to watch you simmer." Dylan tried not to laugh and I tried not to shred their skin like a banshee on crack. Shaking with need and fury, I released a howl of frustration. I close my eyes and counted to ten but it wasn't enough numbers, so I started over, trying to get a handle on my breaths in the process.

"Can I at least put some clothes on, Sirs? The thought of frying bacon in the nude..." I seethed with an indignant huff.

"No," Nick growled. "You don't even get to wear an apron, not with that tone of voice, little one."

"I'm sorry, Master," I mumbled. "It's just that I'm..."

"Wet? Ready? Needy?" Nick taunted.

"Yes. About a zillion times over."

"Good." He smiled.

"How is that good? Sir." I groused.

"Because it pleases us. And because when we finally allow you to come, it's going to be a powerful explosion. Christ, girl, you have no idea how glorious you look and sound when you fragment into a million pieces." Nick marveled as he and Dylan slipped on their jeans.

"Oh," I whispered, at least having something to look forward to—blessed relief.

Their pained expressions as they tucked their swollen erections into their jeans brought a certain satisfaction. It was obvious that I wasn't the only one suffering.

Either I was too horny to care or I was growing accustomed to the plug, but it no longer felt like I had a giant sequoia in my ass. My tender ring continued to throb and I had to remain focused on clenching the base, but I was managing the anal intruder far better than before.

When breakfast was over and the dishes done, Dylan and Nick carried more wood in from the mud room. I held the door for them, shivering as the bitter cold wind wafted into the room. Peeking around the door, I noticed the window in the small room was almost totally obscured in snow. The sunlight reflecting off the white powder suggested warmth. It was a deceitful guise.

"Dammit, Savannah," Dylan scolded. "Your lips are purple and you're trembling like a leaf. Get your ass into a hot bath or back in bed. We've got this."

"Thank you, Sir," I replied as my teeth chattered.

Stretched out in a bubbling pool of liquid heat, I'd finally gotten some time alone. I was used to being alone and it should have relaxed me. But after the past few days with Dylan and Nick constantly at my side, for some strange reason, I missed them. How had I grown accustomed to their presence so quickly?

The question you should ask is how did you fall in love with them so quickly?

I sucked in a heavy breath and closed my eyes. The tiny voice inside my head carried a torrent of fear. I couldn't be in love with them. My brain was confusing love with gratitude. It would only be normal to feel beholden to them after they'd brought out the submissive in me. But I knew I was lying to myself as I tried to rationalize away my feelings. It was becoming more and more apparent that no matter how hard I tried to keep my heart out of the equation, it would be a near-impossible feat.

The bubbles churned and gurgled as I began to dissect the emotions they'd brought to life. By their own admission, they cared about me, but not enough for of them to open their hearts or rearrange their lives to include me. And how narcissistic was it of me to expect them to?

The way they pampered me fed my submissive longings and drew forth the need to please them even more. And the patience they'd shown was quintessential, evolving into a bond of deep and abiding trust. The cognizance that they'd go out of their way to never hurt me physically or emotionally was like a golden net of safety.

So what if I loved them? Loving someone wasn't a bad thing. I loved several people in my life. After all they'd done for me, it was only natural to want to add Dylan and Nick to the list of those dear to my heart.

You love Mellie, Helen and Myron very differently than the love you hold for Dylan and Nick, but go on...blow some more smoke up your ass if you think it will keep your heart from breaking.

That condescending voice of reason held too much truth.

"They're not geared for a serious relationship and neither are you," I mumbled to myself. They probably had more submissives at Genesis than I could shake a stick at. Harboring sophomoric hopes was futile. I might be 'special' to them in some fashion, but no doubt I was one of many 'special' women they used to satiate their Dominant desires. Maybe their opinion was skewed because we were snowed in and I was convenient. By the end of next week, they'd probably not give me a second thought. They'd chalk up our time together as another notch on their proverbial flogger. And didn't that sting like a bitch.

My thoughts swirled like the water around me. I slunk deeper into the tub as I pondered the difference between love and gratitude.

You've known them less than seventy-two hours. That's hardly enough time to make a love connection.

They want a week of "no strings, no promises." So no matter what you feel for them, it's not going to be reciprocated. Don't set yourself up for a fall.

They live in Chicago. Long distance relationships rarely work out.

Yes, the sex is phenomenal, but relationships can't survive on sex alone, no matter how mind-blowing it is.

For all purposes, they're still strangers. You don't know very much about them. Hell, they could have a collared submissive back home and you'll never know. Suddenly, that green-eyed monster reared its ugly head and washed over me in a black oily veil. "Shit!"

"Problem, little one? Or are you anxious to find out what soap tastes like?"

I jumped and turned my head at Nick's gravelly voice, cringing at the look of censure on his face.

"No, Sir. I'm sorry, I was thinking and it just slipped out."

"I see. And what negative thoughts were running through your brain, little one?" He asked as he sat on the side of the tub.

Shit. Shit. Shit. Was nothing sacred with this guy? Wasn't I allowed one or two feelings without be obliged to vomit them out? I cast my eyes toward the water and sighed. If I told him it was nothing, he'd keep prodding and poking until I spilled my guts. Even then, I'd probably be punished. I was screwed either way.

"I was thinking about the fact that I don't know very much about you or Dylan, Sir." It was the truth in a convoluted way.

"Go on," he prompted.

I swallowed tightly. "Do you two have a collared submissive?"

"No, we don't. Next question."

"Do you always share women? I mean, you two seem so…comfortable. Like you've…" I couldn't finish the sentence. I was tripping over my tongue as jealousy spiked again.

Nick was quiet for a long time. I hazard a quick glance to find him staring at the wall with a faraway look in his eyes. After a long moment, he turned and gazed down at me.

"I'm not sure how much of my conversation with George you overheard, little one. So I will tell you a bit about me. I was married for a short time. It was a mistake. One that nearly ruined my friendship with Dylan. And yes, we've been sharing women since the summer we graduated high school."

"That's a long time," I whispered without thinking.

Nick laughed. "We're not *that* old, pet."

"No, Sir. I meant…"

"I know what you meant, girl. Relax, it's all good," he chuckled. "We grew up in the country. It was the middle of June and hot. We were driving home from a party late one night and came upon a girl walking down the road. Her name was Abby. She'd graduated with us. She was one of the cheerleaders at our school, and she was crying. So we pulled over and stopped. Long story short, she and her boyfriend had been parked in a cornfield down the road. She'd been determined to lose her virginity before she went away to college, but her stupid boyfriend got drunk and passed out on her."

"So, you and Dylan…"

"Yes, pet. We took care of her little problem then drove her home."

I wasn't sure if I admired their chivalry or deplored their motive for snagging a convenient piece of pussy.

"What other questions are rolling around in that pretty brain of yours, girl?" He smiled.

"Too many," I confessed with a nervous smile. "How did getting married almost ruin your friendship with Dylan? If I'm being too nosy, Sir, please tell me."

He leaned down and kissed my lips with a tender caress. "No, little one. Your questions deserve answers. I met my ex-wife, Paige right after Dylan came home from Iraq. She was from a wealthy family with old money and thick in society circles. We met at a fund-raiser. Admittedly, I drank too much champagne and invited her back to my house. One thing led to another and a few weeks later we were in a relationship. She's strong willed and while I find that extremely attractive in a submissive, Paige didn't have a subservient bone in her body. But I thought I was in love and could forego my Dominant desires. I may have been able to."

He shrugged and frowned with a sour expression. "Who knows? I never got a chance to test that theory. After the wedding, she changed…almost overnight. There were two sides of Paige. She had a loving, carefree, playful side then a vindictive, hateful and manipulative side. Unfortunately, I didn't discover the latter until *after* the wedding. Dylan was the only one who saw through her façade. He'd tried to warn me that she was only interested in my money as a means to climb her social ladder but instead of listening to him, I got pissed. I accused him of horrible things, of trying to sabotage my happiness because she wasn't the type of woman we could share. I almost lost him over her. I've spent a lot of time kicking my own ass because of it."

"But you thought you were in love." I reached out and squeezed his leg, leaving a wet hand print on his jeans.

"No, I was in love with the idea of being in love, little one. I knew in the back of my mind I was making a mistake as I stood before the Minister. But my own stubborn pride kept me from turning on my heel and walking out the church doors. The marriage was destined to fail before it began. We've been divorced two years, yet she still insists on trying to drag me back to court, contesting the prenuptial agreement."

"Can she do that?"

"She can try, but she'll fail. My lawyer has a box filled with proof that she'd been fucking other men since we got back from our honeymoon. I didn't know it at the time, but her prized Bentley was a gift from one of her rich fuck buddies, an old man she kept on the side because he gave her credit cards to buy whatever she wanted."

"Why did she even bother marrying you in the first place?" I asked in disgust.

"I asked her that, once. She told me it was something she hadn't tried yet."

"Wow." I was speechless. What kind of heartless bitch did that to a guy? I couldn't wrap my head around the fact that she'd used him. My blood began to boil. I wanted to find that nasty snatch and bitch slap her into next week. "God, Nick. I'm so sorry you had to go through that."

"It taught me a lesson, little one, to guard my heart and never get married again."

Paige had damaged Nick so deeply that his entire outlook on relationships had been tainted. She'd taken away all hope of him ever finding a happy-ever-after. And somehow, I knew that if Paige ever discovered how deeply she'd crushed him, she'd find joy in the fact. Women like her gave our gender a bad reputation.

"Do you have any other questions, pet?" Nick asked with a solemn expression.

"No, Sir. Thank you for your honesty," I whispered, wishing I could take his pain away.

"It's part of the exchange, little one. You've been trying to come out from behind your walls and I'm impressed. There's nothing I won't share with you for granting me your gift of trust." A broad smile spread over his lips and his eyes sparkled with pride. The joy I'd brought to him sent a rush of warmth through my body.

"You can relax a bit longer if you'd like, pet, then come on out and join us. Dylan is building a fire. We want to keep you warm. Very, very warm." An evil smile tugged the corner of his mouth as he reached down and plucked a nipple.

"Warm? Is that what you call it, Sir? I call it raging inferno, thank you very much."

"Then we're doing our job, little one." Nick stood and walked out of the room, chuckling as he left.

The emotional torture Paige had put Nick through made my heart ache. And the fact that the evil bitch was still making his life a living hell had me seething with rage. I'd never wanted to hire a hit man like I did then.

Naked and cold, I padded back to the large common area where I was met with two hungry smiles and a blazing fire—not only in the fireplace, but in my veins. Amazed by their ability to ignite my desires with just a look, I darted a nervous gaze between them.

"You're scaring me, Sirs," I giggled as I eased between their warm bodies and sat on the couch.

"Your fears are unfounded, kitten," Dylan winked.

"Thank heavens," I sighed in gratitude.

"We'll remind you that you said that, little one." Nick grinned.

"Remind me? When, Sir?"

"Don't eye me with suspicion, pet," Nick laughed. "We'll make certain you feel no pain at all."

"No pain with what, Sir?" I gulped.

"You'll find out later, little one."

Nick's cryptic reply sent my heart racing. Obviously they had something planned that had the potential to include pain. My mind began to reel with possibilities, none of which brought me one iota of comfort.

"Nick tells me you two had a nice talk in the bathroom. Is there anything you'd like to ask me, kitten?" Dylan smiled.

Oh, they were smooth as silk. Nick dropped a bomb that ratcheted my fears off the damn charts and Dylan swooped in to dust the shrapnel away by changing the subject. And silly me, I let them keep me on my toes like a ballerina in a performance of *Let's Mind Fuck the Submissive*. I liked it better not knowing when I was going to be blindsided versus waiting, wondering and worrying what they planned next.

"Still reinforcing my trust, right Sirs?" I asked with a knowing smile.

"Exactly," Nick grinned. "You're learning fast, little one. Good girl."

Goosebumps peppered my flesh and my nipples drew up tight all from one simple phrase. *Good girl.* Did they have any idea of the heady rush evoked by those two words?

"I'm an open book, kitten, ask me anything." Dylan preened with a bright smile.

"What were your tours in Iraq like, Sir?"

He looked as if I'd asked him to cut off his arm, and I was swamped with guilt for breeching such an uncomfortable subject.

"I'm sorry Dylan...err, Sir. Please don't answer that. It's none of my business," I amended in a rushed apology.

"No, kitten, it's fine. There's much you don't know about us and you'll never know unless you ask. No subject should be off-limits. We know how precious and fragile trust is. I don't want you to feel that we're less than honest with you about everything. Understood?"

"Yes, Sir." I nodded. "But we can talk about something else if you..."

Dylan pressed a finger to my lips, silencing my offer.

"At first I was excited when my Unit Commander informed me he'd recommended I try out for a sniper position. Each time we qualified on the range, I fired High Expert, so I tried out and was accepted to sniper school."

"He had the highest scores in his class. Don't let him fool you, Savannah. He's good."

"That's impressive." I agreed.

"Who's telling this story, bro?" Dylan teased before that abnormally serious expression materialized on his face, again. "My unit was deployed six weeks after I completed sniper school. We flew into Bagdad then got sent to the Anbar Provence. It holds the title of most U.S. soldiers killed than anyplace else in Iraq. Like General Sherman said, 'War is hell'. It really is, kitten."

I issued a sorrowful nod as Dylan scrubbed a hand through his short, spiked hair. Revealing this part of his life was killing him. I wasn't sure I could continue to listen to what he had to say. The tortured tone of his voice filled me with sorrow.

"After Anbar, we spent time in Ramadi. Christ, what a mess. Buildings blown to shit, rubble everywhere, mothers carrying crying, bandaged babies down the streets; their eyes filled with terror. Burned out Hummers clogged the streets with charred bodies of fellow servicemen inside." Dylan closed his eyes and squeezed his forehead with a broad palm. "I lost a lot of good friends in that godforsaken place. If it hadn't been for Nick, I'd have probably eaten a bullet by now--voluntarily."

"Please, Dylan, Stop. That's enough." My voice cracked as a tear slid down my cheek. I soothed my hand over his shoulders and leaned against his strong body, holding him tight. My blood ran cold at the thought of Dylan in such a dark place that he'd contemplated suicide. I was afraid his painful memories would haunt him for the rest of his life.

With a heavy sigh, he nodded. His jaw ticked before he turned and looked into my eyes.

"It changed me, kitten. I'm sorry you didn't get to meet the man I used to be."

I choked back a sob and shook my head. "It wouldn't have mattered. The man I see before me is the one who has touched me in ways I've never known. I'm honored to take him just the way he is."

Tears brimmed his eyes as he pulled me against his chest and held me close. "I don't deserve you, kitten."

"Yes you do," I choked against his warm neck as tears spilled from my eyes. "You deserve someone a whole lot better than me."

"There is no one better than you, princess, and there never will be."

CHAPTER EIGHT

My heart was breaking for his pain and exploding in celebration that he'd bravely exposed his inner demons to me. I held him for a long time in the silence of the room, trying my best to give him comfort.

"Your journey back has been a tough road, bro. But you *are* back, man. Don't lose sight of the work you've done." Nick's words were slathered in praise and admiration. I could only imagine how scared he had been trying to help Dylan cope in those dark days.

"You and I both know life is always worth living, dude. Come on. Let's make it exhausting, too."

Without another word, Nick plucked me from Dylan's side, lifting me into his powerful arms. The carnal smirk on his face left no doubt what he had in mind. It was the shot of medicine that Dylan desperately needed. I watched his desolate mood transform before my eyes. His insipid expression dissolved, giving way to a broad, knowing smile.

I reached out, extending a hand to him. "Please, Master. I need you."

"You've already got me, kitten. All of me," Dylan growled as he stood and laced his fingers in mine.

Side by side, they carried me into the bedroom.

Once seated on the bed, I watched as they began to peel off their jeans. Helpless to do anything but stare at their mouthwatering erections and scrumptious sculpted bodies, I greedily drank in every distended vein and rigid plane.

"It's time for that plug to come out, kitten," Dylan announced in a thick voice of need.

My heart clutched. Were they going to make me endure a bigger plug? Or were they going to drive into my pussy and ass, together? Gazing at their cocks, I was filled with fear that I wouldn't be able to accommodate both of them at once.

"No, little one. It won't hurt, you have our promise," Nick soothed. He'd somehow read my mind again. "Climb on top of me and trust us, pet. We're not going to do anything except make you feel good."

Nick positioned himself in the middle of the bed and extended his hand, helping me straddle his waist. Easing his hands to my hips he glided me down until I was sitting on his washboard abs.

"Kiss me, girl," he growled as cinched a hand in my hair.

With an accepting moan, I lowered my breasts to his chest as he pressed his lips to mine. There was no further guidance from him; instead he allowed me to govern the kiss. The ceding of his control felt foreign yet empowering. I pulled back, question written on my face as I stared into his eyes. His passive expression drew a devilish smile to tug the corners of my mouth. I latched onto his bottom lip, giving a playful tug before sipping the plump flesh inside, suckling it sweetly. And still, he allowed me free reign until I tugged his lip once more. Savagely gripping my hair till my scalp stung, he seized me with a scalding kiss. Undaunted, I gave back all the blistering passion bursting inside.

Dylan moved about the room. The scrape of a drawer dimly registered as I fed on Nick's mouth in wild abandon. The crinkled tear of a condom wrapper prevailed in the quiet room and the bed dipped behind me.

"Here, man, sheath up," Dylan stated as Nick released my mane. I inched forward to allow him room to glove up his hard erection, now nuzzled against my ass. Nick completed his task in short order before sliding his fingers deep in my hair.

"Raise up, kitten," Dylan instructed with a soft caress on my thighs.

I lifted my ass into the air. Nick swallowed my muffled groan as Dylan slid the bulbous plug out. Slick, wet fingers bore through my throbbing ring, granting no reprieve to my tender tissue. With purpose, Dylan swirled and stretched my puckered opening, readying me.

Nick wrapped a hand around my waist, eased me up then slowly guided me onto his steely shaft. The cool, latex-covered tip warmed in seconds as my fiery tunnel fervently sucked at his stalk, pulling him in deep.

Lightning pulsed through my veins as Dylan continued his lurid exploration of my ass. The whole time, Nick thrust up and back in a slow torturous cadence. Anticipation mounted upon anxiety and a soft mewl of fear reverberated in my throat.

Nick searched my eyes with a probing scowl. His expression softened as he issued a compassionate sigh. "No fears. You're safe, little one. Dylan won't enter you until he's got you totally ready for him. I promise."

"That's right, kitten. I'm still working on getting you nice and stretched. There's no rush. We're going to take this nice and slow. Relax, baby. We're going to take good care of you."

Their reassuring words melted away my apprehension. I basked in the rippling pyre of pleasure radiating from my puckered tissue. Nick plucked my nipples as he continued to plow into my fluttering core with long, agonizing strokes. His swollen crest scraped back and forth over that electrified bundle of nerves deep inside.

"You're so fucking gorgeous, Savannah. Your cunt feels like wet, hot silk. So smooth and tight. So fucking tight," he growled, driving deep with a slow languid glide. "Open your pretty little asshole for him, baby. Let him inside. We can't wait to blow your mind, precious."

Dylan pressed the crown of his cock against my dilated opening as he retracted his fingers, one by one. Nick stilled and waited while Dylan pushed determinedly against my electrified rim. The pressure was savage, nearly unbearable. I cried out as his wide flange pierced through the burning rim.

My pussy and ass blazed in a euphoric mixture of pleasure and pressure. Staggered by the onslaught of sensations they spawned, I relinquished all control to them, and they took it. Took it all.

"Fuckkkk," Dylan hissed before sucking in a deep breath. "Relax, baby. You're strangling my cock. Christ almighty!"

"Is he hurting you?" Nick asked, brushing a knuckle over my cheek.

I shook my head as I panted, trying to rise above the searing pressure.

"Slow breaths, little one. Relax and let your body get accustomed to him. We're not going to move until you're ready. You're so fucking beautiful, Savannah, and we're so damn proud of you. You're doing an amazing job, baby. Just keep focused on opening up for Dylan, okay?"

I nodded. I steadied my breathing and tried to force my screaming muscles to relax around Dylan's thick cock. Nick's broad thumb circled my clit and the blinding, burning pressure fused into a fire of demand. I cautiously rocked upon their embedded shafts, captivated by the sizzling currents arcing from my tightly drawn passageways.

Dylan retreated but remained embedded in my throbbing ass while Nick guided his cock up and back, stretching me with each hot, glorious inch. As they alternated their thrusts in salacious choreography, my entire world tipped on its axis. I couldn't tell up from down or left from right. Day and night lost all meaning. There was no hell. I was lost, immersed in total Utopia.

Pristine.

Blissful.

Streaking across the heavens like a shooting star, I basked in the billion shards of ecstasy igniting every nerve ending. Rolling my hips, I implored their driving shafts and welcomed the dazzling bursts of light exploding behind my eyes.

"That's our girl. Work us in, little one. Let us fill you so full, you'll feel what's in our hearts. You're locked inside us now, Savannah. Take us into your heart, little one and never let us go. Never let us go."

Tears filled my eyes. Nick's words felt like a spike through my soul. This wasn't simply tutelage and fabulous sex. They were imprinting themselves inside me. *Me.* The woman who'd never had a lover more than once. The shy loner who'd merely fantasized of having this kind of connection with a man, never allowing myself to imagine it being possible with *two.*

I mattered to them…meant something to them in a way I'd never conceived possible. No longer able to deny the love taking root in my heart, and even if it were only for a brief moment in time, I would brand them to me for all time.

Unwilling to focus on the minute amount of time I would have them in my life, I cast away the disconcerting thoughts before pain could fist my heart. Clearing my mind, I focused on their driving shafts, my trembling legs, the sweat dripping off my body, and the sublime pressure mounting atop itself. Their cocks plunged deep and I was lost in a surreal realm as they brought my darkest fantasy to life.

Consumed in the swirling whirlpool of sensation, I released all inhibition and rode them like a tempest in a sea of carnal splendor. My tunnels rippled and gripped, fluttered and clutched, as grunts, growls and screams echoed in my ears. Surging in and out, they ramped the verve of pleasure. I gripped Nick's shoulders, desperate to remain anchored to their world.

Pulses of fire singed the thin membrane separating their driving cocks, as tiny explosions detonated in my veins. It was the most delicious combination of pleasure and pain I'd ever felt. Hunger begat demand and it was bigger and stronger than I could tame.

My brain was glazed in a silky erotic fog. Possessed by insatiable lust, I tightened on their driving shafts and impaled my quivering flesh in frenzied need. Their curses rent the air. Their feral cries thundered in my ears. I rode them without an ounce of modesty, like a rabid animal. They'd stormed my walls and annihilated any semblance of self-preservation. They'd split my soul in two, yet I remained wrapped in a blanket of safety, protection, and unequivocal love.

I'd passed the heavens, the stars and the sun, and was sailing away to some unknown star system with gaining speed. The inky blackness behind my eyes began to flicker as thunder and lightning collided in my veins.

"Look at me. I want to see every fucking expression as it lights up your gorgeous face. Come Savannah, come for us now!" Nick growled.

High-pitched cries peeled from the back of my throat. His command filtered through my sexual fugue. Heat and demand spun into a giant orb of euphoria and exploded outward in a blinding flash of white. My entire body seized. Suspended in another dimension, I languished in the blissful, pulsating pleasure before an enormous convulsion detonated deep in my womb. Screams burned my throat as the monstrous orgasm ripped me to shreds.

Frenzied thrusts pounded through my convulsing passageways. As my body milked and sucked their driving cocks, their bellicose roars drowned out the sound of slapping flesh and I felt their powerful explosions erupt beneath the twin latex barriers.

Every muscle in my body gave out and I fell to Nick's broad, heaving chest. His arms banded around me in a hold so sublime, tears spilled from my eyes. Overwhelmed by the staggering onslaught of emotions, I sobbed.

Dylan eased from my ass then draped his hot, slick body over my back. His warm lips danced on my shoulders and spine before he burrowed his face close to my neck and nuzzled against me.

Surrounded in their potent heat, I felt loved for the first time in my life. Not as a daughter to my parents, or a sister to Mellie, or even a pseudo child to Myron and Helen; but as a woman. It was unconditional, total acceptance by two unbelievably wonderful men. I felt every ounce of their devotion, protection, and tenderness. And the inescapable magnitude of their love.

Uncontrollable sobs wracked my body. If this arrangement had only encompassed the joys of submission, having to walk away from them might have hurt. But I knew, now, when it came time to leave, I was going to be devastated.

The wave of emotions tearing through me was staggering. Was I insane to feel love for them? Was it right or wrong? How was I going to put myself back together again after allowing them full reign of my mind, body, heart, and soul? How had something so benign evolved into such a tangling of my heart?

Nick held me tighter as if sensing my overwhelming fears. "Shhh, it's going to be okay, little one. We'll figure it out. I'm sorry, love. It's going to hurt like hell...for all of us."

Through my mournful sobs, a humorless laugh escaped. "How do you do always know what I'm thinking?"

"I don't know. Sometimes I can feel your thoughts. I've never had this kind of connection with anyone before."

"Me neither," Dylan whispered. His voice cracked as he issued a curse.

"Hang in there, D," Nick encouraged.

A solitary tear dropped to my skin and slid over my shoulder. I wanted to turn over and wrap my arms around Dylan and share this bittersweet moment. Before I could move, he eased from my back, climbed off the bed and silently walked away. Nick rolled me to my side and held me as I cried tears of redemption...and mourning.

A long moment later, Dylan returned to bed. His rugged chest melded against my back as he wrapped his arms around me. Neither man said a word. They simply swathed me in their steely bodies, as feelings I was helpless to process rushed forth in a flood of hot, wet tears.

I felt raw. Exposed. There were no walls left to escape behind. They'd unfurled me sexually, but more frightening, they'd sliced me open emotionally as well. Though their bodies enveloped me, covered me in warmth and reassurance, I'd never felt so glaringly naked.

Panic took root in my belly. I fought the urge to pry myself from their loving cocoon and lock myself away in the bathroom, to hide like a child. But I was no longer a child. I was a woman who had made the conscious decision to participate in this endeavor. I had to face the consequences of my actions like an adult.

I could spend the rest of our time together counting down the days till emotional Armageddon, or I could bask in the glorious gifts they longed to give. I didn't need a Doctorate to decide which choice to make. Forcing myself to stop crying, I sniffed and exhaled a deep breath.

"I'm sorry, Sirs. I didn't mean to come apart like that. I want to thank you both. That was the most incredible experience of my life."

"It was pretty fucking earth-shattering for us too, kitten," Dylan whispered in my ear. "I've never felt anything like that before and I doubt I will again."

Nick nodded as his warm breath fluttered over my cheek. "Fan-fucking-tastic is what it was, pet."

"Is it going to be like that the rest…" *Dammit!* Why did I have to keep shoving reality in their faces, in *my* face? "If we do it again?"

"You mean when?" Dylan chortled softly. "I sure hope so. We'll have to do it again and find out, won't we?"

"Not yet," I moaned, "I need to recover first."

"Rest, little one. We've got lots of time to practice until we get it perfectly right."

"Oh, mercy," I gasped, wondering how long it would take before the soreness waned.

The sound of a motor running outside snagged our attention. Dylan peeled himself from my back and rolled out of bed. Donning his jeans, he stepped out of the room as the grinding and chugging sound grew louder.

"What is that?" I asked, twisting away from Nick's hold enough to see his face.

"It sounds like a snow blower, pet."

"Yep," Dylan announced returning to the bedroom. "Kit's out there trying to clear off the porch, up at the house. There's at least four and half feet of snow and hell, the drifts are more like six feet. She's never going to get a path cleared."

Nick groaned then leaned down to kiss my lips. "Guess we should go up there and help her."

"You can hang here if you want, I'll do it." Dylan offered.

"No, man. If we both go, we can get it done in half the time." Nick argued as he rolled away from me and stood. The condom still clung to his semierect cock and I couldn't take my eyes off it.

"Kitten?" Dylan stated, drawing my attention away. He cocked his head and looked at me with a strange expression.

"Yes, Sir?"

"Do you have a fascination with soft cocks?"

"Umm." I felt my face warm. "I don't know if I'd call it a fascination. Okay, maybe it is. I've never…"

"You've never felt a cock that wasn't hard, is that what you're trying to say?"

I lowered my eyes and nodded.

"That's nothing to be ashamed or embarrassed about, little one. When we get back, we'll be more than happy to help sate your curiosity. But just so you know, they won't stay soft long…not with you touching them. So inspect fast." Nick grinned.

"I'll do my best, Sir," I laughed.

"You have our permission to say in bed, soak in the tub or curl up on the couch by the fire, kitten. I'll throw some more logs on before we head up to the house."

"Thank you, Sir," I nodded to Dylan.

If someone had told me three weeks ago that I'd accept a line drawn in the sand with docile resignation; I would have scoffed in their face or told them they were on crack. But understanding that I gave Dylan and Nick the power to set my limits was exhilarating.

I opted to stay in bed. My limbs felt like Jell-O and the pungent scent of sex still clung in the air. I hugged their pillows to my chest and breathed in their distinct, intoxicating scents and when I closed my eyes—it was as if they'd never left. As I stretched out in the center of the bed, muscles I never knew I had cried out with a burning reminder of our torrid, mind-blowing session. With a satisfied curl on my lips, I drifted off to sleep.

"Savannah. Savannah, honey?" Kit rousted me from the darkness.

Kit was in my room and I was naked. My arms flew to the empty spaces of the mattress, wondering where Dylan and Nick were. My heart pounded in my chest and it took a moment to remember they were helping her remove the piles of snow. Thankfully, I wasn't going to have to explain to her why I was in bed, *naked* with them.

"Kit." I blinked against the sunlight and clutched the covers to my chin. "What's wrong?"

"Nothing, sugar. I came down to see how you were feeling. The guys are still up trying to dig out the sidewalk. Bless their hearts, they got the porch all cleaned off. Son of a gun, I haven't seen this much snow in years and never this early. I hope that isn't a sign that we're going to have a bad winter." Kit rambled on in a flurry.

"I hope not, too. I have to get back home, eventually." I chuckled.

"Are the boys behaving themselves?" She asked with a tilt of her head.

"Oh, yes. They've been nothing but perfect gentlemen." I nodded and fought back a smile.

"Good. I told them to behave and not to act like a couple of wild wolves around you." She scolded. "Are you doing okay? Are you hurting? Do you need anything, sugar?"

"No," I smiled. "I'm not hurting anywhere." *Liar.* "And I honestly can't think of anything I need." *Except Dylan and Nick right back here, in bed with me.*

"Okay, well, I'll let you rest. If you need anything, you send one of those Neanderthals up to the house to fetch it for you."

I laughed. "I will, Kit. Thanks so much for checking in on me."

"It's the least I can do. I know this vacation hasn't been fun for you and I'm sorry, baby."

Oh if you only knew.

"I'm fine. I know Mellie is safe and sound, so all is right in my world."

"Okay. I'll come down and check on you again from time to time."

"No," I blurted then forced a plastic smile. "I mean, you don't need to do that. I'm suffering no ill effects from the accident or anything. I'm just being a lazy slug today and lounging around. If there's anything I need, you'd be the first to know."

"Uh-huh." Kit issued a look of skepticism then smiled. "Just remember if you need something, you send one of the guys up."

"I will, I promise. Thank you."

With a tight grin still plastered across my mouth, Kit turned and left. It wasn't until I heard the front door of the barn close that I let out a massive sigh.

"Please don't come back down, Kit. God only knows what you might walk in on." I sent up a nervous prayer.

The thought of Kit discovering what we'd been doing for days shouldn't have bothered me, but it did. Not that I thought her a prude, but conventional society wasn't structured around ménages. It was hard enough for gays and lesbians to find states that would recognize their right to marry for shitsakes; it would no doubt take society even longer to accept threesomes, if ever.

The question of how people managed a threesome in their daily lives stuck in my head. From what I'd seen, it was hard enough for two people to work a stable relationship. I imagined three would be next to impossible, especially for someone like me who was used to spending ninety-nine percent of my time alone. I'd probably go batshit with them hovering over me day in and day out. I'd never have a moment to myself. And why was I thinking such ludicrous things in the first place? All this would be just a memory in a few short days.

My stomach grumbled, a welcome distraction from my train of thoughts. As I climbed out of bed, a sweet burn spread from my well used feminine parts. I smiled, savoring each glorious ache.

As I reached for my robe, my mind engaged in a perplexing tug-of-war. If I covered myself, knowing they forbade it, I ran the risk of punishment. But if Kit decided to pop back in, how would I explain my nakedness? Indecision pinged through me and I nibbled my bottom lip. Deciding I could toss on the robe, raid the fridge and hop back in bed naked without them ever knowing. I snagged my robe and put it on.

As I stepped from my room, Dylan and Nick rounded the corner.

Shit!

Nick's brows arched as he stared at me, unhappiness written all over his face, while Dylan tilted his head to the side and scowled.

"You know the rules, little one. What do you think you're doing?" Nick asked as he and Dylan shrugged out of their jackets and toed off their boots.

"Kit was down earlier and I didn't know if she might have decided to come back," I stammered.

"She's back up at her house, kitten. And I'm sure she's seen a naked woman before."

"But it would have been out of character for me to be running around the barn nude. Especially not knowing when you two would wander back in. She would think that very strange, don't you think?"

"Hrmm," Nick grumbled. "Still worried about others' perceptions, I see."

"Come on, Nick. What we're doing isn't the norm. People don't do this."

"It's Sir to you, little one," he barked. "And *we* do it all the damn time."

"Yes Sir," I mumbled as my fingers worried over the sash of my robe. "But I don't and…"

"And you're still not comfortable with the thought of someone finding out what you enjoy. Isn't that right?" Dylan pressed.

"It's my own private business, Sir," I whispered as I hung my head.

"Take the robe off, little one. Now," Nick demanded as he stepped toward me, reaching out a hand. I could feel his impatience and disappointment. It stung.

With a furtive glance toward the hallway, I released the sash and slid the robe from my body. Gooseflesh peppered my skin as I handed him the garment.

"Thank you, girl. Are you hungry?" Nick inquired.

"Yes, Sir."

"Then go sit by the fire. Dylan and I will prepare some food."

With a nod, I hurried to the couch and sat down. The leather was warm but I still wrapped the soft cotton blanket around me and tucked it under my feet. The men talked in low tones and I strained to hear what they were saying, no doubt devising some heinous form of punishment, but I couldn't make out a single word of their exchange. A shiver raced up my spine at the thought of having to endure more edging. A lecture was the punishment I would have chosen, but I didn't have a choice. I knew the risk I was taking when I donned the robe in the first place. And damn, if it didn't come around and bite me in the butt.

During lunch, neither of them said one word about a pending penance. Instead, they talked about the *weather*. Kit had informed them that the freak snow storm had passed and an abnormal warm front was coming in. The newscasters claimed all the snow would be gone in a day or two. From what I'd seen outside, a tropical blast from South America wouldn't be enough to melt the mountains of snow that lay beyond the barn.

#

It wasn't a heat wave from the Equator, but a steady rise of temperatures that set its sights on the expansive farmland, leaving only a few patches of snow on the ground. The snow wasn't the only thing that had melted away. So had the days—far quicker than I'd wanted them to.

"Are you ready yet?" Dylan called through my locked bedroom door.

I giggled, wondering if that poor man had an ounce of patience in him. "Almost, Sir. Just putting on my shoes."

"Nick's about to start gnawing the leather from the couch. Let's go, kitten. We're hungry."

I opened the door and smiled. "I'm ready. Thank you Sirs for allowing me to primp in private. It's not every day I have two gorgeous men taking me to dinner."

"You look…. fantastic. Damn Savannah, you take my breath away." Dylan approved with a wolfish grin. "Too bad we can't call for room service."

"Little one, you look stunning," Nick lauded as his gaze slid up and down my body.

"It's just a pair of jeans and a sweater, Sirs. But thank you." I couldn't help but grin. Their adoring words strummed at my heart strings.

"Well, the restaurant isn't a five-star dining experience, either. It's called Ma's Kettle. I'm sorry but the thriving metropolis of Connor, population seven hundred and two, lacked in elegant dining choices." Nick chuckled as he extended his hand.

Dylan slid his arm around my waist as both men escorted me to the parking lot. The sun was beginning to set and illuminated thin, wispy thin clouds in a golden hue. Nick drove my rented Hummer and as we made our way into town, I couldn't wipe the satisfied smile from my face. When I'd awoken that morning, wrapped in a tangle of heavy arms and legs, I'd made a silent vow not to dwell on the fact that we were down to two days before my dream was over. Shelving the panic, I instead focused on treasuring every remaining second.

Ma's Kettle was even less impressive that its name, but the restaurant was clean. The mouth-watering aromas in the place made up for all it lacked in ambiance. The small sign on the door boasted of home-cooked goodness, and it had been years since I'd had a meal like my mom used to make.

The three of us squeezed onto the wooden bench of an oversized booth situated at the front of the diner. Meg, our waitress who couldn't have been a day over sixteen, greeted us with a warm smile and three glasses of ice water. After rattling off the daily specials, she plopped three menus in front of us, scribbled down our drink orders then scurried away.

Nick's fingers inched beneath my hair, gently massaging the back of my neck as he perused the menu, turning to nuzzle and kiss my cheek from time to time. Dylan mindlessly trailed his fingers up and down my arm as he read the laminated sheet, pressing his lips against mine a time or two, as well. While their affections weren't overt, the muscles of my pussy clenched from their possessive fondles.

When Meg returned, she blinked and rendered a look of shock. Her face skewed as if something bitter lay on her tongue, and she all but slammed our drinks upon the table as she issued a look of disgust. Confused by her sudden change of demeanor, I quickly realized her disapproval had been born from our public display of affection. I lowered my gaze to the menu as my cheeks burned.

"Are you all ready to order or what? The cook wants to go home," She snapped in a curt, tone.

"Meg," Nick smiled. "I sense you're having a bad day. The sign on the door indicates you're open for business until ten o'clock. It's barely eight right now. It might behoove you, tip wise, to put a smile on your face and treat your customers more politely. This is a friendly town, is it not?"

His voice oozed with calm assurance and command. I peeked through dark lashes to see a pink hue color her cheeks as she stared at Nick with adoring brown eyes. I expected her to start drooling at any moment.

"Yes it is," she softened. "My apologies to you, Sir. I don't know what came over me."

"It's all right, sweet girl. We all have days that rattle us to some degree or another. I'm sure you'll be fine, now."

"I will, yes. Thank you." Meg smiled.

I wanted to scoff at the ease with which Nick transformed her from hissing tiger to purring kitten, but knew I'd only be undermining his attempt to make our evening enjoyable.

After Meg jotted down our dinner choices, and scampered back to the kitchen, stopping to whisper to a table full of middle-aged ladies. All four women turned in tandem and gawked at us. Their expressions raged from undeniable horror to blatant condemnation.

I tensed and my heartbeat quickened.

"It's okay, kitten," Dylan whispered as he clutched my hand. "It's a small town. They don't have anything better to do than gossip and judge."

My stomach flip-flopped a river dance of embarrassment.

"With your permission Sirs, may I go to the ladies room?" I asked in a low voice.

"Don't go hiding on us, little one. We have no qualms about dragging you out by your hair. Do I make myself clear?" Nick asked in a warning tone as he stood and helped me exit the booth.

"I'm not going in there to hide, Sir. I just need to use the facilities." I smiled, lying through my teeth. Gathering my nerve, I walked the length of the diner to a small alcove in the back.

Leaning over the ancient, chipped porcelain sink, I splashed cool water over my hands and lightly pressed them to my face. Staring at my reflection in the mirror, I inhaled a series of deep breaths.

"Ignore those women. They're jealous and narrow-minded. They don't know a thing about the bond you have with Dylan and Nick. Let it go. Don't give them the power to ruin the first real date you've had in months." Bolstered by my pep talk, I issued a resolute sigh at myself.

Then the bathroom door opened.

The older woman who entered wore a scowl of censure as she pressed the door closed behind her, stepping close into my personal space. Her bottle red hair shimmered purple in the harsh florescent lights and her lip curled in an angry snarl.

"You and your kind are an abomination. You're a bunch of sick, disgusting perverts. You need to eat your food and leave. We're a respectable, God-fearing town that doesn't cater to whores."

I blinked. Her vile remarks left me stunned.

"Excuse me?" I asked as my mouth hung agape. Anger surged in a red, hot wave. "Just who do you think you are? The morality police? I don't see a badge. Leave me alone and mind your own business, you nasty old heifer."

"On second thought, leave now. You all get out of here or I'm going to call the cops," she hissed.

"And report what?" I scoffed in a humorless laugh. "Friends having dinner? Sorry lady, but that's not a crime." My fists clenched into tight balls. I wanted to knock her on her self-righteous butt. "On second thought, I know what you need. You need to go home and get laid or dig out some toys from your bedside table and give yourself a much needed attitude adjustment."

"Why, I never. Mind my words, missy, you're going to burn in hell, you filthy little whore." Her face turned beet red as she spun on her heel and stormed out in a huff.

I had never lost my temper and spoken so rudely to anyone in my entire life. It felt…strange and empowering, yet my body shook in absolute rage. Suddenly, every glorious moment I'd spent with Dylan and Nick solidified into a black thick slab of shame.

No!

I was not going to allow her to taint the beauty that the three of us had shared. The hateful cow was not going to take away one iota of joy I'd experienced with them.

"God-fearing, my ass," I hissed as I fisted a paper towel and dried my hands. "You can kiss my butt, Bertha, because I'm going to plop my happy ass back in that booth and savor the warmth and affection of those two men *and* enjoy every bite of my dinner whether you like it or not."

A sobering realization filtered through my fury. If our arrangement ever magically evolved into a permanent relationship, we would face a world of people just like Bertha. We'd be assaulted with judgmental attitudes, vile comments, and condemning stares on a regular basis. Reality blindsided me with a powerful punch. Having left the barn and the enchanted realm we'd created, I realized I wasn't equipped to handle the consequences of bringing my fantasy to life. Reality was suddenly much too real. We would constantly be accosted by angry, ugly people slinging insults and passing sentence without a fleeting thought to our feelings.

I was wasting brain cells with such projections. In less than forty-eight hours, it was all going to be a memory. I'd never have to fear being snubbed for loving two men again.

Reminding myself of the vow I'd made, I stepped from the bathroom. With my head held high, I marched toward the booth. The nasty bitch who'd attempted to dictate my happiness, along with her equally pinched-faced friends, sat huddled with their heads together as I neared. Their caustic comments buzzed through the air like a swarm of angry bees. As I passed, I rolled my hips with an exaggerated sway as a broad, proud smile stretched across my lips.

Nick stood, watching me. His eyes sparkled and a wicked smirk tugged the corner of his mouth. "Everything go all right in the ladies room?"

"Of course, Sir," I replied happily as I fought to keep my bubbling anger buried down deep.

"I've decided what I'm having for dessert tonight, little one."

"Me too, Sir. A double-hard-on sundae with whipped cream." I winked then slid back into the booth next to Dylan.

"Only if you beg, kitten; only if you beg," Dylan chuckled.

As the women continued to shoot visual daggers our way, I kept a fake but confident smile glued in place. It was hard to ignore their condescending expressions but I was bound and determined to hide my inner turmoil and not spoil the date.

Meg appeared from time to time, though she never once looked at me. Instead, she lavished Nick and Dylan with flirtatious innuendos as if I were a ghost. I couldn't imagine why she thought she could seduce them. Did she think her girlish wiles enticed either man? The more I watched her, the more I wondered how many local boys had sampled her obvious need for attention. Sadly, I imagined she'd probably had more lovers in the past year than I'd had in my entire life. Why hadn't her parents taught her that happiness wasn't found between the sheets, but from inside. I pitied the poor girl. She faced a lifetime of pain giving her heart to men who didn't want to love her…just fuck her.

That thought made me analyze my own decisions. Was I, too, guilty of trying to find my happiness between the sheets?

"Kitten? Did you hear me?"

I snapped my head and gazed at Dylan, wide-eyed. "I'm sorry, Sir, I didn't hear you. These green beans are to die for."

"Hrmm, I asked if you'd be all right alone in the barn if Nick and I took off early in the morning to do some hunting." Dylan repeated, closely examining my eyes.

"Of course. I'll be fine, Sir. Just don't bring Bambi back in the bed of your truck. Okay? If you two happen to kill anything, I don't want to know." I closed my eyes and shook my head.

Nick laughed. "If we happen to get lucky and find a buck, we'll cover him with a tarp. There. Are you happy now, girl?"

"No, I'd be happy if you hunted rocks or arrowheads instead of poor innocent animals... Sir,"

"But if we take a deer, we can make venison chili for dinner tomorrow night," Dylan insisted.

I stopped chewing in mid-bite. "Ewwwwww," I groaned, wrinkling my nose.

"We'll be getting up early in the morning, but don't worry, we'll be quiet so you can sleep in. We won't be gone long, little one. And when we get back, we'll have the rest of tomorrow and part of the next before we have to pack up and head home."

I took a small sip of water to wash down the ball of anguish in my throat.

"Not a problem, Sir. Since my days of sleeping in are numbered, I plan on staying in bed as long as I can." I tried to keep my voice light and carefree but a part of me clamored to find the mortar and bricks and start resurrecting my shattered walls. I was going to need it.

Nick held me with a probing stare. All the while I prayed he couldn't see the pain that was already seeping into my veins. If I could make it through the meal without my grief spilling over the table, it would be an Oscar-worthy feat. The aromas of the diner now turned my stomach, and I'd barely touched my food. I hoped they wouldn't notice.

Meg reappeared at the table, striking a seductive pose. I wanted to laugh at the young girl's attempt to lure both men, but instead I gritted my teeth as she continued to brazenly flirt.

"Are you all ready for dessert? We've got some gooey pies, smooth and creamy," she purred while batting her lashes.

I couldn't take it anymore. I was livid at her shameless attempts to capture Dylan and Nick's attentions. Pity her or not, I'd had enough.

"No thank you, Meg. See, they want a woman, not a little girl, honey. Just between us, *I'm* their dessert. And I plan to spoon feed them every inch of my body, all night long. But we'll take the check now because I don't think I can wait another minute to feel their hot, slick tongues sliding all over my body."

"Rawwwwrrrr," Dylan laughed as Nick closed his eyes, lowered his chin and shook his head.

Meg blanched, her mouth agape, before she raced away from the table.

"That wasn't nice, pet," Nick whispered in that decadent, whiskey smooth voice.

"She wasn't being nice either, Master. She was all but climbing into your lap."

"Yes, but you're the adult here, little one. She's just a child."

"She certainly isn't acting like one. I don't like the fact that she's looking through me as if I'm not even here," I groused.

Between Bertha the judgmental bitch from hell and Meg the *Playboy* bunny wannabe, my patience and nerves were shot. My hopes for a memorable night out had turned into a macabre episode of *The Twilight Zone*. I wondered if Rod Serling was going to spin around on one of the stools at the counter. At that particular moment, I wouldn't have been the least bit surprised.

Meg stood behind the cash register, her face bright red as she pounded on the keys.

"I'm going to go pay for dinner. I'll be right back," Nick announced as he stood.

"I bet you ten dollars she tries to give you her phone number," I hissed.

Nick spun on his heel and turned. Bracing one hand on the table and the other on the back of the booth, he leaned in. "Put your little green-eyed monster away, pet. It's unbecoming and I don't like it. She's a child and I'm *not* a pervert."

"I didn't mean…"

"Hush. Not another word, girl," Nick hissed as he leaned in and crushed his lips against mine, before he turned and walked away.

"I didn't mean to insinuate…"

"He knows that, kitten. Relax. Everything is okay. You're wound tighter than a ten cent watch. What's wrong, baby?" Dylan nuzzled my cheek, his warm breath cascading over the shell of my ear sending a shiver rippling through me.

"Nothing, I'm fine," I replied on a quivering sigh.

"Not at the moment, but you will be soon," Dylan purred in my ear. "We'll get you back to the barn and make you our good girl."

And there went a flood in my panties. I turned my head and without asking permission, took his lips, his mouth, and his tongue.

"Ah-hem," Nick cleared his throat. "You two ready to go or would rather just go at it right here on the table?"

My muffled laugh reverberated in Dylan's mouth as he reached up and pinched my nipple. I sucked his breath into my lungs with a gasp.

"Home," Dylan mumbled beneath my lips.

Nick gripped my hair and pried me from Dylan's mouth.

"Enough, little one, or I'm going to have to join in, right here in front of everyone." He smiled.

"Yes, Master," I replied in a low moan.

"Look at you, Savannah," Dylan whispered in awe. "Your nipples are all beaded up beneath your sweater like gumdrops. I'm going to chew those hard little pearls all night long."

His hand brushed over my throbbing peaks and my spine turned to jelly.

"Can we go home now, please? Please, Masters. I just want to go back to the barn."

CHAPTER NINE

Back at the barn, clothes began flying through the air, silently pooling on the carpet of my room in our frantic rush to get naked. After a salient dance of hands, fingers, lips and tongues, we fell to the bed in a tangled heap of arms and legs. Our giggles, groans and growls filled the air.

Bathed in their heated touch, my appetite flourished. Alternating between their turgid shafts, my mouth stayed busy worshiping every glorious inch until they forced me to stop amid curses of haggard restraint.

Pinning me to the bed, they feasted on my quivering flesh as I soared to the heavens. It was a thrilling roller coaster ride that gained speed as they propelled me to the peak only to glide me back down in a slow, methodical cadence, over and again. Our sweat-soaked bodies slid, melded, then slipped away as we swayed in a symphony of lust.

With the bottoms of my feet flat on the mattress, Dylan wedged his broad shoulders between my thighs and laid siege to my clit with his teeth and tongue. He delved his fingers deep to burnish upon that fiery bundle of nerves. Nick filled my mouth, coasting back and forth as my tongue drifted over his thick ropy veins. Rolling my hips, I met every stroke, nip and tug of Dylan's sinful pleasures.

Nick hissed as he withdrew from my mouth and fisted his wet shaft.

"I'm going to fill your ass all the way to my balls, pet. Bury myself deep inside you and fuck your tight little hole until you can't take any more. Are you ready for that?"

"Yes, Master. God, please! I need to come. I'm on fire," I whimpered.

His growl of approval was like a soft caress as Dylan eased back from between my legs. My cream glistened on his chin, and the look of hunger etched on his face made my demand spike. Dylan snagged a handful of condoms and a tube of lube from the bedside table then crawled over me. As his cock inched closer to my mouth, I raised my head and wrapped him in my lips. A curse of pleasure rumbled from his chest as he thrust impatiently down my throat.

"Enough," Dylan barked as he reared back. "I need to drive deep in your pussy, girl. Now!"

I coy smile tickled my lip at their impetuous yearning as I scooted to the side of the bed, giving him room to lie down. Nick was usually the impatient one, but Dylan seemed to have reached the end of his rope and had no compunction about showing it.

Licking my lips, I climbed back onto the bed, plucked the condom from between Dylan's fingers then tore the foil packet open.

"Allow me, Master." I winked with a cheeky grin.

"You're trying to kill me, aren't you, kitten?"

"I'd never try to kill you, Master, but I might try to put you in a coma," I giggled. Placing the condom on the end of his wet crown, I inched the latex over his wide stalk with my fist, until the barrier was fully seated.

"Fuck me," Dylan hissed.

"As you wish, Sir." With a devilish laugh, I swung one leg over his waist then eased my hungry tunnel over his wide, turgid cock.

Riding him with a slow, sultry roll of my hips, I could hear Nick behind me sheathing his cock. Pressing his broad hand on the small of my back, I melded over Dylan's wide chest. Nick wasted no time glazing my puckered ring with lube then breaching the taut rim with his thick finger. Explosions erupted from the sensitive nerve endings, bursting outward as Dylan's cock remained buried and inert within my fluttering core.

"Please Master, hurry. I need to feel you inside me," I moaned.

A sturdy slap landed across my ass and I jerked, gasping in surprise.

"Patience my sweet slut. You'll be properly prepared before we allow you to sail to the sun and explode. Besides, I'd rather hear your screams of pleasure instead of pain, little one."

"I'm already on fire, Master," I groaned, impatiently rocking upon his embedded fingers.

"Yes you are, kitten," Dylan growled. "Your silken walls feel like liquid lava. Christ, Nick, tell me you're almost there, man."

"I'm getting there," Nick replied between clenched teeth.

"I don't know how much longer I can hang, bro. I'm losing the fight to drive into her slick pussy."

"Patience, fucker. You can hang."

"Easy for you to say, you're not the one boiling inside her heavenly cunt."

"No, but I'll be blistering in her hot little ass very soon. That's ten times worse and you damn well know it," Nick chuckled as his fingers slid free.

I closed my eyes and inhaled a deep breath, trying to quell the anticipation of his broad crest pinching through my tiny rim. I jerked, and threw my head back. A cry of delight peeled from the back of my throat as Nick sunk his teeth into the flesh of my ass.

"Now she's ready," Nick declared in triumph as the cool tip of his crest slid against my tender opening. "Relax and let me in, little one. Let us take you to paradise, baby." He steadily pressed the bulbous head, breaching my rigid rim.

After having my ass claimed numerous times over the past few days, my muscles knew how to respond. The exquisite burn intensified and coalesced with blinding pressure. A low moan vibrated in the back of my throat as Dylan plucked my nipples, rolling them between his fingers and thumbs.

"Your body was made for us, kitten. You're so goddamn perfect," Dylan murmured.

My body sang in sensory overload. My heart brimmed with joy knowing my submission was giving them such pleasure.

Swimming in their savage indulgence, I tossed my head back and snarled as their synchronized shafts surged. Demand grew with each deliberate scrape of my G-spot, and the exploding nerve endings of my ass.

I felt raw. Open. Exposed. In my heart, I knew there was nothing I wouldn't give them; nothing I could deny to bask in their powerful command. They took me with a demand so sublime and pure, I was helpless to do anything except free fall into the pristine depths of ecstasy.

Wild and wanton, I held nothing back. Grinding upon their driving shafts, I was lost to the primal calling of submission. So many places within me had never been touched, yet they effortlessly unlocked every fragment of my mind, body and soul. They'd set me free.

I could never go back to what I'd been before. There was nothing of my former self left. They'd redefined me beneath their masterful hands. Like a Phoenix rising from the ashes, a new woman had been born.

Bold.

Proud.

Secure.

Willing, ready and able to surrender it all to their fervent demands.

The power was indeed *mine*, but it was hollow… inconsequential without their dominant devotion.

Their passion.

Their strength.

Their love.

And I was safe.

Protected.

Treasured.

Savage heat pooled in my womb, expanding through my limbs. Dylan's chest was glazed in our combined sweat. His dusky indigo eyes sparkled in desire, countering the fierce grimace of restraint curled on his lips. The magnitude of his struggle to stave off release was etched on his face.

Slammed by the force of demand, my heavy breaths were laced with keening cries of need and panic. My mounting sounds of desperation echoed in the room, mingling with their grunts and curses of perseverance. The building pressure soared until I was sizzling with the need to come. Imploring their permission, my control was crumbling, being obliterated by the swelling orgasm.

"Nick?" Dylan barked in a gravelly voice.

"Fuck yes," he hissed digging his fingers into my hips, maniacally thrusting his entire length into my ass.

Dylan narrowed his eyes. His fingers brutally squeezed my nipples. "Now, kitten. Shatter for us. Shatter hard!"

His bellicose roar took possession of my soul and I splintered. I exploded with an orgasm so intense, I was powerless against its consuming fury. Taut muscles gripped and released their driving shafts in rippling spasms as screams of rapture tore from my throat. Their feral cries thundered as they purged and filled the latex barriers. Torrents of hot come spurted against my clutching passageways.

The annihilating crescendo unfurled ribbons of pulsating ecstasy, setting my every nerve ending blaze, but I wasn't coming back down. Their driving cocks thrust me to an even higher peak of sublime pleasure.

"Yes!" Nick roared. "Again, you sweet, insatiable slut. Give us more."

Succumbing to an equally devastating orgasm an inhuman cry rent from my throat as spasms wracked my tunnels, milking the last ropes from their shafts.

I collapsed over Dylan's slick chest, possessed by the twitching aftershocks fluttering within. Long minutes passed before our breathing leveled. When Nick finally eased from my ass and climbed from the bed, Dylan wrapped a sturdy arm around my waist and rolled me to my side. With my body still coupled to his rigid shaft, his fingers smoothed away strands of my sweat-soaked hair before leaning in to lavish a kiss so tender and reverent, it brought tears to my eyes.

When Nick returned, Dylan issued a sorrowful moan then slid his cock from my wet tunnel before strolling to the bathroom. Silently, Nick cleansed my quivering pussy and throbbing ass then climbed into bed, pulling me to his chest with a possessive hug. As we locked gazes, neither of us said a word. We didn't have to. I read his expression clearly. Satisfied. Happy. Content. Cognizant of his capacity to sense my matching emotions, a smile tugged one corner of my mouth.

"My sentiments exactly, little one," he whispered with a wolfish smile then bestowed me with an equally gentle kiss.

When Dylan reappeared, we assumed our usual meshing of bodies. Exhaling a soft sigh, I nuzzled Nick's neck like a sated kitten. It wasn't long before their tandem snores were reverberating through my body. Lingering tingles skimmed through my veins. The intense session we'd shared should have rendered me comatose but I couldn't seem to shut off my brain. The events at the diner kept spooling through my thoughts.

Easing from beneath their heavy limbs and being careful not to wake them, I crawled from the bed and tiptoed out of the room. Snagging the blanket off the couch, I wrapped it around me and started a fire before padding to the kitchen, where I prepared a cup of hot chocolate.

Seated before the roaring fire, I absorbed the blessed heat as I sipped the creamy cocoa. My mind whirled like a centrifuge. This fantasy we'd created was beyond anything I'd ever imagined and I wasn't ready for it to end.

They'd awaken in a few hours and take off in their quest to kill Bambi—I shuddered—then return. We'd share another twenty-four hours of the incredible power exchange, then we'd say our good-byes and go our separate ways.

Tears stung my eyes.

"Come on reality, show your ugly self. I need you now," I whispered to that tiny voice in my head. She didn't appear and honestly she wasn't going to shed light on anything I didn't already know. Walking away from those amazing men was going to be the hardest thing I'd ever had to do. They'd stolen my heart; it belonged to them now, and I didn't want to contemplate the severity of the black and painful abyss in which I'd soon be suffocating.

It was my own fault for falling in love with them. They'd never promised me a thing. Quite the contrary, they'd been absolutely honest with me from the start. My hopeless romantic notions would soon be shattered. I'd let the fairy tale take over my heart, even knowing it never stood a chance of a happy ending. That naiveté had gotten the best of me and did little to soothe my growing angst.

The experience at the diner once again rolled through my mind, and with it, the bleak realization that acceptance of a ménage relationship—beyond the four walls of the barn—was nonexistent. The embarrassment and shame I'd been made to feel made me take pause. Could I handle the constant assault of belittling comments and looks of disgust? While I didn't know of anyone living such a lifestyle, I imagined the complications involved could be insurmountable.

So even if they'd wanted to forge a long-distance relationship, I didn't know if I had the fortitude it would take. Was I equipped to help slay their demons? Nick was determined never to lose his heart again. Did I possess the potion to take away his fear to love again? And Dylan…how long would he struggled with the horrors of his past? Could I help him heal and put the pain he carried to rest?

I knew about artifacts and Native burial grounds; I didn't know squat about the workings of damaged human psyches. My head was probably fucked up way worse than either of theirs, anyway. Why else would I be sitting alone in the middle of the night, allowing pointless scenarios to spin through my brain? If I had stuck to my plan and disengaged my heart in the beginning, I wouldn't be eating myself up inside.

I still wasn't clear what individual fulfillment Dylan and Nick gained in sharing me. Maybe they'd been doing it so long, they'd simply grown past asking why. I'd experienced the way they fed off each other and it felt like the most natural thing in the world. Sharing such an incredible connection with Dylan and Nick, I couldn't imagine ever being with *one* man again. But honestly, there weren't any other men I'd want in my life except the two snoring Doms in the other room.

"I wish I had a magic wand…I'd cast a spell over the three of us so we'd never have to say good-bye," I whispered, staring into the fire and wiping a tear from my cheek.

But the time to for magic was long gone. The hard cold truth was depressing, but it couldn't be changed. Instead of mourning what I could never have, I should be counting my blessings that I was the lucky one Dylan and Nick chose. There was a certain comfort, out of the already blossoming pain, that my life was richer and fuller because of them. I just hoped gratitude would sustain me in the empty days to come.

"After tomorrow, it's all over." More tears slid down my cheeks.

I closed my eyes and drew in a quivering breath as I tried to welcome the familiarity of being alone. This was what I'd grown accustomed to...my own quiet space, a place where I could process my thoughts without interference, without having to confess each and every emotion to be analyzed and scrutinized. It was hard enough for me to process my emotions by myself; sharing them was like an all-you-can-eat-buffet for my insecurities.

But, God, I was going miss them.

I wiped my tears, scrubbed a hand through my hair then took a sip of chocolate. The ache in my heart was inescapable. I needed to formulate a plan if I was to come out on the other side of this with any semblance of sanity.

After hours of joyriding my mental merry-go-round, not one second of which was fun, I still hadn't formulated a painless exit strategy. With a heavy sigh, I closed the glass fireplace doors and crept back into bed. Neither man stirred as I snuggled against their rugged bodies.

Moonlight spilled through the window, illuminating Nick's handsome face. I stared at him for hours, drinking in every ridge of his smooth tawny skin. I focused on memorizing the fine lines at the corner of his eyes, the dark thick lashes that caressed his cheek, and the crease lining the arch of his full, broad lips. I could still taste his kiss. It took every ounce of my willpower not to reach up and trace his exotic cheekbone or thread my fingers through his silky hair.

Dylan snorted then turned on his side, wrapping me with a thick arm. I studied him as I'd done a few short days ago. I could picture that heart-stopping dimple that dipped deep when he grinned and the intoxicating color of his magnificent eyes would haunt my dreams forever.

I had one more night to spend like this, just one. It wasn't enough. It would never be enough. Tears slipped down my cheeks as a lump of anguish lodged in my throat. I softly sniffed, trying to hold back my sorrow, but I couldn't stem the flow. The ache in my heart felt insurmountable and despair gripped my heart in a desolate fist.

Suddenly, Nick's sat phone beeped and he bolted upright. I quickly dried my tears, but my soft sniff drew his attention.

"What's wrong, little one?" he whispered. Concern wrinkled his brow as he cupped my face with his warm hand.

God, I couldn't do it. I couldn't tell him I'd fallen in love with them and I was falling apart at the seams. "Oh, it's nothing, Master. Just a bad dream," I lied. "My parents."

"Awww, pet. Do you want to talk about it?"

"No, Sir. I'll be fine. I have them from time to time and they leave me a little rattled." I was awash with guilt for lying to him.

"On the ride home last night from dinner, you seemed a little... distant... preoccupied. Is everything okay?" he pressed.

"Yes, Sir. I'm fine." I nodded with a slight, false smile.

"We're going to head out and do some hunting. Are you going to be okay until we get back?"

"Of course," I whispered, forcing my smile to widen. "I'm going to roll over and go back to bed and hopefully not dream."

"Okay, baby. We'll be back in time for lunch."

"Please, Master...don't kill Bambi," I begged.

Nick laughed and slapped his hand on Dylan's shoulder. "Get up, man. Let's get this done so we can come back and test some more of our sinfully sweet pet's limits."

"What? Huh?" Dylan jerked and sat up but wasn't fully awake. "Oh, yeah. Hey! Good morning gorgeous. What are you doing awake?"

"I had a dream but it's over now." I smiled as my heart dissolved into a million pieces. Dylan rolled over and caged me beneath him then kissed me with a ferocious growl.

"Keep our bed warm, kitten. 'cause we plan on setting you on fire when we get back."

His blue eyes sparkled with promise and I clung to him a moment longer than I should have, but he didn't seem to notice. As he leapt from the bed, Nick turned and pinned me with an interrogating stare.

"You sure you're okay?"

"I'm fine, Sir," I giggled as I wrapped my arms around his neck and drew him down for a passionate kiss. "Go do your cave man thing. You know…hunt and gather. I'll do my job and keep the bed warm for my Masters."

"All right. But not too warm. You don't have permission to come, little one." He grinned as his gaze delved even deeper.

Keep the mask tight, Savannah. No cracks. No fissures. And NO falling apart.

After a long moment, he nodded and rose from the bed. I pretended to lavish in the big empty space, sprawling my arms and legs out, but in reality I was absorbing the vestiges of their warmth; inhaling the remains of their musky, masculine scent as I died inside.

I curled up in bed, summoning my strength to remain invincible as they dressed and readied to leave. As soon as the front door to the barn snicked shut, I buried my face in the pillow and sobbed.

I listened as the pickup roared to life. The crunch of pulverized gravel beneath the tires matched the shards of glass that pierced my heart. And as they drove away, I felt all peace and happiness inside me…vanish with them.

How was I ever going to keep it together for the next twenty-four hours? I'd barely been able to maintain the short time it took them to dress and leave. Those torturous minutes were but a precursor of what was to come. When they returned, there was no way I could mask my fears and pain of never seeing them again.

My pitiful wails filled the air as I succumbed to the debilitating agony that flooded my soul. It wasn't supposed to be like this. My heart wasn't supposed to be ripped from my chest. Not like this. I couldn't take it. The magnitude of walking away slammed me with crushing emptiness.

Clutching their pillows to my face, I sobbed and breathed in their rugged scent.

Bold and sensuous.

Masculine and virile.

Pungent and perfect.

Commanding yet so tender.

Oh God! Why did it have to be so fucking painful? I jerked off the bed and paced the room as tears streamed down my face. Clutching my stomach, attempting to hold myself together, panic and pain consumed me.

"I wasn't supposed to fall in love with you, two. Goddammit!" I screamed with a sorrowful sob. "I can't do this. I can't!"

I flopped to the bed once more, surrounded in their scent as memories flashed through my mind like strobes of blissful torture. Sobs burned my throat. Despair descended like a black cloak, sucking the light from my soul. I remained there long after all the tears had fallen. After all my mourning, I was finally empty and numb.

Eventually I made my way to the bathroom and splashed cold water on my face. I raised my head and stared at my haunted reflection. Swollen eyes, rimmed red, matched my nose. An errant tear slid down my cheek.

"You've got to get a grip. This isn't the end of the world," I scolded aloud to myself.

It sure as hell felt like it, but I needed to get a handle on my chaotic emotions. The fear of falling apart at the seams in front of them continued to hold me in a ruthless grip.

"I can't pull it off. I know I can't," I whined as I dried my face with a towel. Nick's scent clung to the fabric and another wave of tears slammed me. Sinking to the floor, my back against the tub, I cried some more.

There were only two options I could conceive. I could stay and allow them to see how stupid I'd been for falling in love with them, which would mire them in guilt for not seeing the signs. They would probably think me a player for not confessing my true feelings, but it wouldn't change a damn thing. I'd still be oozing feelings of abandonment. They couldn't fix it with an order or a bandage, the wound was too deep. Open. Raw. Bleeding.

Or…I could pack up and leave before they returned. Go back home like a gutless coward and never reveal how I felt. No strings. No commitments. Hell, those *were* the rules. I'd been a fool for not following them in the first place. If I left, they'd never see how badly I'd fucked up.

Palming my tears, I stood and looked around the room. My toiletries still aligned the alcove, just as they'd been that first night. These men had taken care of me with such devotion, not just the first night, but every hour of every minute we'd been together.

Stop it. You're never going to do the right thing if you keep re-living every goddamn second you spent with them. You fucked up. It's time to go before you make an ever bigger fool of yourself.

Finally, the voice of reason decided to come through loud and clear.

I had no other viable options. I had to leave now and lick my wounds back home, or go down in a ball of fiery embarrassment in front of them. I wasn't about to let the latter happen.

After gathering my toiletries, I marched back to the bedroom. Tossing my suitcases onto the bed, I tried to keep my eyes from wandering over their pillows. I refused to look at the empty mattress where they'd aspired me into the center of their universe. My mournful cry filled the air as I tugged on my clothes. I cleaned out the closet and drawers, stuffing my suitcases in minutes flat. Hastily digging out the rental key, I carried my belongings to the common area.

The couch still sat before the fireplace. So many nights we'd spent curled up by the fire, talking, touching, kissing…fucking.

"Enough!" I screamed, squelching the onslaught of memories.

I rounded the island, pulled a magnet-backed note pad from the refrigerator then rummaged through the utility drawer until I found a pen. Seated at the table, I gripped the pen so tight that my fingers turned white as I pondered what to write.

Tears filled my eyes once again. I blinked them away as I clenched my teeth. The time to fall apart had come and gone. It was time to grow the fuck up. I wasn't some pubescent teen in the throes of a stupid sophomoric crush. I was a grown woman–acting like a child. "Stop it. Just fucking stop it!" I hissed.

Scrawling out the first thing that came to mind, I ripped the page from the tablet then carried it back to the bedroom and propped it atop my pillow. Forcing myself not to look back, I gathered my luggage and made my way down the long narrow hallway.

The rented Hummer sat alone in the gravel lot. It was a stark and haunting reflection of what was left inside me.

"You're taking away exactly what you wanted, Savannah," I whispered to myself in a terse tone. "Memories. That's all you have. That's all you get."

I pressed the fob to unlock the vehicle and heaved my luggage into the back seat. I sucked in a deep breath as I made my way to Kit's front door and rang the bell.

She opened the door, a bright smile on her lips. I mimicked her joy with an erroneous smile of my own.

"Hey, Savannah. Come on in. I'll make us some coffee." She beamed. "Kinda quiet down there with the guys out hunting? I saw them loading up early this morning."

"Actually, it's nice. I miss my alone time." I lied. "I just wanted to pop up and say…see you next year. I'm going to go on home. There's some painting I want to get done in the spare bedroom and I need to check my messages in case something's come up for work. Time to get back into the grind."

The lies rolled off my tongue with ease, but it was becoming increasingly more difficult to keep the tight smile on my face and reign in my tears. When Kit's brows furrowed, I thought the jig was up and my heart pounded in my chest.

"Okay, sugar. You drive safe going home. No more deer. Do you hear me?" She warned.

I laughed, but it sounded hollow and fake. I wrapped her in a gentle hug and promised her I'd be careful.

Once on the road, I didn't stop shaking until I'd hit the four-lane. The sun warmed my skin but my bones were icy cold. I turned on the radio and found a rap station. Cranking up the volume, I was determined not to be sucked in to sappy love songs that would only make me cry.

I tried not to wonder what Dylan and Nick's reactions would be once they returned and discovered I was gone. Would they be relieved that their teaching days were over? I hoped they would welcome a day to relax and do what they wanted instead of what they felt obligated to.

The music blared with the heavy, chest-thumping beat. My head throbbed, a welcome distraction from the ache in my heart.

When I hit the Missouri/Iowa line, I stopped for gas and a cold drink. As I rummaged through my purse for my wallet, my cell phone rang. I clutched the phone, staring at the caller ID. It was Kit. Indecision filled me. Surely they hadn't come back from hunting so soon. I'd only been on the road a couple of hours. My finger hovered over the "answer" display but I chickened out and sent the call to voice mail.

As I climbed back into the Hummer, it rang again. Guilt and dread filled me as I looked at the number on the glass panel. It was one I didn't recognize. After sending it to voice mail, I turned off my phone, started the SUV and pulled back onto the highway.

My hands trembled and anxiety bloomed. Was the unknown number Nick's phone? Were they mad? Were they hurt? Were they relieved? Maybe it hadn't even been them. Maybe it was a wrong number. Maybe they didn't even know I was gone. If I continued to roll every fucking question over and over, I'd go insane before I reached Kansas City.

If I'd had some experience with good-byes, I would have some tools to fall back on, some solid ground for a foothold. But no, I had to be a shy, awkward wallflower my whole life. I had to be the girl that had climbed inside herself after the death of her parents, afraid to love someone for fear they'd disappear on her again and leave her shattered and broken with no way to put herself back together.

It was enough of a risk to love Mellie as much as I did. She traveled endlessly. Every trip she took was a game of Russian roulette. But I'd prepared myself mentally; one day she might not make it home. We'd even made a pact. Each time she had to leave, she would call and tell me how much she loved me. We made sure we carried each other in our hearts, no matter where we went. Of course, there was Myron and Helen—but they'd also die someday and leave me to grieve another parental-type loss. I'd anticipated that day, as well.

"But I wasn't ready for this. I'd given my heart to two men who didn't want it. No. Somehow, I knew they wanted it; they just couldn't accept it. I didn't know how to gather up the shattered pieces and go on. I'd never learned how. Tears slid down my cheeks and the road blurred. I brushed them away and tried to clear my mind but it was a wasted effort.

By the time I pulled into my apartment complex, I was emotionally and physically exhausted. My feet felt like bricks as I unloaded the Hummer. Dropping the luggage on my bedroom floor, I crawled into my bed and cried.

I'd never get to feel their Dominance again. To experience that peace, knowing I'd brought them pleasure. Never float away beneath their masterful touch. Never feel safe within their care. I brought forth their images, in my mind and allowed the unmitigated pain to consume me. I longed to hear their voices one last time but knew it only prolong my heartache. I didn't try to stave off the pain. Instead, I welcomed it, let it consume me so I could purge it from my system. I'd lived my ultimate dream for a few glorious days. But oh how I longed to go back and relive it one more time. To breathe in their virile scent, feel the comfort of their strong bodies next to mine, hear the praise from their decadent voices, and revel in their dominant commands.

"Why does it fucking hurt this much?" I wailed. Tears soaked my pillow. And as I tried to purge them from my heart, a dark fear settled deep in my soul. Fear that I would never be whole again.

Eventually, I dried my eyes and climbed out of bed. In a listless haze, I wandered to the kitchen and made a cup of tea. My movements were mechanical, robotic, and lethargic. I ran on autopilot and felt so dead inside, I wondered if I could get a starring roll in the next zombie apocalypse film.

Looking around the room, I couldn't help but feel there was nothing there for me. Nothing but a way of life I no longer wanted to go back to. My quiet oasis felt like a giant, cavern. The silence that I reveled in before was now a choking weight making it hard to breathe. Seated at the kitchen table, everything pressed against me until I wanted to scream. Gone were the rugged warm bodies that had held me tight. Gone was the thrill of bending to their command and granting them pleasure. Gone were the reassuring touches and the two words that sent my heart sailing…*Good, girl.*

The ring of my land-line phone nearly jolted me out of my chair. I glanced at the message light, pulsating in a slow red heartbeat. My own heart thrummed in double time as I sat at the table and stared at the cordless device. It rang and rang until my answering feature engaged. I held my breath.

"Sanna? Honey are you there? Please baby, pick up if you're home. You're not answering your cell and I'm going fucking bat shit here. Where are you? Come on baby, please pick up!" Mellie's anxious pleas echoed through the room.

Rising to my feet with such force that my chair toppled back and landed with a thunderous crash, I snatched up the receiver.

"Mellie, I'm here. I'm okay. I'm sorry, baby. I'm so sorry." My words tumbled together in a frantic apology as my voice cracked.

"Thank Christ! Goddammit Sanna. You scared the living shit out of me."

"I know, I know. I'm sorry. I wasn't thinking."

"What the fuck is going on? I got a call from your Mr. Dreamy voice, Nick. Sanna, he's pissed to the gills! What the fuck happened between you two?"

"Oh, Mellie. I fucked up. I fucked up big time." Tears rolled down my face as I righted the chair and sunk back down on it.

Through sobs, I explained the whole mess...the Dom/sub stuff...everything. I expected her to be shocked but she wasn't. She understood, which made me cry even harder. Her unconditional love was a balm over my raw and jagged edges.

"Baby, part of submission is being honest. If you don't think they'd understand what you're feeling then they weren't the caliber of Doms you need."

"How do you know that?"

"Let's just say we're cut from the same cloth," she giggled. "You don't think I'm this bossy and hardheaded *all* of the time, do you?"

"Holy shit, Mel. Why didn't you tell me? Like, years ago?"

"Sanna! I know your sexual history," she answered. "I didn't tell you because I was afraid I'd freak the fuck out of you and you'd run for the hills, thinking your sister was some kind of kinky freak."

"Yeah, well if I was in better shape, I wouldn't have told you, either," I sniffed.

"Okay, well we're both out of the closet now. We'll discuss that topic later. What are you going to do about Dylan and Nick? I gotta tell you, sugar, they are *not* happy campers."

"There's nothing I *can* do! I'm not going to call and say, *Oh I'm sorry I didn't ask your permission before I ran away but I couldn't hang.* Jezzzus, Mellie. There's nothing left to say. It was a few days of Dom/sub fun, some amazing, mind-blowing sex but...that's it. We're not going steady. I'm never even going to see them again, so what's the point? All it'll do is make me look like a giant dipshit. I'd rather run away than let them see what I've done to myself."

"Okay, so maybe it's more than you're comfortable confessing to them. They still have the right to know. And you can't just up and walk out on them like that, without a word."

"I had to, Mel. I couldn't stay and fall apart in front of them. It would have been too fucking embarrassing."

"So, you didn't do anything embarrassing with them, say…sexually? Hrmmm?"

I could feel the smile in her words. Logic. She was going to try and trip me up with logic. Damn, that's what Dylan and Nick did. My own sister shouldn't try to pull the same shit.

"Don't go there. This is totally different." I warned.

"Well, *I* have to call him back. So, what do you want me to tell him?"

"*Why* do you have to call him back?" I gasped.

"Because I told him I would, once I found you. Honey, they're honestly worried about you."

"Shit!" I hissed. "Tell them I'm home safe and sound and…hell, I don't know. Tell them I said thanks."

"Thanks?" she choked. "That's it?"

"Yes," I said with a note of finality. "That's it."

Mellie issued a heavy sigh, mumbling that she'd pass the message along.

"Do you want me to fly up there and stay with you for a few days, baby? You sound like you could use some company and a soft shoulder."

"No. I'm fine. Really. This shit will pass. I'll just go back to"

What would I go back to? The life I left behind a week ago was like a wool sweater fresh out of the dryer. Tight and itchy.

"Back to what?" Mellie pressed.

"Back to research."

"But Myron closed the office," she reminded with a hint of doubt.

"I'm working on an article I'm trying to get published. I've got tons to keep me busy. Please, Mellie. I'm fine."

"All right," she sighed in exasperation. "But you'd better call me if you need me, understand?"

"You know I will. I love you sis. Love you so much."

"I love you too, baby. Pour yourself a glass of wine and go relax in a bubble bath. You sound like you need it."

"I will. Talk to you soon."

As I hung up the phone I cringed. Dylan and Nick were mad. That wasn't the reaction I expected. And what exactly did that mean?

"It means nothing other than you usurped their authority as Doms. Don't read anything into it," I groused aloud. Placing my fingers to my forehead, I tried to rub away a pounding headache. I dug my cell phone out of my purse and turned it on. There were at least fifty missed calls from the unknown number. "Nick," I whispered in wistful reverence before I cursed and tossed it back in my purse.

Aimlessly wandering through my apartment, I stopped in the bathroom to take some aspirin but realized I'd not eaten breakfast or lunch. My guts were already eating themselves with anxiety. It would be like adding fuel to the fire if I popped the pain relievers on an empty stomach. With my fridge threadbare and a frozen dinner sounding as appealing as a worn leather shoe, I slung my purse over my shoulder and headed to the store.

Strolling through the aisles, I realized I should have stayed home and fixed the frozen meal; nothing looked the least bit appetizing. I grabbed a package of chicken breast and some vegetables for a salad then swung by the bakery. When in the throes of depression—eat cake! Even that looked disgusting.

You've got it bad if you turn your nose up at cake.

I was about to swing down the ice cream aisle when my cell phone began to ring. Fear gripped my heart as I palmed the device. *Mellie*. Relief washed over me.

"Hello?"

"Hey baby, I'm just checking on you. Are you feeling any better?"

"Mel, stop being a mother hen. I'm fine. Stop worrying. What did Nick say when you called him back?"

"He didn't answer, so I just left him a message telling him you were back home and were fine. I don't mean to pester you, but I know you're hurting. Don't hate me."

"Aww, honey, you know I could never hate you. I love you for being worried, but honestly, I'm fine. I'm at the store...getting cake." I lied.

"Ahhh, the magical powers of flour, eggs, sugar and whatever else they put in that crap."

"Julia Child would be so proud," I teased, hoping a little banter would ease her worries about me.

"You know I can't boil water. Thank God for prepackaged foods."

"Or you'd starve, yes. I know," I chuckled.

"You sure you're okay?"

"Seriously, Mel, I'm fine. Of course, I'm not where I want to be..." I wanted to be back in the barn, wedged between my two Mas--no, they weren't my Masters. I swallowed tightly. "But like mom always used to say, 'this shit, too, shall pass.'"

"It will, baby. And you'll be a whole lot more happy when you find a club in town and get out amongst some other kinky people."

"How do you know there are clubs here?" I asked suspiciously.

"Where do you think I learned about the lifestyle?" She laughed.

"Oh. Well maybe you can tell me where I should go...later. I'm not ready yet."

"I can and will, whenever you're ready. You just let me know."

We said our good-byes before I checked out my groceries and drove back home.

As I slid my key into the lock of my apartment door, I noticed it didn't stick like usual. When I pushed the door open, an ominous presence filled me. Reaching inside my purse, I fisted my Mace can. Flipping it to the unlocked position, I let my groceries and purse slide to the welcome mat. The interior was so dark, I couldn't see into the shadows. Why had I pulled the curtains shut? *Because of your headache, dumbass.*

I opened the door as wide as possible, hoping to shed more light inside, but still failed to reach the murky corners. The hairs on the back of my neck stood on end.

CHAPTER TEN

With a tentative step forward, I breached the portal. The canister of Mace lay hidden in my fist. Even as I tried to convince myself the sinister, prickly feeling was from lack of sleep and my abnormal emotional state, I knew something was wrong.

Only once had I feared for my safety, but never in my own home. I'd been working in an old courthouse, in a bad part of town. It was late at night. Had it not been for the squeaky wooden floors, I never would have been alerted to the drunk coming up behind me. He'd somehow wandered in off the street and decided he was going to have sex with me…in a misguided, alcohol-induced way. Forcing me to the floor by my hair, he reeked in a vile combination of booze, feces and vomit. I knew he was going to try and rape me on the spot. I fought like hell, but not only did the vagrant outweigh me, he was strong as an ox, even for being toasted out of his gourd. My screams alerted the ancient night watchman, who came to my rescue and began beating the delusional drunk with his trusty flashlight. It was the encounter that convinced me to take up karate.

You know what to do. Focus and listen.

Even my inner voice was on high alert. I knew to trust my feelings and they were blaring out a warning. Someone was in my apartment. It was too dark for me to tell where the burglar was hiding. If the thief was thinking about absconding with my jewelry box, he wasn't going to make it past me. The only memento I had left of my mother was her wedding necklace. I'd never let him get past me.

Behind me, a car horn honked. I glanced without thinking . When I swiveled my head back to the apartment's doorway, I narrowed my eyes, trying to peer through the inky darkness. Suddenly, a blurred figure rushed from the shadows. Strong hands gripped my arms and before I knew what was happening, I was shoved against the coat closet door. Now swallowed into the dark abyss, I was unable to see my attackers face.

Crying out in alarm, I bent my wrist and aimed the mace. I squeezed my eyes and pressed the button. The robber began to scream. He released my arms then covered his face with his hands. Feral curses blended with his cries of agony. As I stepped away from the wall, I watched him bend at the waist. Spinning in circles, the asshat tried to escape the fiery burn.

"Get on the ground, mother fucker, or I'll blow your balls off." I prayed he was too incapacitated to realize I wasn't holding a gun, but simply bluffing. "Do you hear me, asswipe? I said get your ass on--"

A second pair of beefy arms wrapped me from behind and squeezed tightly. I was pinned and helpless against a wide chest. Son of a bitch! They were working as a pair. It pissed me off. I didn't hazard to think there might be two burglars.

"Stop!" The prick that had me immobilized growled on the back of my neck.

Thinking fast, I let my body grow lax in his arms. I waited and prayed he'd loosen his hold—as I'd been trained. And the dumbshit did it. I clenched my teeth and sucked in a breath.

"I don't think so, fuck face," I spat as I wrenched from his arms. Balancing my weight on one leg, I spun in the air, and with a round-house kick, I clipped the big bastard on the side of his head. With a howling yell, he fell to the ground like a mighty oak.

Unwilling to stay and see if any more goons were waiting in the wings, I turned and began to sprint toward the door.

"Savannah! Wait!" Came a roar from the man still fisting his burning eyes.

My heart clutched. I froze like a statue. I knew that voice.

Dylan.

"Oh God. Oh Shit. No. No." I spun around and raced to him. I bent and found his face crumpled in pain. "What the fuck are you doing here? Is that…Oh, God. Nick!" I cried as I rushed to the body still sprawled out on my living room floor.

"I'm going to get the goddamn soap and I'm going to make you eat the whole fucking bar, girl." Nick growled as he slowly sat up, rubbing the side of his face.

"Ohmigod! Ohmigod! I'm so sorry," I moaned. "Why did you grab me? How did you get in here? Why are you two here?" I screeched.

"Help!" Dylan cried out. "I can't see a fucking thing. Christ this shit burns!"

Rushing back to Dylan's side, I gripped his elbow and led him into the kitchen. Flipping on the light, I began helping him flush his eyes with cool water.

"Just keep rinsing, I'll be right back," I instructed then raced out of the kitchen to check on Nick.

He was sitting on my couch, holding his cheek and glaring at me as if I'd grown an extra head.

"Where did you learn to fight like that, little one?"

A weak smile wobbled over my lips. "Karate class," I confessed as I snagged my purse and bag of groceries off the welcome mat before I shut the door. I pulled back the curtains, flooding the room with light.

Nick looked like hell. I looked at the worried lines around his eyes as I nervously nibbled my bottom lip. "I thought you were burglars or rapists. I didn't know it was…why are you here?"

"Go check on Dylan. Do you have some ice?"

"Yes, come on." I replied as I rushed to his side and helped him stand.

"I can walk, girl. I don't know if I'll be able to eat for a month, but I can walk."

"Oh, Nick, I'm so sorry. If I'd known it was you…"

"It's Master or Sir, goddammit. You've obviously forgotten how to address us and how to say good-fucking-bye," Nick thundered.

"But…I…thought," I stammered, peeking up at him beneath my lashes. He wore that glorious, disapproving dominant scowl. "Yes, Sir."

Butterflies set sail in my stomach. I wrapped my slender arm around his waist and led him into the kitchen before helping him sit at the table.

"How are you doing, Sir?" I asked rushing back to the sink, smoothing a palm over Dylan's broad back.

"Better. Fuck, this shit is wicked."

"I'm so sorry, Dylan, Sir. I didn't know it was…"

"It's okay, kitten. I'm just proud as hell that you can take care of yourself."

"Easy for you to say," Nick grumbled. "She didn't break your jaw."

"Oh God! I broke your jaw?" I gasped in terror.

"No, but it sure fucking feels like it," he groused.

I dug through the freezer and found a squishy gel ice pack. Wrapping it in a towel, I tenderly pried Nick's fingers away then placed the cold pack against his face.

"I can't apologize enough, Sirs. If I'd known it was you two, I never would have reacted that way. I thought you were here to rob or hurt me."

"So you didn't just kick our asses for fun?" he chortled.

"Never, Sir. Why are you two here?" I asked as my head swiveled between the two like a metronome.

"Why are *you* here and not back at the barn, little one?" Nick challenged, his brows slashed in an angry scowl.

Averting his gaze, I placed a clean kitchen towel in Dylan's hands.

"Let me tell you how surprised--no, surprised is too tame. Let me tell you how *blindsided* we were when we came back early to discover not only that you were gone, but left nothing but a fucking note behind," Nick hissed. The veins in his neck bulged and his face turned a deep crimson.

I'd never heard Nick sound so infuriated, not even that day when I woke and heard him talking to George about his skanky ex-wife. "Christ. The Christmas cards from my accountant contain more heartfelt sentiments than the kiss-off note you left us."

Guilt and fear exploded through my veins as I watched Nick pluck the note from the pocket of his jeans. With a scowl, he begin to read.

"Dear Sirs, thank you so much for a memorable week. I will fondly treasure our time together. Sincerely yours, Savannah." Nick tossed the paper onto the table as if it were on fire. "If you were *sincerely* ours, girl, your ass would have been in bed when we got back, like you'd promised. But *sincerely* you weren't. Is this tripe you wrote how you really feel about us? Or is it another smoke screen to hide what you truly feel?"

I had no idea how to answer his question, except to tell the truth, and I wasn't ready to do that. Luckily, Nick didn't give me a chance to respond before resuming his tirade.

"That's what you were doing this morning before we left, isn't it, pet? Blowing smoke up our asses and feeding us some bullshit story about a goddamn dream? I gotta tell you, Savannah, you had me fooled. I honestly believed you. You looked right into my eyes and lied straight to my face."

Nick stood. Fury rolled off him in a potent wave. I inched back until my butt bumped up against the countertop.

"I'm sorry," I whispered. I felt myself shrinking inside.

"No, girl. I want an answer. Not a goddamn apology!" Nick slammed his fist onto the table. "Is this--this glacial shit you wrote the only thing you feel for us?" His lips curled in an angry snarl as his eyes bore into mine.

Tears welled and spilled down my cheeks. I couldn't speak because I couldn't swallow the lump of pain, and anguish lodged in, my throat. I shook my head in a silent 'No.'

"Finally, we're getting somewhere," Nick crossed his arms over his wide chest. His dangerous were all but peeling my flesh to the bone.

Dylan turned off the water and dried his face with the towel. He wrapped his hand around my elbow and led me to the table.

"Sit down, kitten."

Oh great. It was time for tag-team inquisition. I sat down, steeling myself for the onslaught of humiliation to squash me like an unwelcome cockroach.

"Do you know why we cut our hunting trip so short, kitten?" Dylan asked. His beautiful blue eyes were bloodshot and rimmed red.

I glanced back at Nick with the ice pack to his swollen cheek. A sob eked from my lips. I'd done that to them. I'd inflicted pain on the two men who meant the world to me.

"No, Sir." I blubbered.

"You have no idea why we rushed back to the barn?" Nick asked in disbelief.

"No, Sir," I wailed.

"Come on Dylan, let's go," Nick announced in a defeated tone.

I sat there stunned. Nick and Dylan turned and began to walk toward the door.

"Wait!" I screamed as I bolted from my chair. "Don't go!"

They stopped and turned. Their blistering dominance infused me in a hot wave as they stared at me. Their veiled eyes were dull and lifeless.

"You're going to leave because I don't know the answer to your question?" I sobbed. "What do you want from me?"

"Obviously something you're no longer willing to give." Nick's tone was arctic.

"What? Are you talking about my submission?" I rounded the table.

"Stop," Dylan barked.

I froze. My heart pounded in a combination of panic and confusion. Nick's eyes narrowed in penetrating appraisal. Crossing his arms over his broad chest, his lips thinned to a tight angry line.

"Strip," Nick suddenly commanded.

"What?" I gasped.

"Oh, little one. Do. Not. Make. Me. Repeat. It. You think for one fucking second the rules have changed just because we're on your turf?"

"No, Sir," I whispered, shaking my head wildly.

In perfect synchronization, they squared their shoulders, clasped their hands behind their backs and gazed at me with impatient expressions. Power blasted of them in a formidable wave. They wore their command like sleek, expensive suits and I melted like spun sugar.

I'd been a fool to think I could survive without this...without *them* in my life. Why had they come all this way? Were they seeking some type of kinky closure? And what if they turned and walked out the door...*now*?

I would lose my mind.

The sun beamed through the wide window, casting a halo around their formidable bodies. They looked like angels but their expressions were born of the devil. Angry jaws ticked in irritation. Their bodies were stiff and unyielding as they waited for me to satisfy their demand.

My fingers trembled as I began to unbutton my blouse. Movement at the window drew my attention. My heart slammed against my ribs as my neighbor passed by. I was thankful he wasn't paying attention to me disrobing in my living room. But what if another neighbor passed by, one not as focused, who might glance through the large picture window? I would die a thousand deaths if they spied me stripping. Surely the guys didn't expect me to take off my clothes with the curtains wide open... did they?

"Can I please close the drapes, Sirs?" I asked in a timid voice.

"No," Dylan replied in a cold tone. "It's now or never, kitten. Make up your mind and do it quick."

Dylan's unusual demeanor frightened me. My assumptions of them being relieved had been way off target. All this time, I thought absolving them from the burden of training me would make them happy. But I could see—up close and personal—there wasn't a happy bone in their bodies.

As I began to unbutton my shirt once more, my entire body trembled. Anxiety of a neighbor catching glimpse of my naked body was almost debilitating but I pressed forward, determined to make them proud.

As my clothing fell away, the barriers I'd been reassembling since I'd left the barn began to crumble beneath my feet. That strange, calm serenity began to fill me. I felt as if I'd been brought back to life beneath their command, once again.

When I stepped out of my jeans, I inhaled a deep breath. Casting my eyes toward the floor, I settled to my knees near the kitchen table. An audible sigh wafted from Dylan's direction. I longed to raise my eyes and gauge their expressions, aching to see if I had pleased them, but I remained fixed in my proper position as a formidable silence dragged on and on. Sweat broke out over my upper lip and a tremor skittered through my body.

Please don't leave. Please don't leave. Please don't leave.

I sensed movement, but it was ebbing backward. Fear gripped my heart in a tight fist. Tears filled my eyes as silent sobs shook my body. Whatever they'd come for, whatever test they'd just doled out, I had obviously failed.

The sound of air escaping the cushions of my leather couch lit a flame of with hope within. They hadn't left. They had only sat down. Still, I couldn't shake the feeling that I wasn't out of the woods yet. Warring between keeping my gaze on the floor or risk a peek at their glorious faces, submission won over desire. Pissed or not, they completed me in ways I couldn't fathom.

Emotions whirred, but breaking through the chaos like a beacon of light, there was hope. Luminous hope of possibly spending one more poignant day blanketed in their Dominance. Self-preservation flew out the window. Caution, common sense and logic were hot on its heels. All the heartbreak in the universe would be worth *just one more day* of feeling whole again. Tears streamed down my face.

"Raise your head, little one," Nick demanded in a low, controlled tone.

I inhaled a deep breath then slowly lifted my chin to find both of them seated on the couch, legs spread, elbows on their knees, with matching hunger in their eyes. I swallowed tightly and waited the interminable seconds before Nick finally broke the silence.

"Crawl to us, girl."

His order replayed in my mind—twice. They expected me crawl on the floor, like a damn dog. My knee-jerk reaction was to tell him to go to hell. I wasn't about to crawl to him or anyone. I may have tossed caution to the wind for the chance of one more day, but I wasn't about to throw away my pride. Thankfully, it dawned on me that this was a test, a big one, before I opened my mouth to tell Nick where he could shove his demand.

I drove my swell of humiliation down deep then positioned myself on all fours. The first slide of my knee was the hardest and I choked back a sob of shame as I forced my body to advance. With each glide of my knees, I shoved past my pride and groped for the threads of my tattered submission.

"Head up. Eyes on us, kitten," Dylan commanded, his voice still lacking his usual warmth.

When I raised my head, the unveiled window flashed like a neon of dread. I faltered for a moment then clenched my teeth, determined to see the lesson through.

"Move your ass, pet. You're trying what little patience we have left," Nick growled.

If this isn't a test, you can throw them out. My inner voice railed it in defense of my ego. I issued a small nod, not at Nick's caustic tone, but to my own subconscious as it dealt with their derisive edict.

I gazed into their approving stares. A strange myriad of emotions thrummed within. Anger. Debasement. Servitude. Embarrassment. Arousal. Fear. Contentment. None of it made a lick of sense as I continued to crawl toward them like an animal. As I neared their splayed-out legs, Nick leaned forward, threading his massive fingers into my hair, stinging my scalp. A cry fluttered in the back of my throat as I stared up at him.

"Good girl. You may kneel up now." Those two words made my heart soar even though Nick's voice was cold and detached, void of his usual whiskey smooth timbre.

Releasing my hair, he turned to Dylan. "Can you close the curtains? We'll need her total attention for this discussion."

"Yes, we will," Dylan agreed with a solemn nod before he stood and jerked the drapes shut.

Relieved that no one could gawk at my naked body did little to soothe my pricked nerves. Nick turned on the lamp next to the couch, bathing the room in a soft glow. As Dylan sat back down, he reached out and cupped my chin. With the broad pad of his thumbs, he wiped the tears from my cheeks and issued a heavy sigh. His jaw ticked as he released my face.

"Trust is very fragile. Once broken, it's hard to mend. Don't you agree?" Nick asked in a deep authoritative tone.

"Yes, Sir. I'm sorry." I offered in earnest.

"Don't give me another fucking apology, girl. Give me the goddamn truth. For once, just give me the truth." His eyes narrowed.

"I'll give all the truth I have, Sir."

"Let's hope you do, girl. Let's hope you *finally* do." He speared me with a look of disapproval so intense, I felt it to my bones. "Why did you run away from us this morning?"

My heart picked up as my palms grew moist. "I didn't want you to know that I'd made a mistake."

"A mistake?" Dylan asked in a seething tone. "You think the time we shared was a fucking mistake?"

"No, Sir," I amended quickly. "I meant that *I'd* made a mistake."

"Go on," Nick prompted.

"I did a stupid and foolish thing." I swallowed tightly. I hated being forced to spill my guts. "With my heart, Sirs."

My gaze darted between them. I grew more confused as their expressions softened and slow smiles spread over their lips.

"What happened to your heart, little one?" Nick asked softly.

"I lost it, Sir. To both of you," I confessed, then waited for them to burst into hysterical laughter and chastise me for being so damn pathetic.

"So you fell in love with us, is that what you're saying?" Dylan pressed.

My heart resonated like a bass drum in my ears. I nodded and lowered my head, swamped with embarrassment.

Nick's palm cradled my chin, forcing my gaze to his. Searching my eyes, he issued a heavy, sigh. "Did you ever happen to think that maybe we'd fallen in love with you too, little one?"

My eyes flashed wide as I tried to tamp down the gust of hope exploding inside. "No, Sir."

"You've changed us in ways we never imagined. We came back early from hunting to talk to you, kitten." Dylan began to explain. "But then we discovered you were gone."

"We have to know what's in your heart, pet. The note you left... if that's truly all you feel then we've wasted our time coming here. Are we more to you than a fond memory?" Nick's words sounded tortured. The fear in his eyes ripped my heart to shreds.

"Yes," I sobbed. "I love you both so much. And don't think...I was afraid..."

"Shhh, it's going to be all right, kitten. I promise."

Dylan's soothing words only prompted to escalate my tears. He reached down and plucked me from the floor. Settling me on his lap, he wrapped his strong, thick arms around me. I buried my face in his warm chest, breathing in the manly scent and potent spice I thought was gone forever, and cried like a child.

"We were so afraid that we'd lost you, Savannah," Nick confessed as he threaded his broad fingers through my hair. "We haven't figured how, but we want you in our lives. We want you to come back to Chicago with us. We'll figure out the rest later. Do you want to be with us, little one?"

"Yes," I cried as hope eradicated all my despair, heartache and anxiety.

Nick gripped my hair, prying my face from Dylan's chest. He leaned over and crushed his lips to mine in a desperate, feral kiss. As he swallowed my sobs, drowning me in his passion, Dylan gripped my nape in an exacting hold.

"We love you, kitten. We were afraid to say the words before now, but you've brought us back to life in ways we never imagined."

Dylan wrapped his hand over Nick's, cinching my hair with a double decree of ownership.

Nick reluctantly released my lips before Dylan swooped in, claiming my mouth with a kiss so passionate, the room spun.

My thoughts swam and I could only process chunks of what they were saying. It took long minutes before I wrapped my head around the fact that they loved me. They wanted me. Not just for a week, but maybe forever. And Chicago! They wanted to take me home with them because they'd fallen in love with me.

Me!

They held me as I spilled a deluge of tears, whispering reassurance and promises I knew they would keep. Pressed between their powerful bodies, I began to settle down. Only then did I feel twin erections against my bare flesh.

Demand thundered through my veins.

"Please, Masters, I need to feel you inside me," I begged, wiping my eyes and casting them a hungry gaze.

"Oh, kitten," Dylan growled, low and deep. "We'd love nothing better than to squeeze into your sinful pussy and ass, but there's a matter of punishment we need to see to first."

"Punishment?"

"Yes, little one. You didn't think we were going to let you skate by for leaving without a word, did you?"

"I…"

"Not to mention calling us such vulgar names. I believe you addressed us mother fucker and fuck face. We can't ignore that and you know it." A stern look played over Nick's face.

"But I didn't know it was you or Dylan, Master."

"No, I'm sure you didn't. But that doesn't dismiss your insults, little one."

"We need to work out some other things as well, kitten." Dylan's serious expression worried me more than my pending punishment.

"What things?" I asked in a timid tone.

"About you going with us to Chicago. Is there anything keeping you here until your boss opens the offices again in February?"

"How did you know about that? Did Mellie tell you that?"

"Sat phone. The morning you talked to her, we heard every word. Remember?" Dylan smiled.

"Ahhh, I'd forgotten about that."

"We want you to stay with us, little one, so we can continue your training and see where this road might lead. If you can't, then we'll figure out a way to rearrange our schedules and try to come see you every other weekend."

Every other weekend.

Nick's words knocked the wind out of my sails. I suddenly felt cheapened. Was I nothing more than a booty call to them? The thought left a bitter taste on my tongue. I tensed and shook my head.

"No, what?" Dylan asked in a slightly defensive tone.

"I don't want just a weekend thing. I want it all…but I can't just leave. Can I?"

"Why not?" Nick asked. "You're not working for a couple months. What else is keeping you here, girl?"

I blinked and frowned. Nothing. There wasn't a damn thing keeping me there. I didn't have any animals or anyone to look after, but it seemed frivolous and irresponsible to simply jet off to Chicago. I wasn't accustomed to such spontaneity.

"No Sir, nothing," I confessed as the morose realization that my life was so boring and mundane, no one would miss me.

"What do you need to do before we leave then, kitten?" Dylan's blue eyes sparkled with glee. And that sexy dimple in his cheek grew deeper the more his smile widened. It was no surprise to discover that his humming excitement made it impossible for me to cling to any form of self-pity.

"I have to turn in the rental, go to the post office and forward my mail or stop it…or something. Then, I don't know…pack?"

Everything was moving at the speed of light. While it was exciting and thrilling and more than I'd ever dreamt possible, I was scared. Having aligned my life in rigid routine, such abrupt change was more than a bit daunting. Something niggled in the back of my brain.

Nick said that we would see where this new road would lead us. But he'd also made it clear their desire was to continue my training. They'd both professed to love me, but that was far different from being *in* love with me. Was Nick willing to expose his heart, to try to fall *in* love again? Or would he forever hold back to ensure it never got broken again? And what about Dylan? Was this new arrangement his attempt to heal the scars carried from war? Was he trying to regain the pieces of himself that were lost? They'd said that I'd changed them, but I wasn't sure what I'd done to influence this drastic shift.

I exhaled an inward sigh. There was a little over two months to forge a path. Then what? Anxiety gripped my belly at the thought of enduring another separation, suspecting it would ten times more painful than the few hours I'd endured.

"You're thinking too hard about something, little one. Share what's on your mind, girl."

I swallowed tightly and looked into Nick's eyes. "I'm a little overwhelmed, Master. What happens when I have to come back home in February?"

His expression grew solemn. "Nothing is set in stone yet, pet. We'll deal with logistics in due time. One thing for sure, it won't be the last of *us*."

My lips pursed as I rolled his last comment over in my mind. For a man who vowed to protect his heart, Nick didn't seem to hesitate to toss it into the ring. How had he changed his mind so quickly? I was perplexed and consumed in remorse. Eavesdropping on their conversation that night had come back to bite me in the ass with a full set of fangs.

"We refuse to drag every crumb out of you, kitten," Dylan admonished.

Time to add to your punishment. I clenched my teeth, angry that I'd childishly played possum in the first place. "I need to tell you both something," I began, shooting a guilty glance between them both. "I wasn't asleep that night in the barn, Masters. I was pretending and I heard your conversation."

Their bodies tensed in unison. I didn't have to even look up; I could feel a combination of surprise and irritation rolling off them in a palpable wave.

"Well, well, well," was all Dylan said when they finally broke the heavy silence. "You're just full of surprises, kitten."

"And then some," Nick drawled in curt agreement.

"I'm sorry, Sirs. I knew it was wrong when I did it. But I wanted to learn more about you both and I didn't know how to ask."

Dylan scoffed. "It's easy, kitten. You open your mouth."

"And have you learned how to ask questions yet, pet?" Nick chided.

"Yes, Master...sort of."

"Well, we're getting somewhere, little one. At least now you're being honest."

I bit back the sassy retort that rolled over the tip of my tongue. I'd earned their ire, I just didn't like it.

"What did you ascertain from our conversation that you now have questions about, kitten?"

I was in the hot seat now, and the flames kept growing higher. I took a deep breath and closed my eyes.

"You said that I had changed you both. But Nick, Sir, you were never going to love again and Dylan, Sir, you avoid commitment at all costs. I need to know if you both still feel that way? I...don't know where we...this..I don't know where *I* stand, Masters."

"So your little ploy did nothing but feed more insecurity inside you. Isn't that right, kitten?"

"Yes, Master," I nodded as disgrace suffused my every cell.

"When we told you we loved you, we meant with all our hearts." Nick nudged a finger beneath my chin, his voice so soft and filled with adoration, I found it difficult to look into his eyes. "And when we said you've changed us, we meant that you've changed everything we thought we wanted before you touched our lives. You *have* changed us, little one. Changed us for the better."

Tears blurred my vision as Nick slanted his lips over mine. He'd never pressed his lips to mine with such tender reverence. My heart swelled when he seemed to fuse every ounce of love in his soul into that one staggering kiss.

A tiny whimper escaped my throat as he pulled away. I glanced up at Dylan. His expression looked almost pained.

"Master?" I asked, filled with confusion.

He had always tried to hide his emotions more vehemently than Nick. The fear that it still held true mustered a sudden pang of apprehension within.

"I don't have words to describe it, Savannah. All I know is that the time we spent with you chased away the dark, bleak cloud that has been hanging over my head since I came back home. You've given me hope, kitten. It's something I never thought I could feel again. There's no way I'm going to let you go."

Tears spilled down my cheeks as Dylan pulled me in close. Caressing his broad hand over my cheek, he gave me a gentle smile then kissed me with the same tender intensity that Nick had. All my fears seemed to melt away beneath his lips. I whimpered, basking in the unreserved love given by my two Masters.

I should have been giddy with their newfound commitment. Still, something tugged at my confidence. I closed my eyes for a brief moment to pinpoint the cause of my uncertainty.

The diner.

And there it was. I tensed and my heart pounded in my chest. Had I not been locked in their arms, I would have bolted from the couch.

"What's wrong?" Nick wrapped his broad hands around my face and held me in his stern gaze.

"Nothing," I lied, watching as Nick arched his brows in warning. "I mean..." *Crap.* I couldn't keep pushing them away. The few hours I'd spent alone had been debilitating.

"I'm sorry, Master. Something happened last night at dinner that I didn't share with either of you."

"What happened in the ladies room, little one?"

I wanted to growl. Nick had obviously known I'd had words with the woman even though I'd kept the incident from both of them. I issued a heavy sigh and hung my head.

"A woman came into the restroom shortly behind me. She was one of the women..."

"We remember, kitten. Go on." Dylan prodded.

"She called us perverts and said we needed to leave or she was going to call the cops. She said I was a whore and that I was going to burn in hell."

"She didn't look altogether happy when she left the restroom, kitten. What did you say to her?"

I nibbled my lip. I'd already racked up a punishment for running away. Would they add more for me being rude to the hateful bitch? I had no doubt edging would be their choice of torture, but I worried my confession would only add more fuel to the fire. Ignoring Dylan's question wasn't an option. All I could do was hold out hope that they'd let me come...eventually.

"I umm, called her a heifer and suggested she get laid," I replied in a small, timid voice.

Dylan snorted and began to laugh. Nick threw his head back and guffawed. A reticent smile tugged my lips.

"Our first date didn't go very well, did it, kitten?" Dylan asked when he finally stopped laughing. "We'll make it up to you, baby. There's a wonderful, quaint Italian place not too far from home. Would you like to go there when we get back to Chicago?"

The smile fell from my face. *Great.* Just what I wanted; to be tossed into the ring with a bunch of hungry lions, chomping at the bit to rip me to shreds. Sit there trying to choke down my dinner while narrowminded, judgmental people, slinging rude insults and staring at me like I was an abomination. I had no doubt the restaurant Dylan boasted was far classier than Ma's Kettle's. But would its patrons assume I was a whore, as well? While I knew my Masters wouldn't fuck me on top of the dinner table, I wasn't naïve enough to think they'd curtail their affection in public. It would be like wearing a neon sign. My mind was spinning, and fear was swirling deep in my belly.

Dylan's thick fingers gripped my hair. "Answer us, kitten," he demanded.

"What?" I blinked, knowing I'd missed their question while submerged in dread.

"Where did you go just then?" Nick asked. His mouth set in a tight line wearing his bad-ass-Dom expression.

"To my worries, Sir."

"We're waiting," Dylan pressed.

I closed my eyes and sighed. When I opened my mouth, everything spilled out in a nauseating blob of gibberish. When I was done, neither of them said a word. Their unreadable expressions only served to catapult my anxiety level straight to the moon.

Finally, Dylan slid me onto Nick's lap. "I'll be right back," he announced as he stood and walked out the front door.

"Where's he going?"

"Not another word, pet," Nick instructed.

"But I'm trying to communicate. If I'm not allowed to speak, how can I do that, Sir?"

He slashed me with a look of warning. I pinched my lips together then issued a frustrated huff.

Dylan returned a few moments later, the black duffel slung over his shoulder. I knew then that my ass was in serious trouble.

"Show us where your bedroom is, kitten," Dylan instructed with a scowl on his face. "It's time to pay the piper."

I hesitated just long enough for Nick to lift me from his lap and set me on my feet. My pussy was inches from his face. His gaze dropped to my closely cropped tuft of curls and I felt the moisture gathering over my folds as his nostrils flared.

"I can smell your cunt. Already wet for us, little one?"

"Please, Masters. No punishment. Just make love to me," I begged.

Nick stood and placed his hands on my hips, turning me to face Dylan, who was wearing a wry grin. I opened my mouth to beg for lenience, but before I could speak, a wicked slap landed over my butt cheeks. The ensuing burn rushed down my legs.

"Ouch!" I blurted, when all I really wanted to do was purr.

"That was a sweet cry, but lacked the sincerity we're looking for, little one," Nick chuckled.

"Wh--what? You want me to hurt?"

"You like pain, kitten. We established that back at the barn."

"You know we'd never give you more than you can handle, girl. But there are several things we need to make perfectly clear. First and foremost, you belong to us. Running away is forbidden. You will not trick us by faking sleep or use any other guise again. We will purge the negative body image you cling to, as well as your preoccupation with other people's opinions about our lifestyle choice. Negative thinking has no place in *our* relationship, nor does it promote your submission. And last but not least, you own the responsibility of communicating with us about *everything*. There will be no more yanking it from of you like a goddamn dentist," he growled in a firm voice.

"Looks, like we have enough work to keep us busy for a long time, kitten," Dylan chuckled.

"But… you keep telling me to be quiet. Besides, I wasn't in a frame of mind to explain all this to you at the barn. Don't you understand?"

"And why couldn't you, kitten? Did your pride get in the way of being honest with us?" Dylan asked, eating up the distance between us in two long strides.

"Yes," I mumbled and hung my head. Looking at my beaded nipples, I could no longer ignore the increasing slickness between my legs, either. Their interrogation tactics turned me on like a light bulb. The way they dissected me like a science experiment only made me hotter and wetter.

I was certain there was a psych ward out there, with a whole wing dedicated to me. Normal people didn't get turned on by Dominant cross-examination, did they?

"You keep stepping on your pride instead of trusting us. The submissive road you're on is going to be one hell of a rocky journey until you finally decide to, little one." I raised my head. Nick's expression was severe. "You need to realize that regardless of what people think, what they say, or how they stare... Dylan and I will provide your happiness and serenity. If you don't fucking trust us with your emotions, the good, the bad and the ugly, you'll never find true peace."

"We're not asking for perfection. We know you've been alone for a long time, but we won't tolerate bits and pieces, pet." Dylan scowled. "It's all or nothing. Do you understand?"

"Yes, Masters."

On one hand, I was relieved that they didn't expect me to slough off my insecurities with the wave of a magic wand. But sharing every damn emotion with them seemed daunting. And there was still the matter of my punishment.

"Is it going to be edging again?" I asked with a pained expression.

Dylan patted the bag slung over his arm and grinned. "Not today, kitten. You've earned something far more substantial. Now where is your room?"

CHAPTER ELEVEN

Before I could answer, Nick scooped me up in his arms and followed Dylan as he swaggered down the hall.

"First door on your right, Sir," I announced in resignation as my mind conjured a half dozen hideous and painful scenarios. "Is it going to hurt a lot?"

"Only as much as it needs to, little one," Nick replied in an unnervingly stoic demeanor.

"I've learned my lessons though, Master. I won't run away again. I'll talk to you both about my feelings. I'll do better with my insecurities. You don't have to punish me, I swear."

"Maybe we want to, kitten," Dylan goaded before rounding the corner to my room.

"But all of us making love would feel so much better," I urged.

"Oh, it will…eventually." Nick's lips curled in a feral smile. Little Red's wolf had nothing on him.

"Stop trying to worm your way out, kitten," Dylan warned with a laugh as he dropped the duffle bag next to my bed.

"It won't matter. I can see I'm just wasting my breath," I replied, trying to contain my sarcasm.

"Yes you are." Dylan winked. "I think we put her on her back, bro. What do you think?"

"For now," Nick replied in a cryptic tone as he set me on the edge of the bed. Clasping my shoulders with his broad hands, persuaded me to lie down. "Close your eyes, little one."

A tremor rippled through my body as the sound of the heavy zipper sliced the air. While I knew the bag contained ropes, paddles, floggers, condoms and lube, I assumed it contained some very unpleasant toys, as well. I closed my eyes and tensed.

The sound of releasing zippers gave me the conclusion they were stripping. I wanted to peek but didn't dare, I was in enough trouble. Sending up a futile hope that my punishment might contain more pleasure than pain, I anxiously waited.

Suddenly, broad hands gripped my thighs and spread me open. Warm breath danced over my sodden petals and I moaned.

I gripped my fists into the bedspread. Trembling in anticipation, I waited to feel a warm, wet tongue. Instead, fingers toyed with my folds, plucking and pulling in a maddening cadence. I writhed and whimpered, needing so much more.

My eyes flashed open wide and a trill scream exploded from my throat as white-hot pain engulfed my labia. Flailing beneath the sturdy arms that held my thighs, I tried to escape the searing pain. Tears slid from my eyes and I gasped as I attempted to rise above the caustic fire.

"What the fuck are you doing to me?" I screamed, slashing an angry glare at Dylan, poised between my legs.

Nick's grip tightened around my thighs, growling at my expletive.

"Breathe, kitten. Ride it out. You can do it," Dylan soothed as he rubbed my clit.

"Do you need to use your safe word, little one?" Nick asked in a tone laden with concern. I shook my head. "Answer me, girl. Do you need to stop?"

"No, Sir. What is that? It hurts so bad," I wailed.

A wry smile curled on Dylan's lips as he held up an innocuous clothespin. I blinked. He'd put a damn clothes pin on my pussy lips. *Fuck that!*

"That's just the first one, kitten. You'll take a lot more for me, won't you, baby?" Dylan asked with a wicked gleam in his eyes.

"I don't know," I replied in a small voice.

"Clasp your hands behind your head and breathe, kitten. Let me see if I can make this easier on you."

"I've learned my lesson, Masters. Honest. I have," I pleaded as I tucked my fingers behind my neck.

"Keep your legs open, girl, and don't move or you'll take the whole bag," Nick growled. He released my thighs and climbed onto the bed, beside to me.

I didn't know how many were in the bag, but hazarded it was a hell of a lot more than two. I stared up at Nick as he traced his fingertips in soothing cadence around my areolas. He lowered his head and slanted his lips over mine, carrying me away from the pain with a demanding kiss. We both moaned lowly as our avid tongues tangled.

This was the submission of my dreams, this sweet, tender, possessive tranquility. But I knew what was coming. More searing flashes of pain. *Dylan's pain.* A settling peace surrounded me at the thought of accepting his punishment. The need to please him chased through me. And even as I wondered if I could survive this tumultuous combination of heaven and hell without losing my mind...nothing had ever felt so right.

Nick swallowed my muffled squeal of surprise as Dylan's mouth covered my pussy. Wet sucking noises filled the room as I soared up that glorious spire. Nick cupped my breasts in his palms, and the pads of his thumbs abraded my sensitive nipples. I whimpered and writhed as Dylan tongued, sucked, and lapped my cunt and clit with expert finesse.

They plucked and plunged with busy fingers, encouraging the bubbling orgasm welling inside me, while mitigating the sting of nefarious clothes pins being placed, one after another. With each subtle twinge, Dylan's mouth magically expunged the agony. Grinding against Nick's hot body, his silky seepage glazed my hip. Urgent to be freed from their sexual purgatory, my need to release swarmed like a million buzzing bees.

Easing his mouth from my center, Dylan announced, "All done."

Nick issued a muffled grunt before severing our kiss. "Are you ready, brave pet?"

"Yes, Master." I nodded resolutely.

"Good, girl," he praised.

Those two magnificent words zipped a fiery coil of excitement up my spine. I gazed into his smoldering, seductive eyes. "Get on your hands and knees, little one. We've claimed you, now it's time for you to claim us."

I didn't know what he meant, but frenzied with need, I was more than willing to find out. Dylan stood and extended his hand. As I sat up, a blast of white-hot agony engulfed me. I looked down as I cried out to find half a dozen clothes pins attached to my labia. They dangled and clicked together, making every movement, no matter how slight, jostle the wooden fingers to gnaw my tender flesh. I moaned and begged for Dylan's mouth to soothe away the blistering pain.

It was a slow and agonizing process, but I repositioned myself on all fours as Nick had instructed. My mouth was perfectly aligned with Dylan's weeping purple crest.

"No, kitten. You don't get the treat of my cock, at least not yet." He smiled and slid his thick thumb into my mouth.

Lost in a lust-filled fugue, I licked and sucked his digit as if it were his shaft. The sound of foil somehow registered in my brain, then Nick's nimble fingers began massaging slick, cold lube upon my puckered rim.

"You wear the pins nicely, little one." He reached between my legs, fanning his fingers over the wooden tips. Pain thundered through me like a herd of wild horses. As I rose to my knees, howling in pain, I nearly bit Dylan's thumb off.

Nick's broad hand splayed over my back, forcing me back down on all fours. Tears dripped from my eyes as I sobbed.

"Don't move again, little one," he instructed, emphasizing his command with an open-handed spank across my butt cheeks.

"Owww," I cried. "Please take them off. They burn. They hurt. Please."

Dylan chuckled. "You really don't want me to do that yet, princess."

Nick rubbed my puckered rosette with a wide, wet finger. The irksome pain slowly ebbed, replaced by growing pulses of electric fire. Bidding my tender tissue to relax, he applied more pressure to his circling finger until he breached the rigid center. As he eased a fingertip inside, my muscles involuntarily contracted around his invasion. Retreating, only to begin massaging again, Nick persuaded my gathered ring to expand. He repeated the process over and again, thinning the ultra-sensitized rim. Pleasure centers in my brain exploded as I panted and writhed.

Dylan reached back into his magic bag of tricks and extracted a long vibrating wand. He wasted no time plugging the device into a socket by my bed. The bulbous, round-tipped toy began to buzz and I gazed into his eyes as he sat near my side on the bed. When he pressed the humming toy between my legs, the dangling pins came to life. They absorbed the droning vibrations, setting my pinched pussy lips ablaze in an arduous fire.

Dylan pressed deeper, until the toy connected with my clit. My hiss of pain melded into a moan of delight.

"Such a pretty little slut," Dylan praised as he strummed the vibe against my distended pearl, vanquishing the searing bite from the pins. I launched toward the heavens as Nick squeezed in another finger. Murmuring soft praises, he expanded my surrendering tissue as sinister shockwaves wove a carnal quickening.

Tiny pinpricks of pain sizzled from my tender rim as Nick's broad head pinched through my passageway. The pressure seemed insurmountable and the burn...the sweet, hot burn spread like gossamer webs of pleasure mixed with pain.

My tiny ring expanded and contracted, sucking at his crest in a bewildering contest of consent and denial.

Gasps and moans scratched my throat. My electrified muscles cinched upon Nick's invading cock as he threaded each inch, into my quivering hole. He gripped my hips with a hold so commanding, I wanted to sing. Panting and swearing, he held me captive until he seated his entire shaft deep inside me.

The vibe buzzed and the pins chewed upon my fragile flesh, trapping me in a realm of venerate hell.

"Who do you belong to, girl?" Dylan asked as he repositioned himself and plunged two fingers deep into my quivering core.

"Ahhh," I cried, rocking upon his embedded fingers and sliding back and forth on Nick's luscious cock. "You, my wonderful Masters."

"Yes, you do. And we want all of you, Savannah. Not just the pieces you are willing to share, but *all* of you." His skillful fingers curled, finding that decadent bundle of nerves deep inside. "Do you swear to give us your heart, sweet slut, so that we can shower you in our unconditional love?"

"Yessss," I hissed.

Nick began to quicken his pace. "Do you vow to give us your body to use and treasure as we see fit?" he growled, emphasizing his question by launching deep in my ass.

"Yesss, Master, yessssss," I moaned, trying to ride the rising surge as it layered upon itself.

"Do you entrust your soul to *our* command?" Dylan cajoled as he fanned the biting pins.

A scream rippled in the back of my throat. "Yes, oh god, yessss," I panted through the pain.

"Do you grant your mind to us as well, sweet slave? Open it up so we can climb inside and soothe your fears, slay your demons, and protect you from past and future sorrow?"

Nick's loving words ripped through my heart. Fresh tears filled my eyes and trailed down my cheeks. "Yes, Master," I sobbed.

"You are ours, Savannah," Nick thundered. "You belong to me."

"And you belong to me, precious pet." Dylan growled. "Now come for your Masters, sweet slave. Give us your heart, mind, body and soul. Give us light and life, sweet love."

Catapulted at their command, I succumbed to the swell. It crested and crashed through me as Dylan reached between my legs and plucked all the pins from my enflamed folds.

Lightning streaked from my pussy and shot up my spine. Intense pain, left in the wake of the pins, melded with the electrified pleasure of the vibe. Dylan's gifted fingers and Nick's driving rhythm crushed together beneath each mind-blowing sensation.

I threw back my head as a roar of carnal splendor tore from my throat. Nick shuttled his cock deep in my ass. I combusted beneath the blistering pyre, every nerve ending in my body singing in rapture.

"Ours!" Nick's bellicose roar thundered in my ears. Slamming his shaft through my spasming rim, I felt his seed erupt and spill into the thin latex sheathe.

Quivering, sated, and more replete than I ever dreamed possible, it all paled in comparison to the surge of contentment saturating every cell of my being.

My whole universe was now meshed with my Masters.

They were the air I filled in my lungs.

The blood that pumped through my veins.

The light in my eyes, to help me find my way.

The strength to shield and protect me.

The hope in my heart for a new and better life.

And though I never knew how desperately lost and alone I'd been, they were my salvation.

"I love you, Masters," I sobbed, crumpling to the mattress.

Within seconds, I was nestled between their warm, steely bodies, infused with their unconditional love, and inundated with their praise.

After a long night of conversation, a little bondage and a lot more sex, we woke early and returned the Hummer to the rental agency. Back at the apartment, my five-star chefs began preparing a gourmet breakfast of bacon, eggs and toast. As they cooked, I phoned Mellie, argued with my insurance company, did a quick load of laundry and re-packed my suitcases. After a quick but delicious meal, we made a brief stop at the post office then hit the road toward Chicago.

Of course the long ride was anything but boring. My Masters made great use of my mouth and pussy as they took shifts driving. And only once did Nick have to threaten me with the butt plug, when I got a little sassy.

It was close to midnight before we reached the outskirts of Chicago.

"Our house is about another thirty minutes north of the city, but I'll take us up Lake Shore Drive so you can see the lake," Nick announced as I sat a little straighter, unwilling to miss the sights.

Nick exited the interstate and began driving along a highway parallel to Lake Michigan. Enormous mansions sprawled on the left, and the shimmering lake was illuminated beneath a full moon on the right. I felt intimidated by the ultra-huge homes. I'd grown up in a modest white collar home and while I didn't want for much, we were far from rich. The people who lived in the homes lining Lake Michigan were mega-loaded.

Nick made a series of left and right turns then slowed on a street lined with large, mature trees. Street lights cast eerie shadows through the thick foliage, allowing only quick glimpses of impressive houses set back from the street. Some were totally obscured behind manicured hedge rows while others, daunting and massive, were clearly visible.

When he pulled into a cobblestone drive, the headlights flashed over a monstrous brick Colonial mansion. My eyes grew wide as I viewed the impressive structure. The avant garde metal sculpture situated in the center of the circular driveway and the stately black shutters framing each large window had my mind churning as to what lay behind the mighty structure.

"You live here?" I asked, unable to mask my astonishment.

"We live here, kitten," Dylan chuckled.

"Wow," I whispered in awe. "Do you have maids and such?"

"Yes, Rachel and Pablo live in the guest house out back," Nick replied with such a casual tone, I knew he didn't have a clue how dumbfounded I was to find myself in such superfluous surroundings. "Rachel oversees the cleaning service and prepares our meals. Pablo maintains the landscaping, pool, and makes household repairs, that sort of thing."

"You have a pool?"

"And a stunning view of Lake Michigan, little one." Nick grinned. "Don't let it overwhelm you, pet. It's just a house."

"Yeah, a huge mother…" I coughed. "A big one too, Master."

"Come on, let's go in and crash. We can unload in the morning."

"Can I grab my toiletries, Sir?"

"No. It's late. We need sleep…well, before the sun comes up, anyway." Nick grinned. The knowing look in his eyes told me, sleep would be a long time coming.

Stepping into the wide foyer, I felt like Cinderella at the Prince's palace. Gleaming hardwood floors shimmered beneath a stunning crystal chandelier, flush upon a layered tray ceiling. Dark cherry woodwork garnered a masculine yet inviting contrast against faux beige leather walls.

As they took me on a ten cent tour, I found each room more stunning than the one before. It all looked professionally designed. I knew Mellie would appreciate the attention to detail throughout the elegant rooms. Though overwhelmed by the sheer grandeur of it all, I was fascinated at the dichotomy of the men and their home. Their surroundings were ostentatious, yet there wasn't a pretentious bone in their bodies.

"Come on, kitten, let's get ready for bed."

"How many bedrooms are in this…castle?"

Nick laughed. "There's six but don't get too impressed, little one. We bought it for a song when the market crashed. It's a nifty tax deduction, nothing more."

"It's a little late not to be impressed, Master. I passed that when we pulled into the driveway. And the view of Lake Michigan…whoa, it's breathtaking."

"It soothes our savage beasts, that's for sure," Dylan agreed as we climbed the wide, staircase. "Nick and I laid claim to a couple of the guest rooms. We've been saving the master suite for…well, for you."

"Me?"

"Yes, kitten. We'd always hoped someday we'd find a submissive with whom to share our lives. So the room is a present, so to speak, for the sub of our dreams. And that is, you."

The adoration in his words gripped my heart. Never had I imagined being someone's dream, let alone the dream to two of the most amazing Masters on the planet.

Nick pushed open the double doors to the suite. I felt the weight of his gaze as he watched my reaction. I caught the smile curling on his lips as my jaw dropped at the splendor laid out before me. Stepping into the room, my feet sank into plush white carpet. A massive four poster, mahogany bed was the room's focal point. It was larger than any bed I'd ever seen and had to have been custom built. I couldn't stop myself from gliding my fingers over the ornate, carved accents, imagining what it would feel like to be bound to the sturdy spires.

Making my way across the room, I stopped to admire the white marble fireplace located next to a set of beveled lead crystal doors. Curious, I twisted the shimmering brass handles to discover a large balcony that overlooked a sparkling swimming pool. Behind the exquisitely decorated pool area laid a picturesque view of Lake Michigan.

After returning to the bedroom, I stood in silence, drinking it all in. There wasn't an inkling of masculinity to be found in the room. It was bright and airy and gossamer, as if I'd stepped through a door to heaven. Pale peach and sage green accents highlighted the bedspread and curtains. Cream polished tables were tastefully arranged in the cozy seating area and butted both sides of the big bed. Each elegant table was adorned with a crystal vase overflowing in peach flowers. The room was both functional and aesthetically soothing. Tears stung my eyes as I gazed at the overstuffed ecru couch positioned in front of the fireplace, exactly like the couch in the barn.

"What do you think, little one?" Nick asked, breaking me from my reverie.

"Oh, Master. It's... magical," I whispered with a soft sniff.

"You've not seen the best part yet, kitten." Dylan grinned as he breezed past me and stood before a massive mirrored armoire.

"What's in there?" I asked, having presumed it was a closet.

"It's where we keep the fun toys hidden, kitten." He laughed and pulled the doors open.

"Oh my," I gasped, gazing over the oasis of floggers, paddles, cuffs, gags, whips and vibes. Spying several sizes of butt plugs, I quivered. "You've got a lot of stuff there, Sirs." I gulped.

"Not near as many as we have in our room at Genesis, little one." Nick smiled as he pulled me to his side. "Think of this as the continuing education equipment."

I giggled and brushed my fingers over the soft thick falls of a heavy flogger. My clit throbbed and I sucked in a shaky breath.

Nick plucked my turgid nipple then leaned in close to my ear. "I think our toy closet turns you on, pet. Is your pussy wet?"

"And then some, Master," I exhaled on a wistful sigh.

"Good. That's how we like to keep you, girl. Wet. Ready. Needy. And longing to please us in every way possible."

"Oh, I'm there, Sir. All the way." I trembled as I peeled my attention from the luscious assortment of toys to stare into his dark, dangerous eyes.

The smile fell from his lips as he spun me to his chest, trapping my lips in a torrid kiss.

"If you start this now, bro, we're never going to get any sleep," Dylan warned from behind me.

I felt Nick's lips curl in a smile before he pulled away. "Who needs sleep?"

"We all do if we plan to go to Genesis tonight."

"Genesis?" My eyes grew wide and an excited smile spread split my mouth. "But why do you need a club when you've got so many toys here, Sir?"

"We have toys but it's more fun using the equipment there, kitten. Plus you need to feel the vibe in the air, hear the erotic sounds, smell the leather and the sex, meet the people who share the same kink."

"But I don't have anything to wear. I mean, I don't own fetish wear."

"We'll take you out later this afternoon, after we've had some sleep," Nick explained. "We'll get you some new clothes. Not just club wear, but dresses and whatever else you might want."

"I don't want anything except you, two, Masters. You're all I need and want."

For the first time, I'd confessed what was in my heart without fear of rejection. It was freeing to feel so safe.

Dylan swirled me from Nick's arms and ushered me into an stunning bathroom. I grinned when I spied the oversized whirlpool tub, much larger than at Kit's. Elevated against one wall there was a tier of marble stairs skirting its edge. Sprawled along another wall was a rainforest shower with crystal doors. Against the third wall was a long wide marble vanity. Three ebony marble wash basins with glimmering silver faucets sat poised beneath the biggest mirror I'd ever seen.

"The toilet is in here," Nick stated, opening the door to another large room with not only a stool, but a bidet.

The suite was bigger than my entire apartment. Hell, it had to be larger than mine *and* my neighbor's unit combined. I couldn't wrap my head around the fact that Nick and Dylan lived in these lavish surroundings.

No wonder Nick had Paige sign a pre-nup. Probably a damn good thing, too.

"Oh, and there's one important rule for the master suite, little one."

I could already figure out what rule Nick was talking about by the mischievous twinkle in his luscious eyes. "No clothes. Right, Master?"

Both men chuckled. "You're catching on quick, kitten,"

"I just want to make you the happiest Masters on the face of the earth." I sighed.

"You already make us happy, little one, but pushing your limits will no doubt make us even happier. And finding a way to keep you here forever…that would make us ecstatic."

Forever. I wasn't foolish enough to think it would last forever. All good things came to an end, eventually. And though I didn't want to start thinking about it, the day would come when I'd be forced to leave. Walk away from the two men who brought more joy in my life than I'd ever thought possible. Leave their magical castle and go back to my boring existence. But until then, I would live out this fairy tale as long as I could.

It wasn't like I could turn my back and walk away from the responsibilities that waited for me at home. I had a job and a lease on an apartment. The only saving grace was this time. Now, I had months, not weeks, to spend with them. Maybe it would be easier to say good-bye once I finally got my fill of submission.

And maybe you need to pull that hose out, 'cause sugar, you've never blown that much smoke up your ass. Ever.

I was once again thwarted by that pragmatic inner voice of reason.

Even if I'd tried, I couldn't candy coat it. No matter how many months I spent with them, it would never be enough. I'd fallen hopelessly in love with them both, but eventually I'd have to find a way to live without their abiding love. The gaping hole they'd leave in my heart would never heal. I sent up a silent prayer that somehow, in some way, this fairy tale might have a happy ending. But for the life of me, I couldn't envision that ever becoming a reality.

"Savannah," Nick interrupted my wayward thoughts. "What's wrong? You have that look again."

"What look, Master?" I grinned, attempting to mask my worries. Nick's warning expression and the sound of Dylan's disappointed sigh had me lowering my head and casting my eyes to the floor.

"That 'I'm going to try like hell to pretend everything's all right and hope they don't notice' look," Nick growled as he ate up the distance between us before gripping my chin and tilting my head back up. "You know how we feel about this game, girl."

"It's not a game, Master," I whispered as Dylan swooped in behind me.

"Then what the hell do you call it, kitten?" I gasped as Dylan snarled in my ear then sunk his teeth into the side of my neck. A million pinpricks exploded beneath my flesh and my tunnel clenched in want.

"I don't know how to do this… how to tell you both every thought that flutters through my brain. I'm not used to confessing the mass of crap that consumes my every waking hour."

"Then you'd better get used to it, little one, because that's exactly what we expect."

Nick's eyes were ablaze with reprimand and disappointment. Glancing over my shoulder, Dylan's reflected the same. God, I hated to let them down. Their palpable displeasure felt like a spike through my heart.

"I'm worried about having to leave you two again, in a few months." I confessed it in a tiny voice.

"Hopefully you won't want to," Nick replied with furrowed brows.

"I already know I don't *want* to, but I'll have to, Sir."

"Do you want some popcorn?" Dylan snarled in my ear.

"Huh?" I asked whipping my head around, feeling my face wrinkle with confusion. "No, I'm not hungry."

"That's not what I was insinuating, kitten. It seems to me you've already plopped your ass in the theatre and started projecting the worst. I just thought you might want some popcorn as the movie plays in your head."

Dylan's tone was snarky and condescending, and it pushed a big honkin' button inside. Spinning to face him, I let out a low growl and placed my hands on my hips.

"I'm not projecting the worst. I'm simply stating the facts. I have a job, an apartment and responsibilities to--"

"To whom?" Nick smirked.

"To Myron, my boss. I do work from the office at least one day a week so I can check up on him."

"It's Myron a grown man, kitten?"

"Yes, but he's old and--"

"And you mother him?" Nick asked with a patronizing smile.

"Stop belittling me. Both of you," I huffed.

"There she is," Nick smiled.

"What are you talking about?" I asked, still fuming at their demeaning remarks.

"You," he glowered. "Ever since you realized it was us that you beat the shit out of yesterday, you've been acting like a Stepford sub. It's about time the real you emerged again. You know, the girl with spunk and fire? Trust me little one, she's a whole lot more erotic than the mousy Miss Perfect we rode up here with."

"I'm not perfect and I wasn't pretending anything. I was trying to please you two, if you must know."

"You honestly don't think you please us, kitten?" Dylan asked in amazement.

"I do in bed, but outside of sex, I honestly have no fucking clue."

"Strip," Nick growled as he stepped next to Dylan.

I exhaled a mighty sigh and tore away my clothes. "Kneel as well, Masters?" I asked in a snippy voice.

"No. March your sexy bare ass to the kitchen, pet." Dylan grinned.

"I don't remember how to get there. Sir." I hissed.

"Follow me," Nick instructed with a wicked smirk before he turned on his heel and walked away.

I knew better than to ask what they had in store for me, and I was certain it probably wasn't anything I'd enjoy, at least not at first. With a heavy sigh, I followed Nick out the door and down the stairs, well aware of Dylan right behind me.

When we reached the sparkling bright kitchen Nick opened a cupboard and pulled out a box of rice. I watched as he sprinkled the white pellets onto the pristine ceramic tiled floor.

"What--"

"Not one sound, little one. And if you slip with another curse word, it will be a mouth full of dish soap for you, as well. On your knees, hands behind your neck."

I blinked as Nick pointed to a spot on the floor thick with dry rice.

I clenched my jaw, laced my fingers behind my neck and knelt upon the rice. I'd barely gotten into position before the hard granules bit into my knees with a savage sting. The longer my body weight bore down on the tiny specks, the more painful it became. Trying to reposition myself was futile. The more I wiggled, the more potent the agony became. Both men leaned against the counter, their ropey arms crossed over sculpted chests, watching me as I fought the urge to cry out.

"You please us more than any woman we've ever known. Yet you don't believe that. Not in your heart at least. Do you think we're lying to you when we praise you, little one?"

"No, Sir." I whispered.

"You're not giving us a chance to succeed, little one. It's unfair to our entire relationship. You have to communicate your feelings with us. If you harbor the tiniest doubt about how much we love you, we need to know. Closing yourself off, anticipating good-bye, will only promote negativity. Pessimism will destroy our relationship. If you want us in your life then you've got to give us a chance. None of us know what the coming months will bring. But I can tell you this, neither Dylan or I want to lose you. We will find a way to make this work. We love you, girl. I can't be any clearer about our feelings. It's up to you to decide if you're going to believe us or not."

I closed my eyes and sighed as my shoulders slumped. "I do believe you, Master, and I love you both so very much. I want to stay, honest I do. I can't help but worry. This is all too perfect. I keep waiting for the other shoe to drop." I sucked in a hiss as pain radiated from my knees. "Is my punishment over?"

"No, kitten. Think of the rice as another way we want to drill into your soul everything we've already explained to you. We've been crystal clear from the very beginning what our expectations are. We've coddled, edged, denied and talked. Maybe a little torture will make you finally realize that your trust, honesty and communication isn't something we can take. You have to freely give it to us, girl." Dylan squatted down, eye level with me. "Don't let your worries deny you the chance at happiness, kitten."

Tears stung my eyes. They'd talked to me about releasing my control until they were blue in the face, but I still clung to it. Not only that, I'd tried to slam a door in their face before I'd given them a chance to keep my fairy tale alive.

"They're all I know, Masters. They protect me from getting hurt," I sobbed. My heart was aching ten times worse than my knees.

"Did it hurt when you ran away from us?" Nick asked, squatting next to Dylan and leveling me with a tormented gaze.

I nodded as fat tears slid down my cheeks. "More than I'd ever thought possible, Sir."

"We don't want you to hurt, little one. We want you to grow. To feel safe, protected and most of all, loved."

"Then help me off this da…painful rice, please Master?" I begged with a loud sniff.

"We need a promise, kitten," Dylan warned. "No more keeping destructive and negative fears locked up inside you."

"I'm trying, Master, I really am. It's not easy for me."

"We know, kitten. We know. But you don't have to handle everything alone anymore. You have two strong Masters who can't wait to shoulder your fears. We've been over this time and again."

"I know. I know." I nodded, wishing I could find the magic key to unlock my fucking insecurities. "I promise I'll work on it, Masters. I'll work hard for you both."

"Work hard for *all* of us, sweet girl. This isn't just for our benefit, it's for yours too." Nick brushed the pads of his thumbs over my cheek, wiping away my tears, then stood. Rice crunched beneath his shoes. The sound struck me with a wave of déjà vu. It reminded me of the gravel beneath their car tires as they left Kit's, and the beastly grief that had consumed me. I never wanted to feel that unholy despair again.

Nick's stout arms banded around my waist and lifted me off the rice. Still crouched next to me, Dylan reached out and brushed the embedded bits from my knees.

"I'm sorry I disappointed you, Masters."

"You've not disappointed us, kitten," Dylan reassured as he stood and tangled his arms around us. "Frustrated us? Yeah. There's still a lot we need to teach you. But laying this groundwork is more important than anything else."

"I understand. Honestly, I do." I leaned my head against Dylan's shoulder as his fingers threaded my hair. "I don't like the rice lesson, Masters. I'd much rather take edging."

They both chuckled. Nick kissed the top of my head. "Come on, little one. Let's get some sleep. I think we're beyond exhausted."

When I climbed into the enormous bed, their naked bodies surrounded me, infusing me with their familiar warmth. As I drifted off to sleep, I smiled at the soft snores coming from the two men who owned my heart.

CHAPTER TWELVE

Dawn was breaking when I opened my eyes to find Nick's mouth teasing my hardened nipple. A soft purr rolled from the back of my throat and I stretched, arching into his mouth with a silent plea. Dylan lay snoring with a leg wrapped around mine in possessive claim. Nick tugged the turgid tip between his teeth. My needful moan stirred Dylan awake. A wicked smile played over his lips when he rolled to his side to watch.

"Does his mouth feel good, kitten?"

"Mmmm, yes, Master."

"Is your pussy wet for me, sweet slut?" Dylan taunted.

"Ahhh," I gasped. "Yes, Master. Wet and so hot."

"That's what I like to hear, kitten. Spread your legs for me. I need your sweet honey on my tongue."

Dylan crawled between my splayed legs. Without his usual teasing or torment, his insidious mouth captured my folds and his tongue plunged deep in my core. The tip of his nose burnished my clit, chasing desire through my veins. My soft whimpers of delight floated through the air. Nick eased back, his dark eyes scrutinizing my every response.

"I love to watch you climb, little one. You're expressions are so pure…so innocent…so fucking erotic," he whispered, plucking and pinching my distended nipples.

"Please Masters, make love to me," I begged, writhing beneath the growing inferno.

"I love hearing you beg, little one," Nick growled before he straddled my chest and brushed the slick tip of his swollen crest over my lips.

I stared at his refined, sharp features. His tawny smooth flesh. His seductive dark eyes. His long sleep-tousled hair glistened midnight-blue from the early morning light streaming through the parted curtains. He was beyond stunning. A dreamy sigh escaped my lips as I dropped my gaze to his pulsating cock. I breathed in his heady masculine scent, my mouth watering for a taste of the potent pearl blossoming atop the sensitive slit. Dylan eased away and I whimpered at the loss of his decadent tongue bath.

"More, Master Dylan. Please."

"Easy, pet. He'll be back. He's just running to get some condoms. Now open those plump lips for me, my sweet slut. I need to feel your wicked mouth around my cock."

I parted my lips, engulfing Nick's glistening crown, savoring his potent spice exploding over my tongue. Dylan's hands gripped my hips before he speared deep into my core. My entire body bowed, sending Nick's thick, vein-threaded cock deep down my throat.

Filled.

Loved.

Treasured.

Sensations swamped me. Suffused with their potent and intoxicating force, I wanted to scream to the heavens. Their tandem rhythm ensured I remained anchored to them every sinful second. My tunnel clutched, milking Dylan's surging shaft. His crest scraped over that magic spot deep inside lighting me up with each decadent pass.

Focused on every smoldering sensation they brought to life, I sailed away. I bucked against their driving cocks, granting back every ounce of pleasure they imparted. Locked in the sublime grip of Nick's savage eyes, they were eclipsed in command and replete with love. I ascended toward that glorious summit.

Dylan's nimble thumb strummed my clit as his bulbous head continued to scrape over my electrified nerves. Their guttural praises fused with their grunts and hisses of pleasure, urging me to the craggy edge and magnifying my need to fill them with ecstasy.

Release burned like hot coals as I struggled to hold it back.

"Nick?" Dylan cried out in tight demand.

"Fuck yes," Nick hissed as his erotic eyes flared in a carnal fire. "Now, sweet love. Come," he choked as he bent, gripping my mane, and drove deep into my throat.

Pinching my lips around the base of Nick's cock, the force of his come rippled over my tongue as he erupted, bathing my throat in hot slickness. Dylan clutched my hips, in a savage grip, pounding as he exploded deep in my spasming tunnel. Panting through my nose, I swallowed Nick's offering, gulping and whimpering as I thrashed, conquered by my own obliteration.

Nick eased from my lips, his shaft glistening with saliva. He flopped down on the bed beside me as rippling aftershocks pulsated through me. Dylan remained coupled deep, gliding in and out, easing me down from ecstasy. I stared down at him. Sweat glossed his beautiful, striking face. His mighty chest strained with each gasping breath. But it was his twinkling cerulean eyes, swimming in unequivocal commitment, that took my breath away.

He really *had* changed. He'd torn away the mask and decimated his walls, and stood proud for me to see the real Dylan.

"I love you, Master." The words rolled off my tongue as if I'd spoken them a thousand times. But I sensed he grasped the depth of gratitude that his trust evoked, mingling in my vow.

His loving expression hardened as he tilted his head and narrowed his eyes. Pulling from inside me, he launched onto the bed, pinning me beneath him. His breath was ragged as he delved his eyes into mine. Desperation rolled off his chiseled body.

"Say it again, kitten. I need to hear it again."

My heart swelled and so did my eyes. "I love you, Master. I love you," I whispered.

"I love you, too, kitten. I love you so fucking much." Dylan roared before his mouth stormed against mine, leveling me with a feral kiss.

Nick's hands caressed my face as he moved in, brushing his lips over my cheek.

"We'll never grow tired of hearing that, little one, just as we'll never grow tired of showering you with all the love we hold in our hearts," Nick murmured in my ear.

Tired of asking what I'd done to deserve their astonishing love, I wrapped my arms around Dylan's burly chest and drowned in his torrid kiss.

"You two keep sucking face, I'm going to fill the tub," Nick chuckled as my tongue tangled with Dylan's in a sultry, soulful dance.

Easing back a hairsbreadth, Dylan's lips still fixed to mine as he smiled. "Be there in a sec, man."

I giggled as his words vibrated. He pulled back and smiled down at me.

"You complete us, kitten. You know what that means don't you?"

The smile fell from my lips as the impact of his words slammed me.

"No, Sir." I whispered, a slight bit frightened by the implication.

"We're never going to let you go."

"Oh," I replied on a quivering breath.

"That doesn't mean you have permission freak out, my love. I saw that glint of fear in your eyes. It just means we're going to have some serious discussions about our future. *Our* future," he emphasized.

I nodded, chasing away the icy hands of fear before they pierced my heart.

Dylan rolled away and extended his hand. "Our bath awaits my sweet, sultry siren."

When we entered the bathroom, I couldn't help but grin. Nick was lounging with his eyes closed, in a tub of white, billowing bubbles. His chocolate muscles bore a stunning contrast against the fluffy white suds.

"Not one word, my sweet slut. This is foo-foo scented shit is *all* for you," Nick scoffed, opening one dark eye to appraise my reaction.

As I bit my lips to keep from laughing, he extended his hand. Accepting his chivalrous offer, a giggle escaped as I stepped into the tub. Without warning, he drew back a wet hand and landed a sizzling slap across my ass.

"Owww! That hurt," I huffed in a mulish pout.

"*Owww* is not a safe word, girl. Besides, I look forward to spanking your ass a lot more." Nick smiled. Snaking his leg beneath the water, he clipping the back of my knees and knocked me off my feet. I toppled backward, landing on his chest as bubbles exploded into the air.

"Promise?" I taunted with a cheeky grin, grinding my ass on his erection.

"Indeed," he hissed, thrusting his hips and driving his cock between my tender labia.

Lord, the man had stamina. He was hard as cement. I could have sworn the water heated another twenty degrees as his cock twitched, like a fervent metronome, between my folds.

Scooping me up in his arms, Nick made room for Dylan, who climbed into the tub. I leaned my head against Nick's solid chest as Dylan dipped to his knees and wedged himself between Nick's thighs. I smiled, sated and content, as Dylan wrapped his arms around me.

Neither man seemed uncomfortable entwining me between their naked bodies. Most men I knew would sling insulting gay slurs if they even spied another guy's junk. But these two extraordinary men were unlike any I'd ever met.

Tangled as one—a poignant testament of our commitment to each other.

"How do you feel, little one?" Nick asked as he doused a wash cloth in the sweet, floral scented shower gel.

Searching for words to express the myriad of emotions they cultivated. The warm silky water, their hot steely bodies, and the tender loving care they bestowed was a potent cocktail of serenity.

"Small," I sighed.

Dylan brushed the hair from my neck and leaned in. His warm lips settled on my pulse point, bathing me in reassurance. "Good, that's how you're supposed to feel, princess."

With a languid moan, I closed my eyes as they took turns washing every inch of my boneless body. Passing me back and forth as if I were a rag doll, their reassuring hands never abdicated my skin for more than a millisecond. Nimble fingers, murmured praises, and tender kisses soothed me like warm summer sun.

Finally, they positioned me against the side of the tub. I folded my arms upon the cool porcelain edge as they skimmed the wash cloth over my back and swollen petals. I rested head on my arms and closed my eyes.

Nick leaned in close to my ear as he cascaded a hand over my butt cheeks. "Your milky flesh holds a pink hue so nicely. It's a sight to behold."

My contented moan splintered to a scream of surprise as the jets engaged, pounding in fury against my clit. Fingers cinched my scalp and firm hands pressed down upon the small of my back, forcing me to remain in place as the jets thrummed a beguiling rhythm.

"I can't," I whimpered, snared between exhaustion and demand.

"You can. And you will," Dylan hissed. "You'll do anything we ask, because you live to please us, don't you sweet slut?"

The jets lashed my clit like an incessant tongue. "Yes," I mewled in pathetic accord.

I was soaring in seconds. The strumming water, the staggering need to please, the twin erections grinding on my hips, and their commanding fingers buried in my pussy and ass made it almost impossible to combat the hounding orgasm.

Their deep, hungry voices urged me higher while panic pumped in with ecstasy.

"So, hot. So precious," Nick whispered.

"Let it swallow you whole, kitten. Shatter for us."

Consent tumbled from Dylan's lips and my universe exploded in a blinding orgasm. I shrieked as the thundering release seized me. Clamped around the driving fingers, my entire body stiffened, and I was rolled beneath the blissful, brutal crushing waves.

"Yes," Dylan implored.

I succumbed to the crashing tides, thrashing and screaming as spasms shrieked through me. As I slowly ebbed back to earth, their capable fingers eased from my quivering passageways. The driving jets stung and burned my sensitized clit and it was too much, too intense. The pain was obnoxious. When the jets were finally extinguished, I cried out in relief.

I tried to reign in my breathing as the subsiding aftershocks fluttered through my core. The water swirled as both men moved, but my muscles refused to work. Spent and exhausted, I didn't even have strength to open my eyes. I issued a soft purr as a thick towel encased my shoulders and strong arms eased me out of the tub. Seconds later, I was cradled in safe, protective arms. I knew by his protective embrace that it was Dylan holding me against his steely chest. Even through the heavy scent of bath oil, I could smell his familiar musk.

"Sleep," I whimpered.

Nick chuckled as Dylan carried me from the bathroom. Through slitted lids, I watched Nick sit upon the bed, a dry towel draped over his bulging arm, waiting for me. They dried me with reverence before Dylan eased me onto the pillowy mattress. I closed my eyes and welcomed the dark murky haze that pulled me under.

I woke to the sound of their deep, rich laughter. Squinting against the bright sunlight filling the room, I watched Dylan kick the door shut behind him. Both men's arms were burdened with silver trays brimming with food. The tantalizing aromas hit me long before they'd made their way to the center of the room and placed the trays on the large round table. My mouth watered as I sat up and scampered out of bed, anxious to delve into the steaming assortment of food.

As I reached for a strip of crispy bacon, Dylan swatted the back of my hand.

"Not yet, kitten. There's a few more rules in this room than simply being naked ."

"You're not going to feed me again, are you, Masters?" I whined.

"Should I get the dog bowl out of the armoire?" Dylan asked Nick with a scowl.

"You have a dog bowl in there?" I felt my eyes flash wide and my mouth fall agape.

"Indeed we do," Nick replied with a staunch nod.

I made no effort to hide my repugnance. "I know some subs find great joy in pretending to be a puppy, pony or piggy, and far be it from me to judge anyone, but crawling on my hands and knees is as animal-like as I want to get, Master."

"We've already discovered that humiliation is a trigger for you, kitten," Dylan winked

"Then why did you suggest it, Sir?" I challenged.

Nick smirked. "To help you realize there are far worse things than us hand-feeding you, little one."

"So it was a trick?"

"No," Nick eyes narrowed with his firm tone. "It was push, girl. That's our job."

With a nod, I knelt upon the thick carpet, next to the table.

"Good girl," Dylan praised, running his fingers through my hair. A knowing smirk tugged one side of his mouth as a rush of heat streaked between my legs.

They each took a seat in the matching Parson's chairs, then looked at me with loving smiles. Confidence replaced my trepidation; a blind man could see the pride and joy etched on their faces. I didn't understand their compulsion with feeding me. But as I took the first bite of crispy bacon Dylan offered and licked the tip of his fingers, the heat darkening his eyes was all the reason I needed. But if they ever decided to pluck that damn dog bowl out, we'd have a serious conversation.

As Nick prepared the coffee, a soft chuckle rolled from his tongue. "I still can't get the look of shock on Rachel's face, out of my head."

"What happened?" I asked before taking a sip from the mug he'd lowered to my lips.

"She couldn't figure out why there was rice all over the kitchen floor when she came in this morning," Nick replied.

I felt my face warm. "What did you tell her, Master?"

"I told her what we did to you last night, little one."

"You did what?" I gasped. Mortification filled me. I'd have to face the woman at some point. God, how embarrassing and awkward the introduction would be now.

"Relax, kitten. She knows of our...penchants. She's just never been exposed to any aspect of it until now."

"So you've never brought a sub home from the club before, Sirs?"

"Never, pet," Dylan emphasized with a note of finality. My heart swelled.

"You're the first and the last," Nick added, settling his palm over my cheek.

"I'm honored, Master," I smiled.

"So are we, girl. So are we." Nick grinned, flashing that dazzling smile that always set my blood ablaze.

After breakfast, they carried up the suitcases from the truck and I unpacked my bags. They hauled in clothes and toiletries from their respective rooms, claiming ownership of the suite as a triad. More than once, tears filled my eyes at the significance of our union and with it, the promise of cultivating a stronger relationship.

Nick stole up behind me and wrapped me in his arms. "Yes, sweet girl. You're worth it and so much more."

"How can you *always* read me like a book, Master?" I laughed. Turning in his arms, I pressed a soft kiss to his lips. "Thank you. Thank you for all this and everything you've both given me."

"I'm just lucky that way. And you're welcome, precious." Nick smiled.

"No, kitten. Thank you for being brave and taking a chance with us." Dylan pressed against my back and nuzzled his lips upon my neck. "We've been searching for you for a very long time."

I exhaled on a dreamy sigh.

"A very long time," Nick emphasized. "Now let's go find buy you something to wear tonight."

"Where are we going?" I asked, giddy with excitement.

"Genesis, kitten." Dylan growled low in my ear.

"I know *that*, Master. I meant where are we going shopping?" I giggled.

"We'll hit Gurnee Mills, maybe stop in a few shops along the Magnificent Mile. But first we're going to take you to some special boutiques. Ones that cater specifically in club wear." Dylan winked.

"Permission to get ready?" I asked with a gleeful grin.

"Go, little one. Make it quick," Nick laughed at my over-enthusiastic mien. "Just tell me you're not one of those women who take a day and a half to get ready to go somewhere."

I laughed. "No, Master. I'll be ready in thirty minutes, tops."

Dylan issued an exaggerated groan. "She only takes a half a day, bro."

"Very funny, Sir." I rolled my eyes at his doleful complaint then scurried off to the bathroom.

After my anticipated prickly introduction to both Rachel and Pablo, we set out on our shopping quest. Our first stop was a corset shop. I was fitted and cinched, squeezed and bunched, and wondered how they expected me to breathe or even sit in the rigid garment.

After several adjustments, I was relieved to draw in a deep breath. Nick explained I was to grow accustomed to the garment over time. He promised that neither he or Dylan would cinch it too tight in the beginning. Reason being, Dylan explained, was that they didn't want me passing out during my first visit to Genesis.

I modeled an emerald brocade, corset with hand beading along the gentle sweetheart neck line. I felt like provocative and feminine and blushed at their approval, straining beneath their jeans.

I'd never know such stylish sex shops existed. I'd never set foot in *any* type of adult store. I'd purchased my vibrator from an on-line site. Wide-eyed and gushing at the various types of club wear and enticing toys, it wasn't long before I had more outfits than I could wear in a lifetime. Throughout our entire shopping blitz, neither man complained or grumbled. In fact, they were anxious for me to model each outfit, one after the other. Who was I to let them down?

Nick drove us to Maurizio's, a small Italian restaurant and bar, for lunch. It was nestled between large brick buildings in an older part of Chicago. As we walked through the front door, I prepared myself for the frosty and insulting appraisals. But when we were met with smiles and waves from several of the patrons, I realized they'd brought me to one of their usual haunts. They were protecting me from enduring another episode like the one we'd had at Ma's Kettle. With the anxiety that weighted me down as I'd walked through the doors now vanished. I wanted to pepper them both with kisses.

"Hey, Nick. Dylan. Where the hell have you two been?" cried a sandy haired man who was working behind the bar.

"Hey, Scotty." Dylan waved with a broad smile. "We just got back from our annual hunting trip."

"Glad to know you missed us," Nick laughed, as he wrapped his arm around my waist and led me to the bar.

"And who do we have here?" Scotty asked, a playful smile spread over his lips.

"Savannah, this is Scotty. Scotty this is *our* Savannah," Dylan introduced, his chest expanding.

"So you finally found her, did you?" Scotty nodded with a look of awe.

"Indeed we did." Nick preened.

"Took you two jokers long enough," He laughed before turning his full attention to me. "Savannah, it's a pleasure to meet you. And may I be the first to say that these two fuck-knuckles don't deserve anyone as gorgeous as you."

"Bite me," Dylan growled, as I bit back a giggle.

"Don't listen to him, little one. He's just jealous that we found you first," Nick replied with an arrogant smirk.

"Busted." Scotty winked. "Take a seat where ever you'd like. Carla will be out in a sec to take your order and hey…congratulations."

"Thanks man." Nick beamed.

"Thanks, bro." Dylan nodded.

I just smiled and cast a worshiping glance at my two gorgeous Masters.

After we'd squeezed together in one side of a booth, a short, dark-haired waitress with a bright smile took our orders.

Dylan teased her about her new boyfriend before she scurried away, laughing.

"So you two come here often, I take it?"

"Who are you talking to, girl?" Dylan asked arching his brows.

"Oh, I mean, Sirs." I glanced nervously to the couple seated near our booth and lowered my head. "Sirs."

"What was that, kitten? We didn't hear you."

"I said, Sirs," I whispered. My gaze was glued on the older, sophisticated-looking woman and her handsome son. Silently praying she wouldn't choke on her manicotti. I was confused when the woman simply arched a brow, before a soft smile spread upon her lips.

"Would you prefer to stand on the table and shout out the proper way to address us, little one? We can make that happen," Nick scolded.

I flashed him a look of fear. "No, Sir. I'd rather not do that."

"Then speak up and address us as you've been trained, girl," he instructed.

"I'm sorry Masters, I'm not used to…exposing my submission like this."

"Kitten, there are more lifestylers here than vanillas at the moment. That's one of the reasons we brought you here, so you could get accustomed to being in public with us."

"You mean some of these people are in the lifestyle, too?"

Before either of them could answer my question, an older man with a shiny bald spot came through the door. A petite blonde pixie clutched his elbow, laughing as if her father had just told her some hilarious joke.

"George!" Nick called with a wave in the air.

George and Leagh? I blinked. Neither of them looked anything like I'd imagined. I stared at the couple and tried to envision them together…as in *together*. George was light years older than young Leagh, who was latched to his side, bubbly and vivacious.

"Nick," George cried, a bright smile spreading over his wrinkled face. Seconds later, he and Leagh stood next to our booth. "Glad to see you made it back in one piece."

The older man appraised me for a brief second then turned his attention back on Dylan and Nick. Leagh's focus remained fixed on me. Her eyes flickered as a knowing smile spread across her petite mouth.

"May I, Master?" the young blonde asked in a low whisper.

"After Dylan and Nick have made the introductions, you may ask their permission, precious."

The feisty girl rolled her eyes and bobbed her head back and forth. Her body language screamed, 'get on with it already.' I chuckled.

"She doesn't need any help getting into trouble, kitten," Dylan warned me.

"Awww, I'm not that bad," Leagh protested with an insincere pout.

"No, you're worse," George growled. He pulled a red ball gag from the pocket of his suit coat and allowed it to dangle in front of Leagh's face.

I flashed a nervous look around the restaurant. The prim woman seated next to us looked at the swaying ball gag, then placed her fork on her plate.

"A red ass is what she needs," the woman stated in a droll tone.

"Oh come on, Mistress Ivory. I'm behaving, honest. I've done nothing wrong," Leagh protested with an impish grin.

"Yet, dear girl. And I say that with much faith," chuckled the stylish woman.

Mistress? Wow, Dylan wasn't lying; the whole place was crawling with Doms and subs. Upon further observation, I noticed that the young man seated with Mistress Ivory kept his head down. His attention was focused on the plate of food in front of him. *Definitely her sub.* Watching the young man, the worry that I wasn't showing the proper respect to either George or Ivory skittered through my brain. God, I didn't want to look like a novice, even *if* I was one. I certainly didn't want my actions to reflect badly on Dylan or Nick. Terrified I was somehow embarrassing my Masters, indecision and confusion had me all but crawling out of my skin. I tensed and cast my eyes to the table.

Dylan leaned in, brushing the hair from my shoulder. "You're doing fine, my love. Don't hide from our friends, we don't require strict protocols. Relax."

His warm breath sent a wave of relief. His hand clasped mine beneath the table, instilling was a much-needed shot of confidence. His anchor was a welcome respite from all the nerve-racking emotions blazing through me. I raised my head and smiled as Nick introduced me to George, Leagh, and Mistress Ivory. I cast an inquisitive glance at the young man seated with Ivory, uncertain as to why Nick had bypassed him.

"Ignore him," Mistress Ivory said with a wave of her hand. "My boy, Dark Desire, won't be joining in on this conversation or any other for a few days, I'm sorry to say."

She cast him a blasphemous look. Had I been on the receiving end of such distain, I'd have burst into tears. What dreadful thing had he done to warrant such scorching disapproval? As Mistress turned her attention back our way, the young man peeked at me beneath his dark lashes. I nibbled my lip then issued a weak smile, praying neither of us got caught sharing a subtle greeting. He seemed to be in enough trouble, I didn't want to add to it.

I felt a bizarre bond with Dark Desire, and with the boisterous pixie Leagh, as well. It was something akin to being on the same team, or strangely connected, in some weird way. I longed to pull them aside and find out what it was. But I knew it wasn't the right time.

"Yet, indeed," George agreed, pinning Leagh with an arbitrary look of disapproval before glancing back at Nick. "Hey, we never did get that snow storm you were talking about."

"Consider yourself lucky." Nick shook his head. "It was a bitch."

"Masterrrr," Leagh whined, hopping like an impatient bunny.

"Christ, girl, you're going to be the death of me," George grumbled. "You may ask."

Leagh squealed then bounced up on her tiptoes to plant a wet kiss on George's cheek.

"Thank you, Master." She cleared her throat with dramatic flair before clasping her hands behind her petite frame. Casting a hopeful glance to both Dylan and Nick, she smiled an impish grin. I wanted to giggle at her deferential attempt. "Sirs? May I please have permission to speak to your beautiful sub?"

"Now that didn't hurt at all, did it, Leagh?" Dylan teased.

Leagh clutched her hand around her neck. "Like broken glass lodged in my throat, Sir," she laughed.

"Well I'm glad you didn't choke," Nick smirked. "And yes, precious Dahlia, you may speak to Savannah."

"Oh goodie! Thank you, Sirs." Without warning, she leaned across the table and gripped me in a tight but awkwardly positioned hug. I felt a warm, sincere friendliness bubbling from inside her.

"It's so nice to meet you and it's way amazing that Sir Dylan and Sir Nick have finally found a girl to share." Her excited giggle made me smile, even if her words held a sense of backhanded compliment. But something about her made me realize that wasn't her intent. "There are gonna be submissive hearts breaking all over Genesis now. These two hunks have been making our sub sisters drool for years. They're going to be green. *Green*, I tell ya."

"Leagh." George interrupted. "That's more than enough, my little hellcat."

"Well, thank you, Leagh…I think," I snickered.

"Oh, yeah, it's a good thing they found you. I can already tell you'll be able to handle them. Trust me!" She winked.

"We'll leave you in peace to enjoy your lunch now," George announced with a weary sigh. "Glad you're home safe and sound. Savannah, it's been a pleasure meeting you, girl."

"Likewise, Sir George." I smiled.

Before turning away, George leaned down. "Keep her," he whispered under his breath to both my Masters.

"We plan on it." Nick beamed as George and Leagh walked across the restaurant to a vacant table.

"Just for the record, I totally agree with George." Mistress Ivory nodded with a cheeky grin. "Just sayin'."

Nick started to laugh. "She'll be accompanying us to the club tonight." He announced with a wide, proud smile.

"Oh, I'll look forward to watching you two work her." Ivory grinned.

Suddenly, the bottom fell out of my stomach. *Work her? What the hell did that mean?* I peeked at Dylan beneath my lashes, anxious for understanding.

"She mean's she'll enjoy watching us scene with you, kitten."

"You mean people are going to watch us, Sir?"

"Of course, little one," Nick replied as he turned in the booth, shielding me from the other patrons. "Trust us. We'd never hurt you."

"I know that Master, but can't we do that in your private room, instead?"

"Oh, we plan on it, kitten. That's a given." Dylan flashed an impish grin. "There's no need to worry. We'll always keep you safe."

Before I could begin to imagine what they would do to me in public, the waitress placed our drinks and three heaping bowls of salad on the table. My stomach rolled when the scent of Italian dressing wafted up my nose.

Trust them, Sanna. You've got to let go and trust them. They love you.

I hesitated then picked up my fork. "You okay, little one?" Nick's dark eyes drilled into mine, evaluating and reading my emotions as he always did.

A blanket of peace washed over me as I gazed into his twinkling eyes. "Yes, Master. I'm perfectly okay."

"God, I love you, girl," he whispered as he cupped my chin and captured my lips.

#

In the outer vestibule of Genesis, we stood in a long line. I felt naked in my corset and short ruffled skirt. The room buzzed as members laughed and chatted. Both Dylan and Nick took great pride in introducing me to the people around us. I smiled and greeted each person, and prayed I wasn't expected to remember all their names. Muffled sounds of paddles and whips filled the air, growing louder as members passed through a thick curtain near the front of the line. I was anxious to see what lay beyond, in the next room.

Antsy and self-conscious of my bountiful cleavage and barely covered thighs, I couldn't stop tugging at my trench coat.

"You look stunning, little one. Stop fidgeting," Nick growled in my ear.

"I'm trying Master, really I am," I whispered, nibbling my bottom lip.

"Everyone will love you, kitten. Please don't be nervous. Think of us as a big extended family that enjoys the kinkier side of life." Dylan coaxed.

"Seriously, Master. I doubt my Aunt Emily, the crazy cat lady of Tulsa, is into this stuff."

"I thought you only had Mellie?" Dylan asked in confusion.

"We don't talk to Aunt Emily for a reason," I chuckled. "She's crazy. I mean, full-on bonkers. Like, little white coat with funny sleeves crazy. My own dad wouldn't even talk to her, and she was his *only* sister."

"So does mental illness run in your family, kitten?" Dylan sobered.

"No!" I hissed in a hushed whisper.

He and Nick started to laugh. I rolled my eyes and issued an exasperated sigh.

"Admit it. I got you to relax just a little bit now, didn't I?" Dylan winked with an ornery grin.

I sent him a half smirk then leaned up and kissed his cheek. "Yes, Master. Thank you."

Looking around at the growing group of lifestylers, I found solace that there were so many others like me in the world. The submissives I'd met were welcoming and put me somewhat at ease--at least until I spied a big, burly biker-looking dude who was dressed in leather, standing near a podium at the front of the lobby. Tattoos covered his beefy arms and his expression was tight and stern. A stunning woman with thick red hair and enchanting green eyes stood on his left, smiling and talking to the members as they waited at the podium. On his right was a thin young man with long, silky blonde hair. His infectious giggles and overt gestures made me smile.

"Who are they?" I whispered in Nick's ear, feeling intimidated by the massive man in leather.

"That's Drake, his submissive and life partner Trevor, and the woman is the person we've been anxious for you to meet. That's Emerald."

"Are they a threesome, too?"

"No," Nick shook his head. "Emerald isn't Drake's sub, but she is under his protection. She doesn't have a Master yet, so she goes to Drake if she has a problem or needs help with her submission."

"I bet nobody messes with her. That guy is intimidating," I whispered under my breath.

"Drake's a good guy. One of the best Masters I've ever known. And his single tail skills are impeccable." Nick praised.

"He and Trevor are amazing to watch when they scene, kitten. You've got to see them together." Dylan added with a smile.

I frowned. Was Dylan talking about us watching them have sex? Did *everyone* in the club have public sex? Surely they didn't expect *me* to have sex with them while everyone watched, did they? I had no idea what to expect. My mind was zipping like a lab rat in a maze.

As I continued to stare at the threesome behind the podium, Emerald looked my way. She glanced at Dylan and Nick then a broad smile spread over her full, red lips. I watched as she leaned over and whispered into Drake's ear. Suddenly, he raised his eyes and leveled me with a stare. I felt myself shrink like a violet in the desert. Swallowing tightly, I cast my eyes toward my black stilettos.

"What's wrong, pet?" Nick mumbled in my ear.

"I don't know if I can do this," I confessed.

"Do you trust us to take care of you?" Nick asked, trailing kisses over my jaw and down my neck.

I raised my eyes, melting beneath his touch and his reassuring smile. "Yes, Master."

"Thank you, little one. Then everything else will be perfectly fine."

I felt fine again, until it was our turn at the podium to be checked into the club. Drake's gray eyes sparkled to life as he welcomed my Masters back. I hadn't expected such a drastic change in his gruff demeanor, but I still trembled when he shook my hand. Trevor and Emerald were courteous and I sensed an undercurrent of excitement as Dylan made their introductions.

"Emerald, if you happen to have some time to spare over the next few weeks, we'd like to ask you to help Savannah get more acclimated to submissive life."

"I'd be honored Sir Nick," she respectfully replied.

Emerald's smile could have lit up all of Las Vegas. When she turned and looked at me, I could feel her compassion and wholehearted acceptance. In the ten seconds since we'd met, I knew I wanted to spend a lot more time with her, learning everything she could teach me.

"We have sub meetings every Saturday morning from nine until noon here at the club," she began. "Don't be shy. Come and join us. We talk about a lot of different topics. Some will help you now and some will help you further down the road. Plus, Trevor and I always compete to see who makes the most sinful munchies."

"She doesn't kick my ass often, but she does make the best brownies on earth," Trevor laughed then blew a kiss to Emerald.

"Thank you. I'd really like that, if I get permission," I added, looking between my Masters. Emerald's welcoming mien did more to calm the butterflies swirling in my stomach than I could have accomplished on my own.

"We wouldn't have asked for her help otherwise, kitten." Dylan smiled.

I signed a long waiver filled with legal mumbo-jumbo before Dylan tugged my coat away, tossed it over his arm, then pulled back the heavy velvet curtain.

I held my breath.

CHAPTER THIRTEEN

My heart was in my throat as the curtain slid closed behind us. I tried to take in every sight, sound and sensation, but I couldn't. I was in BDSM overload. Having read about dungeons, it was plain to see that their friend--Michael, Mika, Mitchell; hell, I couldn't remember his name--had spared no expense on Genesis. It was gorgeous. More stations lined the walls than I could count. They were filled with submissives enjoying a plethora of sensations by their Masters and Mistresses.

Numerous tables filled the center of the room, each adorned in ambient candlelight where members sat watching and talking in low voices, sipping drinks. The sweet scent of leather, combined with a hint of vanilla and melded with the musky tinges of sex, hung heavy in the air.

Dylan stowed my coat then he and Nick ushered me toward a gleaming mahogany bar, waving and smiling to members along the way. A tiny blonde woman with twinkling blue eyes and enormous boobs moved efficiently behind the long counter, filling plastic cups with ice, sodas and juices.

Nick leaned in and whispered against my ear. "That's Sammie. She's our resident Domme and bar mistress extraordinaire. Come on, let's get a drink."

I nodded, still enthralled at being in an actual BDSM club. As we sat down on the tall bar stools, I continued to try and watch it all.

"There you two are," Sammie exclaimed with a saucy and sassy smile. "I thought you'd gone off and forgotten us. Oh, and who do we have here?"

Her blue eyes danced over my face then my corset and down my legs, smiling in approval. "Sammie, this is our girl, Savannah," Nick gloated, his smile growing wider.

"It's a pleasure to meet you, Savannah." She extended a petite hand. Her long nails were painted a blood red color.

"A pleasure to meet you as well, Ma'am." I smiled with a soft shake of her tiny hand.

"Oh, such good manners, too," Sammie winked. "You two better hang on to this one."

"We fully intend to," Dylan piped up with a buoyant smile.

"Good to hear. Now, what can I get you all to drink?" She asked with a wink.

Nick ordered sodas for us, then turned the stool I was sitting on until I faced away from the bar.

"Watch, little one," he instructed as he rested his wide hand upon my bare knee. His warmth heated my blood.

Dylan draped his arm around my shoulder and for the first time all night, I felt absolute calm. Sheltered in their protection, I felt brave and safe.

As I sipped my drink, I focused on the different sizes and ages of the subs. Most were naked and none seemed bothered by it. I couldn't understand how they weren't at least a little embarrassed, but if they were, they didn't show it. Not at all.

An extremely large woman and her Master stepped up to a tall, unoccupied wooden frame. As she began to shed her clothing while her Master assembled his toys, I felt the heat rise over my cheeks. She was what was termed, in lifestyle jargon, A Big Beautiful Woman. Soon she was standing naked, awaiting her Master's instructions. Her ankles were almost the size of my thighs. And her pitted flesh sagged in rolls that resembled bread dough. But I found myself awed by her grace; floored by her self-assurance, and envious of her bravery. It shamed me to realize that I lacked the confidence she readily displayed.

The crack of a whip drew my attention to the other side of the dungeon. I blinked in surprise when I recognized the couple. It was Mistress Ivory and her sub, Dark Desires. Tethered to a cross, Dark held his head high. Pride radiated from his posture. Mesmerized, I watched Ivory coil the long leather whip into the air then land it with a deafening *whack* against his narrow ass cheeks. A bright red stripe bloomed before my eyes and his loud cry of anguish chased gooseflesh up my arms.

"It's okay, kitten. Dark enjoys pain." Dylan assured, trying to alleviate my angst.

"I don't think I'd ever enjoy something that brutal, Master," I confessed, feeling my face pinch in a pained expression.

"There she goes," Nick murmured. A hint of admiration resonated in his tone.

I turned to see what had captured his attention. It was the large woman cuffed to the tall wooden frame. Her Master's hand trailed up and down her overabundant flesh as he whispered in her ear. He gripped a long, leather flogger in his fist and when he stepped back and began brushing the leather falls over her back and butt, a wistful smile curled on her lips. Her eyes were glassy and her body glowed in an ethereal serenity. I realized beauty had transcended her physical form; lost in her submission, she was the most breathtaking woman I'd ever seen.

"Oh, wow," I marveled.

"Remember when I told you submission comes in all ages, little one?" Nick paused as I nodded. "Well it also comes in all shapes and sizes. I wanted you to watch so you would understand. It's not the body that makes the submissive, but rather what's inside their heart. That's where the true beauty lies."

Nick's words contained an almost magical cadence. The woman had touched not only her Master, who wore a blatant expression of satisfaction; but emanated her gift of submission to my Master, as well. Caressing his fingers over my cheek, Nick and I continued to watch the woman as she sailed. Her expressions were enthralling. Every clip of the flogger seemed to send her deeper into that silent white space that I'd experienced at the barn. The same surreal place that I longed to be again.

"I'd love to be free like her, Master," I sighed.

"Do you feel brave, kitten?" Dylan asked with a sly smile.

"How brave, Master?" I gulped, realizing I'd just opened a dangerous door.

"Would you like to soar again?"

"If I can keep my clothes on, then yes, Master." I bargained.

"What makes you think you get to make the rules, little one?" Nick's brow arched, his eyes flashed in warning. "You'll need to take your skirt off," he laughed as he no doubt saw the look of terror dancing across my face.

"Technically you'll be covered, kitten. You're wearing that sexy black thong," Dylan growled, then snapped his teeth together like a hungry wolf.

"I don't know if I can get up in front of all these people," I confessed in a thin voice.

"We'll be right there with you, kitten. Just close your eyes and pretend we're all alone. Can you do that for us?"

Dylan's expectant look rocked me to the core. The need to represent them in an outward submissive fashion swarmed me. It was their duty as my Masters to push my limits. I would stagnate if I only submitted to the things I enjoyed. And they had bestowed so much enjoyment on me, granting their desires seemed the only logical way for me to reaffirm my dedication to them.

"Yes, Master. I would love to." The words spilled from my lips before I could think better of it. But when I saw their eyes light up in delight, I realized there was no way I could take back my words; nor did I have any desire to. These were our roles. They defined who we were and what we strived to fulfill. Courage spiked. I eased off the bar stool.

"Hold on a minute, little one," Nick chuckled. We need to discuss the scene first. But your eagerness pleases me, girl. Pleases me immensely." His lips crushed upon mine and I swallowed his growl.

Long minutes passed and I drowned on the taste of his unadulterated happiness. When he released me, his expression turned solemn and his Dominant expression set my blood ablaze.

"You will be cuffed to the St. Andrews cross, similar to the equipment Dark is tethered to. We will flog your backside. The entire time, the club members will only be able to see your back. We intend to only use our hands and the flogger. Your safe word is still 'red.' Do you accept the type of scene I've described?" Nick's words were quiet yet firm.

I had no idea where the sudden shot of bravery came from, but without hesitation, I nodded. I smiled when pride flash in his sexy, dark eyes.

"Very well. I'll be right back," Nick announced as he stood and hurried past the bar then down a long corridor.

"Where is he going?"

"To our private room to get the flogger, kitten." Dylan winked.

"Can we play in there, instead?"

"We will. Later. When we're ready to sink balls deep into your hot little body, kitten."

Dylan leaned in and dusted a slow, sensual kiss over my lips. His tawdry words chased a sizzling visual to my brain of him thrusting his hard cock into my pussy while wearing that intense, focused expression on his face. My body began to hum. As he pulled back, I sighed.

"I think we should start there, now, Master."

"We want you to fly first, my greedy little slut."

Dylan plucked the drink from my hand, drawing me back from my daydream, then stood. "Come on, kitten. Nick's got a spot for us. It's time to go to paradise, my love."

As I eased off the stool, my heart thundered in my chest. My knees shook and I wondered where my bravery had run off to. Dylan secured me against his side, in a commanding hold. Looking across the room, I saw Nick standing next to a cross. His hands were behind his back, his legs were set apart and his shimmering black hair draped over his broad shoulders. I couldn't help but shiver at the palpable command oozing from his every pore. I darted a glance at Dylan as we made our way to the station. He held his head high in regal pride. Everything about him reflected in a powerful Dominant air. When he released me, standing shoulder-to-shoulder with Nick, their faces beamed in a potent reflection of privilege and pride. And I belonged to them.

My Masters.

My guides.

Make them proud, Sanna. Trust them. For once, just trust them without one reservation.

I squared my shoulders and raised my head, hoping to exhibit the courage Dark displayed representing Ivory. They'd selected *me* to be their submissive. And now it was time to prove that they'd made the right choice.

Nick drew me to his chest, his warm breath skimming over the shell of my ear. "Our brave, beautiful slut, you are a sheer treasure. You fill us with such joy. Words can't express how special you are to us. Now take off your skirt."

Staggered by the euphoria and fear his words prompted, a part of me wanted to sing with joy while another part wanted to run and hide. My fingers trembled as I inched the black ruffled skirt from my hips. Dylan stood behind me, protective as promised, shielding my bare ass from prying eyes.

"I think this will help you, little one, at least until we send you soaring." Nick pulled a black satin blindfold from behind his back.

"Thank you, Master." My voice cracked as he placed the soft shield over my eyes.

"We are with you kitten, and will remain the entire time." I shivered as Dylan's breath wafted over my neck. "Remember, your safe word is red. Use it if you need to. Do you understand?"

"Yes, Master. Red. I understand."

"That's our girl. Just relax, baby and we'll set you free," Nick promised in a soothing voice.

They worked in tandem to secure my wrists in downy-lined cuffs. I felt the eyes of the members on me and heard them whispering Dylan and Nick's names. A tremor rippled through me then stilled as a broad hand pressed against my lower back, urging me to lean into the cold wooden frame.

"We're going to warm you up, little one," Nick announced. "Fly as high as you desire, my love. We'll be here to catch you and glide you back to earth."

As soon as he stepped back, I mourned the loss of his body heat, the reassurance of his words and the safety of having him near.

Their hands slapped and squeezed my supple flesh, and their words of encouragement fluttered over me like snowflakes. The first strike of the heavy, soft flogger drew a yelp of surprise from my throat.

"Easy, kitten," Dylan soothed. "Absorb the tranquil rhythm."

Though the blindfold blocked out all light, I squeezed my eyes shut and focused on the tempo of the floggers, landing in supple thuds. It wasn't long before I began to drift away from my apprehension, sliding past the buzzing voices that had filled my ears. Surrounded in peace, all the chaos in my head silenced

Time ceased and conscious thought melted away. I soared in clouds of white light. The lulling rhythm stalled from time to time. The soft leather falls were replaced with the warm, broad hands of my Masters. They soothed my tender flesh as their rich, commanding voices bathed me in praise. Their rugged, hot bodies meshed against mine in affirmation that I was anchored to their chain of Dominance.

Something tugged at my torso, pulling me back from the clouds. Confusion began to sully my brain. Their hands were all over me; up my stomach and arms, down my legs and over my throbbing butt cheeks. And still, the ebb and pull against my back persisted. Suddenly, the constricting corset fell from my body. Long seconds ticked by and the realization that I was naked, except for the tiny scrap of fabric over my mound, crashed over me. Gripped in icy terror, I tried to run but was imprisoned to the wooden cross. Trapped. Captured. Confined.

Obliterated beneath an onslaught of panic, I thrashed, trying to break free.

"RED!" I screamed, jerking impotently against my shackles in a futile fight to cover my breasts.

"Savannah!" Nick's thunderous voice resonated in my ears. "Stop, pet. We're here. It's okay. You're okay."

But I wasn't okay. I was lost in a haze of terror that gripped my heart and stole my breath.

"Back away, Nick. You too, Dylan. You guys know the rules."

Who was that? I had no clue. Someone was issuing instructions to my Masters to leave me. A new wave of panic consumed me and tears filled my eyes.

"No!" I cried, struggling with such force, the cuffs bit into my skin. "Don't leave me! Please don't leave me, Masters!"

"We're right here, little one," Nick reassured, then issued a whispered curse.

Suddenly, the blindfold was removed. A man I'd never seen before was there. He'd stepped behind the cross and had his hands wrapped around my cheeks.

"Don't touch me." I cried. "I don't know you."

"Shhhh, calm down, girl." The stranger's black eyes reflected understanding, but it did little to alleviate the frenzy of emotions that had taken control of me.

"Don't look at me," I sobbed, as tears spilled down my cheeks. "I'm naked."

"I'm not looking at anything except your beautiful eyes, pet." He replied in a soft, calm voice. His gaze remained fixed on mine. "My name is Tony. I'm a dungeon monitor. I need you to relax and listen to me. I'm not going to hurt you and you have my promise that I won't look at anything but your eyes, okay?"

I nodded and tried to suck breath into my lungs. "Where are my Masters?" I mewled.

"We're right here, baby," Dylan responded from somewhere from behind me. "You have to talk to Tony right now, love. Just breathe, everything is okay. We're not going anywhere, I promise."

"See. They're right here with you…Savannah, is it?" Tony asked, never breaking eye contact.

"Yes," I nodded. "Cover me up, please."

"We're working on that, girl. I need you to focus on me for a minute. Can you do that?" His voice was so serene, yet I couldn't grasp onto any semblance of tranquility.

"Tony, can you hurry? Please?" Nick's appeal was fraught with anxiety.

"Hold on, Nick. You know I have to assess."

"Fuck," Dylan spat.

"Dylan," Tony warned, flashing a look of irritation over my shoulder.

"What do you need to know?" I sniffed, trying to wrangle my scattered emotions. I was anxious to for my embarrassing fiasco to end.

"I need to know if you're physically or mentally hurt, Savannah. I have to find out if either Dylan or Nick overstepped their boundaries as Masters."

"I'm not hurt. They'd never hurt me. I'm just being stupid," I hissed, certain that everyone in the club was watching my childish melt-down. "Can you let me go now?"

A broad smile spread over his lips. "In a minute, girl. You've hit a limit and we're here to help you through it."

Suddenly, a soft cotton blanket draped over my bare shoulders.

"Thank you, Emerald," Nick replied, as he pressed his warm body against the blanket, swathing me in his heat and a blessed protective barrier. "Relax, little one. We'll get you back to our room as soon as we can, okay?"

I turned my head and looked into Nick's sad eyes. "I'm so sorry I failed you, Master." My vision blurred as hot tears spilled down my face.

"Oh, pet. You didn't fail us." He buried his lips against my neck, whispering his reassurance. "We weren't going to expose you to the club, baby. We'd never push you in public like that. Not your first time. I'm so damn sorry we didn't discuss it first, baby."

His anguish tore my heart to shreds. He was blaming himself for my insecurities. "It's not your fault, Master. It's not."

Dylan moved in beside me as Tony began releasing my wrists from the cuffs. "We'll talk it through in a few minutes, kitten. But baby, you didn't fail. You did everything right."

"No, Master. I didn't," I whined. "It's all my fault. I failed you both."

"Pet, you could never fail us," Nick assured, wiping the trailing moisture from my cheeks.

"We need to have a chat, you two." Tony issued a heavy sigh as he fixed a serious gaze on each of my Masters.

"We know," Nick growled and pulled a key from his pocket. "Emerald, will you please take Savannah to our room. We'll be along in a couple of minutes."

"Of course, Sir," Emerald replied as she accepted the key. Stepping up to the cross, her smile was filled with understanding.

"But I want to stay with you, two." I prayed they weren't in trouble because of me.

"This is only going to take a couple minutes. We'll meet you there, pet," Nick pressed with a grim nod.

"Come on sis, they really won't be long, I promise." Emerald smiled, tucking the blanket around me before she slid her arm around my shoulder and began leading me away.

I cast a frightened glance over my shoulder. Both my Masters looked decimated by guilt.

"Hurry, please?" I begged.

"We will, kitten. We will." Dylan nodded.

I kept my head down as Savannah escorted me through the dungeon. I couldn't bear to look at any of the other members as my embarrassment blazed. She led me down the same long hallway I'd watched Nick take earlier.

"One sec and we'll be inside, sis." She shoved the key into the knob and turned it. Flipping on the lights, we advanced into the big, bright room.

Seeing my Masters' private chamber for the first time wasn't the experience I'd envisioned. I was led in by another sub and blubbering like a loon. No, that's not at all how I'd pictured it would be.

"Here, sweetheart. Put this on." Emerald held out a white silk robe with the word "*Genesis*" embroidered on the breast pocket.

"I feel like such a fool. Oh my God, how can I face anyone here again?" I sobbed, wondering if I'd ever gain control of myself or my fears.

"Stop that. You didn't do anything wrong," Emerald scolded as she tied the silky sash at my waist. "Come on, sit down. Let's talk."

She plopped down on a huge bed, patting the mattress beneath her long slender hand.

"They'll never want to bring me here again," I groused, wiping my eyes.

"Savannah, honestly, stop. You did exactly what you what you were supposed to do, you safe worded out."

"But they didn't hurt me. I only called my safe word because I was embarrassed."

"You hit a limit. It doesn't have to be a physical limit, honey. It can be a mental one, as well. Hell, we all have limits and triggers and buttons that bring up ugly feelings inside. It doesn't mean you failed, and it certainly doesn't make you a bad submissive. It makes you human."

"But I got them in trouble with that dungeon manager...Tony."

"Dungeon *monitor*. And they're not in trouble. They just have to explain to him what happened. By the looks of both of them, they're kicking their own asses and drowning in guilt about it."

"That's what I *don't* want them to do. It's not their fault, it's mine," I huffed as guilt and insecurity continued to swirl out of control.

The fear of them rejecting me, of deciding I wasn't capable of submitting to them; at least not the way they needed, swamped every cell in my body. I knew that Emerald was trying to help, but until Dylan and Nick walked through the door and held me in their arms, nothing on the planet was going to erase my panic.

"Listen to me, Savannah. I would never lie to you or anyone else. You're *not* the first submissive to use their safe word and I can guarantee you won't be the last. Safe words are there for a reason. Sir Dylan and Sir Nick will be proud you weren't afraid to use yours. Too many subs don't. They end up getting hurt or making their Doms not trust them. Your Masters are just going through the safety precautions that Genesis has in place. Without them, none of us would be able to play in a safe, sane and consensual environment."

"You seriously think they're not going to be mad at me and want to dump me as soon as they walk in that door?"

"Not in a million." Emerald shook her head with a sorrowful. She wrapped me in a tight hug and pulled me close. "Honey, they'd never do that. I've seen the way they look at you. God, Savannah, they're so in love with you. I've never seen them so happy in all the years I've known them. You bring light to their eyes. They're not going to release you. Ever. Especially not over this."

Relief tried to break through my grieving haze as Emerald hugged me tight. I wanted to believe her... She was so certain about how my Masters would react, and I wished like hell I could share her conviction.

I didn't even know the girl, yet she showered me with so much acceptance and understanding, it blew my mind. When she pulled back, I palmed my eyes, sniffing as I struggled to regain my composure.

"I'll make you a deal. If they decide they don't want you, I'll have Daddy Drake kick their asses, how's that?" She grinned.

"I've already done that," I groaned.

"You what?" Emerald gasped.

"Long story. Let's just say it was an all-star example of my act-first-think-later stupidity. Just like what I did out there." An exasperated huff rushed from my lips.

"You'll have to tell me about that one of these days, but first you need to stop beating yourself up. Or I'll be forced to bring Daddy Drake in here to convince you that you did the right thing."

"No thanks, he's a scary-looking dude." I sobered, hoping she wasn't serious.

"Oh, pfffhh," she dismissed my comment with a wave of her hand. "He's nothing but a giant teddy bear. He just looks bad-ass because he likes to intimidate people."

I couldn't help but chuckle at the way she described the leather-clad Dom. It would take me a long time to see any teddy bear-like qualities in that man.

"Listen to me. Stop worrying. I know what I'm talking about. Everything is going to be okay." She issued the assurance just as Dylan and Nick came bursting through the door.

They froze, staring at me. I knew I looked all snot-nosed and blotchy-faced. My heart leapt to my throat. Tears spiked once again as I jumped from the bed and ran to them, scared of how I'd be received. When they spread their arms and crushed me to their rock-hard chests, I fell apart.

"I'm going to leave you three to talk things out now, with your permission, Sirs?" Emerald beamed.

"Of course, pet, and thank you," Nick choked as Emerald hurried toward the door.

"Anytime, Sir. Savannah is a love of a girl. I look forward to seeing her again on Saturday," Emerald replied before darting out of the room and closing the door behind her.

"Yes, you are a love. *Our* love," Dylan decreed before laying siege to my lips.

"Come on. We need to discuss what happened out there," Nick announced.

I moaned in regret when Dylan released my lips. I didn't want to talk. I wanted to stay right where I was: wrapped in their safe, loving arms.

I tried drying my eyes as we sat on the bed. Nick kissed my temple then cleared his throat. But before he could speak, I charged ahead of him.

"You're mad at me, I know. I'm sorry I embarrassed you and screamed my safe word."

Nick shook his head. "First of all, we are not mad at you. You did nothing to embarrass us. Trust us, little one; it's reassuring to know you won't hesitate to call your safe word. But…"

There it was; a big fat ugly *but*. I knew what was coming next.

"But you don't want me as your submissive anymore, right?" I asked in a fearful whisper.

"What?" they both thundered, slashing me with identical looks of disbelief.

"No. But I'm going to get a ball gag to keep you quiet, and maybe a hammer so I can knock the insecurities out of your system," Nick growled.

I closed my eyes wishing we'd never come to Genesis after all. We could be rolling in our big bed and making love 'till the sun came up, instead of dealing with my fucking fears.

"Do you trust us?" Dylan asked. The distress in his voice was unmistakable. "Think long and hard before you answer me, pet."

Of course I trusted them. How could he ask such a thing?

"Yes, Master. I trust you with my life."

"We don't think you do, little one. If you trusted us, you wouldn't have freaked out. You would have realized that although we'd removed your corset, we never would have turned you around and exposed you to the club," Nick explained. "We'd fully intended to keep your body flush against the cross until the session was done, then wrapped you in a blanket to bring you back here."

"We know your buttons, kitten. We were not intentionally pushing them. Not in your first public scene." Dylan interjected.

Their words felt like an anvil upon my heart. I may have done all the right things during the session, but I'd failed them by not trusting their Dominance. Drowning in guilt, I bit back a sob.

"That's right. We were not pushing, pet. We simply wanted to flog your back. Your ass was getting so red and Christ, you were flying so damn high. We wanted to keep you suspended for a good long time," Nick continued. "Tell us what happened in your head when the corset came off."

I sucked in a ragged breath. "I wasn't thinking about anything. I was floating then it was like I was pulled back into my body. As soon as I realized I was naked, I freaked out. I'm sorry. In my head, I wasn't thinking about Dominance or submission, it was all a knee-jerk reaction brought on by fear."

"We're sorry, too, kitten. We handled the scene badly. We handled *you* badly," Dylan professed.

I turned and wrapped my hands around Dylan's sad face. The contrition in his eyes stabbed my soul. "Oh, Master. No. No. No." I sobbed. "You didn't handle anything badly. It was me. Please forgive me. I love you. I love you both so much. I wanted to be brave and make you both so proud. But instead I …I freaked out. God, I'm so sorry."

"Shhh, kitten," Dylan soothed. He pulled my wrists from his face then placed a tender kiss in each palm. "Stop feeling like you failed us. You've never failed us. This is nothing more than a learning experience. Nick and I now know that next time…"

I gasped as my eyes grew wide.

"Oh yes, there will be a next time," Nick chuckled. "But next time, we know to bring you back down. Explain exactly what we're going to do, until our relationship has had a chance to grow more substantially. I think if we can circumvent those fears of yours, you'll stay in the moment and trust us not to let you fall."

It sounded good in theory and I wanted to believe they had the power to keep my stupid fears at bay. But what if I never grew past the insecurities? What if they were hardwired into my psyche or something?

"I'm not sure how to lay my insecurities to rest. But I promise I'll try and keep instinct from taking over. I'd like to see if Emerald can help me, if you two don't mind?"

"We don't mind a bit, kitten. That's why we plan to bring you here every Saturday. We hope that by talking with other submissives, you'll see the exchange in another point of view. And maybe it will help you better understand some of the fears you carry."

"Agreed." Nick nodded. "Come. Lay down, little one. We definitely need to hold you."

Wrapped in their arms, the feel of their lips against my flesh and soft spoken words of reassurance vanquished the fears and insecurities that had lingered. Yet I couldn't stop apologizing, until finally Dylan commanded I put the incident behind me and move forward. Voicing my worry that I'd gotten them into trouble, Nick assured me that Tony understood the situation, and all was well.

"He seemed like a compassionate man," I commented in regard to Tony.

"He's an amazing person. Another well-respected Dom and a bit on the sadistic side, but a top-notch guy." Dylan appraised.

"Sadistic. You mean like Mistress Ivory?"

"She goes by Lady Ivory here, but you're addressing her correctly as Mistress, kitten." Dylan reaffirmed. "But no, Ivory isn't even in the same ballpark as Tony when it comes to doling out pain," Dylan chuckled.

"Ouch. He sounds scary."

"He's not. In fact, he has quite a stable of pain sluts that thoroughly enjoy him," Nick replied. "Speaking of being thoroughly enjoyed, are you up for some private fun, little one?"

A broad smile spread across my lips. "With my two amazing Masters? Always," I purred.

Nick leapt from the bed and extended his hand. "We want to watch you fly again, pet. Can you do that for us?"

"Oh, yes, Master," I gushed and slipped my hand in his.

Nick tugged me off the bed and Dylan tumbled behind me, peeling away my silky robe. He trailed soft kisses over my shoulders and down my spine, sending ripples of pleasure over my body.

Nick pulled a wooden suspension frame out from against one wall as a devilish smile played on his lips. "We're alone, but you still have the responsibility of using your safe word. Understood?"

I admired his arched brows and commanding mien. "Of course, Master. But I know I won't need it now."

"Don't be too sure about that, kitten," Dylan growled as he reached up and tweaked my nipple.

I hissed as shards of fire rippled through my breast and centered in my core. "Yes, Sir." I grinned with a saucy wink.

"Arms up, kitten. I've wanted to do this for a long time," Dylan announced, gathering up several bundles of rope.

"Shibari," I whispered on a wistful sigh.

"Yes, kitten. Shibari and a little bit of torment." He chuckled as Nick positioned me under the large frame.

Chills skittered through me. I closed my eyes as Dylan wrapped the first strand of rope around my wrists. Nick framed my face beneath his broad hands, skimming his lips over mine. He bathed me in reverent, tender passion. Sailing higher beneath each knot, I floated away as the rope secured my arms and bound tight against my torso.

When Dylan cinched the soft cotton upon my clit, I cried out and quivered. Nick paid infinite attention to my throbbing nipples. Fiery need thundered through my veins and I wiggled upon the clustered bundle of rope, burnishing it against my clit.

"Delight all you'd like in that hard little knot, sweet slut. Just remember, you don't have permission to come," Nick growled in command.

"Yes, Master," I whispered breathlessly, rocking and soaring.

A squeal of surprise tore from my throat as I was hoisted into the air. Suspended to the frame and poised like cupid, I hovered on my side, spinning in a slow circle. Dylan and Nick stood back, admiring their work. Lust danced in their eyes and hungry smiles adorned their handsome faces. The confinement of the rope, coupled with floating in a languid swirl, served to heighten my increasing journey into sub-space.

"How do you feel, kitten?" Dylan asked as they began to remove their clothes.

"Incredible, Master," I sighed. "The ropes are tight. Don't hurt. Flying in heaven." Finding it hard to string my sentences together, I felt drugged and fought the desire to close my eyes. Even, the inviting clouds of light weren't incentive enough for me to miss the opportunity to watch them strip.

Once nude, they stood before me. Their sculpted bodies and rigid cocks were a breathtaking sight to behold. With sturdy hands they gripped my bound limbs, making me sway back and forth as they guided their glistening cocks deep inside my mouth. With a mewl, I sucked their swollen shafts, breathed in their potent musk, and collected their unique flavors on my tongue. Their combined essence was like sweet ambrosia.

The bisecting knot chaffed my clit with each punishing thrust. Sailing toward the stars, I gave myself over to them, welcoming my mounting need. Dylan swiveled me back toward Nick and I focused on his sturdy cock as he thrust it between my lips. Tempering my frustration at not being able to touch them the way I desired, My vexation vanished when Dylan wedged his head between my thighs and tugged the knot with his teeth. I moaned and rocked against his mouth as much as my limited movement allowed. Sucking deep, I worshiped Nick with compelling vigor. But when Dylan teased my bisected folds with his talented tongue, I tore my lips from Nick's cock and cried out in a desperate plea. My cries were left unanswered and I whimpered in their denial.

Nick cinched a mighty fist in my hair, pulling my mouth back to his turgid shaft before shuttling his cock between my stretched lips, until I felt him swell upon my tongue. His loud roar of ecstasy resonated in my ears as he showered my throat with slick, warm seed. Dylan continued to nip and lick my aching center, and as I swallowed Nick's offering, I felt the familiar numbness consume my tethered limbs.

I keened over Nick's shaft as I swallowed the last of his milky treasure. He pulled from my mouth with an abrupt halt. Cradling my face in his hands, his loving voice fell over my skin like smooth whiskey. "Open your eyes, little one," he coaxed. His voice was hoarse but his command resolute. "I want to watch you shatter, sweet baby."

Peering at him through slitted lids, I found him kneeling in front of me. His expression was soft and filled with such vivid love, I wanted to weep.

"Now, our beautiful girl. Come now for us."

Nick's mouth claimed mine and he swallowed my cries of deliverance as Dylan launched me to oblivion. I thrashed helplessly upon the massive frame as wave after wave crashed through me. All the while, Nick held my mouth captive, drinking down my screams and moans.

Nick finally released his claim, spinning my convulsing body away. Dylan gripped my hair now, and speared his slick shaft past my lips. Pumping in a manic rhythm, his feral cry soon filled the air as he showered my throat in a torrent of spicy, slick come.

My body quivered in aftershocks as I sucked the vestiges from Dylan's cock. Nick began to release the ropes with great care then eased me down, back on my feet. Flying and sated, I sagged against my bindings. Dylan's hot body supported mine as Nick extricated me from the ropes. They carried me back to the bed, and snuggled close.

Swathed in their potent aftercare, I closed my eyes, marveling at the absolute joy and completeness they brought to my life.

After several long hours nestled in their arms, we dressed and left Genesis. As we departed, we walked past Emerald. She sat at a table, chatting away with a large group of people, her bright smile and animated mien filling me with honor that she'd been the one to help me through my first submissive crisis. I already felt a bond with the woman that I hoped would grow stronger. She seemed to have her submissive shit so together, it amazed me that she didn't have a Master. I hoped one day she'd be as lucky as me and find the Master of her desires.

Once back at the house, the three of us sat around the kitchen table. The pre-dawn breakfast my Masters created was nothing short of Nirvana. I scarfed down everything on my plate as we laughed and swapped stories of our lives before destiny aligned us at Kit's.

#

Waking in their arms was a feeling I would never grow tired of, no matter how many times I had to pinch myself to make sure it wasn't some fantastic dream. I smiled and snuggled deeper against my two Masters, who both still snored softly even as the sunlight peeked through the curtains and casted light over their stunning features.

Nick's hair lay tangled across his pillow. I threaded my fingers through the silky black edges, sighing in contentment.

"Morning, little one," he whispered, startling me with a sly smile.

"I thought you were asleep," I replied softly.

"We're both awake, kitten," Dylan confessed as he growled like a lion then rolled over, pinning me beneath him.

"I need to pee, Master," I giggled as he continued to make feral noises while nibbling my neck.

"So go," Nick laughed.

"Not that again, Sir," I chuckled.

"We're not into water works, kitten. Go!" Dylan chortled as he pushed me toward Nick.

"Thank gawd. I don't think I'd enjoy that kink." I grinned as I climbed out from beneath the covers and scurried toward the bathroom. After washing my hands, I quickly brushed my teeth. As I rinsed my mouth, both men came swaggering into the spacious bathroom.

"Grab a shower and get dressed, pet. We're meeting a friend for breakfast," Nick announced as he reached in and turned on the water in the shower stall.

"Who, Sir?"

"It's a surprise," he replied cryptically.

A short time later, we bundled up and began walking along the shoreline of Lake Michigan. It was a short walk before we climbed the stairs of a wooden deck to a big beautiful mansion.

A dark skinned bald man opened a set of etched glass doors. His bright white teeth glistened as a huge smile spread upon his handsome face. Embracing both Dylan and Nick in a robust hug, he stared down at me.

"She's just as gorgeous up close and personal as she was last night." The man beamed, still gazing at me.

His eyes were the most gorgeous shade of amber I'd ever seen, and sparkled with merriment. I couldn't help but smile. I didn't remember meeting him the night before, but obviously he remembered me.

"Savannah, this is Mika. He's a good friend of ours who also happens to own Genesis," Nick announced with a broad smile.

"Oh." I blinked. "It's an honor to meet you, Sir. Genesis is…it's amazing."

"Thank you, pet. It's a pleasure to meet you, as well. But for the record, you've never met me and you don't know who I am." Mika arched a brow while still wearing his dazzling smile.

"I beg your pardon?" I asked, confused by his words.

"Remember when we discussed anonymity, kitten?" Dylan asked.

I nodded, wondering what that had to do with the owner of Genesis.

"Mika is a phantom," Nick interjected with a chuckle. "He guards his anonymity at all costs, little one. No one but a chosen few know his true identity. He wishes to keep it that way. So we're trusting that you'll honor his wishes."

"Oh, but of course. I understand now, Sirs. I won't say a word to anyone. I promise."

"Thank you, sweet girl." Mika nodded with a wink. "It'll be our little secret."

"You're welcome, Sir." I nodded and hoped that we were back home, I would get the answers to the zillion questions fluttering through my brain.

As Mika led us to the dining room, I was once again overwhelmed by the opulence of such ordinary people. The mansion was gorgeous and screamed Dominance with its rich masculine décor. I kept expecting a harem of submissives to descend the wide staircase and fall at his feet. But none appeared. Did he live in this massive kingdom alone? I wondered.

A buffet table laden with food awaited us in the formal room. Expecting servants or maids to appear, I was stymied to find it was just us four. I wondered if I'd ever grow accustomed to such grandiose surroundings, but I tried to relax and enjoy breakfast.

It didn't take long before I found myself laughing at the playful conversation of the three Doms. Mika was as down to earth as my Masters, and that alone eased my anxious mien.

At least until the discussion broached my freak-out in the dungeon the previous night.

"Have you ever tried to analyze why nudity is a hard limit for you, Savannah?" Mika asked. Warmth and understanding reflected in his face and words.

"No, Sir. I haven't. There's no reason for it as far as I know. I've never been de-pants or streaked across the high school football field while people pointed and laughed."

All three men chuckled and Mika shook his head. "Sometimes there are no *reasons* for triggers. They just are. Don't let it bother you, girl. Everyone has them and it's nothing to be ashamed or embarrassed about."

It was if Mika reached inside my skin and actually felt my discomfort.

"That's what we've tried to tell her." Nick nodded. "It's something we plan to work through, though. Little by little." As he looked at me, I knew he could see the fear pumping through me. "But we'll be taking baby steps from now on, girl. Nothing but baby steps."

"It's not going to be anytime soon is it, Sir?" My faced wrinkled in a pained expression.

My plea set off another round of laughter. "Rest assured little one, we learned from the experience as well, and plan to make good use of our private room for a long time. But there will come a day when we cuff you to the cross in the main dungeon and use you hard. Make no mistake about it, girl."

Nick's decisive promise zapped me with a bolt of lust and anxiety that raced all the way to my toes.

"I'd be happy to observe if you'd like your Masters to take you to the dungeon down the hall, sweet one." Mika offered with a predatory gleam in his eyes.

"Your what, Sir?" I choked.

"My dungeon. It's here in the house. Right down the hall," he chortled.

Was he serious? My face grew hot as embarrassment burned down my neck and over my chest. Would Dylan and Nick accept his offer? And why did the thought of Mika watching me feel far more intimate than a whole club of strangers? The jovial breakfast had taken a wicked turn. Fear succeeded in producing its usual knee-jerk reaction within me, but remembering the words of my Masters from the night before, I stopped to dig deeper into my soul. If they wanted to display me in Mika's dungeon, I knew they would do it with my insecurities in mind. They would shroud me as they'd planned to the night before and keep me safely ensconced in their Dominant care.

"Savannah?" Nick's voice broke through my churning thoughts.

"Yes, Sir?"

"Come, sit on my lap, little one," he instructed as he pushed back from the table and patted his thigh.

I eased onto him. No sooner had I situated myself before his arms wrapped around me in a fierce hug. "You just did it, didn't you? You stopped your fears from consuming you."

I smiled at the wonderment in his voice and the pride reflected in his eyes. After I issued a timid nod, Nick planted a euphoric kiss on my lips.

"Fucking phenomenal, kitten," Dylan praised on a grateful sigh, before rising from his chair and claiming my mouth when Nick was done.

"Stunning breakthrough, sweet girl," Mika praised with a wide, shimmering smile.

We adjourned to Mika's study, the decor dripping with even more masculinity. If there were ever a contest to measure testosterone by home design, Mika would win hands down.

After hours of conversation and yet more ribbing between Doms, we said our good-byes and made our way toward the monstrous wooden deck.

"Oh, hey, you and Drake and Trevor are coming for Thanksgiving again this year, right?" Nick asked, turning toward Mika.

"Wouldn't miss it for the world."

"Will Emerald be there?" I asked with a hopeful raise of my brows.

CHAPTER FOURTEEN

"NO," Mika barked with a fierce scowl.

"Umm, sorry. I was just curious, Sir," I replied in meek confusion.

Mika exhaled with a powerful huff. "I'm sorry, girl. Emerald doesn't know who I am, and she never will." He frowned.

"I'll keep your secret, Sir." I nodded, unsure of his drastic change of demeanor. One more curious thing to ask about when we got home.

"Come along, pet. We need to spend the afternoon working that big breakfast off... in bed," Nick rumbled as his mouth tugged in a mischievous grin.

A shiver rippled through me, not from the cold, but from desire. As we walked along the sand, lurid images filled my mind, and the slow pace we kept was frustrating.

"Race you!" I threw out the challenge and started running toward the house.

"Minx!" Dylan roared on a laugh.

Glancing over my shoulder, I saw they were chasing me. Dylan's sexy dimple and Nick's dark flowing hair made it hard for me to draw air into my lungs. Their incredible beauty was stunning and I no longer wanted to run from them, but *to* them. I stopped and turned as they approached at breakneck speed. Stretching out my arms, I surrendered and burned to feel them surround me. I did not expect them to pass me, laughing like a couple of loons. I scoffed when I realized they weren't racing me; they were competing against each other.

"Hey! A little hug would be nice," I yelled in a dejected voice then shook my head and sprinted after them.

Nick was the first to slap a palm on the banister of the deck. As I came up behind them, I started to laugh when Dylan shoved him away and declared himself the victor. Nick crouched and charged a shoulder into Dylan's ribs. They both sailed into the air and landed hard on the sand.

"Now who's the winner, fucker? Huh?" Nick taunted, gripping the railing and wearing a broad triumphant grin.

"Yeah, yeah. Kiss my ass," Dylan laughed as he stood and brushed the sand from his clothes.

My big bad Doms were acting like a couple of six year olds, and all I could do was laugh. For the first time in a very long time, my soul was filled with absolute happiness.

#

Rachel had prepared a Thanksgiving feast of biblical proportions, and as I mashed the potatoes, I felt as nervous as a cat on a hot tin roof. Drake, the powerfully intimidating Dom, was coming for dinner. He had been more than amiable in the few times we'd exchanged words at Genesis. But just the thought of him seated at the same dinner table had my nerves singing the jitters. A soft smile curled on my lips as I remembered Emerald regarding him as a big teddy bear. It worked to calm my anxiety. Well, a little.

As the mixer whirred, I thought of last Thanksgiving in my small apartment, preparing the usual holiday dinner with Mellie. I missed her. It was our first Thanksgiving apart. She promised to try and visit over Christmas, but Enrique was still her "flavor of the month" and they'd talked about spending it with his family in South America.

The sound of the doorbell drew me from my reverie. As our Thanksgiving guests began to arrive, Rachel shooed me out of the kitchen, sending me off to play *hostess*.

I remained quiet through most of dinner. Thankfully, with Trevor's gregarious personality and never-ending energy, my reserved mien went unnoticed. It was easy to see why he and Emerald were close friends; they had the same glass-half-full disposition. I felt honored that they were fast becoming dear friends of mine, as well. They had both held my hand when I'd needed them the most.

Sitting at the table my mind wandered back to the second submissive session I'd attended. The only subs that showed up were Emerald, Trevor and me. Leagh had stopped by for a few minutes, but left after she'd whined and pleaded for Master George to let her go shopping.

"Don't be like Leagh," Trevor warned after she and George had left.

"Trevor!" Emerald gasped.

"I didn't mean it like that," he said with a dramatic wave of his hand. "I just meant there aren't many Doms who would put up with her antics. I know, I know; MG loves her to death. But if I pulled half the crap she does, Daddy would blister my ass so hard, I wouldn't be able to sit for a month."

Emerald shook her head then leaned in with a clandestine look around the room. "George isn't a bad Master. He's just very lenient. Their exchange is perfect for them. But trust me, don't behave like she does around *your* Masters, Savannah. You'd be in a world of trouble."

I nodded in understanding, assuring them both I already knew where my Masters' line for bad behavior had been drawn. With the three of us huddled around the small table, I gathered my nerve and began to solicit their help in finding a way to wipe away my fear of public nudity. After several long minutes, Emerald looked up, searching the room for someone. She stood, announcing that she'd be right back then hurried toward the bar. After a brief conversation with my Masters, she made her way down the corridor toward the private rooms.

A few minutes later, she returned, with Sir Tony, the Dungeon Monitor who'd helped me through my meltdown. He took a seat and joined our little sub group, but I didn't know why.

"Hello again, Savannah." Tony smiled. "Emerald has asked me to sit in for a bit. I'm not sure if I'm here in a Dominant capacity or a professional one."

"Oh, sorry, Sir. Umm, professional if you don't mind," Emerald replied with a shaky smile, then reached beneath the table and took my hand. "Sir Tony is a psychologist. I thought that if you're willing to tell him the things you've told Trevor and me, he might be able to help you."

My mouth suddenly went dry as I flashed an anxious glance to my Masters, still seated at the bar. Nick smiled, giving me a barely perceptible nod of permission. I exhaled then began to spill my guts.

"After your parents died, did you begin actively looking for men to date?" Tony asked in a discreet, low tone.

"No, Sir. I…"

"If you'd rather to talk to Sir alone, sister, we can leave," Trevor volunteered, no doubt sensing the sky-high tension rolling off me.

"No, please stay. I don't have anything to hide," I reassured then clutched his hand beneath the table, Anchored to them both, I gained strength from my newfound friends.

"I've not had boyfriends, Sir. My Masters…they're my first…boyfriends…lovers? I don't know what you'd call them, but they're my first relationship." I struggled for an appropriate label.

Tony leaned back and stared at me for a long time. He wore an intent expression, as if pondering one of the great mysteries of the world. And maybe it was. Maybe I was so fucked up, even the professionals couldn't fix me. Finally, a smile tugged the corner of his mouth before he leaned in again and steepled his fingers. "Could you take off your clothes in front of Emerald?"

His question caught me off guard. I blinked then cast a considering glance at Emerald. "Yes Sir. I wouldn't have a problem with that."

"How about Trevor?" he asked again, still wearing that tiny smile.

"Yes, I could do that."

"But he's a man." Tony challenged.

"He's a submissive."

"And I'm gay," Trevor tossed out on a giggle.

"And he's gay." I grinned.

"What about Drake?"

"No, Sir. He scares the crackers out of me." I shook my head.

Tony chuckled. "What about me?" His brows arched as his pearly white teeth sank into his bottom lip, nibbling and watching my reaction with great interest.

"I can't do that, Sir."

"No, you can't. Your Masters would have my balls, but more importantly, you'd freak the fuck out again. Wouldn't you?"

I nodded, confused as to why I didn't feel threatened around Emerald and Trevor but the thought of stripping in front of Tony sent a coil of panic through me. "But *why* would I freak out with you, Sir? That's the part I'm trying so hard to work through and understand."

"Think about it, girl. You don't trust me and you shouldn't, because you don't know me. When your parents died you, pulled the proverbial shutters in and closed down. By your own admission, you've not allowed yourself to love many people, for fear they'll die and break your heart again. But when you tied up your heart and your ability to share love, you also locked up vulnerability, as well. Subconsciously, I think you knew that being vulnerable had the potential to devastate you as much as loving someone and having them ripped from your life."

"Little one?" Nick placed his hand atop mine, drawing me back from my reminiscences.

"Yes, Master?" I blinked, fearing he'd asked a question I'd need him to repeat.

"Would you go in the kitchen and tell Rachel we're ready for coffee in the study, please?"

"Of course, Sir." I nodded then stood and excused myself from the table.

As we sat by a roaring fire in the study commiserating about our full bellies, I sipped my coffee and listened to the flow of conversation.

I'd realized that my manufactured fear of Daddy Drake had been for nothing. He and Trevor were two of the funniest and friendliest people I'd had the pleasure of spending time with. Snuggled between Dylan and Nick, I listened as the group of Dominants chattered like a bunch of gaggling geese.

Mika had a wicked sense of humor. He was far less reserved then the first time I'd met him. Dylan and Nick had answered *most* of my questions about the club owner, but not all. Mika's relaxed mien in the company of Drake and Trevor made perfect sense; they'd been friends for years, longer than Genesis had been in business, in fact. The bond the three men shared was easy to see. I knew they'd shared many experiences, good and bad. Several years ago, Mika had lost his slave to brain cancer. Having loved and lost, he'd made a vow to never claim another submissive. If anyone understood the need to protect your heart at all costs, it was me.

But the one question that remained unanswered was Mika's vehement reaction when I'd mentioned Emerald, a few days before. His aversion to my new friend seemed over the top. I supposed it was none of my business, but there was something peculiar about the whole thing.

#

The days passed in a blur and the weather turned bitter. I spent every Saturday morning learning volumes about submission. My Masters were pleased with my growth and seemed eager to answer my questions evoked by the classes. Before I'd realized it happening, my trust in them had soared to new and reassuring levels, and I felt more secure than ever before.

Christmas morning, I woke to an empty bed and the sound of the doorbell's incessant ring. Vaulting from beneath the covers, I rushed to the bathroom, quickly donned my clothes, and bounded down the stairs.

When I reached the foyer, I plopped down on the steps, consumed by a fit of laughter. Standing in the entryway was Drake, dressed in a red velvet Santa suit. Trevor danced around my Masters, giddy with excitement and wearing a green elf costume.

Suddenly Drake turned and pinned me with a big, bad, Santa-Dom glare.

"And just what do you think you're laughing at, pet?" Drake growled. "You know Santa has a list for insolent subs. If your name is on it, girl, then Santa knows how naughty you've been and you're likely to get something you don't like."

"Oh, I'm sure I'm on that list Santa, because I've been a wicked, naughty girl…numerous times." I laughed so hard, tears leaked from my eyes.

"That's it!" Drake barked as he slung the big red bag off his shoulder then set it on the marble floor. "There will be no bunny floggers for you."

"I can't help it, Sir," I choked through my howls of laughter. "I've never seen a Dominant Santa before. It's…it's…hilarious." Laughing even harder, Drake narrowed his eyes and began to dig through the large red bag. Trevor was standing behind him with a hand pressed to his mouth, smothering his grin. Dylan and Nick watched with expressions of disbelief while merriment danced in their eyes.

"Hilarious, am I? You may not think so when you're cuffed and helpless beneath this wicked whip." Drake pulled a plaited red and black single tail from his Santa bag.

"Uh-oh, sister, you're in trouble now," Trevor warned with a child-like giggle.

"Oh, Santa," I begged as I scurried off the step. "Please don't give my Masters a whip. My lily white ass will never survive."

"We already have three, kitten," Dylan announced with a devilish gleam in his eyes.

"But not for me, right, Masters?" I asked with a nervous grin.

"Not today, little one, but soon. We'll work you up to it in no time. I'm sure." Nick replied with a sudden serious conviction.

I didn't have time to lament before the bell rang again. Trevor pulled back the door as Mika brushed the snow from his wool coat before stepping inside. His eyes grew wide, blinking at the outrageous outfits Drake and Trevor wore.

"What kind of fucking holiday spirit got into you two?" Mika laughed.

"Don't laugh at him, Mika Sir. Santa will give you horrible gifts. Like a nasty whip," I cautioned, nodding to the single tail Dylan held gripped in his fist.

"Got tons of them. But I would like to see if Santa brought me a bottle of Glenfiddich. Whatcha got in that bag for me, man?" Mika asked, peering into Drake's satchel.

"Well, even though you've been a bad boy, I think there's something in there for you." Drake wrapped Mika in a tight hug. "Good to see ya."

"I'm always a bad boy." Mika grinned as he sloughed off his coat to my waiting hand. "Thank you, Savannah. You're such a good girl, regardless what Santa thinks."

I laughed and began to hang up Mika's coat when the doorbell rang yet again.

"I've got it," Trevor announced with a happy grin as he danced toward the door.

"And you're such a good little elf, I'll have to see what's in my bag for you, dear boy," Drake praised, scratching at the white faux beard adorning his face. "Damn thing itches like it's full of lice or something," he muttered.

"Gross, and I fucking hugged you, dude. What the hell?" Mika laughed.

Sammie crossed the threshold, her arms burdened with gifts.

"Let me help you, Mistress," Trevor offered as I dashed to help him relieve her from the packages. "Under the tree, Sirs?" he asked Dylan and Nick.

"Please, dear boy." Nick nodded.

"What tree?" I asked in confusion, trailing after Trevor.

"The one we put up in the study this morning, kitten," Dylan called out behind me. "Next year you'll have to get your sexy ass out of bed and help us."

"A Christmas tree?" I squealed in delight, racing past Trevor.

With the love of my Masters and their entourage of friends, I'd not been consumed by the magic of the holiday since my parents were alive. Christmases spent with Mellie were cozy but subdued. They didn't compare to the level of excitement I felt in the air. And although Enrique had taken Mellie to South America, I wished she was in Chicago to celebrate with me. When we'd chatted on the phone the day before, she was nervous. Enrique had made mention that he was anxious for her to meet his parents. She'd never been introduced to any of her other lovers' families. I wondered if it might be a precursor to something more permanent. By the tone of her voice, I suspected Mellie might accept a ring...if Enrique offered.

I skidded to a halt in the study, staring at the massive, beautifully decorated Christmas tree. A mound of presents lay stacked beneath the twinkling lights.

"Here, please take these, Trevor. I'll be right back." I stacked more presents in his arms before I turned and ran.

Racing to the media room, I grabbed the gifts I'd hidden from my Masters and hurried back to the study, where I placed them under the tree. Trevor and I arranged Mistress Sammie's gifts as the Doms assembled into the room.

"It's a beautiful tree, Masters. Thank you," I gushed, wrapping them both in a powerful hug.

"Glad you like it, princess." Dylan kissed the top of my head.

"Is Emerald spending Christmas alone?" Mika asked Drake. A hint of anguish flashed over his amber eyes.

Drake tugged off his beard with a shake of his head, then peeled off the bright red Santa suit and sat down. "No. She's spending it with George and Leagh," he replied solemnly.

I watched as Trevor lowered his head, an unusually pensive look lining his fair complexion. There was a hell of a story between Mika and Emerald; I just didn't know what it was. Out of all the people assembled in the room, I had the sneaking suspicion I was the only one left in the dark. Trevor's expression seemed so forlorn, I fought the urge to reach out and hug him. Emerald was his best friend, and it was evident that he missed her.

"Savannah, Trevor, would you two please go to the kitchen and bring in the coffee and sweet rolls for us?" Nick asked, breaking the awkward silence that had settled over the room.

"Right away, Sir." I smiled, dragging Trevor out of the room in a tight hug.

Once safe inside the kitchen, I pulled him next to me. Giving a cursory glance around the room, I leaned in. "Okay, what the hell is up with Mika and Emerald?"

"Nothing and don't ask me anymore about it, please," Trevor begged in a tiny whine.

An immediate rush of guilt slammed me. "I'm sorry. It's none of my business. I shouldn't be prying."

"No, don't be sorry. It's just...I can't even talk to *her* about it. Master is the only one I can discuss it with."

"So there *is* something going on," I whispered.

"No. Dammit, sis. Leave it alone, please." The pained expression on his face pierced my heart.

"I'm sorry, baby. I won't say another word." I hugged him tight.

"It's better that way." Trevor replied after our hug, but the sorrow in his eyes remained.

"Come on, before they come looking for us," I insisted with a reassuring smile. "Last one in the study gets to serve."

"Hell no, I'm not racing you. I'll drop something." Trevor shook his head in mock fear. "Are you trying to get my ass whipped?"

"Like you wouldn't enjoy it?" I scoffed, lifting the heavy silver platter weighed down with mugs, sugar, creamer, spoons, and a large carafe of coffee.

Making it back to the study without dropping the tray, I served Mistress Sammie and the other Doms seated upon the long leather couches. Trevor knelt at Drake's feet and I followed suit, settling in between Dylan and Nick's legs. Immersed in their loving caresses, they trailed their strong, warm fingers over my face, shoulders and hair.

Hands down, it was the best Christmas I'd enjoyed in all my whole adult life.

I listened as the Dominants discussed every topic from toy techniques to politics. The tone became quite heated when religion was broached. Trevor held up his hand.

"What is it, boy?" Drake thundered after a long rant about zealous, homophobic hate groups hiding under the guise of religion.

"Can we open presents now, Master? Pretty please?"

"Are you trying to circumvent our discussion, boy?" Drake scowled.

I eyed the two men, worried Trevor was getting into serious trouble.

"Indeed I am, Master. It's Christmas. I don't want you to stroke out on Jesus' birthday," he railed with an impish grin.

"I'm going to fire up your ass, you insolent brat," Drake teased with a broad smile before gripping his mighty paw through Trevor's hair. Pulling his boy's head back, Drake planted a sizzling kiss on Trevor's lips.

Trevor beamed with a heated grin after Drake released him. "Oh, good. Santa got my Christmas list, after all," he snickered.

"And therein lies the problem with pain sluts," Drake sighed. "The only way to punish them is to ignore them."

I couldn't help but laugh as Drake scowled in feigned annoyance, though it fast became a wicked smile. "You may ask permission to distribute the gifts my sweet, mouthy slut," he ceded.

Trevor launched from the floor, wiggling his slender butt right in Drake's face. A giggle of delight tore from his throat as we all laughed. Drake pulled his hand back and landed a hard, echoing slap over Trevor's ass.

"I sure do love you guys," Mika laughed, shaking his head at their antics.

Sobering quickly, Trevor somehow managed to hold his exuberance inside and placed his hands behind his back. Lowering his gaze in a stunning display of respect, he cleared his throat.

"Master Dylan and Master Nick, if it pleases you, may I have permission to hand out the Christmas presents?"

"He *does* know how to be a good slut, after all," Drake sighed with teasing exasperation. His words may have been fraught with sarcasm, but no one could miss the absolute pride that filled the burly man's eyes.

"Trevor, sweet lad, you may." Dylan smiled with a nod.

As soon as Dylan issued permission, Trevor's protocol flew straight out the window. He let out a squeal of excitement then grabbed my hand, yanking me from the floor. "Come help me, sister. There's so many presents! It'll take me hours to get them handed out."

"Boy!" Drake bellowed in a scary, feral cry.

Trevor froze. All the excitement drained from his body and the jubilant smile fell from his lips. He turned toward Drake and cast his gaze to the floor. You could have heard a pin drop, as everyone waited for Drake's next words.

"Did you have permission to touch Savannah?" Drake asked in a tone slathered with reprimand.

"No, Master. I'm sorry. I let the moment carry me away."

"It's fine, Drake. I appreciate your concern on our behalf, but I could never be insulted by anything your Trevor does. He never disrespects and is a treasure to us all. Plus, we love him," Nick lauded.

"Very well. Thank you, Nick. Trevor?"
He raised his head and issued a soft smile at Drake. "Yes, Master."

"Enjoy yourself, boy." Drake beamed.

Trevor's entire body lit up brighter than the tree. "Thank you, Master," Trevor jumped up and down like a kangaroo on crack. Spinning around, he flashed a wide grin. "Thank you also, Master Nick."

"Okay, you two, let's get this show on the road." Mika smiled, waving us away with his hand.

The next hour was a whir of ripping paper and flying bows, as everyone unwrapped the mountain of presents. For the first time in ages, I felt like a child again.

My Masters were speechless when they opened the custom-made floggers I'd ordered for each of them. And their eyes lit up at the matching boxes of pervertibles I'd scoured long and hard to find. Dylan held up the innocuous wooden pasta paddle I'd found at a gourmet foods store, then flashed a smile filled with the promise of a red ass.

"I wanted to give you each something to remind you of our time at the barn." I smiled shyly.

"It means the world to us, little one. Those days were the catalyst of where we are now. Thank you, my love." Nick smiled. He leaned down and captured my lips in a poignant kiss.

Mika stood and pulled a stack of envelopes from his back pocket. He began to pass them out to the Dominants. "Please wait and open them together, if you don't mind." He asked as he wove his way around the couches.

When all the envelopes had been handed out, Mika smiled and nodded.

"Oh holy hell," Drake blinked, reading the message on the small square of parchment.

"What is it, Master?" Trevor asked, easing up and tilting his head toward Drake's hands.

"Oh, Mika," Sammie giggled. "This is going to be a blast!"

Craning my neck, I tried to see what was on the paper that Dylan and Nick held in their hands.

"A fucking kinky cruise?" Nick choked as he stared up at Mika.

"I've rented the whole damn boat. So keep the week of August fifteenth open, because we'll be spanking our way through the Caribbean. The club members are invited as well, but you all will be my honored guests." Mika announced with a broad smile then started to laugh. "But all that's going to get you is the biggest rooms on the ship."

My heart skittered with excitement and died in a grip of despair. As everyone began to chatter with enthusiasm, I sat in silence. A fake smile spread across my lips and I focused to keep my body relaxed. I was determined not to let reality spoil this special gift for my Masters and their friends.

August was a long way off, and I would be a distant memory. The odds of me accompanying my Masters on the cruise were between slim and none. Blinking back the tears that prickled my eyes, I sensed someone watching me. I looked up to see Trevor staring at me, his brows drawn together in question. I issued a subtle shake of my head and flashed him a look of plea, hoping he wouldn't say anything to draw attention to my struggling emotions. A bright happy smile quickly spread over his mouth as he gave me a short nod.

"Oh, I almost forgot. You have one more present, little one," Nick announced as he palmed my nape. "Climb on up here, love."

I couldn't imagine another gift as I took inventory of the presents spread out before me. There were nipple clamps and sexy lingerie, various vibrating toys that came with strict warnings to never be used without my Master's presence--and a scary-looking set of butt plugs that made me blush. I turned and gazed up to both he and Dylan, wondering what I'd missed.

Climbing onto Nick's lap, I watched as Dylan reached into his shirt pocket and pulled out a square velvet box. My heart drummed steadily in my chest as he placed the soft red box in my hand.

"We love you, girl. No matter what the next few weeks hold in store for us, we always want you to remember how deeply you've captured our hearts." Dylan's smile waivered as he spoke about our uncertain future. He claimed me with a kiss suffused with such love, it stole my breath.

As Dylan released me, Nick gripped my hair and turned me to face him. Déjà vu flooded back of the day they'd come to my apartment and held me in this same way.

"We're going to find a way to make this last, little one. Make no mistake about that," Nick vowed before he, too, captured my lips with an equally beloved kiss. I fought back tears as I returned his potent kiss. Try as I might to cling to his words of hope, they slid through my hands.

Ending the kiss, Nick nodded toward the box. My fingers trembled as I carefully eased it open. Tears filled my eyes and I blinked, sending them to spill down my cheeks as I gazed upon a necklace of three golden hearts, intertwined.

"This is us, kitten. Connected. Joined together, no matter what." Dylan whispered.

"Wear this always, little one. Wear it and think of us no matter where you are or what you're doing. Will you do that for us, girl?"

I nodded as tears continued seeping down my cheeks.

"Good girl." Nick whispered.

Those magical words tossed all my fragile emotions to the four corners. Sobs rent from my throat as my Masters worked together, clasping the delicate chain around my neck.

"Thank you, Masters. I love you both so much." I choked through the coil of emotions that pulled me under.

"Who's ready for Christmas pizza?" Trevor exclaimed, wiping tears from his own eyes.

"Christmas pizza?" I choked out a laugh.

"Yeah," Dylan smirked. "We don't expect Rachel to work on Christmas. And we sure as hell don't want to cook a big huge dinner for our little perverted group. So it's Christmas pizza for everyone."

"They're heathens," Sammie denounced with roll of her eyes. "But I humor them. After all, they're just men." She couldn't maintain her sarcasm any longer and let go with a long, loud belly laugh.

"You could always cook for us, dear," Mika countered Sammie's insult.

"Oh for shitsakes, Mika, you know I can't boil water. Me, near a kitchen? That's a recipe for disaster."

I wiped my cheeks and stared at the beautiful necklace nestled between my breasts. Suddenly, the doorbell rang again and the room fell silent.

"I'll get it," Dylan said as he launched off the couch.

"Are you expecting anyone else?" Mika asked Nick. His sudden worry was palpable.

"It's not anything to be concerned about," Nick replied in a cryptic tone.

All eyes turned expectantly toward the study's double doors. A moment later, Dylan reappeared carrying an envelope. Fighting back a smile, he held it out to me.

"It's for you, Savannah."

"Me?" I blinked and took the large manila envelope. There was no return address, just a label with my name on it. "What on earth is this?"

"Open it and find out, baby," Nick whispered as he wrapped me tightly in his arms.

I tore open the seal and pulled out a handwritten letter. I immediately recognized the handwriting; it was from Myron. As I began to read, my heart lodged in my throat.

My dearest Savannah,

Words can't begin to describe how thrilled Helen and I are that you have found two young men to fill your life with love. While it's outside the conventional ways, I applaud you for sharing your heart with two upstanding young men. All I have ever wanted for you, dear, is to find love--the kind of love Helen and I have shared all these years.

When I received calls from both Mellie and your young men, Helen and I nearly jumped for joy. Both Dylan and Nick explained their longing for you to stay and build a life with them in Chicago. They sung your praises for hours, Savannah. Since I hadn't heard a word about either man from your own lips, I placed a call to Mellie to make sure they were on the up and up. Once she confirmed that you were head over heels, I knew it was time to make some decisions.

That leads me to the reason for this letter. Dylan, Nick, and I had several conversations, and in turn, Helen and I have spent long hours discussing the company on a personal level. Our wish is that you build a life of love and happiness with both men. So I'm writing to let you know that I've decided to retire, sweetheart. I've put off closing the company for years, mainly, because I couldn't in good conscience leave you high and dry; unemployed. Although Helen has been pestering me for years to retire and travel abroad, I could never find it in my heart to shut the company down. Your two young men assured me that if you wanted to find a new job in Chicago, they would support your decision one hundred percent. Their reassurance helped me make my decision. I have one condition that is non-negotiable. We expect an invitation to your wedding. If you need anything... anything at all, dear Savannah, we are just a phone call away.

Best wishes to you three and may you find as much happiness as Helen and I have been blessed with.

All our love,
Myron.

I sat dumbfounded for several long minutes, re-reading the letter over and over again.

"Nick? Dylan?" I mumbled in a whisper of confusion as the paper trembled in my hands.

"I know you're probably upset with us, little one. But it was the only solution we could think of to keep you here. I know we broke your trust and weren't honest with you when we went behind your back. We understand if you're mad, but...we couldn't let you go. There's no way in hell we could let you walk away from us, again."

"What did you say to Myron?" I asked in a soft, even voice, trying to remain calm.

"I told him you swept us off our feet, little one. That our week at Kit's was the single most spectacular time of our lives and that neither Dylan nor I would ever be happy if we didn't have you."

"He put us through the wringer for the first thirty minutes. He knows more about my family than my own parents did, I think." Dylan flashed that sexy dimple in a pleading, scared smile. "Don't be mad, Savannah. We want you. We need you. We'll do anything in our power to make this work."

"I don't have a job anymore," I mumbled. My head reeled with the implications that Myron felt obligated to put his life on hold to ensure I was taken care of. Then it hit me. "I don't have to leave. I don't have to go back home. Do you know what this means?" A giggle escaped my throat as I dropped the paper and bolted from Nick's lap.

Dancing around the room like a woman possessed, I pulled Nick from the couch and wrapped my arms around my Masters with a tight hug. Trevor's infectious giggle filled the room as I closed my eyes and exhaled a massive sigh of relief.

"This is the best Christmas present I could have ever gotten, Masters. Thank you. Oh, God. Thank you so very, very much." I peppered their faces with kisses.

Their matching exhales made me laugh. "Thank God you're not pissed." Nick murmured in my ear.

"I could never be mad at you for this, Masters. Never." Tears of joy slid down my cheeks as I was slammed by another revelation. "I get to go on the cruise with you two!" I squealed and started jumping up and down.

"Of course you do, girl." Dylan laughed. "We'd never have gone without you."

Nick landed a hard slap across my ass and I jumped and issued a cry of surprise.

"Keeping your feelings from us again, little one?" He asked with an arch of his brow.

"No, Master. I was going to confess it all to you both, later," I vowed, making an x over my heart.

"Good girl." Nick smiled.

"Masterrrrrr," I whimpered. "You know what that does to me."

Nick began to laugh. "Why do you think we say it, little one?"

A strange expression fell over Dylan's face. He turned to Nick and grinned. "She's stayin', man. She's really fucking stayin'."

Nick's deep laugh rippled over me. They bumped fists and let out a resounding, "Fuck yeah!"

I turned and looked at all the smiling faces beaming around the room…all except for Mika. He stared out the window with a bittersweet expression lined on his face. My heart felt heavy for him, knowing he'd had this joy in his life once upon a time but no longer. The emptiness he felt had to be staggering.

"So who's ready for Christmas pizza? I promise next year *I'll* cook you all a proper feast!" I giggled.

"And I thought you didn't know how to cook, kitten?" Dylan teased.

"That's why I have my two talented Master chefs, to help me." I winked with a sly smile.

"Conniving little minx," Nick muttered.

#

My feet didn't touch the ground for weeks after my life-altering Christmas surprise. No longer plagued by the worry of having to leave my Masters, I felt as if the world had been lifted off my shoulders. The freedom of knowing my life was set on a course I'd only dreamed possible was like a breath of fresh air.

The last week of February, there was a break in the winter weather. We traveled back to Kansas City to clean out my apartment. Before we made the trek back to Chicago, we enjoyed a delightful dinner with Myron and Helen. There were only a few cases that Myron needed to wrap up, then he would officially close the office. He and Helen planned to fly to Paris. Thrilled to finally meet both Dylan and Nick in person, they spent hours discussing construction companies and artifacts.

Helen joined me on a trip to the ladies room and I was flabbergasted when she pulled me aside and asked what it was like to be loved by two men at once. I was sure our girlish giggles could be heard throughout the lush restaurant, and my face burned when I told her it was beyond incredible. While it was harder than I expected to say good-bye to them, Dylan and Nick extended the invitation for them to stay with us when their travels brought them to Chicago. It helped ease my feeling of loss. After reassuring us they would, I shared one final but poignant embrace with them both.

As soon as we breeched the door of our hotel suite, Dylan and Nick began stripping off my clothes. A tingle of excitement zipped up my spine and a smile spread over my lips. I was hopelessly lost when they undressed me with such tender care.

"I hope I'm as good a boss as Myron," Nick smiled as he loosened his tie.

"You're a wonderful boss, I'm sure," I placated, helping slide his tie free and unbuttoning his crisp shirt.

"Would you like to take some dictation to find out, little one?"

"It's a conference call, so you'll have to take it from both of us," Dylan announced, swaggering out of the bathroom.

"I'm assuming I won't need a note pad or pen, Sirs?" I asked with a saucy grin.

"No, you won't, kitten. It's all going to be by memory."

With a sassy wink, I eased to my knees and spread my legs in proper submission fashion.

"Your preparation is luscious, Miss Carson. Now let's see if you can handle the work load," Nick growled in a hungry voice.

"Whatever you slam me with, Mr. Masters, I'm sure I will fulfill my duties."

I bit back a giggle. I'd *so* wanted to call him Master Masters, but wasn't sure he'd find it half as funny as I did. Peeking up beneath my lashes, I watched Dylan undress. The thick muscles on his arms rippled and bulged, and a contented sigh escaped my lips when his hard cock sprang from his trousers.

"I see you're getting comfortable for this round of dictation, Mr. Thomas."

"Indeed I am, kitten. I don't want anything to hinder your expert oral abilities."

Six months ago, I never would have imagined engaging in any type of role play, much less doing it as I served two Masters. So much had happened in such a short amount of time, it sometimes felt as if I'd taken over someone else's life. Or maybe it was because I had changed so much, opened myself up for new experiences knowing I was safe and protected by their unconditional love. The need to please them had grown exponentially. Nothing I'd read in the past about the lifestyle had brought it full circle. But living it day in and day out, I understood the meaning of the power exchange…the meaning of my submission.

"You know, Sirs, this would be a whole lot more realistic if you allowed me to get dressed again."

"No!" They both barked at the same time.

"Alrighty, then." I smirked.

"Wipe that devilish smile off your face, Miss Carson, and present yourself for inspection," Nick growled, stepping closer as he stroked his impressive thickness. "We'll need to see if you're up to the task we have designed for you."

I raised my ass high in the air then slid my arms above my head, lowering my forehead to the carpet.

"Well, well... what do you know," Dylan *tsked* as he swiped his fingers up my exposed center. "Slick, hot and seeping already, Miss Carson?"

"Yes, Mr. Thomas," I replied, wishing he'd glide his fingers over me one more time.

"Explain why you're wet?" Dylan asked as he drew indiscriminate patterns with his fingertips over the cheeks of my ass.

"You excite me, Sirs."

"We excite you, hrmm? And when did this first start happening, Miss Carson?" Nick inquired brushing his cock down my spine.

"Since the first time I saw you both." It wasn't a line I'd devised for the role play, it was the truth.

"Do you have fantasies about us?" Dylan's lips tugged in a sensual smile as his finger enticed tiny tremors to ripple through me.

"All the time, Sir."

"Tell us about them, Miss Carson, and don't leave a single detail out," Nick whispered close to my ear.

"Oh, please," I mewled, wishing they'd just shut up and fuck me.

"Tell us, princess," Dylan cajoled before he plunged two fingers deep in my core.

"Ahhhh, that Sir. I dreamed about your fingers, your tongues and your cocks. Devouring me. Claiming me. Driving deep inside my pussy and ass."

"Is that what you want us to do, Miss Carson?" Nick asked with a soft chuckle.

"Yes, Sir. Please. All that and more."

"More? Do tell, Miss Carson. Obviously you've thought of more than us simply filling your tight little cunt and ass."

"Oh gawd, please Sir."

"Tell us," Dylan ordered as he withdrew his fingers and slapped my ass.

"That, Master...errr I mean Sir. Spank me. Hard. Fuck me. Hard."

They'd driven me half out of my mind. The room was thick with sexual tension. My tunnel contracted against the emptiness. It was maddening.

"You want us to use you, Miss Carson? Is that what you're saying?" Dylan asked as his thick thumbs spread my labia.

"Ahhhh, yes Master. Please. Please don't stop." I cried as he drove his tongue deep inside my quivering center.

"Stunning," Nick whispered from somewhere beside me. His silky hair fanned over my back. His fingers gripped my mane, raising my head from the floor. "On all fours, girl. I need to feel my cock sliding down your throat."

Dylan spread the cheeks of my ass and I growled like an animal when his soft tongue swirled over my exposed asshole.

"Oh God, Master," I whimpered at the lewd sensations crawling up my spine.

"You like Dylan's tongue on your tight puckered hole, girl?" Nick asked in a low, sultry voice.

"Yes, Master. Yes. More, oh god, please."

Gliding his tongue in and out, over and around, Dylan sent me spinning on a carousel of carnal splendor. The ride so sublime, I never wanted it to end.

Nick knelt in front of me. His angry shaft wept and I couldn't take my eyes of the enticing pearl poised on the crest.

"Take me in your mouth, little one. Worship your Master's cock."

Butterflies swooped in a tumultuous tumble. They'd put the role play to rest and awakened my fantasies with their dominant command.

Opening wide, I swallowed him to the base, delighting in the groan of pleasure that rumbled from his russet chest. Nick's curses floated in the air as I swirled my tongue along the smooth, sensitive ring beneath his purple crown.

"My sweet slut, you keep doing that thing with your tongue and this is going to be over before it begins," he warned before thrusting his hips and gliding to the back of my throat.

Dylan's fingers delved deep into my core and his thumb burnished my swollen clit. All the while, he danced his decadent tongue over the sensitive ribbed flesh of my ass. Nick wasn't the only one who was primed for detonation. Dylan had me on the cusp of release in seconds flat. Trying to focus my attention on the driving cock in my mouth was futile. Keening out in muffled cries of distress, I wiggled my hips. I was going to topple over if Dylan didn't ease up a bit. His only response was a low chuckle that vibrated over my puckered hole, catapulting me even higher. Struggling to contain the blistering orgasm bubbling too close to the surface I disengaged my mouth from Nick's cock with an audible pop.

"I can't hold it, Masters. Please. It's too big."

"Not yet, kitten," Dylan growled as he breeched my electrified rim with the tip of his tongue.

Nick gripped my mane and invaded my mouth with his turgid shaft once again. White flashes of light detonated behind my closed eyelids and I surrendered to the blinding release. My body thrashed and spasmed, consumed by the powerful explosion, I knew my failure to hold back was going to cost me…something big.

CHAPTER FIFTEEN

Nick held my lips to the base of his cock, releasing a thunderous cry as he showered my throat with thick ropes of come. My spasms began to subside as I swallowed his milky seed. Dylan moved away for a brief moment then returned to slam his cock deep into my quivering pussy.

As Dylan glided his finger to my hypersensitized clit, I squealed as I cleaned the remnants of come from Nick's silky shaft. Dylan drove mercilessly into my simmering core as if he had a point to make. It was unusual for him to be so punishing and rough, but it turned me on like a freaking light bulb.

"You didn't have permission, kitten. So now you get to keep coming and coming until we've decided you've had enough."

Nick pulled from my mouth. "Keep sucking, sweet slut. I want to be nice and hard when I fuck your ass after Dylan explodes in your cunt."

Oh God. They're going to fuck me to death.

"So. Fucking. Hot. And. Tight." Dylan choked out with each thrust.

Dylan danced his fingers in a lurid waltz over my clit, driving me up the craggy peak once again. My tunnel clenched around his driving shaft as I continued to plunge up and down over Nick's turgid shaft. Without warning, Nick yanked his stalk from my mouth and stood. I heard the sound of a condom wrapper rustling as Dylan gripped my hips, driving into my pussy with brutal force. All at once he froze as I was seized by another powerful orgasm. We shattered together, our cries of rapture intertwined.

As Dylan spilled into the latex barrier, I dropped my head to the carpet, gasping for breath as my powerful orgasm subsided. Dylan eased from my core and dropped to the floor beside me. But before I could steady my breathing, Nick spread his broad hand over the small of my back. A glob of cold lube landed over my anus. Without a word, his broad crest began to pierce my tender tissue. Pain and pressure exploded as my delicate ring tightened in denial.

"Master!" I screamed. Pain stabbed like a thousand needles as he continued pressing, intent on gaining access. He'd not prepared me in the usual way and my mind waged war with my body as Nick continued to wedge his shaft into my unyielding ass.

"Open for me, little one. Take my cock." Landing his broad hand over my orbs in a succession of hard slaps, I felt electrified and dazed and bombarded with sensations I couldn't process. Gripping the carpet, I was desperate to find an anchor as my body spiraled into another dimension.

Lust and demand ripped through me like a panther's claw.

"Yes, fuck yes!" I yelled when Nick's bulbous crown breached my screaming ring. "Harder Master, fuck me harder. Give me all of your thick, hard cock."

"Fuck me," Dylan mumbled, kneeling beside me to pluck my nipples and my hungry clit. "Tell him more, Savannah. Tell him how you like it, baby. Tell him how good it feels."

"Dylan," Nick roared.

"No worries bro, I'm hard as granite just listening to her talk like this." Dylan said with a soft laugh.

"Thank Christ," Nick growled. "Talk to me, sweet slut. Tell me how you want it, baby."

Struggling against Nick's fierce hold of my hips, I bucked hard, forcing his cock to drive deep where I needed him. "Please, Master. Please. I need you deep, and rough. Hammer me, please. I can't take this. Don't hold back, please. Take me hard and fast. I need…I need to feel your balls slapping my pussy."

As more lurid words tumbled from my lips, I begged Nick to defile me in every way known to man. Lost in a free fall of lust, I'd never spoken in such brazen fashion. It was if I was possessed by their carnal need, unable to temper the consuming demand they bred within.

I met each of his solid thrusts with my own brutal slams. With all inhibitions tossed aside, I fucked him like an animal. Wild. Willing. Unrestrained.

"Rub her clit, man. I've got an idea." Dylan announced as he jumped up and hurried away.

"Hurry," Nick barked. "I'm not going to last. Her ass is too tight, too fucking perfect."

As Nick pounded deep in my ass, he circled his fingers over my clit. I'd stopped wondering how they could draw so many orgasms as another one sliced through me. And as my muscles constricted around Nick's shaft, an inhuman cry tore from his throat. I could feel his spasms along the tender walls of my clutching tunnel as he filled the condom.

As he released his biting grip of my hips and eased from my ass, my legs gave out. Melting against the carpet, I gasped and panted as my body continued to hum.

"Not yet, kitten. You still have an orgasm to atone for," Dylan chided as he flipped me over and positioned two high-backed chairs near my feet.

Blinking through a haze of sexual vapor, I watched as Dylan hoisted each of my legs onto the chairs then secured my ankles to the wooden rungs with the rope from our toy bag.

I sighed at his sexy dimple as a devilish smile spread across his lips, then blinked and gasped as he held up the big electric vibe.

"Oh yes, kitten. Forced orgasms."

"But, Master..."

Before I could beg for mercy, Dylan flipped the switch and pressed the vibe against my clit. Nick reappeared and gripped my wrists, smiling as he secured my arms above my head. Bound and splayed, I was helpless and at their mercy--a mercy I knew they would not grant. The toy burned. I writhed beneath its droning assault.

"You always have a safe word, little one," Nick soothed, as he captured both my wrists in one of his beefy paws. He used his other hand to pluck and pinch my nipples, one after the other.

Dylan coxed another blistering orgasm with the fiendish toy and I screamed, my torso levitating off the floor. My clit was on fire but he kept the toy pressed against it, soaring me up and over, again and again.

Time had ceased to exist. My mind refused to process anything other than the endless loop of orgasms. My voice was gone; my screams conveyed on strangled whispers. Sweaty and limp, my muscles and limbs had long surpassed their ability to work, and still my Masters demanded more. The multitude of orgasms rolled one into another, no longer defined. Tears spilled from beneath my lids, my eyes no longer able to focus.

Then there was silence. The droning of the vibe ceased and I felt a wide palm brush the sweat-soaked hair from my forehead.

"Will you have more control over your release next time, little one?"

Nick's handsome face came into focus and I tried to reply to him but I could only respond with a slow nod of my head.

"Good girl," he praised, lifting me off the floor and into his strong arms. My legs had been released from their bindings but I had no memory of when.

My head lolled against his chest and my arms flopped from my sides. Nick carried me across the spacious hotel suite toward the sound of running water. Fragmented images sprung into focus then retreated as my head swam in a thick, gray fog.

"Such a gorgeous, hot mess," Dylan cooed, brushing his lips against mine. "Keep floating, kitten, we've got you and we're going to take good care of you."

Floating. Yes, I was floating, but in a much different place than I'd ever been before. In the throes of subspace, I felt as if I were deep inside myself, soaring in an ethereal, primordial splendor. But this felt like I'd been torn from my own body. Disconnected. Patchy. Surreal. It wasn't a disquieting sensation, but I didn't feel altogether like myself.

Nick gently lowered me into the tub. I was immersed in a heavenly buoyant bath. Raising my heavy lids, I realized we were clustered in a massive whirlpool tub. It was not as large as our tub at home, but comparable to the one at Kit's. Still nestled in Nick's arms, I closed my eyes, appeased in the soothing, hot water.

Indulging me with soft words of praise, they filled me with serenity. I had paid my penance and pleased them, and that awareness made everything right in my world. Floating in the tranquil bliss, they suffused me beneath their lips and their hands. I smelled the sweet scent of jasmine as a soft cloth glazed over my flesh. A hoarse sigh escaped my lips as they washed my body. Next a tangy citrus essence filled the air as strong fingers massaged my scalp. I closed my eyes and let the darkness carry me away.

#

Spring turned into summer with my days spent by the pool and our nights spent exploring our Dominance and submission at Genesis. Their promise of pushing my limits held true. And as they drove me to new and exciting levels, they did so with care and consideration for my ugly trigger.

Finding a job had fluttered through my mind a few times, but I was finding far more satisfaction cultivating a domestic side that I never knew existed. Every task or act of love I bestowed up on my Masters was met with reverence and joy. They were truly happy and so was I, basking in giving them all the pleasures they desired.

Dylan and Nick opened me up to so many new and exciting experiences, both in and out of bed, that it was sometimes difficult to remember how void my life was before I'd met them. They wined and dined me at exclusive restaurants where nary a brow was raised at their affection, and I found the fears I'd manifested while at the barn had been a waste of time.

All was right in my world. Mellie was beyond the moon at my happiness. While no longer with Enrique, she didn't mourn the demise of their relationship, but simply poured herself into work and play. She'd visited a few times between trans-Atlantic jaunts, taking in the sights and sounds of Genesis with wide eyes brimmed in delight.

Everything was spectacular until one bright summer morning.

Nick's cell woke us from a sound sleep. I could tell by the expression on his face that something was dreadfully wrong. Dylan obviously picked up on Nick's tension, because he climbed out of bed and got dressed without a word.

"We'll be there in a couple of minutes," Nick replied in a voice fraught with concern, before ending the call. "Mika needs at his place for a while."

"I'll get some clothes on," I announced then pulled back the sheets.

"Sorry, love. He asked for just Dylan and me. You snuggle back down and get some more sleep. I'm not sure when we'll be back, but I'll give you a call later, okay?"

His voice was even and calm, but worry and fear blazed in his eyes. Nick's dishonesty stung and I covered myself with the sheet, craving security even it was only a thin layer. I didn't know whether to slap him for his betrayal or cry. Anger won over hurt feelings.

"If I was holding back from you, you'd spank my ass. Or make me endure a day of edging. Don't patronize me with fluff about going back to bed. You've forced me to be honest since day one. Is honesty a two-way street or just a submissive requirement? Tell me what's going on, please."

Nick exhaled a heavy sigh. His reflection was grim and I knew whatever he was holding back, was bad. He scrubbed a hand through his hair, tossed his head back, and briefly gazed at the ceiling.

"What the fuck is it, Nick?" Dylan asked in a low, tense voice.

"Emerald was attacked in Drake's private room last night at Genesis."

"What?" I gasped as my stomach twisted in a knot of fear. "What happened? Who attacked her?"

"No fucking way. Is she okay?" Dylan whispered in disbelief.

"That new guy that just joined, Jordon something-or-other. The one that's been sniffing after her, asking everybody questions about her. Turns out he's nothing but a fucking player. He played up to Drake to get next to Emerald. The prick used a razor blade flogger on her ass. Cut her up pretty bad. Mika, Tony, James and Drake rescued her. Mika called in his Doctor friend Martin and he stitched her up right there in Mika's office."

"Oh my god," I cried as tears stung my eyes. My stomach continued to swirl.

"Mika?" Dylan repeated. Incredulity resonated even stronger in his tone.

"Yeah. Evidently, Mika spent the night at her place last night, to take care of her." Nick nodded.

"Mika stayed with Emerald last night?" Dylan's words began to take on a more ominous tone.

"Can you two please just stop for a second? Is Emerald okay or not? And what is the big fucking deal if Mika spent the night with her? Will someone *finally* tell me what is up Mika's ass when it comes to her?"

"Language, little one," Nick growled.

"I'm sorry, but my best friend has been attacked. And Dylan's about to go into shock because Mika *revealed* himself to Emerald, like that's some kind of cardinal sin. Tell me what the hell is going on?" I railed, frantic in worry and confusion.

"I understand you're upset, girl, but if you don't watch your mouth, you're going to get edging for a full day and forced orgasms the next. Do I make myself clear?" Nick bellowed.

"Crystal, Master," I hissed.

"Now, if you can calm down long enough to let me explain, I'll tell you what I know. Do you think you can do that for me, pet?"

His condescending tone reminded me of every lawyer who had talked down to me for being a woman. They always treated me like a blithering idiot, and all but patting my head while insinuating that my expert opinions didn't matter and the *big boys* could handle things. Nick had pushed a button that got my back up. Even if he didn't mean to provoke my anger, it was on.

"I think I can manage that Master, thanks."

His brows slashed in an angry scowl at my cynical reply.

"Time out, you two. This is getting *way* out of hand, *way* too fast," Dylan interjected, being the only voice of reason in the room at that moment. "We're all worried, but jumping down each other's throats isn't going to do us any good."

Nick sat down on the bed and massaged his finger and thumb against his forehead. "I'm sorry, little one. I didn't mean to snap at you like that. Mika has been...humph, *infatuated* with Julianna--err, Emerald--for a long time."

Emerald's real name was Julianna. But I'd grown accustomed to calling her Emerald so I wouldn't slip at the club and divulge her real name. I thought it sweet of Master to think of her as not just a submissive, but all aspects of her, as a woman.

"But I thought she didn't know who he was?"

"She didn't. Not until last night. It's a long, convoluted story. I promise we'll share it with you when we get back home but right now, Dylan and I need to get over to Mika's. He's in bad shape and needs us."

"Okay." I nodded, my blood still pumping with ire. "I'll wait here until you both get back, Sir. Can I at least call her and see how's she doing?"

"No, pet. Trevor is with her now and Drake's on his way back to her place. Let them take care of her today. We'll see what tomorrow brings, okay?"

I opened my mouth to argue then closed it, pressing my lips together.

"Kitten, it's upsetting to all of us. We're not asking you to ignore your friend, just for you to be patient until we have all the details of what happened last night. We'll share everything we know once we get back home." Dylan smoothed a hand over my hair. His loving touch diffused all the hostility that had me ramped up.

Nick said nothing as he dressed. His silence was like a hot knife to my heart. Hurt and in need of space, I grabbed my robe and left the bedroom. I found solace in the kitchen with a cup of coffee, at least for a few gratifying moments until Dylan joined me.

"He's not mad at you, kitten."

"Yes, he is," I replied in a dejected tone, as I stared into my mug.

Dylan reached out and tugged my arm. In silent perception, he drew me to his lap. I wrapped my arms around his sturdy chest and buried my face against his neck. Soothed by his familiar scent and warmth, I clung to him like a lifeline, anchored against the unknown.

"I got mouthy because I was scared," I explained in a shaky voice. "And now he hates me for being so unsubmissive."

Dylan's smooth chuckle rankled. "So you're saying that the first argument you've had with one of us holds the power to ruin the love that's in our hearts for you, pet?"

"I don't know," I whined.

"You're wrong, kitten. So, so wrong. I don't know of any couples who go through life without a bump or two in the road. We've been lucky so far that we mesh better than most. We're all scared because we're dealing with a lot of unanswered questions. But as soon as Nick comes down, we're going to get all the details. And while we're gone, I want you to forgive yourself for being human and bury the thought that Nick hates you. Put it in a lead vault surrounded by my chains."

"Oh, little one," Nick moaned as he entered the kitchen and quickly ate up the distance between us. "Is that what you think, love?"

He knelt next to Dylan and me then reached up and cupped my chin in his broad palm. The sorrow in his eyes felt like a sledgehammer to my lungs. Tears burned and I struggled to blink them away.

"I'm sorry for making you mad, Master," I choked.

"Little one, we're going to make each other mad from time to time. But, Christ, baby. I could never hate you. I love you far too much. Don't you realize how deep I've got you imprinted in my heart? One little tiff isn't going to change that, pet. Not ever."

"Oh, Master," I wailed. His words were a balm of salvation that filled me with relief. Twisting on Dylan's lap, I grabbed hold of Nick. Melding against his chest, I scrambled to repair my erroneous perceptions and realign his connection to my soul.

"It's okay, little one. Our relationship can withstand anything as long as we're together. There's nothing we can't weather. All right?"

I nodded and sniffed as I held tight to the power of his convictions.

They stayed at Mika's for hours. No amount of pacing curbed the antsy feelings crawling through my veins. As I swam laps in the pool in hopes of burning off my nervous energy, they suddenly appeared. Watching me from the deck toward the deep end, their faces bore a look of haggard exhaustion. Gliding through the water with powerful strokes, I neared the ladder.

"Wait, kitten," Dylan instructed, holding up his hand. "Stay, we're coming in."

In seconds flat they'd stripped naked and speared through the water like Olympic divers. With a playful tug of my legs, Nick yanked me under the water then wrapped me in his arms and jettisoned us up to the surface. Dylan was waiting, his expression serious and body language impatient. When he gathered us in his arms, a sigh that with echoed relief exploded from his chest.

My mind raced with a million questions. But before I could ask, they trailed their hungry hands over my body, revealing the details of all Julianna, aka Emerald, had endured. The emotional aspects of Mika's discontent were complex. I kept my opinion that he was being a complete douchebag to myself. My feelings weren't a part of the equation. The man was going to have to pull his head out of his ass on his own. What I didn't understand was the fact that Julianna was off limits to everyone except Drake, Trevor, Mika and Sammie. Being sequestered from all her friends seemed more like punishment for being victimized. I wanted to see her, help take care of her. But every appeal I lobbied to enlist due process and help Julianna was met by their ardent gag order. I was not to contact her until Mika granted permission.

Mika's directive was wrong on so many levels. Piqued with the injustice of it all, I wanted to march down the beach and give that misogynistic prick a peace of my mind. Who did he think he was, issuing such ridiculous orders? He wasn't her Master. Hell, he'd hid in the shadows, watching her like a sick pervert, for years. Then after succumbing to his pent up desires, he used her sexually. What kind of monster did that to a woman who was already in such a vulnerable state? But the fact that he tore out of her house like a scared pussy when he'd taken what he'd wanted had to have damaged her even more.

Dylan and Nick knew I was livid, and did everything in their power to talk me off the ledge from doing something irrevocable, like tell Mika where he could shove his so-called Dominance. With a begrudging promise, I vowed not to interfere, and let the mighty Masters who'd decided it was their right to handle my friend put their plan of action into place.

It was an insufferable, long week. The few nights we visited Genesis, it seemed as void and empty as my old life without Julianna there. Drake looked like he'd aged a hundred years. I'd never seen him so distraught, but the aura of Dominant impotence surrounding him was the most disturbing. He tried to reach out to Julianna every day, only to be met with lies. She'd broken his big ol' teddy bear heart and he wore it on his sleeve. Of course, a part of me deemed he'd deserved it, but another part ached for the pain he was going through.

The whole situation was a cluster-fuck of biblical proportions. I felt helpless and a horribly inept friend to Julianna, being figuratively bound and gagged by the mighty and oh-so-powerful Mika. Trevor was under an even stricter gag order than me. Drake had shut him totally out of the loop. His face wore a constant expression of torture and the dark circles under his eyes appeared even more defined against his porcelain skin. My opinion of Mika reached an all-time low.

Nick's cell phone sliced through the stillness of the night. Bolting upright, I looked at the clock. Who was calling at three in the morning? In a groggy, angry voice, he answered, then launched from the mattress and flipped on the bedside lamp. Dylan sat upright too, gazing at Nick.

"George, what's wrong? Are you all right?" Nick asked in confusion.

"No. Fuck. No. Is he alive?" The anguish in Nick's voice made my blood run cold.

"Who? What's happened?" Dylan demanded, tearing out of bed and rushing to Nick's side.

"Mika. He's been shot."

"She didn't get shot, too, did she?"

"She who?" I cried. Fear pumped like fire through my veins.

"Julianna. She's okay. She's at the hospital with Drake and Trevor. George just got word that Mika's father has arrived, as well," Nick relayed. "Sorry, George. Go on."

Nick dropped on the edge of the bed as if his legs refused to support his weight. He pressed the speaker option on his phone and we all huddled around the device as George's grief-ridden voice filled our bedroom.

I palmed my eyes, silent sobs wracking my body as George retold the horrific details. Mika had died in the ambulance, en route to the hospital. The monster who had attacked Julianna had returned, seeking vengeance. Mika had enlisted Sammie and Drake's aid in hopes of disproving Julianna's conviction that she was no longer a submissive. Mika had Sammie escort her to the club for days, in an attempt to reach her broken soul and bring her back to the fold. There had evidently been a breakthrough earlier that night, and as Mika and Julianna traversed the empty parking lot, Jordan appeared out of nowhere. He'd threatened her with a gun before Mika pulled his own weapon. He'd killed Jordon but not before taking a bullet to the chest. Mika had made it through surgery but was in critical condition at St. Agnes Hospital.

Nick asked several questions as did Dylan, which George answered as best he could. I couldn't gather my thoughts long enough to think of any aspects that hadn't already been covered. Julianna was alive and safe but Mika…all the horrible things I'd thought and felt about the man filled me with guilt. The lengths he'd gone to, in an attempt to repair the damage done to Julianna, were benevolent and adoring. He'd not been a misogynistic prick, but a devoted Dominant pursing every avenue available in order to save her. I'd been a narrow-minded bitch, filled with anger and venom, thinking the worst of Mika when all he wanted to do was save her.

"Mika is a hardheaded bastard. He'll get through this, George," A note of conviction bled past the anxiety in Dylan's voice. "Get some sleep, man. We'll meet you at the hospital in a few hours."

Mika's father, Emile, along with Julianna, Drake, Trevor, and Sammie, were in the ICU waiting room when we arrived. Hell, most of Genesis was there lending what support they could. Julianna sat curled and sleeping against Sammie. I glanced at Nick, who nodded solemn approval, before I made my way across the room and gave Mistress a weak smile.

"Wake up, baby. Someone wants to see you." Sammie rousted Julianna gently.

"Oh, Mistress, please don't wake her," I interjected but it was too late. My friend's lids lifted and her stunning emerald eyes gazed up at me.

Her chin quivered as she extricated herself from Sammie's arms and stood. She seemed so defeated as she hugged me tight. She was thin and frail, like a strong wind would shatter her into pieces. It broke my heart that she'd been through so much in such short time.

"How are you holding up, honey?" I whispered in her ear as she continued to cling to me.

Pulling away from the embrace, she patted the tears forming in her eyes. "I've been better," she snorted. "Mika was so brave and I was so scared. I've never been that terrified in my whole life."

"I can't imagine. I can't wrap my head around any of it. I wanted to come see you over the past week, so many times, but..."

"It's okay, Savannah, I wasn't fit for company. It's been a--" Julianna paused as if trying to find words to describe the hell she'd crawled through.

"That's fine, hog all Savannah's lovin' for yourself, sister. I know how you are," Trevor teased as he joined us.

"I'm getting coffee. There are way too many subbie butts in my face. Makes me want to grab a whip," Sammie snickered with a teasing wink. "You three sit down and visit, I'm going to head down to the cafeteria. Do you want something to eat yet, Julianna?"

"No thank you, Ma'am. I'll get something later," she promised with a shake of her head.

Sammie leaned down after we'd taken our seats. "You need to eat, girl. I'll sic Drake and Emile on your ass if you don't down some nourishment soon, are we clear?" Sammie's brows arched as she whispered it. The look of warning in her sparkling blue eyes reminded me of Dylan when he wore that "bad-ass-Dominant" look.

"Yes, Ma'am." Julianna sighed in resignation.

Trevor and I did our best to help support Julianna through her dark days at the hospital. Mika was indeed strong-willed, and recovered at a pace that floored the medical staff. Soon he was home and recuperating with Julianna at his side. The man who once dismissed his feelings and had closed himself off to love again blossomed into a doting Master with Julianna, his devoted slave.

EPILOGUE
August 15th

With champagne flowing as we left the port of Miami. Mika stood on deck, dressed as a dashing pirate, wearing a smile that rivaled the sun. Nestled against his side, wearing a sexy wench costume and glowing with pride, was Julianna. The golden collar that adorned her throat cast shimmering reflections from the sun.

Surrounded by his extended kinky family, Mika raised his glass. "To all you scurvy landlubbers, I can't tell ye how it warms me heart to share this day with ye."

"Master," Julianna giggled. "You keep talking like that I'm going to beg you to rape and pillage me."

"Aye, me sexy wench. I'll be driving deep into your hot little booty soon." Mika grinned and waggled his brow.

"Oh my God," Julianna gasped, as her cheeks flashed a bright crimson.

Mika claimed a powerful kiss upon Julianna's lips then smiled. "Seriously, I'm glad you all could be here to share a week of debauchery on the high seas." His face sobered as his eyes danced over the crowd assembled. "Words don't give justice to the appreciation in my heart for everything you guys have done for Julianna and I over these past few months. While being shot was one of the worst things that have happened in my life, it brought an awakening inside me. Life is short and we all should spend it doing what we love with the people that we love."

Mika dropped his gaze to Julianna, who quickly wiped a tear from her cheek.

"I just want to say thank you, and I love you guys." Mika raised his glass again, swallowed down the bubbly liquid then tossed his glass over the side of the ship. While the rest of us imbibed our champagne, Mika growled before he swooped Julianna into his arms, and kissed her for a long, passionate moment. When he released her lips, he raised his head and grinned. "Let the spankings begin!"

A loud cheer went up among the crowd and I laughed. It was surreal being aboard the luxurious ship, surrounded by my likeminded family. But the light and love reflecting in my Master's eyes was more breathtaking than the sun sinking against the crystal blue water.

The dinner buffet was to die for and I ate until I ached. As we dressed in our spacious suite before going below deck to join in the dungeon festivities, I begged Nick, who was cinching up my corset, not to make it too tight.

"No worries, little one. If you're going to suffer, it will be beneath *our* hands."

His deviant chuckle made my blood heat.

Both men stood before me, looking dashing in their dark suits. I couldn't help but stare as I admired my gorgeous Masters, welcoming the flames of arousal that flared inside.

We didn't stay in the dungeon long and when we returned to our suite, they kept their promise about me suffering beneath their hands. And suffer I did, over and over, until finally I lay tangled in their limbs; a sweaty, sated, boneless mass of quivering submission. It was sublime rapture.

Rousted awake by the sound of voices followed by a bizarre noise outside our state room, I wiggled out from beneath my Masters' warmth. Tiptoeing across the room, I peeked out the curtains over our spacious balcony. Julianna was leaning over the side of the ship. Trevor held her riot of auburn curls in his fist.

Oh no, she's seasick. I tossed on my robe, grabbed my room key along with a bottle of water from the mini fridge, then slipped out the door. Winding my way through the main deck, I approached my friends and brushed a loving hand over Trevor's back. He met me with a weak smile and look of worry in his eyes.

"Awww, honey," I commiserated as Julianna heaved once again. "Seasick?"

She shook her head as she wiped her mouth with the back of her hand. She raised her head and looked at me, fear blazing her eyes. My brows furrowed as I offered her the bottle of water.

"Thank you, Savannah."

"Ohmigod!" I squeaked in a whisper as I my gaze darted between Julianna and Trevor. "Are you pregnant?"

"She won't do the test." Trevor sighed with an overexaggerated flip of his hand.

"Why not?" I asked keeping my voice low.

"I don't know if Mika wants kids or not. And I have no idea how to even bring up the subject. God, I can't be pregnant!" Julianna whined.

"Oh baby. He'd be thrilled."

"You think so?" She asked as a fat tear slid down her cheek.

I wrapped her in a hug and planted a kiss on her forehead. "Come on. Follow me."

"Where are we going?" Trevor asked, wrapping his arm around Julianna's waist.

"The first aid room. They've got to have one of those pregnancy kits on board."

"Savannah, I can't," Julianna whimpered. I turned and saw the fear in her eyes.

"Yes, you can. It'll be all right. Hell, Trevor and I will hold your hand while you do it. And we'll be right by your side when you tell Mika, if you need us to. Right brother?" I pierced Trevor with a stern gaze.

"Oh, I'd get my ass handed to me on a silver platter. But hell yes. I'll be there if you need us for moral support, sweetheart. Count me in."

Julianna issued a pained sigh as we snuck down the hall and ducked into the first aid station. I shut the door behind us then began to rummage through the cabinets until I discovered the kit.

"Come on," I whispered as the three of us wedged into the tiny bathroom. "Pee on the stick, sugar. No matter what the results are, we're with you all the way."

Julianna's worried expression tore at my heart. She flipped up her robe and sat on the toilet.

"I don't know if I can pee with an audience," she moaned.

"This will help," Trevor beamed as he squeezed sideways and turned on the tiny sink's faucet.

We all started to giggle as Julianna finally got her own water working. She closed her eyes and thrust the stick toward me. I held it up as Trevor peered over my shoulder, holding me in a death grip as a blue plus appeared.

"Ohhhhhhhhh, sister!" Trevor squealed with glee.

"What is it? What is it?" Julianna lamented as she quickly wiped and stood.

"You're gonna have a baby." I grinned and hugged her tight.

"I'm gonna be an Uncle," Trevor announced with glee.

Julianna's face turned a pasty white. Her eyes rolled back in her head as her entire body slumped against mine.

"Oh fuck!" I cried. "Trevor. Quick. Go get Mika."

Packed like sardines in the tiny bathroom, Trevor somehow wiggled his way out and sprinted from the first aid room. I could hear his bare feet thudding on the carpet as he raced down the hall.

I struggled to get Julianna's unconscious body out of the tiny cubicle and onto the small bed against the far side of the room. Sweating, I lifted her feet onto the mattress as I gently caressed her face.

"Come on, baby. Wake up." I whispered in a frantic voice.

Within seconds Mika rushed into the room, fear flashing in his amber eyes as he spied Julianna unresponsive on the bed. I stepped back as he dropped to his knees next to her.

"Baby. Oh God. Come on Julianna, speak to me. Please!" His tortured tone drew tears to my eyes. "What happened?" He barked over his shoulder as Trevor and I clung to one another.

"She passed out." I replied.

"Why? What were you three doing in here?" He demanded as his gaze narrowed on Trevor and me.

"I can't tell you that, Sir." I whispered.

"What the fuck do you mean you can't tell me?" Mika growled as he stood and advanced toward us.

Trevor and I trembled. The fierce anger distorting Mika's face was chilling. I swallowed back the terror that was lodged in my throat just before Julianna moaned.

Mika swirled around and dropped to his knees, trailing a dark hand over her pale face. "Baby. Easy, love. I'm here. I'm right here," Mika soothed in a calm and reassuring voice. "Trevor, I want you to go wake up Drake, Nick and Dylan. Tell them I need them in here. Do it NOW, boy!" Mika barked, without even glancing over his shoulder.

"Shit," Trevor hissed, blanching at Mika's directive. "It was nice knowing you, sis." He groaned as he left the room.

"Master. Please don't be mad at them. It's my fault," Julianna begged.

"What is?" Mika asked, gazing into her green eyes, still gently brushing the hair from her forehead.

Julianna raised her head and looked at me with a pleading gaze. "Show him, sis."

"Are you sure?" I asked

"For the love of God, somebody tell me what the fuck is going on here!" Mika thundered.

I jolted at his intimidating cry and raced into the bathroom. Plucking the stick off the back of the toilet, I thrust it toward him. He snatched the plastic tester from my hand just as Drake, Nick, Dylan and Trevor rushed into the room.

"It's my fault, Master. I'm sorry." Julianna whimpered as tears spilled down her cheeks.

"Pet?" Dylan's brows slashed, confusion written all over his face.

"I… I…"

"Fuck. Me. Holy. Shit," Mika screamed.

Julianna covered her face with her hands and began to wail.

"What is that?" Drake thundered over Julianna's mournful cries as Mika's eyes filled with tears.

"I'm going to be a father!" Mika beamed, thrusting the test strip toward Drake. He turned back to Julianna, who had balled her body into a fetal position on the gurney, bawling her eyes out. Mika frowned.

The room filled with laughter and cries of congratulation. There was more chaos than I'd seen in my life. And all the while, Julianna howled with tears.

Mika lifted her from the bed and cradled her in his arms, trying to quiet her incessant cries. Finally, he laid her on the floor and stood. "Slave. Present!" He barked, adjusting his body in the exact stance I'd grown to love from my own Masters.

"I can't..." Julianna sobbed.

"You present to me now, or I'll..." Mika's threat sputtered and died on his lips. He turned to the Doms behind me, wearing an almost comical expression of indecision. "What the fuck can I do to a pregnant sub?"

"Shower her with love, bro," Nick laughed.

"Fuck. I already do." Mika grinned. "Present, or you'll go nine months without an orgasm, girl."

His threat lit a fire under Julianna. She scurried to her knees in a perfect submissive pose.

"Much better," Mika praised. He knelt in front of her and cupped her chin in his palm. "Look at me."

Julianna opened her red swollen eyes. The last time I'd seen such fear in her beautiful face, it was the day after Mika had been shot.

"I love you, pet. I love that our baby is growing in your belly. You've showered me with gifts, but this is absolutely the most magnificent present you could ever give me."

Julianna didn't respond. She simply opened her mouth and bawled louder than before. Mika laughed and pulled her up into his arms, peppering her face with kisses.

As he walked toward the door, Drake stepped forward, his mighty paw wrapped tightly in Trevor's hair. "What do you want us to do with these two?"

Mika paused and pursed his lips as his gaze darted between Trevor and me. "Hrmm," he pondered. "They *were* accomplices to my pet's subterfuge. I'll leave that up to you, gentlemen."

I raised my chin and issued a heavy sigh. "It was my idea," I confessed. "Julianna was scared to find out. I forced her here. I forced her to take the pregnancy test. Trevor didn't do anything except hold her hair while she barfed. If anyone should be punished it should be me, not him."

"Obviously, I'm not keeping you busy enough to keep you out of trouble, am I boy?" Drake growled, cinching his fist tighter in Trevor's mane.

Trevor didn't reply. His face skewed in pain.

I managed a guilty glance at my Masters, immediately wishing I hadn't. Both their mouths were set in firm, tight lines.

"I'm sorry for disappointing you, Masters," I mumbled as I dropped my gaze to the floor.

Mika laughed. I peeked at him from beneath my lashes. Julianna's face was nuzzled against his neck as intermittent sobs shook her body. "I'd say take her back to your room, or the dungeon below deck, and use her hard."

My eyes grew wide.

"I think that can be arranged." Dylan's feral grin sent a shiver coiling up my spine. "Come on, kitten. I think you've caused enough trouble for one day."

Nick arched a brow as a devilish smile tugged his sensual mouth. "Maybe we need to push a button or two, little one. What do you think?"

He stepped closer and began to glide the silk robe from my shoulders. I squeezed my eyes closed and sucked in air. "If it will take the disappointment from your eyes, I'll do it, Master."

Dylan's rugged body pressed up behind me. He pushed the robe back over my shoulder. Nick leaned in, his warm breath fluttering over my ear. "I think we'd rather sink balls deep into your hot little holes, pet. Practice for the day when you will give us the same glorious gift Mika now has."

I raised my head. My mouth fell agape. I launched my arms around his neck. "Really, Master? Really?" I giggled.

"Not today, but soon, little one," Nick laughed.

"Very soon," Dylan growled.

I reached out for Dylan then hugged them both tight. Their hard, hot bodies urged on my simmering need. "Use me, please Masters. Use me hard for hours," I whimpered.

"Not so fast, kitten," Dylan warned with a scowl. "You have a punishment to take. And you have all day to think about sticking your nose in other people's business. About how you should have encouraged Julianna to talk to Mika instead of pseudo-Domming her actions and forcing her to take the pregnancy test."

"Let's go, little one," Nick growled.

My heart raced in a combination of lust and fear. Their lecture started as we left the first aid room and continued well past breakfast. After they'd put me through the emotional guilt-laden wringer, I was left alone for two hours to "Think about your actions," as Nick had eloquently instructed.

With a heavy sigh and a pout, I sat on the bed, praying to everything holy that they wouldn't make me endure another session of forced orgasms. I'd learned my lesson well that night. I couldn't wipe my cooch without wincing for days and I thought my poor little clit would never stop aching.

Picking at the food on my plate at dinner, my stomach felt like a teeter-totter. They were going to punish me in the dungeon. Push my buttons. Or so I'd been warned.

Everything from whips to public nudity plagued my timorous thoughts. Panic swelled as the dining room thinned. I knew everyone was assembling in the dungeon to witness my punishment.

Although I didn't think it would do any good, I set my fork down and raised my head. I had to give it one last try.

"I'm sorry for what I did today, Masters. Can you please forgive me and not punish me?" A fat tear slid down my cheek.

"You've already been forgiven, kitten," Dylan assured as he leaned forward and brushed it away.

"Then why am I still going to be punished?"

"Let's go, little one," Nick directed as he stood and extended his hand. "We'll explain before we hand out your discipline."

My bowels turned to liquid as fear slammed through my chest. Forcing my legs to support my weight, I stood and wobbled down the hall with my all-too-silent Masters and into the dungeon.

The room was packed. Everyone was seated and facing an empty cross. I felt as if I were being led to the gallows. Death would be a welcome respite over standing before all the people staring at me.

My chest rose and fell in frantic breaths as I gazed at the floor. Nick and Dylan stood by my side in their prevailing Dominant stances.

"Thank you all for coming here this evening to witness Savannah's punishment." Nick began. Suddenly a commotion in the audience caused me raised my head.

"Go easy on the girl, Nick. Thanks to her, I just found out I'm going to be a grandpa," Emile, Mika's father cried out with a fist pump.

The entire room began to laugh and applaud. Even my Masters were laughing. I, on the other hand, was too frightened to even crack a smile.

"Congratulations, Emile," Dylan called back. "But as is with all of us Doms, Dommes, and Tops, we sometimes have to do things we'd rather not be forced to do. Such is the case with Nick and me tonight."

"We've talked to you about trust before, little one," Nick interjected. "Remember?"

"Yes, Master," I whispered with a slow nod of my head.

"Once trust has been lost, kitten. It's hard to regain."

"Yes, Master, I remember. I'm sorry for what I did," I pleaded, hoping this time they would hear the sincerity in my voice and opt to forego my humiliating punishment.

"I don't know, Dylan. Do you really think she means it?" Nick asked, scrubbing his fingers over his chin.

"I do, Master," I insisted with a whispered plea.

"Silence, little one. I was speaking to Dylan."

"I don't know Nick. I don't know that I can trust her to tell the truth."

Dylan's words hurt more than if he'd pierced my heart with a knife.

"I don't know if she can make this up to us, man," Dylan added, his words slathered in sorrow.

Make it up to them. Make it up to them. Do it now.

It had been a long time since that little voice in my head had captured my attention. And as if a light had been turned on in my brain, I knew what I had to do to earn back their trust. Regain their faith. Bask in their honor.

I took a step forward, my gaze fixed on the back wall. There was nothing I wouldn't do for the love of my Masters. Nothing I wouldn't give to live the rest of my life enveloped in their adoration. And there were no fears too strong to keep me from drowning in their Dominance.

Clenching my fists into the filmy silk of my gown, I lifted it over my head and tossed it to the floor. I heard a gasp in the crowd and as I swallowed a lump of anxiety, I looked out over my friends…my family. Their faces bore the truth in tears, smiles, and reflections of love.

I was safe.

I was whole.

Julianna stood, tears streaming down her face. "You are gorgeous, Savannah!" She screamed on a sob.

Tony stood up near the back of the room, wearing a smile so wide I thought it would split his face. He raised his hands, gave me a thumbs up, then began to clap.

Suddenly the entire room began to applaud as screams of encouragement filled the air. A startled gasp of laughter exploded from between my lips and a shy smile tugged the corners of my mouth. There was one more thing I had to do.

I turned and faced my Masters. Their expressions were choked with emotion.

"There is nothing I wouldn't do to earn back your trust in me, Masters. Nothing on earth."

Nick's nostrils flared as tears welled in his eyes. "I love you, darling. I love you so much and I'm so damn proud of you," he whispered as he gripped me in his arms. Burying his face against my neck, he murmured the same words over and over against my naked flesh.

Dylan pressed his warm body over my back, his mouth nuzzled close to my ear.

"Forever, kitten. You are ours forever. You were sent from heaven, Sanna. Sent to save me from myself. Sent to teach Nick to love again. You're our salvation, kitten and I love you so much. I'll never stop loving you."

Tears of joy spilled down my face. "I love you both. I'll love for you for all time," I cried.

Nick scooped me into his arms, capturing my lips in a torrid kiss.

"Sorry folks, but…ahhh, oh fuck it. Punishment is off," Dylan stammered. "You all have fun. We're going to go enjoy our brave and beautiful slave."

The whole room erupted in laughter as Nick carried me out the door, down the hall, and back to our suite. Dylan closed and locked the door behind him. And as Nick laid me onto the bed, they stood and gazed down at me. I could see every emotion, so very clearly in their eyes.

Pride.

Hunger.

But best and brightest…

Love.

ABOUT THE AUTHOR

Jenna Jacob is married and lives in Kansas. She loves music, cooking, camping, and riding Harley's in the country. At thirteen she began writing short stories and poetry and dreamed of one day becoming an author.

Now that her four children are grown, she has time to paint with words, the pictures in her twisted mind. Outgoing with a warped sense of humor, she's never once been accused of being shy or introverted. With close to twenty years of experience in the dynamics of the BDSM lifestyle, she strives to portray Dominance and submission with a passionate and comprehensive voice.

Connect with Jenna online:
Website: http://www.jennajacob.com
Facebook: http://www.facebook.com/jenna.jacob.author
Facebook Fan Page: http://www.facebook.com/#!/pages/Jenna-Jacob/236316889830812?fref=ts
Twitter: http://www.twitter.com/@jennajacob3

Also Available from Jenna Jacob:

THE DOMS OF GENESIS SERIES
Embracing My Submission – Book One

DOMS OF HER LIFE SERIES (by Shayla Black, Jenna Jacob, and Isabella LaPearl)
One Dom To Love – Book One

COMING SOON

The Young And The Submissive - Is the second in the BDSM Erotic Romance Series titled: *The Doms of Her Life* and will be available July 23, 2013.

Jenna is co-author with New York Times Bestselling Author Shayla Black and Isabella LaPearl. The three have created a toe-curling, knock-you-off-your-fcet erotic treat. Here's a peek:

Raine Kendall has everything a woman could want...almost. Sexy, tender Dom Liam O'Neill is her knight in shining armor, but Raine keeps pinching herself. Is he too good to be true or is this growing connection one that could last a lifetime? She's constantly torn by her abiding feelings for her commanding boss, Macen "Hammer" Hammerman, especially in the wake the mind-blowing night he cast aside the barriers between them and ravaged every inch of her body.

Hammer, Liam's former best friend, can't stop coveting Raine. But Liam is determined to hold and guide the woman he loves and see if she can be the submissive of his dreams. However, he's finding that her trust is hard won and he needs a bloody crowbar to pry open her scarred soul. So he risks everything to win her once and for all. But once he's put his daring plan in motion, will it cost Liam his heart if he loses Raine to Hammer for good?

Master Of My Mind - Is the third in Jenna's BDSM Erotic Romance Series titled: *The Doms of Genesis* and will be available in the fall of 2013. Here's a peek:

I stood beneath the faded green awning staring at the gleaming mahogany casket. The elegant brass handles glowed mocking the warmth that had been ripped from my soul. A cold rain splattered upon the canopy as somber faced friends gathered beneath it to show their respects. Well rehearsed tears spilled down the cheeks of his ex-wife as his hateful snatch of a daughter tried sooth the ice queen's theatrics. They weren't there to mourn the loss of the man I loved, but to masquerade as grieving victims until the fat inheritance landed in their laps.

    The monotone voice of the Minister droned in my ears. None of his words of comfort penetrated the numb consuming void within. I was all but dead inside. Just as dead as my beloved Master who would soon be lowered into the black earth hollowed out below him. And God help me, I wanted to go with him, I couldn't imagine a life without him.

Check out these other fantastic stories:

Dangerous Boys and Their Toy
By Shayla Black
Available Now!

Trading orgasms for information isn't their usual way of doing business, but when a missing criminal-turned-star-witness and fifty grand are on the line, bounty hunter R. A. Thorn and Detective Cameron Martinez are prepared to put their bodies to the task and give gorgeous Brenna Sheridan everything she needs.

An exchange they never anticipated becomes an experience none can forget—or walk away from. Sexual hunger sizzles the threesome, but the stakes and danger rise as a mafia bad-ass stalks Brenna.

Soon, their "deal" is no longer about information—or sex. Emotions bind Brenna, Cam and Thorn together more tightly than they ever imagined as the men protect—and serve—the beloved woman neither can live without.

* * *

"Detective," she cried. "Thorn broke in, tied me up in my sleep and fondled me without my permission."

"Not exactly true. I used the key under the flower pot on the front porch to let myself in, and I touched you with your permission—more or less. I asked you if you'd tell me what I wanted to know if I made you come, and you said yes."

"I didn't mean it."

"How was I supposed to know that? You were wet as hell when I touched you. As far as I'm concerned our bargain still stands."

"Even if it did," Brenna argued. "You didn't make me come."

Thorn flushed red. "I came damn close. Besides, you didn't specify that I personally had to make you come, just that I had to make sure it happened. Cam will take care of the technicalities."

Cam sighed and opened his mouth to refute Thorn.

Brenna shot back, "He can't make me come, either."

Normally, Cameron would let such a comment slide off his back. He didn't have the chest-beating, macho caveman instincts Thorn possessed. But somehow, Brenna's bald statement riled him a touch.

"Actually, I think, under normal circumstances, I could. I'm a patient man willing to take the time to discover what my partner needs during sex." He cocked his head and stared at Brenna. An odd sort of longing crossed her face. He remembered the night by the pool, watching her frustrated attempt to orgasm. "But what you're talking about is deeper, right?" He crossed the room to sit on the bed beside her. "Have you ever had an orgasm?"

Brenna flushed twenty shades of red then turned away.

He took that to mean no.

An orgasm deficit to most would not be a huge tragedy. Through most of high school and college, Cameron had gone without. Too many people underfoot for self-pleasure. In his mostly white school, too many folks had been unwilling to get naked with someone half Apache, half Hispanic. In Arizona, that century and a half year-old prejudice against Indians and Mexicans still quietly lived on in more than a handful of people.

But Brenna... Her deficit wasn't a mere case of going without. It was an inability, her shamed expression told him. And Cameron ached for her. What would it be like to be an adult and not know the joy of sexual satisfaction?

Tragedy.

"See? She's frigid," Thorn mouthed off.

Cameron whirled on him. "Has anyone ever told you what an enormous prick you are?"

Thorn grinned. "No, but I hear frequently what an enormous prick I have."

Cameron rolled his eyes then turned back to Brenna. "Ignore him. When the phrase son of a bitch was coined, they had Thorn in mind."

"You're not much better. Pinching me so hard it brought tears to my eyes."

So he had. Totally unlike him. This stupid plot of Thorn's wasn't getting them anywhere, but he may be onto something.

"Key." He held out his palm to Thorn.

"Ah, shit. Man, you're going to uncuff her? She looks hot, bound and ready."

She did. No refuting that. But Thorn couldn't see the long-term benefit of uncuffing Brenna beyond the short-term benefit the view provided his dick.

"I'd hate to have to arrest you. You'd have to call your brother to bail you out."

"Oh, hell no!" With another curse, Thorn slapped the key in Cam's palm. "You ruin all the fun, you know that?"

"I'm the original party pooper."

With a quick turn of his wrist and a few tugs, Brenna's wrists were free. He untied her ankles. Just as she would have leapt from the bed and reached for the robe on the floor beside it, Cameron placed a palm between her bare collarbones.

"Not just yet." Once he had her pinned to the bed, he said, "I am sincerely sorry that no man has taken the time or care with you to give you the pleasure you deserve. I'm sorry you have yet to figure out how to bring yourself to orgasm." He brushed a stray curl from her cheek. "I know it must bother you. You must feel somewhat left out and…defective."

Tears flooded Brenna's eyes, and Cameron sucked in a shocked breath. He'd hoped that he was close to the truth, but hadn't imagined that he was dead on. Her tears and pained expression said, however, that he was.

"It's okay," he whispered. "You're not. It's wrong for you to go on suffering needlessly. We will help you discover what you need to find fulfillment, if that's what you want. But…" Cameron sighed, hating what he had to say next. "Thorn is right. We need your help in return. Lawton worked with a man named Julio Marco and others to traffic humans across the border and sell them into slavery. I was Lawton's arresting officer. Thorn is his bail bondsman. We need Lawton to live up to his word to turn evidence for the state so the victims can have justice. He must come in and provide the testimony he promised. You're our only hope of finding him."

Brenna blinked. Tears ran down the sides of her face. Cameron hurt for her. She was clearly confused, didn't know who to trust or what to do. He understood.

For more information visit: *www.shaylablack.com*

Handcuffed By Her Hero
Book 2 of the W.I.L.D. Boys of Special Forces
By Angel Payne
Coming July 18, 2013!

"Ssshh," he murmured again. "Rayna, it's all over. You got the gun, remember? And you got the bad guy. You got him, honey."

"No. No. He's going to get in again! He's going to get me again!"

"Ray-bird—"

"He's coming!" Her torso shuddered as her lungs struggled for air. "He's bringing the guards with him this time!"

"He's not here. He's not—"

"They're going to hold me down. He's going to let them put that needle in me. No! Not there. *Not down there*!"

Z's muscles went to sludge a second time. Relief had liquefied him the first time. Rage was the villain now. He forced his way through it, wrapping her hand tighter in his.

"Needle?" he demanded. "What needle, Rayna?"

He prayed this was some strange glitch of her nightmare, and not a remembered reality. If it was, so help him God—

"Don't let them do it. Oh, God!"

He pulled her up, cradling her against him. He needed her closer, needed to help her fight off the demons, even if they were only in her mind. "I won't let them do it." He pressed his lips to her temple. "I won't, okay?"

She whimpered and struggled at him. "Zeke!"

"Here," he assured. "Right here, Rayna."

"I need Zeke!"

He frowned. She'd started to blink her eyes, but her gaze swept the room without seeing it. Shit. She was still subconscious. And pleading for *him* from that misty mental realm. His reaction was a double-edged blade. Hearing his name on her lips jolted him with elation. The panic in it brought him back to earth. Painfully.

Fuck it.

"Time to wake up, Sleeping Beauty." He gave her a gentle shake. A second one, harder and longer. She batted at him again.

"Zeke!"

"Honey, I'm *here*."

Her breath hitched in her throat. Her frame froze then softened. She blinked with slow confusion. Her free hand curled into his camouflage top. "You—you really are," she whispered.

Her lips parted on a slow, sweet smile. The expression fascinated him so much, Zeke wrestled with his reaction. He liked to smile, right? Then why couldn't he remember how to do it now? Why couldn't he think of *anything* to do right now?

Finally, he forced his mouth around one syllable. "Hi."

Her smile became a full grin. "Hi." Jolt of elation, the sequel. "How was the mission?"

Was she kidding? He already knew the answer to that. She really wasn't. The question was typical Rayna, filled with concern for everyone else, despite how the tears from a post-traumatic nightmare still gleamed on her cheeks. "Time of my fucking life," he cracked. He wouldn't be able to reveal anything beyond his cynical tone, so he squeezed her shoulder to indicate he was changing the subject, whether she liked it or not. "You were having a pretty shitty episode, honey."

Rayna dislodged her hand from his top in order to wipe the moisture off her face. "Yeah," she muttered. "Probably."

He still held her other hand. If she thought she was getting that one back, she could also think it snowed in hell. Zeke squeezed those fingers harder. "The episodes weren't this bad before I left."

"I know."

"You were also staying on your meds before I left."

"Zeke—"

"You don't have to be on them forever, Rayna."

"I *know*, okay?"

"Apparently, you don't."

"Stop it." She tried to jerk free again. Zeke gripped her

tighter. "I don't want to talk about it. About any of it."

He treated that statement like a badly-hung door on a drug lord's hut. Kicked it into non-existence. "You went on about King for a while."

She sighed and looked away. "Yep. Sounds right."

Strands of her brilliant, near-burgundy hair fell into her eyes. Zeke let her hand go so he could brush them back. Change of tactic. There were occasions for busting down doors, and then there were moments made for silken steps. Especially when they came before the questions he asked next.

"Have you ever dreamed about the bastard's guards, too?"

Her shoulders wiggled on a semi-shrug. "Of course."

"What about them using needles on you?"

She tensed again. He'd anticipated that and made sure he had her tucked in tight, but his bird laid a turd of shock on his precautions, turning him inside out by grimacing through fresh tears. But one thing about her expression dug at him the most. The tremor of her chin. It said everything. That valiant, determined wobble…fighting back images that weren't dreams. Memories. He knew it as fact now. They were memories.

His gut writhed in a bath of acid. "Holy shit."

She slammed a hand on his chest. "No. Don't. Don't go 'holy shitting' me, Zeke. It's done. It's in the past and I'm leaving it there."

"Right," he countered. "And that's why you're still having screaming nightmares about it."

He watched her wrestle with that, before she pushed at him again. This time, Zeke let her roll back to her pillow. A time and a place for everything—including the silence he allowed to roll into uncomfortable stillness.

Rayna squirmed and huffed. Her chin didn't tremble anymore. She was too busy glowering up him. "You going to sit there and gawk at me until they ship you out again, Sergeant Hayes?"

He let her stew as he got back to his feet in one precision move. He unzipped his jacket and unlaced his boots then placed both on the floor near her little reading chaise. On his way back across the room, he shut the door with a quiet click. "I'm respecting your request not to talk about it."

Her eyebrows high-fived her forehead. "You are?"

He nodded once. "Yep."

She pushed herself up until she leaned against the headboard. "Thank you."

He joined her again on the bed. "Hmm," he finally said, stroking the top of one of her feet through a cute bootie sock. "That may be premature."

Her foot flinched. He maintained his grip on it. "Premature?" The syllables were laced with suspicion. "Why?"

Zeke carefully schooled his features before looking up from her ankles. He'd honed the talent since the age of ten. When he was a teen on the streets, his facial wall saved his hide countless times. As a sensual and sexual Dominant, it had submissives taking numbers for sessions with him. As a Special Forces mission leader, it came in handy in so many ways, the team gave him a new callsign: Zsycho.

Right now, it bought him a much-needed ten seconds. He used them well. By the time he issued his reply to her, he'd swung all the way up on the mattress and gotten both her feet beneath his hands. He leaned close, hovering his jaw over her knees in order to let her see two distinct truths in his gaze. One, for the sake of her well-being alone, he wouldn't accept her refusal as an answer again. Two, he was more than ready to back that assertion up, even if it meant waiting her out all night.

"Because you're not going to like what you'll do in place of talking, Ray-bird."

Comprehension began to shimmer against the forest depths of her eyes. Her lips pursed and she flattened harder against the headboard. "Wh-what do you mean?"

Zeke didn't move. He kept his hands atop her feet in a gentle but firm embrace. He barely blinked as he willed her stare to him with equal command. Her nostrils flared and she curled her arms in, surely sensing what he was about to say.

And dreading it. Probably hating him a little for it. Like that was going to change one word of what he ordered.

"Show me, Rayna. I need to see what they did to you."

Check out more at: *www.angelpayne.com*

The Diva And The Dom
By Isabella LaPearl
Coming July, 2013

Christina wanted to walk out. Wanted to rail at Haden and tell the self riotous prick exactly what she thought of the swinging games he liked to play. Then Jack, the other guy in the group tonight, whose wife was currently perched over Haden's face, ran a confident finger or two along her shoulder and quietly breathed in her ear, "So have you ever been tied up?"

And just like that, something had slid into place in her mind.

She'd shivered like a pup. Felt the tremor run through her nerve endings in a delicious roll from one end of her to the other, and suddenly she was instantly wet. Not damp either, but drenched at the sudden thought of being tied up and...more by this man. A scarlet flush rose up from her chest and colored her neck and cheeks as she felt his chuckle hot against her skin.

"I think you like that idea, shall we?"

Visit Pearl at: *www.isabellalapearl.com*

Thug for Hire
A Beautiful Destruction Novel
In the New Adult genre by: Kylie Gray
Available August 27, 2013

Suffocating under the impossible expectations of her cruel, iron fisted parents while struggling to deal with her abusive past, Nikole Masters has no other choice but to abide by their rules and suffer in silence until she can escape to college. When the seemingly charming Lucas Peterson comes to her rescue, the saviour she is secretly so desperate for thrusts her into a chilling, dangerous game of deceit, riddled with skeletons, leaving Nikole at the leniency of a thug who has no mercy left to give.

Crude, obnoxious and uncaring, Andrew 'Ajax' Jackson is one of the youngest criminal masterminds of the underworld, getting exactly what he wants, when he wants it. Without a past for an anchor and only a bleak existence as his future, he understands only one thing; survival. Ajax has no time or compassion for humanity, much less the damaged broken girl he has kidnapped and yet...

Connect with Kylie Gray on Facebook -
https://www.facebook.com/kylie.gray.794?ref=tn_tnmn